AFTER-DINNER CONVERSATION

TEXAS PAN AMERICAN LITERATURE IN TRANSLATION

Danny J. Anderson, Editor

After-Dinner Conversation

THE DIARY OF A DECADENT

by JOSÉ ASUNCIÓN SILVA

Translated with an introduction and notes
by Kelly Washbourne

UNIVERSITY OF TEXAS PRESS, AUSTIN

Requests for permission to reproduce material from this work should be
sent to:
   Permissions
   University of Texas Press
   P.O. Box 7819
   Austin, TX 78713-7819
   www.utexas.edu/utpress/about/bpermission.html

⊗   The paper used in this book meets the minimum requirements of
ANSI/NISO Z39.48-1992 (R1997) (Permanence of Paper).

Library of Congress Cataloging-in-Publication Data

Silva, José Asunción, 1865–1896.
   [De sobremesa. English]
   After-dinner conversation : the diary of a decadent / by José Asunción Silva ;
translated with an introduction and notes by Kelly Washbourne. — 1st ed.
       p.   cm. — (Texas Pan American literature in translation series)
   Includes bibliographical references.
   ISBN 0-292-70698-7 (cl. : alk. paper) — ISBN 0-292-70979-X (pbk. : alk. paper)
   1. Silva, José Asunción, 1865–1896. De sobremesa.   I. Washbourne, R. Kelly.
II. Title.   III. Series.
   PQ8179.S5D413   2005
   863'.64—dc22
                                                        2004030275

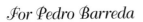

For Pedro Barreda

CONTENTS

ACKNOWLEDGMENTS

First I would like to thank the editors, readers, and all those involved with this project at the University of Texas Press. Next, Francisco Fagundes for all I learned from him at the University of Massachusetts at Amherst, and Edwin Gentzler for his support and collegiality at the Translation Center. Also, Nico Suarez at Smith College for the opportunities to discover the Amazon and to translate its works. I want to acknowledge Suzanne Jill Levine at UC Santa Barbara for her generosity in helping me find my sea-legs as a young translator. And of course, my colleagues at Kent State University, especially my mentor, Carol Maier. I am indebted to my professors at the Monterey Institute of International Studies, particularly Carl Fehlandt.

Special thanks go to Fred Niditch, who started me on my way in languages and cultures. Finally, my gratitude to all the authors who have entrusted their work to me, all my translation students, and of course, those who have been most supportive of me: my mother, and Camelly.

I want to thank José Asunción Silva for a haunting, beautiful work, and the readers and critics who have kept it alive.

TRANSLATOR'S INTRODUCTION

In the hands of the masters the novel and criticism are means of presenting to the public the terrifying problems humanity must confront, and of distinguishing psychological complications; the reader no longer asks of the book that it amuse him, but rather that it make him think and see the mystery ensconced in every particle of the Great All. —*After-Dinner Conversation,* 14 April

I dreamt back then of fashioning a poem
Of an art both nervous and new, a daring, supreme opus
—"A Poem," José Asunción Silva

Against the impossible, what good is desire? —José Asunción Silva

"AN ART BOTH NERVOUS AND NEW"

It is perhaps regrettable that the full fin de siècle flowering of Latin American prose should not appear until 1925, well into avant-garde times, a belatedness that may help account for *After-Dinner Conversation*'s status as a "lost novel." The work actually is thrice lost: first literally, in the wreck of the *Amérique;* second in its rewritten manuscript; and third in critical discourse, at least until very recent times.[1]

The work's ontological status as a re-created entity is perhaps too much with us as we read; no reader fails to let Silva's tragic biography intrude on the text. We read a text that mimics a shadow-text left somewhere on the ocean floor.[2] Is it necessarily inferior to the original draft? We must ask ourselves if it is valid to compare an existing work to a conjectural one. Regardless, the novel was long deemed incomplete or chaotic—read "failed"—by critics, an assumption that now is being challenged by a chorus of readers.

This introduction will give the reader an indication of José Asunción Silva's life and times, particularly the latter. Its purpose is twofold: on the one hand, to collect and to some extent critique the main currents of thought on a key work of Spanish American *modernismo;* on the other, to offer possible avenues of further inquiry, and to delve deeper into aspects that may have been overlooked or unduly neglected, and to connect them. In the order treated, these are the areas covered in the pages to follow: the life and work of Silva; the context of *De sobremesa*'s composition and the myths around it; a few words on the phenomenon of *modernismo* in Spanish America; the work's setting, including a discussion of Paris in the imaginary of the day; a consideration of genre and language, leading to a broad definition of Decadence; a tour of the interior spaces of the novel, particularly the opening and closing scenes, illustrating Decadent sensibility and the treatment of time in the novel, experimental for its day; the reception of the work; erotics and naming;

religiosity; illness, including madness, nerves, and tuberculosis; energy and its primacy; the representation of doctors and medical discourse; the economic context and material culture in which Fernández moves; and finally, a word on the translation. Let us begin, then, with Silva himself.

José Asunción Silva's life is the stuff of legend, and, all too occasionally, of fact. Born José Asunción Salustiano Facundo in 1865, Silva was the precocious son of a well-to-do father who was also known as a writer of *artículos de costumbres,* or manners and customs articles. Pulled from the democratically integrated schools, he was then educated amid the wealthy Bogotá youth; scornful, proud, and apparently something of a Fauntleroy in dress and manners, he soon earned the nicknames *el niño bonito* ("pretty boy") and "José Presunción" ("José the Conceited," a pun on his name). In 1870, his sister Elvira was born, who was exceedingly close to the poet and with respect to whom Silva's reputation would be suspect for years as insinuations of an unnatural relationship persisted. Some say these rumors began with a legend surrounding an illustration in his posthumous *Poesías* in 1908.[3] Matters were certainly not helped by the intimacy of his internationally famous "Nocturno," which was unquestioningly understood to be a grieving rumination on Elvira's loss and lingering presence in the sensitive youth's life. He began helping in his father's store (1878), and reading French Romantic works, which he translated (1882). In 1885 he was sent to Paris to establish commercial ties; he read books on medicine voraciously. He traveled, as his protagonist later would, to London and Switzerland. After much frequenting of salons, where he socialized with the likes of Stephane Mallarmé, Oscar Wilde, and Paul Verlaine, Silva was transformed like Lucien in Balzac's *Lost Illusions,* returning dandified and mocking, stifled and alienated by the provinciality of *fin de siglo* Bogotá. In 1886 he was left at the head of the family business; his father died the following year, and the business suffered. By now, though, Silva was a star of the first order in *tertulias,* or literary gatherings, attended by such figures as Baldomilo Sanín Cano, Emilio Cuervo Márquez, Roberto Suárez, E. Rivas Groot, Clímaco Soto Borda, Isaac Arias Argáez, and D. Arias Argáez.[4] Eight of his poems appeared in 1886 in the important Colombian anthology, *La lira nueva* ("The New Lyre"), compiled by José María Rivas Groot for publication in Bogotá, but perhaps only one—"Estrofas" ("Stanzas"), popularly known as "Ars"—hinted at his uncommon talent.

In 1890, the year Oscar Wilde's Faustian novel *The Picture of Dorian Gray* appeared, Silva wrote "La protesta de la Musa" ("The Protest of the

4

Muse"), a plea to end satiric poetry, a genre which he himself would later perfect in his "Sinfonía color de fresas con crema" ("Strawberry-and-Cream-Colored Symphony"), an artful and scathing lampoon of the devices and *preciocité* that had gone to extremes in the work of Rubén Darío's followers. The year 1891 would bring an irretrievable loss: Elvira, his muse and only confidant, fell ill with pneumonia and died. He was devastated, emotionally and financially; the latter state he had hidden from even his closest friends. The next year the court seizures began; Silva had next to nothing to be confiscated, yet there were fifty-two claims against him, including one by his own grandmother. He continued writing occasional critical articles and poems, and was named to a diplomatic post in Caracas (1894).

It was in 1895 that Silva's life took one more ill-fated, heartbreaking turn. The steamship *Amérique,* on which he was traveling, was wrecked. Silva's reputedly greatest works were lost: all twelve of his *Cuentos negros* ("Black Stories"), the *Cuentos de razas* ("Stories of Races"), meditations, criticism, and poetry, which he had divided into *Sitios* ("Places"), *Versos para ella* ("Poems for Her"), *Para los niños* ("For the Children"), and *Psicopatología* ("Psychopathology") (Camacho Guizado, 310). Also, a treatise he had written on will and energy in a letter to Paul Bourget was gone forever.[5] He also lost novels, including *Ensayo sobre la perfumería* ("Essay on Perfumery") and *De sobremesa.*[6]

Shortly after, Silva, distraught beyond imagining at his losses, wrote "Lázaro," a poem in which the resurrected Lazarus weeps inconsolably, envying the dead. The poem gives us insight into his state of mind during this would-be recovery. At his friends' urging he feverishly reconstructed one of the lost writings, *De sobremesa,* which he had been writing and expanding since 1887, possibly having already decided his fate as he wrote. His friends would be divided as to the work's merits. With his financial situation perilous, he visited his doctor friend Juan Evangelista Manrique days later and asked him to draw the exact outline on his chest of where the human heart is located. His friends met at night at his house. In a *sobremesa* (a lingering after-dinner gathering for conversation) that evening, he scoffed at the notion that he would ever kill himself. They disbanded around midnight. Sometime in the small hours of 24 May 1896, he shot himself once through the heart with a rusty revolver. Arias Argáez found Silva completely lifeless, the hurriedly rewritten manuscript of his only novel on his desk like a protracted suicide note for those who would read it as one. The next day's newspaper in Bogotá related the death laconically, noting that Silva "apparently wrote poetry" (Serrano Camargo, 213–214). On 1 June, Pedro Emilio Coll would write in *El Cojo Ilustrado,* a principal organ of Modernist sensibility:

> In Bogotá, the city of melancholy convents and austere stone temples, José Asunción Silva, the misanthropic dandy, after having laughed at a worldly party, has committed suicide in his room full of books, bottles of scent and rare orchids.   [1 June 1896]

Silva was buried in unhallowed ground set apart for suicides. Another indignity would follow in 1907 with the publication in Colombia of Lorenzo Marroquín and José María Rivas Groot's scandalous novel, *Pax.* In it appears a character, the poet "S. C. Mata" (pronounced *ese se mata*—"that one kills himself"), some of whose poems are unflattering, veiled satires of Silva's nocturnes, allegedly revenge for a slight Silva had made of Marroquín in a newspaper *crónica.*

Like a Borgesian catalogue of imaginary works, Silva's legacy upon his death became hypothetical, full of unrealized potential, thus mythifying him. Several theories about his death have been put forward in the ensuing years, some more outlandish than reasonable. Sanín Cano catalogues and dismisses them: The first legend, supported by a roman à clef reading of the passages in the novel that depict the ravages of despair and *horror vacui* on the antihero, runs that Silva feared he was going insane (Silva, *Obra completa,* 97). Sanín Cano claims the scenes in question were written back in 1892, when Silva received word of Maupassant's insanity.[7] A second legend claims the insularity of a mediocre environment led its denizens, jealous of Silva's superiority, to spread the word that he was mad, which amounted to character assassination in that milieu; Sanín Cano dismisses this (99) as strange and unfounded, since in his view Silva was the very picture of mental balance. Probably the most famous explanation—and correspondingly, perhaps, the most "romantic" one, in Sanín Cano's phrase—has Silva stretched out, like the painting of the stylized, lifeless Chatterton in his garret, we might say, and with Gabriele D'Annunzio's *Il trionfo della morte* ("The Triumph of Death") open on the bedside table. Many began to view D'Annunzio's novel with superstitious horror, and as a causal agent of the death. On close inspection Maurice Barrès's *Trois stations de psychothérapie* and an issue of *Cosmopolis,* a trilingual journal in which Silva was researching Leonardo, appear also.[8] Silva's friend likewise rejects this complicity: It would be beneath the poet to be swayed in fundamental beliefs by readings.

Countryman Guillermo Valencia was to write a paean to Silva, who would "sacrifice a world to polish a verse"; the long poem culminates in a plea for forgiveness for the poet's self-annihilation. In recent years, no resolution to the controversy has been forthcoming; in fact, apologist Santos Molano published a massive tome, *Corazón del poeta* ("The Poet's Heart"), speculating that Silva's burgeoning debts, both inherited and contracted, had more to do with his death than meets the eye.[9]

De sobremesa (1887–1896)—the full title of Silva's novel—was not published until 1925, by Cromos in Bogotá, the year after José Eustasio Rivera's regionalist novel *La vorágine* ("The Vortex") and three years after César Vallejo's radically innovative volume of poetry, *Trilce*. Silva's book would not make an impression. An irony of literary history: A work can be more out of date thirty years after its conception than one hundred.

MODERNISMO

The approximate dates of Spanish American *modernismo*—which should not be confused with Brazilian Modernismo or Anglo-American Modernism—are from 1882, the appearance of José Martí's *Ismaelillo*, to just after World War I, circa 1917, when the avant-garde "isms"—Futurism, Creationism, Cubism, Ultraism—came into vogue. It was, simply put, a sensibility in Spanish America and Spain that held dear the autonomy of art and the cult of form, and practiced an aggressive cosmopolitanism.

José Asunción Silva is frequently considered among the major figures of *modernismo*, a movement of revolutionary pedigree but whose demise left its aesthetics distinctly passé, its repertoire of swans and fleurs-de-lis exhausted by countless imitators of Rubén Darío (1867–1916), the Nicaraguan innovator who "translated" the Spanish language into forms that had been more properly the domain of the French. Darío was accepted among writers of the time as an inspired master of the New World and scion of the Old, and set the agenda for *modernista* sensibilities. Silva, too, had caught the admiring attention of Spanish writers such as Miguel de Unamuno. The Colombian's poetry was highly influenced by Bécquer, Heine, and Hugo. His "Nocturno" is an apparently formless but exquisitely wrought masterpiece of assonant rhymes in verse that are multiples of four; it is instantly recognizable anywhere there is a Spanish-speaking poetic tradition, and was hailed (and reviled) at the time for its innovations:

Una noche,
Una noche toda llena de murmullos, de perfumes
 y de músicas de alas . . .

One night,
A night full of whispers, of perfumes
and of wing-songs . . .

The *modernistas* were a highly diverse group. Any list of the indispensable members would have to include Rubén Darío, first and foremost; also José Martí (1853–1895), the Cuban patriot, essayist, poet, and translator; Silva; and the tubercular Julián del Casal (1863–1893). Also in the first generation is included the Mexican Manuel Gutiérrez Nájera, who wrote verse, short stories, and important essays on art and materialism. Key writers in the epoch emerged: Julio Herrera y Reissig (1875–1910); Amado Nervo (1870–1919), a deeply spiritual writer who has wide popular appeal even today; Delmira Agustini (1886–1914); Salvador Díaz Mirón (1853–1928); Ricardo Jaimes Freyre (1868–1933); and Leopoldo Lugones (1874–1938), though the latter developed into a vital link between modernista aesthetics and the vanguard that was to come. The Peruvian José Santos Chocano (1875–1934) was important in the *mundonovista* ("new-world-ist") phase of *modernismo,* in which simplicity and the autochthonous prevailed over Europeanized, self-consciously "artistic" values.

Silva's age, following Parnassianism's prizing of musicality, sought the precious, the *recherché,* the exotic, and the strange, and Silva's work is virtually a compendium of *modernista* strategies and concerns. Though deeply influenced by Parnassianism and the first "moderns," such as Charles Baudelaire and Paul Verlaine, *modernismo* was the first manifestation of a uniquely Spanish American literature, fulfilling the goal on the one hand to join universal literature and on the other to *descastizar,* or "de-Castilianize" its letters, exactly when Spain was losing its last colonies. The movement is known largely for its poetry, though its prose displayed many of the same traits. The literary current's basic outlines could be said to include many of the following articles of faith: (a) a preoccupation with the marginalized status of the writer and his or her fall from legislator to "non-producer"; at the same time, a recognition of the writer's interpretative role in the universe—the artist as shaman, magus, bard, artisan of the verbal object; (b) disdain for the acquisitiveness of the philistine classes and all that was admired by bourgeois values: the mass-marketed, accessible, emotionally dishonest, crass, commercial productions ruled by the judgments of the class Baudelaire called the "mediocracy"; (c) art as a new source of faith; (d) language as incantatory, orphic, and the means to transgressing, transcending, and creating a "double" of the universe; (e) formal refinement and innovation; (f) an aspiration toward beauty, understood in a Platonic sense; (g) a cultivation of the vague and suggestive over the concrete, highlighting mystery, uncertainty, pessimism, and ephemerality; and (h) the awareness of Latin America as a presence emerging from exotic "Other" to exploited source of resources and victim of the foreign policies and cultural hegemony of colonial aggressors. This last point may help inoculate the newcomer to this literature against the long-standing critical misconception that *modernismo* was somehow "apolitical" or *torredemarfilista* ("ivory-tower-ist" or "elitist"). Especially in its latter or "heroic" phase, *modernismo* was committed to the dynamics of the "real world." Indeed, societal concerns mattered; note Aníbal González's point that

> Silva believed that entropy was eroding history and society; "progress" was an illusion, world history appeared to be returning to its chaotic origins, and it was difficult to see the direction society would take in the future.   ["Modernist Prose," 103]

In some ways, the *modernista*, like the Decadent, often sought in interiority a wealth of impressions to shield him from the anarchistic realities of the time. It is a mistake, though, as we suggested, to assume he was disengaged from them. Some *modernistas'* Pythagorean erotics, for example, may on the surface seem an escapist dodge, but in reality such pursuits can and should be seen as counter-ideals in a world of ever more threatening, and desacralizing, mercantilism.

Then, as now, there was great pressure to be "modern," against the pull of tradition and the pride of cultural heritage. *Modernismo* finally gave way just as globalization, modern cities and city life, and capitalization and its discontents brought with them new forms of writing and of conceiving the world.[10] It was above all a nondogmatic current, as Gómez Gil indicates (405), and thus we should be careful not to call *modernismo* a movement so much as a "moment" or "consciousness," one of great ambiguity about the role of art and the cult of change now holding sway, and one that was heterodox in its many approaches to art.

SETTING

As a novel of exile, or travel novel, *After-Dinner Conversation* invokes the libertinism and moral freethinking that were set against a narrow Victorian ethos and the old religious order. Paris would be the screen on which countless Latin American writers would project their fantasies, making of the city a siren, a utopia for frustrated dreams at home. It is also a site of ambiguity. Marcy Schwartz notes that "depictions of Paris vacillate between images of orgiastic decadence and ennobling tradition" (11). She suggests that *modernista*-era writing expands the aura of prestige around Paris, developed by Domingo Faustino Sarmiento, to include the sensual and sexual. In Ventura García Calderón's view, Paris is an "Athens that would be Cythera[11] . . . and sometimes Lesbos"—that is, the classical, the mystic, and the erotic (Schwartz, 14). Paris becomes, by antonomasia, the extramoral, the supermundane, at least in thought; witness Rubén Darío's famous "my wife is from my country; my lover, from Paris" (Schwartz, 17), voicing the double and divergent arc that the real and the dreamed would trace for so many Latin Americans who had the means at the turn of the century to journey there. Julián del Casal, for instance, loathed the "bourgeois Paris" but loved the "rare, exotic, refined, sensitive, brilliant and artificial Paris," the Paris unsuspected by foreigners, the "theosophical, magic, satanic and occultist" Paris (Franco, 25). For Silva, the city shares the elusiveness of Helen herself, the ideal, but also a disassociated and destructive life, home of the artificial paradises that would lead to disease and disenchantment. The urban space allows a "dense cartography of . . . autonomous behavior" as set against the affectation and small-mindedness of the provinces (Moreno-Durán, 50). In Silva we can see revealed what Schwartz perceives as Paris's inevitable move from "an aesthetic of pleasure and luxury toward a revelation of urban modernity's high cost" (Schwartz, 20). Paris is, of course, an ideal vantage from which to criticize the aspirations of certain classes then in formation, and the novel thus continues the centuries of dialogue between and about the "old" and "new" worlds and their identity formation. Silva, though, invokes little of the physical, historical Paris, an absence that seems to give credence to the idea of Paris as a topos or theater for certain values to play out—Paris as the spirit, in other words, of what could not be found in the provincial Bogotá of the times.[12] Silva's Fernández takes the idealization of the city even further, voicing his desire (20 June) in a Faustian rumination to see the city of lights refined even further: "[I dream] of a larger, more beautiful Paris, one richer, more perverse, wiser, more sensual, and more mystic" (41). In many respects, then, *After-Dinner Conversation* is a novel of ideas, and Paris plays a key role in the construction of its imaginary, rewriting Europe as the pole from which the Utopia of the Americas is (re)constructed. Importantly, Fernández's diary is read in Latin America.

After-Dinner Conversation is a hybrid—part disquisition, part memoir, part *modernista* manifesto—written at a time when mixing genres still provoked resistance in certain quarters. In large measure, too, it is a nervous, frantic prose poem, unmistakably modern and full of flights both lyrical and cantankerous. Interludes appear of what we might call "pure prose" (after *poesía pura*), language that serves only the aesthetic end. The reader may find something of the love note, the séance, the Greek dialogue,[13] prayer, the religious confession, pamphleteering and speechifying, and doses of parody and pastiche. As a general point of departure, though, it might be useful to term it an early example of the psychological novel, in which external events are subordinated to the inner life of the protagonist. Orjuela notes the forsaking of Romantic realism and an orientation toward a French tendency: to study decadents, neurotics, and maladroits (*De sobremesa,* 16–17). The work is, as critics such as Gómez Ocampo have shown, "essayistic," discoursing ("digressing") on art, love, philosophy, and medicine. As Rafael Gutiérrez Girardot explains in his introduction to the Biblioteca Familiar Colombiana edition, *After-Dinner Conversation* is a marriage of the "sentimental journey" and the "artist novel" (3). Nuancing further, he notes that the Spanish language had lacked these traditions, and that the only diary novels until this novel's appearance belonged to one of the two loose categorizations of diary, *anecdotal,* whereas Silva's novel partakes of the "*reflexivo*," roughly the intimate or *journal intime*.[14] In truth, *After-Dinner Conversation* shows elements of both, although the protagonist's (or "agonist's," to borrow Miguel de Unamuno's term for his own characters) state of mind is chronicled more rigorously than the events surrounding it. While the artist novel, or *Künstlerroman,* traditionally shows the *development* of an artist from childhood, the novel at hand depicts not so much a becoming as the crisis, entropy, or inertia of an age and of a man. The tradition of confessional literature, both as a form and in examples—Augustine, Rousseau, De Quincey's *Confessions of an English Opium Eater,* Rilke's account of an impressionable aristocrat living an anxious Bohemian life in Paris, *The Notebooks of Malte Laurids Brigge,* Maurice Barrè's *The Cult of the Self* (also known as *The Cult of the Ego*), Edmond de Goncourt's *The Goncourt Journals 1851–70,* James Hogg's *The Private Memoirs and Confessions of a Justified Sinner,* Musset's *Confesion d'un enfant du siècle* (which Fernández echoes consciously in calling himself a "child of the century"), George Moore's *Confessions of a Young Man,* and of course Goethe's *Sorrows of Young Werther*—certainly find continuity as well in Silva's work. Not only sin but insanity was in vogue: for example, *Memoirs of My Nervous Illness* (1903), a schizophrenic's by turns lucid and raving account of reality, a work that allows glimpses into the workings of the modern mind. Another fictional exploration in diary form is the philanderer's memoir, Søren Kierkegaard's "Diary of a Seducer" (from *Either/Or,* v. I, 1843), the meticulous recollections of an "eroticist's" conquest, the record of which, like the impressions in Fernández's diary, seems to be the goal and justification of the hero's manipulative arts.[15] Coetaneous diaries also include Grossman's *Diary of a Nobody* (1894), Constant's *Journal Intime* (1887–1889), and the discursive "installments" of Oliver Wendell Holmes's *The Autocrat of the Breakfast-Table* (1857), which are a structural analogue to Silva's novella. Orjuela (*José Asunción Silva,* 26) adds Amiel's diary as a widely read book at the time.[16] Also, the Russian tradition was internationally in full force: Dostoevsky's *Diary of a Writer* and *Notes from the Underground,* Gogol's *Diary of a Madman,* and Turgenev's *Diary of a Superfluous Man.*[17] *After-Dinner Conversation* often is invoked with other Spanish-American *modernista* works that explore the artistic temperament, such as Eugenio Cambaceres's *Sin rumbo* ("Directionless," 1885); José Martí's novel, *Amistad funesta* ("Ill-Fated Friendship," also known as *Lucía Jerez,* 1885); Manuel Díaz Rodríguez's *Confidencias de Psiquis* ("Confidences of Psyche," 1897), *Ídolos rotos* ("Broken Idols," 1901), and *Sangre patricia* ("Patrician Blood" or "Blue Blood," 1902); and Pedro César Dominici's *El triunfo del ideal* ("The Triumph of the Ideal," 1901). In Spain we have the examples of Azorín's *Diario de un enfermo* ("Diary of a Sick Man," 1901) and Ramón del Valle-Inclán's four *Sonatas* (1902–1905), the memoirs of the Marquis de Bradomín. The "voice" behind Fernández's diary, of course, is that of Russian diarist and painter, Marie Bashkirtseff (1860–1884), who appears in the novel as both a "character"—a heroine to Fernández—and a historical personage. Bashkirtseff's diary (1887) is one of the most revealing of the late nineteenth century, and offers clear affinities with Silva's novel in style, thematics, and sensibility.

As a "frame" novel (*Rahmenerzählung*), circularity organizes Silva's work, and emphasizes the futility of the search. Wanting Helen, Fernández attains only her representation,[18] the portrait, her "relics," and the "verbal portrait" of her in the diary itself; wanting cosmopolitan stimulation, he winds up back in the unnamed South American provincial capital. Note that the novel tautologically opens and closes with the words "secluded" and "fairy tale," underscoring the *literaturization of*

KELLY WASHBOURNE

experience, experience captured for the sake of literature, akin to Marie Bashkirtseff's self-conscious discovery: "I am the most interesting book of all." In considering the narrator's reliability in such a text, it should be remembered that, although we have no indication *how* it is read, the diary itself—what we are basically reading when we read the novel—in the interdiagetic plane is a kind of artistic performance as much as a confession, a *texto público* ("public text") in Trigo's phrase (139). This observation raises the question: to what extent does Fernández's diary represent his "true" psychology, i.e., to what extent does it represent something revealed, something transparent, and to what extent the deliberate posturings of a self-conscious polemicist? Diaries, like letters, were formerly written with third-party recipients in mind. In short, we must consider to what extent we are witnessing the theatrics (rhetoric) of reading and to what extent a transformative act of "sorcery" (Trigo's word; see his discussion of memory and reading in this connection, 114–115). The very title of the novel points to the spoken—the oral tradition.

Critics have been anxious to focus on *After-Dinner Conversation*'s apparent eluding of genre; indeed, until the 1960s and even afterward, they compulsively argued over whether or not it even qualified as a novel, and many dismissed it out of hand, feeling it was unworthy of the great poet. Edgar O'Hara called it a *divagación* ("rambling") (221). Sanín Cano, a close friend and *contertulio,* or fellow man of letters, was an early detractor, calling it defective in construction and arbitrary and subjective in its judgments, as if it were an essay (Maya, 81). A disjointed, disarticulated body is an apt metaphor for a novel in which the dissembling body plays such an important role. And yet this nonlinearity is the very protocol of conversation, of "table talk," and of the diary form. The flux of experience replaces the old teleology of the novel, which made of life and character an almost scientific coherence. *After-Dinner Conversation* shares what Robert Heilman calls the "catharsis of rascality," to wit, the "secret inclination to discontinuity, to hit-and-run raids on life, the impulse to shun the long and exacting unity, to instead live by episodes" (Wicks, 44). Further:

> A fiction in the romance mode offers a word-world construct
> in which harmony, integration, and perfection prevail: dream-
> like wish fulfillment. The picaresque mode offers a word-world
> construct in which *disharmony, disintegration and chaos prevail:*
> *nightmarish anxiety.*   [45; emphasis mine]

We can see where the antiheroes of the two genres converge: the Decadent owes much to the picaresque tradition in form, worldview, and sociology. As Porter sees it, "As a negative version of the picaresque (one that ends in the protagonist's degeneration instead of success), the episodic structure of the decadent novel reflects a frustrated quest for a bad goal" (94).

DECADENCE, THE DANDY, AND NEUROSIS

Decadent precedents are everywhere advertised in the novel—from Baudelaire to Moreau. Silva's Fernández belongs to the lineage of this character type: Pater's Marius (*Marius the Epicurian*, 1885), D'Annunzio's Andrea Sperelli (*The Child of Pleasure*, 1889), Huysman's Des Esseintes (*Against the Grain*, also known as *Against Nature*, 1890), Villiers de l'Isle-Adam's Axel (*Axel*, 1890), and Wilde's Dorian Gray (*The Picture of Dorian Gray*, 1891). Lorrain's Phocas (*Monsieur de Phocas*) would appear in 1901. There are, too, untold precursors of a modern, neurotic, divided self, the essence of the decadent: Don Quixote, Hamlet, Dr. Jeckyll and Mr. Hyde, Don Juan, Faust, Werther.

The discourses of modernity, disease, and morality seem to converge in the style, topics, and values of Decadence. The very root of the word implies a declining, a fading, an exhaustion, and a failing. Arthur Symons, who famously set forth the principles of the Symbolist movement in art, notes that Decadence is "really a new and beautiful disease . . . a moral perversity . . . an unreason of the soul" (Beckson, 135–137). Let us take a cursory glance at some of the tenets of Decadence, and hold them up against the example of the novel. I will argue that Fernández is largely, but not archetypically, Decadent.[19]

The first of these principles we will consider is style. Decadent style is monotonously artificial, introspective, contradictory, riotous, and boundless in referentiality and imagination. The Decadent searches out the rare word that has the feel of an arcane curiosity plucked from an alien context. In Decadent prose we typically are assailed with long catalogues of artistic and cultural heroes, Byzantine passages adorned with every artifice, fixations on every detail, details which threaten to engulf the whole (indeed, disproportion is primary to the Decadent's art). In Paul Bourget's words:[20]

A decadent style is one in which the unity of the book is disarticulated to leave room for the unity of the page; in which the page is decomposed to make way for the autonomy of the phrase, and the phrase to give free reign to the rebelliousness of the word.

[Maya, 77]

Bourget also stresses extreme individualism in Decadent style, that is to say, a license for the breakdown of traditional unities and conventions. Porter notes (102) the paramount use of digression.[21] This technique can bring the *fabula* to a halt at every turn, while the *récit,* to use the Formalist terms, rambles endlessly into non-sequiturs, plotlessness, or the use of outrageously contrived coincidences and correspondences. This feature is vital: For what seems like the first time, the writer refuses to satisfy public demand for continuity and closure, which helps explain the initially adverse reception of Silva's novel and the importance of the mode to later "postmodern" experiments. Porter further notes the use of "rare and precious objects (unavailable to and unappreciated by ordinary people) harmoniously arranged in luxurious interiors" (102). That is, even if the Decadent was a social outcast or his claim to nobility was growing remote, which was often the case, the material realm—plants, gems, heraldic symbols, art, delicacies of the table—was available to him through art, through mimesis. Lasowski perceptively captures the image of the word in this type of text thus: "word is bibelot" (Watson, 137). And finally Hanson observes a "tendency to vague and mystical language, a longing to wring from words an enigmatic symbolism or a perverse irony" (2). Consider in this light Fernández's preoccupation with the "manibus date lilia plenis . . ." invocation throughout the novel.

Second, let us take note of the overriding valorization of artificiality. With respect to the natural, when Fernández notes that "the sublime has fled the earth" (1 September), he is explicitly overturning the Romantic conception of nature, of the presence of the Infinite in the sublunary realm. For some critics, the Decadents' paradoxical acceptance of Rousseau (nature is good, civilization is bad), while enjoying the foul fruits of the latter, characterizes their reading of the Romantics (Weir, 4). The Decadent shuns nature as incomplete, too democratic and common. We see evidence of this embracing of the unnatural in Fernández's dismissal of the fledgling tourist industry and its masses; his descriptions of the European tourist "engaging" nature are nothing if not comic *grotesques.* On the other hand, Fernández does relate some sublime moments in nature (note the lovely Niagara Falls rumination), but he cannot resist interspersing them with a diatribe on the profanation represented by the railroad and the anticipated hordes it would bring. He also finds solace in nature, for example in his hideout. However, these are very atypical scenes for a true Decadent novel; here Silva seems still under the spell of Romantic countryman Jorge Isaacs.

We might also, in this vein, point to the Decadent's frivolity, his embracing of the in-itself, or the object extraneous to bourgeois functionality. Baudrillard's *Simulacra and Simulation* lays out four successive stages of the image, of which the fourth we might say typifies the Decadent interior:

> it [the image] is the reflection of a profound reality;
> it masks and denatures a profound reality;
> it masks the absence of a profound reality;
> it has no relation to any reality whatsoever; it is its own pure
> [simulacrum]. [Watson, 183][22]

In the Decadent we typically see a perverse reveling in the breakdown of society accompanied by a yearning for pre-modernity, an irreligious religiosity, even as the new religion of science holds sway over its adepts. Perhaps the ancient and the modern are reconciled in a kind of transitional Utopian vision of the future in which technology serves some enlightened material ends. Fernández's long delirious prophesy (10 July entry)—which significantly is but one more of his pipe dreams—obeys the exigencies of what Poggioli calls "the task of Decadence," which consists first of " 'a denial of culture' (or the assertion of an entropic culture's ruin), and secondly, in a kind of re-cultivation of—or from—such ruins [into] 'a culture of negations, a flower of both evil and ill' " (cited in St. John, 212). In other words, a regeneration of sorts derives from a degeneration.

Next we come to hypersensitivity. The Decadent has an almost fetishistic predilection for intense sensory experience, especially the novel or perverse, a feeling that Art has replaced Ethics, and a conviction that the outside world is but a pretext for the work of art (Mallarmé's "tout au monde existe pour aboutir à un livre"—everything in the world exists to result in a book); indeed, these beliefs are reflected formally in the use of *transpositions d'art*, so overwhelming in Silva both of existent works and of notional ones. Drugs, too, and their attendant altered states are part of the Decadent arsenal in that they are deliberate exacerbations of sense. Walter Pater provides the watchword: "Not the fruit of experience, but experience itself, is the end" (Beckson, 289). Readers of Huysmans, for instance, will recall the synaesthetic "mouth-organ" of liqueurs with which Des Esseintes mixes sound and taste to heighten experience, to produce new flights of harmony. These indulgences depend on a cultivation of a voluptuous distance from the world: *seclu-sion*. The Decadent's solitude is a kind of quarantine, an aristocratic convalescence. Correspondingly, action in the world is a problem. The Decadent's hypersensitivity nevertheless allows for the coexistence in him of an ironic distance that makes him capable of detachment from his own acts of cruelty or callousness, or rather, an amorality born of scorn for common morals. Note how Fernández praises the anarchist not for the ends of his actions, but *because he acts*. The impressionable exile's conquests are nevertheless Machiavellian, and occur in controlled climates—hothouses, boudoirs, galas. They also occur on morally am-biguous grounds: the Decadent hero's overtures to woman—so intense, unconnected, and contradictory—often confuse the reader as to their sincerity. Moral corruption, however, is seen as the privilege of aesthetic superiority, a feeling of what one critic calls "spilt aristocracy" (Porter, 99). Fernández diverges from the model in that he does not scorn travel as redundant to art; he is too robust to be a complete Decadent, but too Decadent for concerted action. Meyer-Minnemann calls him part of the "heroic phase" (73) of Decadentism. An objection to this contention may rest on the fact that all Fernández's vitality is squandered; the diary is proof of failures of action.

Tied to the hypersensitive and hyperaesthetic is a fascination in Decadence with psychopathology. Fernández is both a reader of works on personality disorder and a victim of them. He is susceptible to ner-vous illness, as proof of passage into this "elite," illness being a mark of distinction in the logic of the turn-of-the-century aesthete. And there is a tendency to attempt to trace degeneration of lineage in Decadent works; note how Fernández attributes his animal nature to the "ata-vism" of the Andrades—particularly his sexual predation and eroticism. William James's chapter "The Divided Self" may serve virtually as the profile of Fernández, whose decadence takes the form of an atomization of personality, a *schizoid* state:

A 'dégénéré supérieur' is simply a man of sensibility in many directions, who finds more difficulty than is common in keep-ing his spiritual house in order and running his furrow straight, because his feelings and impulses are too keen and too discrepant mutually. In the haunting and insistent ideas, in the irrational impulses, the morbid scruples, dreads, and inhibitions which beset the psychopathic temperament when it is thoroughly pronounced, we have exquisite examples of heterogenous personality. [169]

Though ill, Fernández does not embody the "typical" emasculated Decadent hero: he is far closer to the Romantic physically, but is "typically" modern in his dividedness. Edmond de Goncourt diagnoses the maladies of the type based on bodily manifestations, to wit, arising from:

> individual or collective pathological disturbances . . . : the decline of nations exhausted by the senility of civilization; the physical instability caused by the ever more artificial conditions of modern life; and the exacerbation of their nervous sensibilities that led artists to live in a state of mental erethism; an atrophy of the will eventually resulting in the triumph of uncontrolled association of ideas and anarchic reverie. And . . . most decadent heroes are clearly abulic in character, unable to make any decision, gnawed by doubt, living wholly isolated from society. [Weir, 84]

Indeed in the Decadent period there was an apocalyptic sense of time; the Decadent hero is that ironic figure who meets the contradictions of modernity and the "deliquescence" (to use a favorite word of the time) of values with a spectacular surrender into that decomposition.

OPENING AND CLOSING SCENES

The parallel scenes that frame the work invite reflection on *After-Dinner Conversation*'s valuing of inner spaces, and the bricolage of private composition—the home as a work of art, the self at its center:

Opening

Secluded by the shade of gauze and lace, the warm light of the lamp fell in a circle over the crimson velvet of the tablecloth, and as it lit up the three china cups, which were golden in the bottom from the traces of thick coffee, and a cut-crystal bottle full of transparent liqueur shining with gold particles, it left the rest of the large and silent chamber awash in a gloomy purple semi-darkness, the effect of the cast of the carpet, the tapestries, and the wall hangings.

Closing

The crimson semidarkness of the room grew drowsy. The tenuous smoke from the Oriental cigarette curled in subtle spirals in the circle of lamplight, dimmed by the old lace lampshade. The fragile china cups were whitened against the blood-red velvet of the rug, and in the bottom of the cut-crystal bottle, amidst the transparency of the Goldwasser, the gold-leaf particles stirred, dancing all in a luminous ring, as fantastic as a fairy tale.

The novel begins with the word *recogida* ("secluded"), which connotes "enclosed," "withdrawn,"[23] and ends with *cuento de hadas* ("fairy tale"), creating a frame for the hermetic fictionality and self-consciousness of the scene. Two of many shrine-like spaces in the book (the cemetery, the studio, boudoirs, etc.), the first and last scenes seem almost to etherealize themselves into fantasy, leaving the diary—and Helen—as the reality. Silva invites us into the novel with a chiaroscuro effect, highlighting what we might call a "visual epicurianism." Like the Impressionists' enlightened attention to everyday objects such as food, the use of light here (1) works as a narcotic and (2) heightens the transitory perception of objects, especially the décor—its ensemble effect but also its miniaturist detail. In this case we are clearly in the *modernista* interior: sensual, precious, refined, crepuscular, cosmopolitan, deliberate, disparate. Note too the use of dream-effects and private space that literalizes Aestheticist ideal images such as Walter Pater's "House Beautiful," and anticipates such famous metaphysical sanctuaries of harmonic thought as those painted in José Enrique Rodó's *Ariel* (1900).[24] We are presented with a similar scene in the opening to Silva's recently recovered short story, "De sobremesa," in which the privileged male spaces of both action and contemplation are clearly drawn:

We had hunted all day. A true hunting party through cultivated fields, leafless vineyards, the fox at our heels and the dog behind the fox; shotgun at the ready, amidst a cloud of partridges that suddenly rises, and warrens of scampering hares; the true exhausting hunt, in which all one's sorrows, all one's worries are forgotten, and for which one is as passionate as for a game of baccarat. After dinner—one of those dinners with only men in attendance—in which there is hard drinking, the putting of elbows on the tablecloths amidst heated arguments through cigarette and pipe smoke, the subtle aroma of coffee and the strong emanations of alcohol, Pedro de Entreves began talking about all that was inexplicable that arose in life, of the marvelous, the hidden, with which we have such frequent brushes, of the mysteries in which we are made anxious as if in a lake of dark shadows, of the sickly attraction that mystical journeys to the beyond hold for restless spirits, of the accursed sciences, of colloquies with the invisible, and in these times of unbelief, of calculated or brutal debunkings, which have given me something akin to a soul from the Middle Ages.

[from *Cuentos negros*]

For García Márquez, the first scene in the novel is "filmic," a device obviously predating developments in cinematic technique (13).[25] There is a certain "pan" effect in the claustrophobic interior as the details are revealed in their still-life state.[26] Action is replaced by languor. Compare the novel's opening to a setting from a passage in Rachilde,[27] for example, a comparable "simulated reality" (Jullian, 112):

The countess's room was lit by a magnesium lamp which spread jeweled varnish over everything it touched. The walls were hung with apple-green plush, framed in whorls of iridescent mother-of-pearl; from the ceiling, painted in enamel to imitate a cathedral rose-window, the bright light fell like a meteorite. The bed was very low, lacquered . . . , and curtained only by a canopy of gauze studded with Bohemian garnets; the counterpane consisted of three hundred blue points . . .

Behind this scene we sense a painter's palette, in the colors and light particularly. Rendered artificial by juxtaposition, the aesthetic paraphernalia are *props,* counterpoints to the natural world, where chronology and the elements—the extensions of time and space—oppose them, where movement is banished. In Silva's interiors, Byzantine flourishes obscure all outside space, save the past, which is assembled achronically inside in a kind of *cabinet de curiosités,* the museum-house. The effect of such a space is to *dehistoricize* the artifacts, and to constellate around their artificer, the collector or *bibeloteur,* whose mastery over the natural diachrony and dispersal of things is made plain. The "cult value" of objects, in Walter Benjamin's terms, is superseded by their "exhibition value." The aristocrat's cabinet, moreover, is antidemocratic, an exclusionary space, unlike the museum. Finally, there is a directed chromatism at work; here we have red, white, purple, and gold, colors of heraldry and nobility. Also all the contrasts and indistinctness beloved of the Symbolists, half-lights, silhouettes, dimness, twilights, light on dark and dark objects against light, the sculptural dimensionality of bas-relief in words, all these are bound up in physical settings as constituent parts of mood.[28] Language itself takes refuge in the darker tones.

Not only spaces are highlighted in *After-Dinner Conversation*, but also time. Time in the novel is treated variably as a utilitarian enslavement (witness disaffected Nelly's tirade against the North American concept of it, claiming it exists "for the body"), and as a source of mysterious synchronicity (Fernández's fainting fit at midnight, a response to Helen's fate). The subjectivization of time in the novel, the emplotment of events and their pacing, remain to be studied.[29] Striking proleptic pages leap out at the reader, such as the revelation of the aftermath of the knifing before it happens; little wonder that the novel has been regarded as disjointed by traditionalists. In general what holds sway in *After-Dinner Conversation* is the time of Decadent fiction, which, as Reed points out, "is not a consequence of sequential acts in a temporal field but a transformation of emotional and psychic energy through the tension created by changing forms of desire" (46). Thus is time in the novel—studiously Bergsonian. Many artists of the age "sought to cancel time by dislocating action to the non-spatial 'place' of the mind" (46). Or as Weir sums up magnificently, "The decadent novelist, in short, occupies his time with style" (12). This is consistent with the idea that time in the novel revolves around *excess* (Battilana, 35), the hallmark of Decadent style. Battilana notes that the *sobremesa* itself is a remainder, *leftover time* to waste.

RECEPTION OF THE WORK, EROTICS, AND NAMING

As we will discuss in greater detail below, the body and its representation, both in the domain of erotics and in that of disease, which are not mutually exclusive in *modernismo,* play a fundamental role in the novel and its reception.

Osiek notes that *After-Dinner Conversation* treated with frankness certain themes that were sensitive in the Colombia of the day, and suggests that the delay in the work's publication may reflect that fact (94–95). Too, some early readers dismissed its excesses as unworthy of Silva's crystalline poetry. (See Mejía, 493, for a fuller account of the work's initial reception.) Clearly the book demands of the reader an unusually active participation. The self-referential epigraph from 14 April above provides this aesthetic of reception: "the reader no longer asks of a book that it amuse him, but rather that it make him think . . ." Like Joyce's *Ulysses* or other novels suppressed on account of a freewheeling or amoral protagonist (Fernández is aggressively—beyond the more genteel "implicitly"—atheist, though with nuances, as we will see), Silva's novel flouted contemporary standards of decency on several fronts, even conjoining religious and profane ecstasy. Silva even treats the topics of lesbian love; Fernández, during the episode in question, is enraged at such a "perversion"—but in fact, significantly, he never names the act he sees.[30] This instance of restraint would seem to stand in contradiction to the novel's reputation for distastefulness. Jaramillo Zuluaga notes ("Desire," 42) that despite Silva's novel's exercising an "aesthetics of modernity" in which the body is not elided, postponed, or censured, neither was it embraced, but rather relegated as, in his felicitous phrase, a "Wandering Jew of language":

> In the [1920s], the principle of decorum still managed to hold tenaciously to the conviction of its own invisibility. This conviction may be described as the belief that what was said was not at odds with the speakable and that the system of restrictions on which it rested was part of a normal way of behavior or written expression. Any works that could possibly contradict this opinion, such as *De sobremesa* . . . were relegated to the margins of the literary canon with the argument that such works could only please readers of poor taste or only interest literary historians. . . . The principles of decorum eventually wound up revealing the system of restrictions (albeit ambiguously and awkwardly). [42]

I would venture the objection to those who see sexualized bodies in the novel that what we actually read are the *metonymies of acts* that in fact hide their physicality; "sobs of voluptuosity" but not voluptuosity, a lesbian act but not the word *lesbian* applied to it. In other words, Silva stresses the *impression* of the act on Fernández.[31]

Another word is elided: *adultery* in Fernández's conquest of Consuelo, who confesses her fears to José (1 September) about the "crimen sin nombre" ("unspeakable crime," literally, "crime without a name") they are committing. Is the crime attenuated for contemporary tastes, one wonders, by making her husband an unloving cad (and not coincidentally, a businessman), turning de facto adultery to a kind of poetic justice?[32] The literally "nameless" crime stands as a counterpoint to the novel's *proliferation of names* in the medical, or in Lacanian terms, symbolic, order. Much could be made of the protagonist's overarching desire not merely to experience sensations, but to qualify them, to historicize and *order* them—that is, to name them, however arbitrarily, with the immediacy that naming provides.

Indeed, naming is the only "seeing" that occurs in the novel, particularly where doctors are concerned. Trigo notes, following Foucault's *Birth of the Clinic,* that "the medical gaze only 'sees' a disease after it has classified it, after it has drawn an 'imaginary picture . . .' Words configure bodies, in short, and by extension, their 'crimes'" (5). We might offer a stanza from Poe's poem "Sonnet to Science" to capture the nineteenth-century artist's scorn for this menacing, mundane gaze that "alterest all things":

> Science! true daughter of Old Time thou art!
> Who alterest all things with thy peering eyes.
> Why preyest thou thus upon the poet's heart,
> Vulture, whose wings are dull realities?   [33][33]

So, seeing, implicitly, is tied to naming, and naming, in this aesthetic, is corruptive, since the Symbolist ideal is "not to name but to suggest." Finally, if the doctor's gaze is damning, Helen's is salvational, and so the novel can be said to present an "opposition of gazes": the *trans*forming artistic gaze and the *de*forming medical one.[34] Nevertheless the two are merged in the work, as when Helen returns his gaze as a doctor would look on an ulcerous patient.

After-Dinner Conversation is "the first Colombian heterodox novel to clearly unfurl the fundamental devices of erotic expression: pretext, digression, verbosity, and a more skillful articulation of action and description" (Jaramillo Zuluaga, "Desire," 48). In fact, the diary both organizes suspense around the consummation of Fernández's conquests, or his taking possession (or not) of things and people desired, and forms a kind of *modernista ars amandi,* cataloguing the metaphysical and social "types" of women, real and ideal, goddess and dilettante, that occupy the fin de siècle artist.

Critics today, as we suggested, embrace the novel as a watershed work, a Rosetta stone of sorts for deciphering the *modernista* mind. Gerald Martin called the novel "one of the most characteristic prose works provided by the fin-de-siècle mentality" (Martin, 64). Allen Phillips: "*De sobremesa* is . . . key and testimony of a whole era. . . ." (268, cited in Jrade, 54). The work was precursory to the diary and confessional novels of the pre-boom and boom—for example, Juan Onetti's *El pozo* (1939), Ernesto Sábato's *El túnel* (1948), and, in particular, Mario Benedetti's *La tregua* (1960).[35] Critics rightly have seen the outlines of Cortázar's *Rayuela* ("Hopscotch")—the cornerstone of the *nueva narrativa*—in Silva's novel. *Sobremesas* appear frequently in the novel as well.

Moreno-Durán[36] is instructive on this score, noting the search for la Maga in *Rayuela* as a parallel of Fernández's obsessive search for Helen, displaced muses both.

"Holy Water and Spanish Fly"

Excedunt enim spirituales consolationes, omnes mundi delicias et carnis voluptatis.
Nam omnes mandance aut vanae sunt turpes.

—*Imitat,* Book II, ch. X[37]

The Catholic piety that motivated them endures in me, transformed into an atheistic mysticism.

—*After-Dinner Conversation,* 20 November entry

The subtitle above—"holy water and Spanish fly"—could well serve as a title to Silva's novel itself. Like St. Augustine's two souls that dwell within his breast, holy water (the spiritual impulse) and Spanish fly (sign of the exaggerated erotic urge) are at war in the protagonist. This doubling led Rafael Maya to declare that Fernández seems educated by the satyr Chiron (*Los orígenes,* 87). Indeed, the lower order of pursuits coexists with a constant desire to *transcend,* to free himself. This desire, in the fallen secularity of the fin de siècle, the era Edith Wharton called the "Age of Anxiety," could not be consummated, almost as if religious beatitude were closed to him, but not the rites of religion; Oscar Wilde's penitent confession in *De profundis* could be that of Silva's Fernández:

> I deliberately went to the depths in the search for new sensation. What the paradox was to me in the sphere of thought, perversity became to me in the sphere of passion. Desire, at the end, was a malady, or madness, or both . . .   [37–38]

Consider Fernández's long lament of 1 September, which culminates with love displacing belief:

> And in what will you believe, my melancholic, fervent soul, if . . . the gods have all died?
> Perhaps Love had bitter and ecstatic flavors that could replace faith.

Much of the novel is contained in the passages of the 1 September entry: the "nameless malady" of life, the backward-looking, longing gaze to a nobler time when faith was possible (importantly, the faith of *nobles*), the lamentation of enduring a homogenizing and base era, the sense that "the sublime has fled the earth," the impenetrability of the laws of an inhuman universe (and indeed, the this-worldly search for otherworldly presences at the same time there is a Pythagorean correspondence between realms), the parodizing forms of real belief that the modern spiritual impulse takes.[38] And again, *the desire to believe is not abandoned;* it is displaced, and variously misdirected by Fernández, who is an "abandoned church," in his phrase, but a church nonetheless, a temple or a body fallen from grace. Yet he knows "there is nothing to sate the hunger to believe, except with belief itself." This is the central crisis of *After-Dinner Conversation:* belief in belief, and its neurotic sublimation.

The so-called therapeutic ethos came into force during this time, replacing the ethos of salvation through self-denial (see "Fernández as *homo economicus*" below). In keeping with this development, the therapist becomes priest and "lay confessor," ministering to the parishioner-patient's moral failings. Darwin and the cult of science edged their way into the prevailing discourse. Next to the artist—who replaces God in that his creations are more intentional than "mere" nature—the doctor is the highest hierophant; he may not create but he is privy to creation's laws. In the case of *After-Dinner Conversation,* critics have glossed at length the pantheistic, Rosicrucian, theosophical, or otherwise occult presences that underlie its symbolism, yet none has systematically shown how *the novel retains an apparatus of remnant Catholicism,* and to what effect.[39]

To support this contention, let us look into Fernández's vocabulary. Though he takes from all possible registers, time periods, languages, and systems of thought, clearly the religious discourse is overwhelming, and this is significant in that, being ostensibly a "mystic atheist" (20 November), he *nevertheless ritually appropriates the liturgy and sacraments* of his forebears' Catholicism, often in the very consciousness of "pagan" acts.[40] Most obviously, his reverence for Marie Bashkirtseff is conveyed in the formula of veneration reserved for the Virgin: Our Lady of Everlasting Desire.[41] He refers to Helen, the object of his reverence, as Her Worship, which is ambiguously appropriate either for royalty or for an exalted sacred figure; she inspires hope in him like a "mystical music" in an "abandoned church." He uses the word *devoted* (a semi-dead religious metaphor, as is *to adore*) when speaking of his feeling for her; she pros-trates herself at the feet of the Savior in a kind of religious voluptuosity (Paris, 3 June 189–. . .). He praises Nietzsche as the "new gospel." The portrayal of Jesus himself, following Strauss and Renan, is secularized; he is seen not as a divinity but as the paragon of human kindness (Paris, 3 June, 189–. . .). Fernández's grandmother is not only his "saint," but a *patron saint,* in that her prophesies are designed to protect him. Moreover, she is tied intertextually to Dante's Beatrice, a clearly heav-enly presence and source of *grace,* which is the precise state Fernández seeks.[42] She is also preserved in the unction of memory as Helen is pre-served in a cult-like shrine, and jealously, recalling Rossetti's lines from "The Portrait": "Her face is made her shrine. Let all men note / That in all years (O Love, thy gift is this!) / They that would look on her must come to me" (Rossetti, 262). And perhaps most fruitfully for our consid-eration here, he uses the term *ecstasy* indiscriminately in both religious and amorous contexts. Examples of this aesthetic religion are legion, and we will offer only a few: The doctor in the final scenes (16 January) pronounces him "salvado," which means both "recovered" (body) and "saved" (soul); Fernández even had prayed to the anachronistic "god of my childhood" (Geneva, 9 August). His erotic conquests occur in beds "ornamented like an altar"; he surrenders to "the well-nigh religious gravity of all those minutes consecrated to love," as if with a priestess performing the sacred "Act" (30 June, "The next day"). When he falls to his lowest point, it is for a "priest of science" that he asks (London, 17 November), and it is the latter who counsels action over the "car-ryover [ideas] from the Catholicism of your ancestors." Ironically it is the doctors who, offering a rational explanation for Helen (the "camera obscura" effect), while combating the irrational impulse in their patient, give him a steady stream of advice that falls well in line with orthodox Christian teachings (marriage, hygiene, moderation, humility, absti-nence). His Don Quixote–like epiphany in the end, in the morbo-erotic cemetery scene, is a quasi-religious awakening to "Mystery," which is not unreality but a *super-reality.*

Second, Fernández attributes the causality of his world to a vague, esoteric Catholicism (and one, certainly, wherein the meek shall not inherit the earth).[43] In effect, superstition (perceived connections made causal) rules his passions; note the scene in Constanza Landseer's bed-room when the icon of the "saint," his grandmother, apparently recrim-inates his behavior. This is doubly functional in that a work of art—the aesthetic—effects a religious "conversion." What is the effect of this strong, atavistic religious framework? We may offer a simple reply that sinning is performed the more consciously, the more dramatically, when it is done as a refutation, as a flouting of norms and precepts; as Richard Le Gallienne's line from "The Décadent to His Soul" (1892) phrases it, "Sin is no sin when virtue is forgot" (Landow, 1). However, though Fernández is conscious of sin, it is my contention he does not sin as a pose (as his consumption is a pose), but out of a perverted religiosity.

Another interdependent binary similar to sin and virtue (or redemption) is that of pleasure and pain, which strike a note of abnegation and martyrdom (a religious condition which Fernández explicitly claims for himself). The sick man's symptoms acquire transcendence in the novel as stigmas, inverted stigmas, if you will: physical proof of sensibility of a higher order. In "London, 17 November" we read: "I must tell you that in moments of suffering a pleasure greater than pain itself arises within me, that of *feeling the pain*, that of experiencing the new sensations that it brings me." Compare Marie Bashkirtseff, who finds, in William James's phrase, "luxury in woe":

> In this depression and dreadful uninterrupted suffering, I don't condemn life. On the contrary, I like it and find it good. Can you believe it? I find everything good and pleasant, even my tears, my grief. I enjoy weeping, I enjoy my despair. . . . It would be cruel to have me die when I am so accommodating. . . . [I]n the very midst of my prayers for happiness, I find myself happy at being miserable.
> —*Journal de Marie Bashkirtseff,* i.67, cited in James, 83–84n2

It may help to consider these apparently masochistic tendencies in the light of Lionel Trilling's remark on "how pervasive and deeply rooted is the notion that power may be gained by suffering" (161) and indeed, "[I]n the nineteenth century the Christianized notion of the didactic suffering of the artist went along with the idea of his mental degeneration" (162). Knowledge gained through suffering in part is encoded and revealed through nerves, or sensitivity, in the work (see "Nerves" below).

Clearly, Fernández criticizes the facile traps that alternatives to orthodox Christianity provide: mass-consumable, "ready-made," fashionable systems (Jrade, 62) and pseudo-scientific parlor amusements.[44] While Nietzsche provided the model for an abolishment of reigning orders, Christianity, as Hanson notes in his chapter on Huysmans, "could still hold sway over the imagination as a kind of archaic aristocracy, a poetic possibility in decline, ever losing ground to bourgeois materialism and modern psychology" (111). Moreover, the entire quest for purchase into the unearthly can be seen as a desire to transcend, to return, as in this almost Gnostic fragment of Baudelaire:

> Our unquenchable thirst for all that lies beyond, and that life reveals, is the liveliest proof of our immortality. [Poetry and music] bear witness . . . to an aggravated melancholy, an appeal from our nerves, our nature exiled in imperfection, which desires to enter into immediate possession, while still on this earth, of a revealed paradise. [cited in Hanson, 4]

The pageantry of the Church itself had its allure; as Hanson notes, the Decadents, cultists of overabundance, were taken in by its "sheer excess":

> its archaic splendor, the weight of its history, the elaborate embroidery of its robes, the labyrinthine mysteries of its symbolism, the elephantine exquisiteness by which it performs its daily miracles—[have] always made it an aesthetic and fetishistic object of wonder. The decadents had much to say about the gothic and Byzantine architecture of the great cathedrals, not to mention the sumptuousness of church vestments, chalices, altars, even the symbolic grandeur of the Mass itself. [6]

Not only the visual but the invisible trappings were prized as well: the erotics and beauty of its texts, for example.[45] Hanson concludes by proposing art not as surrogate religion, but as an "incitement" to it; he even goes so far as to call all decadent works "narratives of conversion."[46] This is difficult to dispute. Fernández quite arguably does want to overcome his decadence, even when he most incorrigibly and amorally refuses responsibility for his acts ("No one seduces anyone"). We might rather call them narratives of reversion, since they frequently respond to old inherited nostalgias; witness Des Esseintes's dying words:

> O Lord, pity the Christian who doubts, the sceptic who would believe, the convict of life embarking alone, in the night, under a sky no longer illuminated by the consoling beacons of ancient faith. [Huysmans, 331]

Barbey d'Aurevilly famously critiqued *A Rebours* by suggesting that the only options remaining for Huysmans were "the barrel of a pistol and the foot of the cross"; after finishing *Là Bas,* he in fact converted. Georges Bataille's contention that "sacred things are constituted by an operation of loss" (119) is borne out by Silva's novel. Loss is the premise of the book, and the will to faith its refrain.

THE TROPES OF ILLNESS: MADNESS, NERVES, AND TUBERCULOSIS

> . . . and all disease is only love transformed.
>
> —Thomas Mann, *The Magic Mountain*

Madness and Its Revalorization

Let us examine more closely a few of the most prevalent diseases and their representation in the work, beginning with mental illness. In many ways the disjointed narrative sequencing of the novel plays off the protagonist-narrator's own psychic multiplicity. Each of the four aspects, or fragments, of Fernández, which Trigo (137) names the artist, the philosopher, the pleasure-seeker, and the nihilist (perhaps representing heart, mind, body, and soul), can be said to account for different narrative styles and subgenres. The association of dissipation and madness explicitly functions as an organizing principle, and crisis, in the novel.

Fernández is characterized using precisely the lines of the discourse that had come into vogue—the vocabulary of the occult sciences, the fledgling field of clinical psychiatry, and pathology: neuropathy, neurasthenia, hyperaesthesia, etc.[47] The most pernicious, or most notorious, of the root-seekers in pathologies was certainly Max Nordau (Hungary, 1849–1923). Nordau practiced the taxonomer's art with an obsessive, almost parodic dismissiveness; virtually all of the great spirits of the age to him were degenerates. William James employs the term *medical materialism* to describe those, like Nordau, who adhere to the simple-mindedness of

> [c]alling [Saint Paul's] vision on the road to Damascus a discharging lesion of the occipital cortex, he being an epileptic. [This ideology] snuffs out Saint Teresa as an hysteric, Saint Francis of Assisi as an hereditary degenerate. . . . All such mental overtensions, it says, are . . . mere affairs of diathesis (auto-intoxications most probably), due to the perverted action of various glands which physiology will yet discover. And medical materialism then

thinks that *the spiritual authority of all such personages is successfully undermined.* [13; emphasis mine]

If we substitute "aesthetic authority" for "spiritual authority" in the last line, we have the dogma of Max Nordau in sum. The topos of *the sick artist,* as Lionel Trilling writes in his classic essay in *The Liberal Imagination,* was employed, however, on both sides of the representational divide; the critic notes that "[t]o the artist himself the myth gives some of the ancient powers and privileges of the idiot and the fool, half-prophetic creatures, or of the mutilated priest" (158). The poet, deprived of his former status as law-giver and news-bringer, metaphorizes the demoted status and marginalization in the most persuasive physical emblem possible: the artist as unfit for social life. Trilling here arrives at the crux of the sick artist's position, and the fascination with the pathological:

> By means of his belief in his own sickness, the artist may the more easily fulfill his chosen, and assigned, function of putting himself into connection with the forces of spirituality and morality; the artist sees as insane the "normal" and "healthy" ways of established society, while aberration and illness appear as spiritual and moral health if only because they controvert the ways of respectable society. [155–156]

There is much implied by this passage: The artist's illness is a tracing of boundaries apart not only from respectability but, by extension, from the *insensitive,* the philistines. Notice that when Fernández wishes to deride the vacationers in Europe (Interlaken, 26 July), he details their inadaptiveness and petty nationalistic routines, silly provincial traits and self-absorbed imperviousness to their surroundings; but the coup de grâce is his acerbic declaration that Nordau would likely find them the picture of health and equilibrium.

The essence of Nordau and his legacy is laid out in *After-Dinner Conversation,* and a number of critics have taken up this aspect of Silva's book for comment.[48] Greenslade highlights the importance of Nordau's work and the strange place it occupies. For the reader unfamiliar with Nordau, a few details should be kept in mind. *Degeneration,* or in its original German, *Entartung,* appeared in 1892. Much of Nordau's condemnation fell on those whom Fernández—and the *modernistas,* in such homages as Rubén Darío's *Los raros* ("Oddities")—would look to as models, among them Wagner and the Symbolist artists. Nordau used a style of reading that was rigorously and persecutorially ad hominem; that is, he sought passages from works of art that supported his adverse diagnosis of a given author. At bottom what Nordau saw in these writers was an exaggerated cult of the "I" (Greenslade, 122), and some critics—not all of them contemporary—seized upon him to condemn literary trends of the time or shore up their own conservative take on them (124–125). In short, time has revealed Nordau's attacks for what they are: character assassinations disguised in objective language and aimed at reducing the status of their targets. In many respects he falls in with the very positivist doctors whom Fernández reads and to whom he resorts with almost hypochondriacal desperation.

Let us turn our attention to madness. We would do well to consider madness first in terms of its cachet, not as degenerative but in its ecstatic or aesthetic potential. Clearly Fernández's revulsion in the doctor's waiting room, where *his* malaise is felt to be of another, higher, aesthetic order than that of the broken and pathetic patients assembled there, points to an unwritten code whereby the artist's distemperments are superior in that they are *a product or catalyst of aesthetics*. In London, 20 November, he asserts the noble line of madmen who have died mad, and significantly calls himself a "degenerate," appropriating Nordau's coinage just as the "Decadents" appropriated that condemnatory epithet. Evidence of this identification is found in the number of times in the novel that suffering is aestheticized. Another clue in this connection might be found in the figure of Charcot (the namesake for Silva's doctor, Charvet).[49] Charcot found parallels between the mystical exaltations of saints and the symptoms of "hysterics" at the Salpêtrière hospital, a state that later artists, including the Surrealists, would seek to exploit (Balakian, 161). Madness, hysteria, and ecstasy are seen as kindred, heightened states that, as Plato knew, provide access to creativity.[50] Fernández's praise of a litany of misfit artists (3 June, 189 – . . .) attests to this codification of illnesses. It is telling that one of the most accomplished and revealing images of the work comes about in Fernández's hallucination of Madness. In it a phantasmagoric *coincidentia oppositorum* operates, metaphorizing the forces vying for his soul— vitality on the one hand, and death on the other, an essential *modernista* bipolarity:

> Madness! Good God, Madness! . . . How many times have I seen
> her passing by, dressed in shimmering rags, . . . beckoning me into

the unknown! . . . She had a horrible head, half twenty-year-old woman, smiling and healthy but crowned with thorns that bled her smooth brow; the other half, a desiccated death's-head with hollow black eye sockets, and a crown of roses, . . . was saying to me: "I am yours, you are mine, I am madness!"

[London, 20 November]

Madness, then, is painted as an hermaphroditic seductress, a burlesque figure mocking both life and death. In this, one of the more expressionist scenes in the novel, Silva here uses the grotesque—which by nature yokes together the exaggeratedly heterogeneous—to represent to Fernández his own mind.[51] This is a variant on the Decadent motif of the sphinx, and one of many hermetic unions in the novel, which oscillates between and sometimes conjoins the illusory and the real, the real and the "extra-real," the antigravitational and the heavy, the beautiful and the beastly, dissipation and crystallization, the elusive and the unshakable, the traditions of the past and the chimeras of the future. Silva, according to P. E. Coll, sought to forge in prose both the "verdores de la descomposición" ("salad days of decay") and the "fragancia de la juventud" ("fragrance of youth") (Camacho Guizado, 312), a new, Baudelairean aesthetic ideal.

As we can see in the *modernistas* in general, sin—of which sensuality and sexuality are markers—is embraced thematically as the possibility for transcendence, but also with a horrible price. Sin and disease, according to Sontag, are linked in the popular imagination. Fernández's sins, then, may be said to be *secular* and *historical:* he is an idler and a dreamer in a world of remunerative action. In the new morality of industrial and material accomplishment, his sins are as much against practicality as against the God of his fathers (note the doctor's chastisement of Fernández's "sins against hygiene," a bizarre and revealing confluence of two discourses). Our fascination with the protagonist's sins, in turn, is the fascination of *After-Dinner Conversation:* we are equally attracted and repulsed by him.[52]

As Villanueva-Collado notes, Silva has fallen victim to narrow gender expectations and the imposition of "the bourgeois concept of artistic 'normality' as expressed in a medical discourse" ("Gender Ideology," 121), at bottom ideological traps that have hampered insightful criticism of the Colombian's writing. On the narrative level Fernández is subjected to the same ideology; there we see the doctor in the role of legislator, not of morality but of health and (ab)normality. Doctors are represented as inveterate philistines, false prophets, surrogate priests, impassive interrogator-torturers, and clownish objects of satire, and this despite Fernández's fascination with the medical order, perhaps for its nominal power but just as likely for its residence in the dark spaces of the soul, in the unknown. This duality, as various commentators have noted, characterizes the novel's ambiguity.[53]

Nerves

Nerves, nerves! O folly of a child who dreams
Of heaven, and, waking in the darkness, screams.

—"Nerves," Arthur Symons

Our nerves are whips held in the hands of time. —Tristan Tzara

One element of pathology crucial to understanding the novel and its age is *nerves*. In part a side effect of the rigors of mechanization, urbanization, and the pace of business, nervous suffering increased generally and dramatically in the late nineteenth century. *Nerves*, however, is also an ambiguous code word signaling any number of physical states; nerves appear in the novel as rare, disordered, overstimulated, "set on end," "high-strung"; nerves are fed special diets to "soothe" them. But they are also the sign of strength and vigor, and above all, they stand for, and contour, sensibility, the spirit, superior consciousness, and the aesthetic response.

The notion of aristocracy (real or assumed) is fundamental to the era; examples abound in the novel in which predisposition—biology—plays a key role in the assertion of class: In the 30 June entry, for instance, Fernández marvels at how the humble origins of Lelia Orloff could have produced in her an "aristocracy of the nerves," a phenomenon "rarer perhaps than that of the blood or the mind." The modernity of this notion is striking: *nervous aristocrats are born into every station,* an idea that does violence to the old orders. G. S. Rousseau stresses that nerves "were neither the signs nor symptoms of ephemeral illness but an inherited condition that, if undetected, would eventually surface" (243). The nerves, in short, are where a metaphorical claim to special sensitivity, and the real danger of succumbing to their excess strain, converge; oversensitivity is thus configured ambiguously—both as a privilege and as the price of privilege. Where Fernández writes: "I have the nerves of an artist, not a man of science" (30 June entry), it is Charvet's boast and lament both.

In his chapter titled "Towards a Semiotics of the Nerve," G. S. Rousseau notes a "nerve craze" in the late Renaissance that theologized nerves (they were signs of grace or punishment), metaphorized and tax-onomized them; by the eighteenth century nerves were "medicalized, academized, globalized, climatized, electrified, genderized, and sexualized" (220–221).[54] An example of the latter is found at one point in the novel where Fernández ridicules contemporary poets as "enervated mandarins" the solution to whose poems is the word *nirvana*. Recognizing that "enervated" means enfeebled by a loss of vigor, we observe that many prevailing discourses about masculinity and class are bound up in this characterization. A primary manifestation of nerves is *nervous style,* characterized by strength of thought, in Fernández nurtured by an optimistic spirit and faith in progress, and his continent's material development.[55] Not only the style but the very impetus behind the diary is nervous: According to Logan (2), the nervous body is *narrative* in structure. He surveys Trotter's *A View of the Nervous Temperament* (1807), which describes how the nervous narrator, an "overly inscribable body," is compelled to narrate its story, its impressionability, to "act out its nervous fit" (29).

A second, very important meaning of *nerves* is its *status:* just like *spleen* and *melancholy* before it, *nervous sensibility* became chic, aris-tocratic, and was mythologized as the touchstone—or the image at least—of true class in an increasingly mobile and unstable social hi-erarchy (Rousseau, 226–227).[56] This "gentrification" of the nerves, in G. S. Rousseau's phrase, was a mark of being Romantic, even suicidal, and coincided with the rise of what Veblen termed the *leisure class.* The doctors of the day seem to have been in league with this class (Rousseau, 229). Not surprisingly, ailments of the nerves fed the new hypercon-sumerism: pills, spas, resorts, and of course "nerve doctors" (Rousseau, 232). For almost all the instances where we find nerves in *After-Dinner Conversation,* there is a corresponding number of high-class treatments chosen for "tonic" effect. In short, delicacy, genius, sensibility, imagina-tion, discriminating taste, and sexual appetite (Rousseau, 245) are the bounty of the nervous in the discourse evolving into modern times. Just as madness is a prestige ailment for the artist, nerves are a mark of dif-ference. Like an invisible, internal tuning fork predisposing one for re-ceiving impressions—or not receiving them: Fernández in "Interlaken, 26 July" criticizes "those made in haste by the Great Creator," whose nerves lack a "tuning"—nerves were a sufficiently vague category to allow for claims of distinction in a time of middle-class ascendancy and mounting alienation. Too, the "nervous conditions" and nervous excitability to which the artists of the day were heir were co-symptomatic with an addictive desire for the drug of novelty and with the rise of consumer culture.

The question arises: Why use the metaphor of the "nerves" to represent aristocracy? Part of the answer lies in that, discursively, the sick individual is seen as someone outside the order of things, alone, unique; nerves, then, are intimate, alienating, the barometer of excess. The reality of illness, however, cannot be fully contained by the metaphor. Inevitable dissatisfaction contributed to suffering that had nothing metaphorical about it: the anhedonia and listlessness ("neurasthenia"), the hypochondria and anxiety of the times—and at the extremes, nihilism and despair.

Tuberculosis

From Susan Sontag's incisive meditation, *Illness as Metaphor* (later *Illness as Metaphor / AIDS and Its Metaphors*), we can derive many insights into the portrayal of illness not as a mere biological phenomenon but as an event that partakes of mythology, class, gender, and psychology. Sontag's characterization of TB as metaphor shows how a linking of disease and sexuality, in a way that "decriminalizes" sexuality, actually romanticizes illness:

> The metaphor of TB was rich enough to provide for two contradictory applications. It described the death of someone (like a child) thought to be too "good" to be sexual: the assertion of an angelic psychology. It was also a way of describing sexual feelings—while lifting the responsibility for libertinism, which is blamed on a state of objective, physiological decadence or deliquescence. . . . Above all, it was a way of affirming the value of being more conscious, more complex psychologically. *Health becomes banal, even vulgar.* [25–26; emphasis mine]

While Helen is rendered back to mystery in death, Fernández cannot accept her physical decomposition, which is even worse than her absence. In fact, he had never really accepted her physicality; his discourse is full of desexualizing images—angels and the like. So illness, and the discourse of medicine, become important cultural signifiers that describe and inscribe the polar values of the times. In fact, bourgeois norms are controlled through this modern ritual; note Ruben Darío's discussion in *Los raros* of the process that eschews artistic reverie as abnormal (178, cited in Villanueva-Collado, *Encuentro*, 357):

> After the diagnosis, the prognosis; after the prognosis, the therapy. Once the disease is determined, [follow] its progress; then [find] the means of curing it. The first therapeutic treatment is to remove the ideas causing the disease.

Note that many of the diagnoses given Fernández in the novel adhere to this very conception of deviant thought—he is advised constantly to be practical and moderate. Silva's poems cast this doctor-patient relationship in the mold of an initiate-hierophant hierarchy, even while ironizing, undermining, the priestly authority the doctor presumes to represent.[57] Silva's poem "Psicopatía" ("Psychopathy") includes the very image from *After-Dinner Conversation*'s 12 April entry—calloused hands—that is Fernández's symbol of the manual laborer[58] in his diatribe on slave morality; the doctor in the poem orders him to:

> move, shout, strive and sweat,
> look at the storm when it looms,
> and tie and knot the stern lines
> *until you have earned ten calluses on your hands*
> *and cleansed your mind of ideas . . .*   [emphasis mine]

Here the prescription is clear: (1) healthy (read: moderate) activity that participates in the material realm; (2) concerted movement that has a purgative effect on an overstimulated brain (namely, Darío above: "to remove the ideas causing the disease"); and (3) leisure-class activity, that is, not manual labor but manual *play*, in this case, boating. Clearly, the positivist regime is advanced here as a curative to the aesthetic, or "degenerate," contemplative realm.[59] In another pithy poem, "El mal del siglo" ("Mal-de-siècle"), the "patient," a homologue of the disenfranchised poet, is held out a nostrum of the same sort to treat a disease of the spirit, to ironic effect: his disease is *life*, consciousness; he rejects all possibility of treatment or recovery, and yet the doctor prescribes a bourgeois, vitalist self-regimentation just the same. Clearly there is a certain heroic, quasi-religious martyrdom in the assertion of his illness:

MAL-DE-SIÈCLE

Patient
—Doctor, a loss of heart to live
in my innermost being is taking root and growing,
the *mal-de-siècle* . . . the same ill that Werther suffered.
. . .
A weariness of it all, an absolute
disdain for things human . . . an incessant
disowning of the meanness of existence
worthy of my master Schopenhauer;
a profound malaise that worsens
with all the tortures of analysis . . .

Doctor
—That's a matter of regime; walk
at daybreak; sleep long, bathe;
drink well; eat well; take good care,
what you have is hunger!

In a similar vein, in "17 November" the secret fallibility, insincerity, and dehumanization behind medical discourse are parodied: "Judging by the symptoms / the animal shows, / it could well be hydrophobic, / or just as well not."[60] Note, also, the subtle parody of having Rivington despair at the thought of his name being linked to an "unglamorous" disease. Nevertheless the Victorian-era doctor's counseling of restraint echoed the general shift away from Protestant ethics (or their "modernization") toward a search for reaping the marginal utility of morals, not the attaining to them for their own sake. Commensurately, energy was thought of in economic terms of scarcity and abundance. Hence the "rest cure" and the principle of moderation (which appears in *After-Dinner Conversation* in various forms). In Lears's words, the reigning therapy placed

> insistence on careful husbanding of resources, [and] expressed the
> persistent production orientation within the dominant culture.
> The Victorian morality of self-control was surviving, but on a
> secular basis. Therapists counseled prudence because it promoted
> well-being in this world, not salvation in the next. [13]

Countless references to energy appear in the novel; in fact a superabundance of energy is, or leads to, Fernández's malaise. At one point (Paris,

26 December) Fernández is even likened to an electric boiler and battery, and on various occasions energy is expressed in economic terms—*expending* energy, *stockpiling* or *storing up* impressions (of which he has an "annuity"). Sontag saw early capitalism shaping how TB was verbalized, but her characterizations apply to health in general and elucidate Silva's novel:

> Like Freud's scarcity-economics theory of "instincts," the fantasies about TB which arose in the last century . . . echo the attitudes of early capitalist accumulation.
>
> *One has a limited amount of energy,* which must be properly spent. . . . Early capitalism assumes the necessity of regulated spending, saving, accounting, discipline—an economy that depends on the rational limitation of desire. TB is described in images that sum up the negative behavior of nineteenth-century homo economicus: consumption; wasting; squandering of vitality.
>
> [62–63; emphasis mine]

Melancholy, too, despite its degenerative force, is similarly productive in Silva, as it is in Bashkirtseff. For example, in the following early poem, where it is the name given to the vehicle leading on from the concrete to the perception of higher forms. Like madness, melancholy is a "defensive disorder" for the poet, against crass Victorian materiality, mechanized relationships between things, and prescribed relationships between bodies:[61]

MELANCHOLIA

From all things veiled,
Tenuous, mysterious, remote,
A vague melancholy rises up
To lead us from the ideal to heaven.

. . .

Airy chain of gold
Which unseen sympathy,
Seething in the depths of the unknown,
Links soul to soul with its filaments

And that in the concrete forms of life
Is lost and swallowed up

Like a dewdrop is lost
In the blades of grass that overlie the tomb.   [24 April 1883]

Fin de siècle ailments are best considered in light of what Lears called
the "therapeutic ethos" of the Victorian era (4). Essentially this involves
the growing authority of medicine and its professionalization, which
effectively linked moral values and health on more and more fronts,
therewith offering the perfect strategic backdrop for the consumer culture. With the urban-industrial revolution in swing, "real life" receded,
market interdependence grew, and the alienation of city life took hold
(6). Neurasthenia, or "nervous prostration," was an affliction of the urban bourgeoisie, causing paralysis of will and an alignment of comfort
with "over-civilization," anxiety, and insulation from direct experience
(7). At the heart of Fernández's desire for experience lies this crippling
contradiction: comfort, in modern, urban terms, enervates mind and
body, and disables the vitality he needs to seek experience; dissipation
is inevitable. Fernández, additionally, has a very slight relationship with
nature—the body's "double"—and its tonic effects.[62] The novel is largely
urban. The ill effects the city causes in Fernández in part are as elusive in
nature and name as is Helen.[63] Part of Fernández's search is a harmonic
wholeness of self, an *integration*. Jackson remarks on "all the anxious ear-
nestness which often seemed—by the late nineteenth century—to lack
clear focus or direction" (8–9). Like Fernández's fragmented identity,

> [t]he autonomous self, long a linchpin of liberal culture, was being
> rendered unreal . . . [in part by] a growing awareness of the con-
> straints that unconscious or inherited drives placed on individual
> choice.   [ibid.]

In this connection, Fernández feels bound at times by the Andrades' an-
imalism, their "rage for action." Silva himself seems to have internalized
this biological and hygienic gospel of the times, even if he questions it;
note, for example, his genetic metaphors and mind-body connections
in his description of his own writing process:

> To produce perfect literary work the *body* must have the *normal
> and physiological sensation* of life; neuroses do not *engender* but
> *sickly children,* and without . . . study of the secrets of art, *regular
> calisthenics of the mind,* literary labors will not have the needed
> foundations to have staying power . . .
>   [Camacho Guizado, 312; emphasis mine]

Writing itself as an "ingested" influence is the topic of Silva's poems, such as "Avant-propos," which opens *Gotas amargas* ("Bitter Drops") and takes the tone of a "prescription." The poems caution against Romantic sentimentalism and offer the collection itself as a fortifying "dose of . . . bitter drops"; i.e., irony as antidote. "Psychotherapeutics" ends on a similar note: "And apply solid cauteries / to the sentimental chancre." Hygiene provides the pretext for Fernández's very reading of the diary: one of the friends assembled requests "disinfecting" from his worldly concerns.

Fernández as Homo Economicus

It is important to root Fernández in the historical times of which he is a product, as we have suggested, and particularly in the emergent consumer culture, the rise of capitalist competition, the integration of Latin America into modernization and global import-export economies, and, importantly, the displacement of humanism from modern neoclassical economics in the last decades of the nineteenth century.

Let us consider some examples of Fernández's economic psychology from the novel. Unlike his cousin Monteverde (1 October), Fernández uses purchasing power as the instrument of his insatiable whims, while Monteverde cynically extorts "gifts" from acquaintances through flattery. The latter follows a kind of protocol of trading on the ceremony of one's host, and perhaps, the inclination to be owed favors or the goods one desires. Ironically, it may be Monteverde who has developed the best economic strategy for a prototypical dandy, since he has broken the mundane system of exchange, and in Benjamin's phrase, stripped things of their commodity character (cited in Glick, 143). Frequently, for example, sexual politics and economics mix, as when Fernández, during a conquest, accuses a libertine woman of merely adopting a pose, of secretly belonging to the class structures of the status quo and tradition. Through all these relationships economic and amorous, Fernández's continuity is his impracticality; he does not give up working—to Monteverde's dismay—even though he can.

Fernández can be viewed as an exaggerated consumer of a certain type: an unrepentant pursuer of luxury and of positional commodities, a Hobbesian creature not less a part of the system for all his wealth; on the contrary, he is often worried about matters of conspicuity, such as whether his investments in the silver box will be laughed at, or the impression his exclusive party made. He is status-conscious in a way that depends on consumption; the role of the poet having declined in modernity, he must commodify his impressions in the object of the diary. The diary is a legitimizing enterprise of what would otherwise be, to the bourgeois ethic, even to his coreligionists assembled to hear it, aimless bohemianism; there is the expectation that a life is diarized either because it deserves to be, or because, in being produced, it becomes deserving along with its producer. Fernández—and his circle—invariably either note the *place of manufacture* ("Moroccan leather") of a good, or name its *maker* ("portrait painted by Whistler"), or employ luxurious adjectivization ("malachite candlesticks"). This consciousness of the quality of goods allows for a pointed passage involving Consuelo in which the mystique of Parisian wares is downplayed relative to Colombia's; the scene is a comment on nationalism, as well as scarcity and distribution and their role in the demand for consumer goods.

Beauty alone, then, cannot be said to motivate Fernández; he enters the market impractically, even improvidently, to be sure, and shows signs everywhere of what the Greeks termed *pleonexia*, "the insatiable desire to have more." Disproportion is a key feature of the decadent, as Roberto González Echevarría's observation underscores: "[E]xcess is at once being and an impulse towards death, being towards death" (60). In our consideration of the psychology of this decadent character, we might use one of Silva's own figures from his poem "Futura," in which he decries humankind's new materialist "god," the base and gluttonous Sancho Panza (a figure with whom, incidentally, Monteverde identifies explicitly). But what is the Decadent but a Sancho of the soul, a *discriminating* Sancho who seeks the immaterial *through the material*? In "Futura," idealism ironically has been banished from the earth and "digestion" (the body) is exalted. Perhaps the emblem of the battle of material and immaterial in the novel is Helen herself, who, "not touching the ground," partakes of the noumenal and the phenomenal alike; she is also repeatedly referred to as if she were a bibelot, the crowning collectible.

Consumer fetishizing, personified in Fernández, may be seen as an extension, and a historical locating, of his outsize appetite for the world—sensations, experience, and their material (and fleshly) conveyances. Fernández is a modern man at his most saturated, fallen into material history, irrational in economic and psychological terms, and a case supporting Thorstein Veblen's notion of how man—even the wealthy man—does not develop consumer tastes in a vacuum, but within a system with various feedback mechanisms.[64] Partly he may be said to be suffering from what Emile Durkheim described in 1897 as anomie, the dissolution of social bonds; if the atomization of society is to be remedied in modernity, it now can occur only through the economic nexus. In the end, in a kind of Quixotic lucid interval, the protagonist even seeks his very salvation *in the market,* where the senses have denied him fulfillment:

> I am going to ask of common commercial operations and of the incessant employment of my material activities what neither love nor art would give me: the secret for enduring life . . .   [16 January]

Hence, Fernández's autonomy is illusory, simply mystique, which is continually purchased as a kind of utility. He is part of the move from creation to consumption; *he does not produce, he re-produces.* Furthermore, he goes against the literary and economic grain of the times: He implicitly resists the new phenomenon of the professionalization of the writer.[65] Gutiérrez Girardot terms him *anfibio* ("amphibious"): both within and without the bourgeois order ("Prólogo," 2). However, the character's modernity should not obscure his historical precedence. He is essentially a dislocated feudal lord. The roots of the *modernista* décor, which we discussed above, and the artist's relationship with objects may be traced precisely to the feudal system and its hostility toward commercial rationality. Max Weber (1106):

> The need for "ostentation," glamour and imposing splendor, for surrounding one's life with utensils which are not justified by utility but, in Oscar Wilde's sense, useless in the meaning of "beautiful," is primarily a feudal status need and an important power instrument. . . .
> . . . [P]ositively privileged feudal strata do not view their existence functionally, as a means for serving a mission. . . . Their typical myth is the value of their "existence." . . . [F]eudalism is inherently contemptuous of bourgeois-commercial utilitarianism. . . .

The Decadent's utility is what allows for his distancing from those values, even if he must make use of their logic and marketplace to gain that apparent distance.

This is but one of the contradictions of the Decadent which Elisa Glick's essay "The Dialectics of Dandyism" details neatly. The consumerism of the day, she notes, is tied to the discharge of energy in an infinitely unfulfilling loop (141). Since *After-Dinner Conversation* assumes a *sed non satiata* philosophy—that of insatiable market economics—it can be read as a model of that era's consumer psychology, a secular materializing of Our Lady of Everlasting Desire's motivations. The fundamental failure of Fernández lies in his consumption of simulacra, of copies, when his discriminating taste runs to originals; what he winds up with is a copy of a copy (of Rivington's painting) of Helen, who even for her father is a "copy" of an effaced "original"—Helen's beloved mother. Fernández himself is alienated from his origins, like his collections. In some sense even his impressions are grafted or assumed literary poses or paintings; like the hero in Alejo Carpentier's novel, *The Lost Steps*, Fernández lives in a prison-house of Western culture.

NOTE ON THE TRANSLATION

The translator works with units of meaning large or small to create *analogues*,[66] doubled texts that are and are not new, are and are not "other." One of the conscious considerations in these operations is *foreignizing* (bringing the reader to the text) versus *domesticating* (bringing the text to the reader).[67] It is my view that a text like *After-Dinner Conversation* should retain its historical place as a document of the period, and not strain to conform to contemporary conventions or tastes, as, indeed, early versions of the novel were expurgated to account for contemporary sensibilities. This translation is most foreignizing *in the very choice of text*. It avoids concessions to a readerly public; it is a writerly novel, as many Decadent novels are. In the sense that "the past is a foreign country," pastness is retained in the formality of tone and syntax, bespeaking a certain strangeness.[68] The translator inevitably interprets, as an actor does, and always with an eye to relevance for an audience.[69] There were countless translational problems in this work. One is the fact that the source text was already an affront to storytelling for its disorderly, uneconomical language. Long, irregular passages had to be made more consumable for a modern public to whom such "word mass," in Steiner's phrase, is disagreeable. Another problem is voiced in Steiner's dismissal of Rossetti's "Sonnets for Pictures" (14–15). He claims that the Pre-Raphaelites' gestures often are now empty, subject to "a suspension of natural reflexes in the interest of some didactic, polemical, or antiquarian aim"; further, that we are "word-blind" to the era's production due to our changed sensibility (15).

We know that the translator is no mere scribe of the source text (or author, which is especially important to stress), but that even if he or she wanted to remain "faithful," he or she could not entirely, since "faithfulness" is better applied to intentionality. Also, what is in play is more: *an actual interdependent series of real, mediated operations,* or praxis. The present edition, for example, shows a didactic bent; it goes further in annotating than any other edition, and offers a few key glosses. So to consider this edition (as all translations are editions) from the vantage point of *skopos,* or purpose, we recognize that for one type of translation user this version is cumbersome or somehow "impure," but for another this hypercultural, highly allusive, and self-contradictory novel could have been well served only by an annotated text, particularly for an academic setting.

One camp may claim that, just as streamlining foreign phrases into English tampers with Silva's original effect, endnotes or footnotes are a *supplement* the author never authorized; another camp may reply, rightly I think, that Silva's audience, or audiences, had a much greater sense of the references—and foreign phrases—than we could hope to have now.[70] So, a tentative conclusion would be that we can never read *After-Dinner Conversation* exactly how *De sobremesa* was read; the work has to be *doubly translated*—linguistically and culturally. Silva himself was "translating"[71] literary currents—harsh Naturalism, arch European Decadence—into prose. In some ways, translators, *preservationists*[72] in their majority, would have us read innocently, as if we were somehow there at the moment of creation, but now there is a sense of that impossibility: *the recognition of belatedness without acceding to a secondariness* is one of the fronts on which the translator takes up arms against those who would have him or her be a mute witness of culture. One Borgesian author-translator, Willis Barnstone, impishly rejects the primacy, the fetish, of the original, and suggests throughout *The Poetics of Translation,* inverting the paradigm, that the translation is the mechanism for making new originals. In an article on Severo Sarduy, Roberto González Echevarría notes the Cuban author's inversion of Platonism: "[T]he copy is the strongest because it is what generates movement, what awakens the subversive capacity of the model. The model only survives in the copy"; this is what Sarduy considers, in González Echeverría's phrase, "the aggression of the copy against the original" (60). Of course, the implications of this idea for the translator tie in to post-colonial images of translation—as evinced in the predominance in modern times of colonizing metaphors in talking about translation: conquest, aggression, captivity, plunder, invasion. These circumstances—or effects—of the translation proper are often impossible to foresee or gauge accurately, but translation can be a means of "fixing a read" on how an era approaches a given text in all its renegade or conservative renderings; each reading, each translation, reflects its own times, and allows for new readings.[73] So, what a competent translation does is something it does *not* do: limit future readings. In this sense the source text is not consumed, but neither is it ever left unaffected by the existence of a translation, in the same way an author, once translated, is not the same author he or she was before.[74]

A great irony is that the translator often translates for the same reason many biographers choose their subject—out of a sense of duty to the subject, even if that duty is to write against the grain—but it is axiomatic that the result plays uncontrollably into larger social, commercial, and aesthetic forces. Lawrence Venuti's terms *invisibility* and *visibility* are perhaps the larger categories into which these considerations fall, although visibility may not simply be restricted to textual presence, but may include the general status of the translator in cultural production. The translator may feel the nostalgia, the anxiety of influence, the Oedipal (or Elektral) usurpation of the father's domain, if you will, but this may be simply a function of overwhelming training as consumers of anonymity in our translations. Yet today in an age of intertexuality, even hypertextuality, the translation is quite often expected not to behave like a translation; that is, it is the only kind of text that is presumed to arise magically, immaculately, from latent possibilities in the "original" (and *original* is an aura-heavy Romantic notion to be sure; likewise its noun, *originality*).[75] The translation is not expected to *evoke* or *reference* the original, but—as in some mystery rite—to somehow *be* that text. This is especially true in a utilitarian society in which all forms of "mediation" are suspect, somehow seen to be adding another remove between the "true" experience and the apprehension of it, as if a work of fiction were not already a "translation" of experience, and Decadent fiction considerably more so. It is a telling note that in Silva's very novel, translation (17 November) is included in a test of dexterity on a level with the other tasks in a physical exam; by implication, to be sane, the healthy are expected to render source texts unproblematically and *univocally*, the way one with healthy lungs blows up a balloon; the insane translate *a rebours*. In another scene, Fernández comes to be known to Nelly through translation. Having judged the English language unmusical in comparison to the original, the poet restores his work to Spanish, and the conquest is under way.

Translation is a reenactment—not in the sense of *ritual*, which stands outside of time, but in the sense of *performance*, which inescapably *stands in relation*, like the painting declaring "This is not a pipe" (or, for that matter, one that declared "This *is* a pipe"), or like Decadence itself, which sought to reproduce the fall of Rome. Translation, however, stands alone also, forging a new horizon from two receded or undesirable ones—the source text (which it is impossible to revive) and the translator's own target language (which it is pointless to mimic). An ideal, then, is to erode the limits of the language in currency *through* the source text—why translate if nothing is to be gained? So I believe translators should choose texts that have a linguistic dimension whose importation, even partial or artless, *upsets the domestic tranquillity of the host language*. Once the process has multiplied, the national literature is enriched.

On the textual level, a few observations are in order.[76] The most pressing of these involve the novel's heteroglossic nature, which critics have noted. Fernández offers a key to the text in this respect when he describes (25 October) "my being, mysterious composite of fire and mud, ecstasy and moans." Indeed, *composite* could be the figure to describe the novel's very structure, and a helpful one in considering translation, for what is a translation but a composite? A heterogeneous discourse—not only heterogeneous, but multilingual—is fitting for a heterogeneously occupied Decadent, in that it thwarts all economy of expression, i.e., that of bourgeois commerce. One clear thread amidst these multiple voices is scientific discourse, even in imagery. In the London 13 November entry, for example, Fernández writes, literally, "Come, my very globules of blood [or "hemoglobin"] cried out to me. . . ." "Globules of blood" is of course a positivist incursion into Romantic discourse, which would have preferred simply "blood." Such passages must be rectified sometimes by ear.[77] These "discursive invasions" parallel one of the central figures of the novel—the *monster,* by nature a grotesque composite. (Dis)proportionate images dominate the discourse; the adjective "monstrous" is a constant. Moreover the very "monstering" of the images is consistent with the distortions typical of the Decadent, for in the grotesque there is generally

> a process of decay or disintegration or a progression from the
> beautiful to the ugly, the harmonious to the disharmonious,
> the useful to the useless, the meaningful to the meaningless,
> or the healthy to the diseased. [Iffland, 30]

The grotesque even plays into certain ideologies, as when Fernández frets over Helen, his *"vision deformed by maternity"* (my emphasis). *Maternity,* moreover, should not be rendered *pregnancy,* a word far too indelicate even for a shocking novel.

Lexically, a few specific examples may be offered to show how a translation can foreground certain constellations of meaning. One is the use of the word *fleshly,* to which I tried to be attentive in order to deliberately echo the "Fleshly School of Poetry."[78] Also, the word *nerve* was used in cases where strength, vigor, or courage was suggested, and in cases requiring a deprivation of the same, or in order to upset, I sometimes opted for *to unnerve,* in order to stress the predominant preoccupation with "nerves" in the era, which I discuss above. In the Spanish, the verb *crispar* (to fray, make tense, or exasperate) is even used to suggest nerves in unexpected instances where nerves are not explicitly present; on one occasion, it occurs in the guise of a collocation (what translators call "natural" or conventional word pairings) with "imagination." Some terms I used that also mirror the time period are *overwrought* for *anxious,* and others in keeping with the presumed high level of learning of a contemporary audience (the Hellenic epithets for doctor—"Zoilo," etc.). I worked in coinages that were new in English at the time of the novel's action—e.g., the adjective *crackpot* (1880s). On one or two occasions I used the mildly anachronistic[79] word *pep,* which was something of a marketing word around World War I, for matters of "energy." Some translations are derived from Edgar Allan Poe's ideolect: For *etéreo,* the word *supernal* was more than once employed; for *pupilas azules, azure orbs;* for *sobrenatural,* almost invariably *unearthly.* "Hearing" Nietzsche, I used *the herd* for *el vulgo* in the first scene. And finally, subtly interwoven in the text are many instances of synaesthesia, particularly in verbs; laying bare this *modernista* device took high priority.

On the question of the title, a *sobremesa* is polyvalent in Spanish, and quite culture-specific. The obvious translation of *De sobremesa* is *Table Talk;* I resisted this, since there is a whole literary tendency, if not a genre, implied by this term: From Hazlitt to Martin Luther to Coleridge, this tradition of the colloquist, or talking essayist, has been practiced; usually they are private editorializations on given topics, often for the purpose of being collected by a biographer. In other words, table talk is the record of a real writer. Strictly speaking, complicating matters further, the novel presents much more of a monologue with slight "choral" characters, and is really a diary with implied readers; in that sense, and in the sense that *no one is actually at the table,* a *sobremesa* references the subject matter more than anything. The translator tries to retain here the notions of *class* and *culture*—and their attendant postures—implicit in a *sobremesa.* Manuel Gutiérrez Nájera's poem "La Duquesa Job" ("The Dutchess Job"), for example, begins "En dulce charla de sobremesa . . ." ("In pleasant after-dinner conversation . . .") (Olivio Jiménez, 100). This consideration proved a challenge. However, the most important con-

After-Dinner Conversation

TRANSLATION OF *De sobremesa*

$\mathcal{S}$*ecluded by the shade of gauze and lace,* the warm light of the lamp fell in a circle over the crimson velvet of the tablecloth, and as it lit up the three china cups, which were golden in the bottom from the traces of thick coffee, and a cut-crystal bottle full of transparent liqueur shining with gold particles, it left the rest of the large and silent chamber awash in a gloomy purple semidarkness, the effect of the cast of the carpet, the tapestries, and the wall hangings.

In the back, dimmed by diminutive shades of reddish gauze, the light from the candlesticks on the piano did battle with the enveloping half-light, while on the open keyboard the brilliant whiteness of its ivory squared off against the dull black of the ebony.

On the redness of the walls, covered with an opaque woolen tapestry, shone the engravings of hilts and the smooth steel blades of crossed swords in a panoply over a shield, and standing out from the dark background of the canvas, bordered by the gold of a Florentine frame, the head of a Flemish burgomaster, copied from Rembrandt, smiled good-naturedly.

The smoke from two cigarettes, the fiery tips of which burned in the darkness, curled in tenuous bluish spirals in the circle of lamplight, and the sweet enervating smell of opiate tobacco from the Orient mingled with that of the Russian leather in which the household furnishings were covered.

A man's hand ran along the velvet tablecloth, struck a match and lit the six candles arrayed in a heavy bronze candelabra beside the lamp. With the brighter light the group that sat in silence came into view: the fine Arabian profile of José Fernández,[1] accentuated by the dull pallor of his complexion and his curly black hair and beard; the Herculean frame and serene features of Juan Rovira, which were rendered very attractive by the contrast between his large eyes with their childlike expression and the gray hair of his thick mustache set against the darkness of his sun-tanned skin; the lean, serious face of Oscar Sáenz, who, with his head sunken in the cushion of the Turkish divan and his body stretched out on it, twisted his pointed blond beard and seemed lost in endless thought.

"Some after-dinner conversation *this* is! We've been as silent as three corpses for half an hour.[2] This half-light you like, Fernández, feeds the silence and is a narcotic," Juan Rovira burst out as he chose a cigar from the box of open Havanas on the table, near the bottle of Dantziger Goldwasser. "A fine after-dinner conversation for a feast splashed with that Burgundy. I already was feeling some congestion coming on!" With that he began pacing with large steps across the room, his right hand stuck in his vest pocket, drawing from the cigar the first puffs of smoke.

"What do you expect? This is what the poets call 'the silence of close friendship'; also, the fact is that Oscar's ailment has rubbed off on us—the hospital mice have eaten his tongue . . . You haven't joined in three words since you got here. You're tired," he said, speaking to Sáenz, who sat up upon hearing him.

"I, tired? . . . no; I'm a bit worn out. But realize, Juan," he went on, focusing on Rovita his small penetrating eyes, which out of professional habit fixedly observed the speaker's face, as if seeking in it the symptom or expression of a hidden malaise, "realize that I spend the entire week in cold hospital rooms and in bedrooms where so many incurably ill people are suffering; there I see all the anxieties, all the wretchedness of weakness and of human pain in their saddest and most repugnant forms; I breathe in nauseating stenches of filth, decomposition, and death; I don't pay visits to anyone, and on Saturdays I come in here to find the dining room lit *a giorno*[3] by thirty diaphanous candlesticks and perfumed by the profusion of rare multicolored flowers, moist and fresh, that cover the table and overflow their Murano crystal urns; the dull shine of the old silver dinner service imprinted with the coat of arms of the Fernández de Sotomayor family; the fragile china hand-decorated by famous artists; the tableware that has the appearance of gems; the dainty morsels, the blond aged sherry, the dry Johannisberg Riesling, the Bordeaux and Burgundies that have slept thirty years down in the depths of the wine-cellar; chilled Russian-style sherbets, the honey-flavored Tokay,[4] all the refinements of those Saturday repasts, and then, in the sumptuous environment of that room, the coffee, aromatic as an essence, the choicest cigars and Egyptian cigarettes that impart their scents to the air. . . . Add to the impression that all those material goods make on me—who am used to seeing dying people—the surplus of physical vigor and the superabundance of that man among men," he said, pointing to Fernández, who smiled triumphantly, "add that to my day-to-day tasks and to the lowly, pedestrian environment in which I live, and you'll understand my silence when I'm here. *That's* why I keep quiet, and for other reasons too . . ."

"What reasons are those?" inquired Fernández.

"Your love affairs, which we all secretly envy you," Rovira insinuated with a paternal air. "And the unsanitary side has this don Pedro Recio Tirteafuera[5] worried."

"No, the rest is that I've understood how pointless it is to implore you to return to literary work. And for you to devote yourself to a writing worthy of your energy, and that every time I'm here, I'd rather not talk so as not to have to tell you again that it's a crime to have at your disposal all the means that you do, and to let the days, months, and entire years go by without writing a line! Are you resting on your laurels, content with having published two volumes of poetry, one as a child and another seven whole years ago?"

"Does that not seem like much to you, having written books of poems like *First Verses* and *Poems from the Beyond*?"

"I don't know about such things, but it seems to me Fernández's verses are worthy," Rovira chimed in, sounding annoyed.

"For anyone else I would think it quite a bit, but for Fernández it's nothing . . . Remember how long ago he wrote them . . . Everything you've done," he went on, turning toward the poet, "all the most perfect aspects of your poems amount to nothing. It's inferior to what we have the right to expect from you, we who know you well, inferior to what you know all too well you can do. And yet, it's been two years since you've produced one line . . . Tell me, do you plan to spend your whole life as you've spent the last months, squandering your abilities in ten opposing directions; exposing yourself to the vagaries of war for the sake of defending a cause you don't believe in, as you did in July when you fought under Monteverde's orders; promoting political rallies to rile up your countrymen, at whom you

laugh; cultivating rare flowers in the greenhouse; seducing hysterics dressed by Worth;[6] studying Arabic and undertaking dangerous
jaunts to the most unfamiliar, unhealthy regions in our territory in
order to further your studies of prehistory and anthropology? Let me
lecture you, since I have held my tongue for so long. In your frenzy
to widen the field of your life experiences, in your zeal to simultane-
ously develop the many faculties with which nature has endowed
you, you are steadily losing sight of the place where you are headed.
The look of your desk yesterday morning would lead one who did
not know you as well as I do to think you suffer the onset of incoher-
ence. On your worktable there was an ancient majolica vase filled
with monstrous orchids;[7] a copy of Tibullus[8] handled by six generations, and which held amidst its yellowed pages the translation you've
been working on; the final book by some English poet or other; your
dispatch from the General, sent by the Ministry of War; some mineral
samples from the Rio Moro mines, the analysis of which worried you;
a perfumed cambric handkerchief that you doubtless snatched away
the previous night at the Santamaría ball from the most aristocratic of
your conquests; your Anglo-American Bank checkbook, and presiding
over that motley assemblage, the Quechuan idol that you hauled out
of the floor of an Indian temple on your last outing, and a little Greek
statue in white marble. Sitting at your desk, already whiplashed by a
cold shower and exhilarated by three cups of tea, you would begin
your day. You had already written a perverse musical stanza intended
probably for one of your victims; from what you told me, you had
already drawn three checks to cover the week's expenses; phoned to
give orders to the Villa Helena architect; begun a lab test on the Rio
Moro minerals; you had already read ten pages of a monograph on
the Aztec race, and while they were saddling the most spirited of the
horses, you kept yourself occupied by studying a battle plan. My God!
If there is a man capable of coordinating all that, that man, dedicated
to a single thing, would be monstrously great. But no, that's outside
the realm of the human . . . You will dissipate yourself in vain. Not
only will you spread yourself thin, but those ten paths you wish to follow all at once, will come together on you, into a single one."

Quental[10] came the sonnet sequence I later called "The Dead Souls";
in "Diaphanous Days" any intelligent reader can detect the influence
of the sixteenth-century Spanish mystics, and my masterpiece, the
"Poems of the Flesh"[11] that form part of the "Songs from the Beyond"
that have won me the admiration of the penny-ante critics and five or
six ridiculous imitators—what else are they but a mediocre attempt
to convey in our language the sickly sensations and complicated
sentiments that in perfect forms Baudelaire and Rossetti, Verlaine and
Swinburne already expressed in their own? . . . No, my God, I'm not
a poet . . . I dreamt before and I still dream of mastering form, of
forging stanzas that suggest a thousand obscure things I feel seething
within me and that perhaps would be worth saying, but I cannot
devote myself to that. . . ."

"After listening to you I understand why Máximo Pérez says that
the critic in you kills off the poet . . . that your analytical faculties are
superior to your creative powers," said Sáenz.

"Could be, I'm the one least in a position to say," Fernández
went on. "Poet, maybe, that's the label that stuck. In the public's
mind you have to be *something*. The herd puts names on things in
order to speak of them and sticks labels on people in order to clas-
sify them. Afterward the man undergoes a sea-change but the label
remains. I published a volume of bad verse at age twenty and it sold
well; another of average verse at twenty-eight and it didn't sell at all.
They called me *poet* since the first, after the second I haven't written another line and I've practiced nine different professions, and in
spite of that I still have the label stuck on me, like a bottle that when
opened in the drugstore contained *myrrh,* and that later, full of Spanish fly, linseed, or opium, says *balsamic gum* on the outside. Poet! But,
see, no, it's not my analytic faculties, which Pérez overstates, that are
the secret source of the unfruitfulness you accuse me of; you're well
aware of what is: the fact is, just as poetry fascinates and attracts me,
so too does everything fascinate and attract me, irresistibly; all the
arts, all the sciences, politics, speculation, luxury, pleasures, mysticism,
love, war, all life forms, material life itself, the very sensations that my

senses demand be ever more intense and exquisite . . . What do you expect—with all those ambitions can a body set to chiseling sonnets? Under those conditions a fellow's not in his right mind."

"Especially when he wears a mask—as you do—of perfect worldly uprightness, when he isolates himself as you live isolated among the treasures of art and the lavish creature comforts of a house like this, and only interacts with a dozen loons like us, your friends; with the exception of Rovira, the others serve to isolate you from real life . . ."

"Real life? . . . But what *is* real life, tell me, the emotionless bourgeois life, the one devoid of curiosity? . . . It's true there are only ten close friends who understand me and whom I understand, and a few departed souls in whose circle I keep constant company . . . The rest are skin-deep friends, to coin a phrase; as for my life today, you well know that, although different from the way in which I have lived at other times, its organization boils down to an adherence to what has always constituted my most secret aspiration, my deepest passion: the desire to experience life, to know life, to possess it, not like one possesses a woman to whom we help ourselves during moments of her weakness and our recklessness, but like a worshipped woman who, convinced of our love, confides in us and surrenders her most delicious secrets. Do you think I get accustomed to living? . . . No, with every passing day the savor of life grows stranger to me, and the eternal miracle that is the universe astonishes me more. Life. Who knows what it is? Not religions, since they consider it a step toward other regions; not science, since it merely investigates the laws that govern it without discovering its cause or its purpose. Perhaps art, which copies it . . . perhaps love, which creates it. Do you think the majority of people who die, have lived? Well, don't be too sure; see here: most men, one group in constant struggle to meet its daily needs, the other locked in to a profession, to a field of expertise, to a belief, as in a prison that has only a single window open always onto the same horizon, most men die not having lived it, not having taken from it more than a blurry impression of fatigue . . . Ah! To live life . . . that is what I want, to feel all that can be felt, to know all that can be known, to do all things possible . . . The months spent diving for pearls, not seeing the sand on the beaches and the sky and the greenish waves, breathing deep the salty steep of the sea; the age of orgies and earthly pell-mell in Paris; the months of retreat in the old Spanish convent, between whose thick grey walls are heard echoing only the monotone prayers of the friars and the solemn music of the plainsong; my restless stint in Conills's office, with my fortune tied up in the dizzying machinery of Yankee business, and my head full of prices and calculations, a complete grind;[12] the refined residences in Italy, in which, locked away from the world and having no thought for myself, I lived cloistered in churches and museums and dreamt for hours on end in loving contemplation of the works of my favorite artists like Il Sodoma[13] and Leonardo. All of these are five roads taken with crazed enthusiasm, traveled frenzily, then diverged from for fear that death would catch me unawares on one of them before I could head down others, down those other new ones I try to travel now and down which you say I've been vainly squandering my energy . . . Ah! To live life! To get drunk on it,[14] mix all its palpitations with the palpitations of our heart before it turns to frozen ash; to feel it in all its forms, in the shouting at the rally where the disordered soul of the rabble is stirred and floods its banks, in the acrid perfume of the strange flower that is opening, fantastically multicolored, in the warm atmosphere of the hothouse; in the guttural sound of the words that, made into song, have for centuries accompanied the music of the Arabian guzla;[15] in the divine convulsion that chills the mouths of women as they lie in the throes of voluptuous death; in the fever that seethes from the jungle floor where the last worldly remains of the savage tribe are hidden . . . Tell me, Sáenz, are all those conflicting experiences and the clashing visions of the universe that seek me out, all that is what you want me to give up in order to set about writing quatrains and carving out sonnets?"

"No," the other man answered, unruffled. "I never said not to think but rather not to overdo it. You contend that what I call overdoing it is to you what is strictly necessary, and you scoff at my sermonizing. Clearly, if the result of all your labors seemed up to your

standards, I would applaud you, but what you want is to *enjoy,* and
that is what you pursue in your studies, in your business affairs, in
your loves, in your hatreds. It's not your intellectual complications
that don't let you write, nor your great critical faculties that would
require that you produce masterpieces in order to satisfy them, no,
that's not it; it's the demands placed on you by your exacerbated
senses and the urgency to satisfy them, that's what rules you. Why,
if it were up to me I'd remove one by one all the things blocking
you from writing and from making a name for yourself. You want to
know what it is that holds you back from writing? Enervating luxury,
the refined comfort[16] of this house with its enormous gardens full
of flowers and populated with statues, its hundred-year-old park, its
hothouse where, as in the poisoned atmosphere of the native forests,
grow the most singular species of tropical flora. You know what it is?
It's not so much the tapestries fading in the hall, nor the sumptuary
salons, nor the bronzes, marbles, and paintings in the gallery, nor the
Far East room with all those loud silks and flamboyant gimcracks, nor
the collections of weapons and porcelain, not to mention your library,
nor the watercolors and drawings that you shut yourself in to see for
weeks at a time. No, it's the other things. The things that stimulate
the body, the weapons, the strenuous exercises, your wild hunts with
the Merizaldes and the Monteverdes; your complicated business dealings; the hydrotherapy salon, the bedchamber and boudoir worthy
of a courtesan. They are the new vices you say you're inventing,
those jewels in whose contemplation you spend your time fascinated
by the sparkle, as a hysteric would be fascinated; the tea dispatched
directly from Canton, the coffee Rovira sends you, chosen bean by
bean; the tobacco from the Orient and the cigarettes from Down
Under, the Russian kummel and the Swedish krishabaar, all the nice
touches of the princely life you lead, and all those little dainties that
have replaced the poet in you with a pleasure-seeker who by dint of
pleasure is headed fast for depletion . . . Man! Here you are as healthy
as a horse and strong as an ox, and you've taken to drinking tonics
of the sort that they give to paralytics, and that only to feel more full
of life than you already are! Look, if it were up to me I'd take away all

your refinements and your sumptuosities with which you surround yourself, I'd weaken you a bit to calm you, I'd send you off to live in a little town, in a poor, peaceful environment where you'd converse with countryfolk and wouldn't see any other paintings than the church icons, nor would you get your hands on any other books than *The Christian Year*,[17] lent by the priest. If it were in my hands I would save you from yourself. After six months of living in that environment you would be a new man, and you would set about writing a poem like those you *should* write, like those it is your *duty* to write."

"Ah, so it's my duty to write them, is it?" asked Fernández, laughing. "Well, now, that's rich!" And suddenly becoming serious: "Happy you who knows what each man's duties are, and who fulfills those you think are yours, as you do. Duty! Crime! Virtue! Vice! . . . Words, as Hamlet says[18] . . . I'm in the situation in which that shoemaker supposed us to be, that fellow who, when he would get drunk, would keep us at the school exit, remember?"

"Ah, Landínez the shoemaker," answered Juan Rovira, as if he were talking to him. "The day before yesterday I came across him drunker than ever and he stopped me with his eternal singsong: 'Give me a peseta, sir. You don't realize the position you hold in society; you don't know right from wrong.' So, José, what do you have to do with that sloven?" he said, questioning Fernández.

"You don't understand these things," he responded. "It's an inside joke I have with Sáenz. So tell me," he asked, turning to the doctor, "do you really think my duty is to write poems? Well, look at that skull," he added, showing with his slender, nervous hand a death's-head[19] whose hollow eye sockets where the shadows pooled seemed to stare at him from the pedestal of the Venus de Milo where it was placed. "That skull tells me every night that my duty is to live with all my might, with all my life!

"And yet, verses lure me, and I should like to write—why hide the fact from you? In these final days of the year I dream constantly of writing a poem, but I can't find the form . . . This morning returning on horseback from Villa Helena I seemed to hear inside myself some finished stanzas that were fluttering to find a way out. Verses make themselves inside one, one does not make them, one simply writes them down . . . Do you not know that, Rovira . . . ?"

"No, how should *I* know those things!" answered the addressee. "I like yours and they're certainly good, since a man of taste who has horses like the dappled pair in your carriage and the Arabian you ride, and a house like this and so many paintings and so many statues and cigars of this quality," he said, showing the long ash of the nearly black cigar that he was smoking, "it's as plain as plain could be that he can't make bad verses!"

"Why don't you write a poem, José?" Sáenz insisted.

"Because you wouldn't understand it, maybe, just as you didn't understand the 'Songs from the Beyond,'" said the poet listlessly. "Don't you remember Andrés Ramírez's article in which he called me a disgusting pornographer and said my verses were a mix of holy water and Spanish fly? Well, that'd be the fate of the poem I'd write. The fact is I don't want to *say* but rather suggest, and for suggestion to work, the reader needs to be an artist.[20] In imaginations lacking in faculties of that order, what effect would the work of art produce? None. Half of it lies in the verse, in the statue, in the painting, the other in the brain of the one hearing, seeing, or dreaming. Drum your fingers on that table, and clearly only a few blows will sound; run them over the ivory keys and you'll produce a symphony: And the public is nearly always a table and not a piano[21] that vibrates like this one," he concluded, sitting at the Steinway and playing the first notes of the prologue to the Mephisto.[22]

"Fernández," said Rovira, holding up his endless pacing to approach the table and shake the ash from the cigar he was smoking into an embossed copper ashtray. "Look, Fernández: don't fret over this doctor's lectures; he just wants to be your don Pedro Recio Tirtea-fuera, nor over writing a few verses more or less, so your admirers proclaim you a genius the day after your burial! It's better to live the good life for three days, than three centuries in the heart of poster-ity . . . Pay no mind, my boy, have fun, take care, get more Arabian horses and more weapons if that sounds good to you, buy more old relics and more gewgaws, get involved up to your neck in politics, be loved by all the women who fancy you and let yourself love all those whom you fancy, don't write a single verse again if you don't feel like it . . . For all that I give you permission, in exchange for your satisfying tonight a whim I have had for some time . . . I want to hear you read some pages that, as you once told me, have to do with the name of your estate, with a trifolium design and a butterfly several volumes of your library have stamped in gold on their soft covers, and that painting by an English painter . . . What do you call him? Decadent? No . . . Symbolist? No, Pre-Raphaelite? That's it, Pre-Raphaelite, which you have in the gallery and which I cannot manage to understand no matter how much I look at it every time I pass by it . . . Do you know what I'm talking about? . . ."

"Yes, I know what you're talking about," Fernández answered, rising upon hearing the sound of voices and steps in the next room.

The heavy red cloth door-curtain trimmed in gold that closed off the right entry was drawn back, opening the way to Luis Cordovez and Máximo Pérez.

"Good evening, I brought you this man for you to entertain," Cordovez said, stretching his hand out to Fernández; "Juan, Oscar," greeting informally the friends with whom Pérez was speaking. "And I've come to be disinfected of all the coarseness I've heard in these last two hours . . . Give me a glass of your driest sherry, and sit down here," he added, motioning at an armchair next to his. "I need to hear fine poetry to disinfect my soul . . . If you only knew where I've been! . . ."

"Well, it doesn't seem impossible to guess; from a meal at which you were near a blonde . . . your coat gives it away . . . Irreproach-able! . . ." Fernández added, noticing the fresh gardenia that Cordo-vez was wearing in the buttonhole of his tailcoat and the thick pearls that buttoned up his shirt front.

"You see there, you're mistaken! Poets are forever dreaming delightful things. Not at all, man, I'm coming from a dinner given by Ramón Rey for Daniel Avellaneda, in which we spoke of politics in the beginning and religion and women toward the end. Thus I'm telling you I need you to read me verses by Núñez de Arce[23] to disinfect me. No, not verses," he added, directing a glance at Fernández in which was betrayed his almost brotherly love and his fanatic enthusiasm for the poet. "You know what? Not verses by Núñez de Arce . . . it's your prose that I want . . . I've come to ask you to *dream* as you say . . . it's been three days since I've asked anyone to *dream* out of fear they ill serve me and I was thinking every minute, let this night arrive so I can beseech you to read some notes you took on a journey through Switzerland, which you have never shown me . . . You'll read them to us in a while, won't you? . . . If you knew that I spent a horrible day today thinking about you, with the *idée fixe* that you were ill . . . But you're well, right? . . ."

"I'm never well in the last days of the year," answered Fernández, as if his mind were on something that preoccupied him. "I'm never well in the last days of December."

The freshness and liveliness of Luis Cordovez, whose delicate features and budding brown beard recalled the profile of Scheffer's[24] Christ, without the dark curls that fell down his narrow forehead, nor the tails that gave shape to his bust, managing to diminish the likeness, formed a strange contrast with the meditative lethargy of the pale semblance and spiritlessness of Máximo Pérez's grey eyes. The latter man's thinness, hardly concealed by the light cheviot he had on, could be discerned in the lines of his body stretched out on the neighboring divan, in a posture of sickly fatigue.

"You're still not doing well, eh? . . . Your pains are getting worse? . . ." Sáenz asked him, fixing his inquisitive eyes on him.

"The horrendous pains are still there, in spite of the bromides and the morphine . . . Tonight I felt so bad that I was already on my way out of the club when I came upon Cordovez and he was kind enough to bring me . . . Your colleagues don't know what I have . . . Fernández, tell me, could they not give a precise diagnosis of what you suffered in Paris either? A nervous disorder that Marinoni spoke to me of . . . Tell me, did you describe it somewhere in your diary? . . . If you were to read it to us tonight . . . I think the mere reading of something novel and that interests me greatly would manage to dispel my dark thoughts a bit."

"I had prompted José earlier to read us something related to the name of the estate, to Villa Helena," Rovira said, out of sorts and as if fearful of not attaining what he was after; "now you and Cordovez come along, each with his own idea, and it'll turn out that José won't read us anything. Fernández, what do you say?"

"You wanted to read Pereda's[25] latest novel, right, Cordovez?" said the writer absentmindedly. "Remind me to give you the volume."

"No; I had entreated you to read us some notes written in Switzerland, but it turns out that Rovira wishes to hear some pages that he says are connected with Villa Helena; Pérez, others that apparently describe a disease that you suffered in Paris, and Doctor Sáenz has no opinion, he's kept silent as the tomb since we came in . . . Say something, Sáenz!"

"Fernández never listens to me when I talk to him. I've been telling him for four years to write and he never listens to me. José, don't you have a short story or something that takes place in Paris on New Year's Eve?" the doctor insinuated . . . "Why don't you read it to us?"

"That's all Her . . ." said the writer, as if lost in a dream; "this morning the white roses in the wrought-iron gate at Villa Helena; at midday the fluttering of the white butterfly that came in the study window . . . Now four conflicting desires come together for me to mention her . . ."

He passed his hand over his forehead and then remained quiet for ten minutes in which he seemed to forget about everything and fall into deep meditation, without any of the friends daring to rouse him.

"Fernández, aren't you going to read us anything?" asked Rovira impatiently, stopping at the former's armchair . . . "Do you have a headache? . . . It's the work from today . . . What do you work for? . . . Will you read us something after all? . . ."

José Fernández, after searching in one of the dark corners of the room, where in the reddish dark only the whiteness of a bouquet of irises and the outline of a bronze vase were suggested, after dimming the lights on the chandelier, sat near the desk, and placing a closed book on the velvet tablecloth, remained looking at it for a few moments.

It was a thick volume with dull gold locks and corners. Over a background of enameled blue, encrusted in the black morocco of the covers, there were three green leaves on which fluttered a butterfly with its wings wrought in tiny little diamonds.

Fernández settled into his chair, opened the book, and after leafing through it for a long while, he read the following by lamplight:

Paris, 3 June, 189–...

The reading of two books that are like a perfect antithesis of intuitive comprehension and systematic incomprehension of Art and life, have absorbed me these days: they form the first thousand pedantic, pseudo-scientific elucubrations which a German doctor, Max Nordau, titled *Degeneration,* and the other, the two volumes of the diary, of the written soul, of María Bashkirtseff, the incomparably gentle Russian girl dead in Paris of genius and of consumption, at age twenty-four in a Rue de Prony hotel.

Like a nearsighted Eskimo in a museum of Greek marbles, full of glorious Apollos and immortally beautiful Venuses, Nordau wanders among the masterpieces the human spirit has produced in the last fifty years. He wears thick black lenses over his eyes, and in his hand is a box full of file cards with the names of all the manias classified and enumerated by modern alienists. He lingers at the foot of the masterpiece, compares its lines with those of his own ideal of beauty, finds it deformed, chooses a name to give to the artist's imagined disease that produced it, and sticks the classifying label on the august white marble. Seen through his black spectacles, judged in the light of his aesthetic canon, Rossetti is an idiot, Swinburne a superior degenerate, Verlaine a fainthearted degenerate with an asymmetrical cranium[26] and mongoloid face, vagrant, impulsive, dipsomaniacal; Tolstoy, a mystic, hysteric degenerate; Baudelaire, an obscene maniac; Wagner, the most degenerate of the degenerates, graphonomer,[27] blasphemer, and erotomaniac.

moods. He paints her as an adolescent, on the frozen savannas of Russia, allowing to develop within her the spiritual and sensual vigor that give impetus to her life; in mid-youth, forming the background of the portrait with dark branches, through which the music of an orchestra quivers at nightfall, where the waters of Bohemia lay, and touched by the cold hand of consumption that lends luster to her eyes with an artificial shine and flushes her pale cheeks with the stir of her impoverished blood, under the sun of Nice, smiling and with her bodice decorated with a tiny bouquet of mimosas and anemones. None of the ideologue's disparagements satisfies me. I close my eyes and I envision her thus, following the pages of the Diary: It is late at night . . . The family, tired from the day's trivial difficulties, sleeps peacefully. She, in the silent room where she is surrounded by her favorite books, Spinoza, Fichte, the most subtle of the poets, the most caustic of the modern novelists, leaning on the desk, the warm lamplight falling on her mass of brown hair, her head resting on her pale hand, she stays up and goes over her day. She rose at daybreak, and as she ran down the balcony blinds, seeking an artificial night conducive to study, the passing of a group of workers down the street, a street full of the pre-dawn mist and lashed by rain, moved her as she thought of those wretches' lot. After several hours of reading Balzac during which she communed with that enormous spirit, the project of the painting she dreams of, the painting that would immortalize her, has sent her to Sèvres,[31] where the model awaits her, and there in the luminous landscape of spring, her hands trembling with artistic fever, her eyes open wide to see everything, her nerves stretched taut to work the miracle of translating to oil the freshness of the budding new growth, the warmth of the sun that lights up the countryside, the rosy flesh of the model, over which floated the diaphanous shadows of the branches of a peach tree in bloom; the damp green of the tender grass, the purple of the violets and the yellow of the buttercups that glaze[32] the meadow, the blue of the pale sky on the horizon, she has worked, losing herself in activity, frenziedly, in a mad fit of art, hour after hour, the day long. In the afternoon, exhausted, disenchanted to the depths of her soul with painting, convinced that all her efforts to reach the dreamt-of goal will be in vain, there was an instant in which she had to contain herself in order not to tear up the oil she was working on with her every ounce of strength. An elegant gesture puts her momentary anguish out of her mind. Doucet, the dressmaker, is waiting for her to try on a pink silk crêpe dress for him, which has as its only adornment a garland of Bengala roses. The two have been coordinated so that, when she wears it at the next dance, when the gathering sees her cross the modern ballroom among the propriety of black tuxes and white shirt fronts, they have the illusion of beholding the most beautiful of Greuze's[33] paintings, smiling and brought to life. And how the dress excited her! For an hour she forgets the artist she is, the philosopher that works inside her and that analyzes life every minute and whom the eternal problems preoccupy . . . No, that is not what she is, she feels that she was born to concentrate in her all the graces and refinements of a civilization, that her true role, the only one equal to her talents, is that of a Madame Récamier,[34] that her theater will be a salon where the exceptional intellects assemble and whence the double light of supreme worldly elegance and the most high-flying intellectual speculation emanates . . . The most illustrious men of the day will be the guests of that center; there Renan[35] will smile suavely, moving his great kindly head with an episcopal motion; Taine[36] will come from time to time and will hold forth, a bit wrapped up for brief spells in his incessant thought, other times lively, asking questions in phrases as short, neat, and precise as formulas; Zola, potbellied and pallid, will tell the outline of his future novel; Daudet[37] will rove the curious gaze of his myopic eyes over the old faded tapestries that showcase his sketches, and rest against the brocade of the ashlars his long tangled locks; the painters, Bastien Lepage, the favorite, tiny, pug-nosed dynamo of a man, with his adolescent blond beard; Carolus Durán,[38] with his air of a swashbuckler and a ladykiller; Master Rohault de Fleury,[39] he of the tender Arab countenance and the sleeping eyes; the poets Coppée, Sully Prudhomme, Theuriet,[40] all of them will be welcome there as in a house of art, and they will feel indulged and pampered as if by a sister. She will hold the scepter in her hands, she will be the Vittoria Colonna[41] of tomorrow, encircled by that court of thinkers and artists . . .

Oh, fruitless dreams burst like soap bubbles that are born, take on color, and pop in the air! . . . Upon leaving Doucet's house, the idea of speaking with the doctor, of telling him the truth about the affliction devouring her, prevails upon her. She has felt so unwell in recent days, the pains that have tormented her have been so sharp, so intense has the fever been that has scorched her veins; so profound the decay that has laid her up for hours on end! . . . In the grave silence of the doctor's office the Æsculapius[42] slowly auscultates her, taps her with soft little blows of his slender fingers, attentively applies his ear to her silky smooth skin, her delicate bust, and after the thorough examination prescribes caustics that burn her bosom, plaster applications that stain and disfigure, horrible drugs, a trip to the Mediodía that was tantamount to giving up everything—art, society, pleasures—and to justify the rigid prescriptions and with his coldness of a man of science used to others' pain, he utters the brutal words. *She's consumptive . . . the right destroyed by tubercules, the left already encroached upon, the deafness that has been torturing her for months will steadily worsen; the cough that wracks and pains her, the awful bouts of insomnia that deplete her, all that will grow, gaining strength, and spread like wildfire, doing away with her . . .*

She's consumptive! Yes, he's sorry, he knows. There was a moment in which as she left the doctor's house she succumbed to despair and felt close to death, but for two hours she forgot her illness . . . Through the studio's large open window, near the little room where she is now, the nighttime sky could be seen, a deep, transparent blue; the moonlight filtered through there and flooded the darkness with its pacifying spell. As she sat there at the piano, the ivory keyboard quivering under her nervous fingers, the music of Beethoven stretching out into the dormant air, and in the semidarkness, evoked by the pained notes of the nocturne and by a reading of Hamlet, floated the corpse of Ophelia, Ophelia, pale and blonde, crowned with flowers, pale and blonde, swept along by the melody as if by the treacherous waters of the murderous river . . . the pale blonde corpse crowned with flowers, carried off by the gentle current . . .

It was true that two hours ago the magic of the music had made her forget everything, herself and her consumption, but now, the charm faded, alone, seated in front of her desk, leaning on it as the warm lamplight fell on her mass of brown hair, her head resting on her delicate hand, now, as she went over her day, her reading of Balzac, the fury of artistic activity in Sèvres, trying on her dress, the dream of worldly greatness, the past moments at the piano, all of it vanished before the cruel reality of the illness that advanced in the great religious silence of midnight; the sinister prophecy of the man of science fills the field of her inner vision, lonely, dark, and evil as a cloudy horizon . . . To die, dear God, to die like this, tubercular, at twenty-three, just as she was starting to live, not having known love, the only thing that makes life worth living, to die without having carried out the work she dreamt of, which will save her name from oblivion; to die leaving the world without having satisfied millions of curiosities, desires, ambitions she feels inside her, when the knowledge of six living languages, two dead languages, eight literatures, the history of the world, all the philosophies, art in all its forms, science, the voluptuosities of civilization, all the luxuries of the spirit and the body, when the trips all around Europe and the assimilation of the souls of six nations have served only to desire life with infinite passion and to hatch plans whose execution would require ten lifespans. To die thus, feeling like the embryo of oneself, to die when one adores life, to be undone, to disappear in the shadows! Impossible! . . .

The idea of fighting the disease possesses her now . . . she had to struggle . . . a year devoted to overcoming it should suffice. With her health fully restored later on she will make up for lost time; diaphanous tulles and white mimosas and camellias will mask the stains from the plasters and the iodine on her turgid breast, and her entire body will betray the subtle coloration of blood intensified by the warm salty air of the Mediterranean. She must fight, she must live! She must paint the Holy Women guarding the tomb.[43] Mary Magdalene seated, in profile, elbow resting on right knee and chin in hand, her lifeless eye, as if seeing nothing, fixed on the rock that closes off the tomb, and with her left arm fallen in a position of infinite weariness. In Mary's posture, seated, covering her face with her hand, and with her shoulders raised in a sob, highlighting her dark outline against the leaden pre-dawn sky, one must infer an explosion of tears, of desperation, of surrender, of permanent depletion. Far off amidst the semidarkness of the tragic hour that blurs the contours of things, the forms of those who have just buried Christ can fiery, broad, in such a way that one who sees the painting feels what she felt as she wielded the brushes. There is so much work to do to get there! All those paintings require studies beforehand, complicated compositions, preparation of details, and she would want to be working on them right away, to have them done, to not waste one minute . . . There is so much to do and life is so short . . . She loves sculpture projects because sculpture is honest and does not deceive the eye with colors, nor admit shams or dodges . . . She will model all that she dreams: dying of love and sadness, fallen on the sands of the beach as she sees fleeing on the horizon the sailboat carrying Theseus,[48] an Ariadne[49] with her breast heaving with sobs; then a bas-relief with six figures caught in graceful poses, and the sculptures will be such that Saint Marceaux himself will be thrilled and the paintings will be so artful that the imbecilic jury will not be able to help giving it the first-prize medal in an upcoming salon. Ah, the medal! How it has pursued her, how she sees it in her dreams; the medal will make her understand that she did well to devote herself to painting, that she has not made a mistake, that she is someone, that she can love, think, live as all people live, relaxed, not tormenting herself with so many ambitions. When they give it to her she will be able to live like everyone else does, and then her energy, expended in another direction, will take her far, very far, she will give herself over to the delicacy of feeling, a profound passion for a superior man who understands her will consume her, she will go and breathe for long spells the warm, perfumed air of Nice, of San Remo, of Sorrento, she will return to Spain, to Toledo, to Burgos, to Cordova, to Seville, to Granada, to stand spellbound before the polychromy of the Arabian architectures, with the fresh foliage of their pink laurel and of their gigantic chestnut trees, with the blue of the sky; to Venice, where among the ruined palaces of marble a subtle fever from the greening canals rises toward the vault of heaven, to see the melancholic feast that is Tiépolo's paintings;[50] to Milan, where the creations of Leonardo smile, and to Rome, above all to Rome, the mother city, the metropolis, the only place in the world that has filled her heart, for as the sun goes down behind the cupolas of the Basilica, the center of Christianity, it floods with light the trail of art from twenty-five centuries past, revealing the complication of our more lavish and wide-ranging modern life and suggesting to pensive souls the shape of what tomorrow's sensibility will be.

Ah! My God, and Russia, Russia, the mother, the homeland, the land of nihilism and tzars, with its semicivilization so different from the Latin civilization, its peculiar customs, its superstitious, half-savage populace, its pleasure-seeking aristocracy; its own art and its singular literature; Russia is calling her back: she will go to St. Petersburg, where the Court will receive her, then to Moscow, to Kiev, the holy city, full of cathedrals and convents; she will once again breathe in the sunny fields the air that in her childhood induced the fever that drives her, and those many journeys, she will alternate those experiences so opposite to life with stays in Paris, in that salon full of men of genius; with her days portioned out between worldly parties, where her elegance will enthrall everyone, and reading philosophers and listening to the music of Handel and Beethoven and continuing her studies, other new studies she dreams of, the sociology, politics, Oriental languages, history, and literature of nations she does not know well and whose soul will be assimilated to broaden her view of the universe. Thus will she live and all that will she do with all her mettle, with all her soul, with all her being, wresting from every sensation, every idea, a maximum of deep vibrations!

Now an inner death overtakes her; she felt a sting there in the place that the doctor pointed out as the seat of the disease eating away at her, and the shooting pain once again brings her back to reality . . . Ah, yes! The cough, the sweat, the insomnia, the caustics, the iodine ointments, the trip to the sanatorium, annihilation . . . death . . . the end, all that is nigh. And what of God, where is He to let her die like this, in her prime, feeling this exuberance of strength, this mad zeal to see everything, to feel everything, to understand the Universe, His work? . . . God, where is He to let her die like this, after having been good, after having never had an unkind word to say about anyone, nor having uttered a complaint for the bitterness that has been her lot, after having shed gold around her to mop up tears, after giving away her favorite emerald for the enjoyment of someone who does not love her, after an instant's suffering? . . . After having cried for others' pains, having taken her piety to the point of loving the lowly animals? If He exists, if He is the supreme good, why does He kill her this way, at twenty-three years of age, before she has lived and when she wants to live? . . . Where is the Almighty, the Heavenly Father of His creatures? . . . Ah, He does not exist! Spinoza has taught her so; the scientific readings have shown her the universe as an eternal meeting of atoms, bound, from the millions of suns that shine in the deeps of the infinite to the secret center of human consciousness, by dark, implacable laws that reveal no supreme will tending toward the good . . . yes, a whirlwind of atoms in which forms emerge, are accentuated, filled, and undone to return to the earth and be reborn in other forms that will die in turn, swept up in the eternal tide . . . No. That cannot be. She is not an atheist, she wants to create, she wants to believe, she believes. The Bible holds words that calm and comfort; the verses from Psalm 91, "His feathers shall thee hide; thy trust / under his wings shall be," sing to her in her memory; the Savior, with his haloed head and his arms open, walks now over the choppy black waves out on the ocean of her thoughts and speaks the gentle words that pour into her soul an ineffable divine peace: "Blessed are those which do hunger and thirst after righteousness: for they will be filled."[51] And faint with mystic emotion, she mentally prostrates herself at the feet of the Divine Master . . .

A sudden association of ideas is conceived in her brain and that sweet image flees, dissipated by the memory of the works of Renan and Strauss.[52] The latter, analyses by conscientious exegetes, show Christ through the texts, interpreted with strict discernment, not as God the Son incarnate to purge sin from the world, but as the highest expression of human kindness. The books of criticism and religious history that she has read right there in the silence of that shabby little study where she is now seated, set to flight the holy ghost of the consoler of men . . . There is no one to invoke in moments of despairing anguish . . . and death is on its way, death is nigh. A cold sweat drenches her brow, fatigue doubles her over, and in the cold, diffuse light of dawn that filters through the windows and steadily dims the warm lamplight that lit the pensive evening she feels a chill that forces her to rise, to take two teaspoons of opium syrup to catch some sleep for an hour and to pile up on the golden bronze bedstead the soft silky-smooth eiderdowns, to bring warmth back into her frail little frame, undermined by tuberculosis, which now will sleep in the warm nest for a brief spell, and forever, after a few months, in the depths of the tomb, under the wet grass of the cemetery . . .

Tomorrow she will be up early, she will smile at herself as she gazes in the mirror at her complexion, as velvety and roseate as a ripe peach, her large brown eyes that smile back as she looks at them; her thick hair that falls down the gracious curves of her shoulders, and drunk on life, hungry for sensation, she will begin the day full of the same fevers, the same dreams, the same endeavors, and the same disappointments as the previous.

Thus did I see her as I read the Diary. That is the *composition of place,*[53] which to proceed according to the uplifting methods of Loyola, the subtle psychologist, I have performed in order to feel the full charm of she whom Maurice Barrès proposes we venerate under the worshipful dedication of Our Lady of Everlasting Desire . . . Never has any figure of a maiden dreamt of by a poet—Ophelia, Juliet, Virginia, Graziella, Evangeline, Mary—seemed more ideal to me nor more moving than that of the marvelous creature who left us her soul written in two volumes, which lie open now on my work desk and on whose pages falls, through the curtains of Japanese gauze that cover the balcony windowpanes, the diaphanous light of this cool Parisian summer morning . . .

20 June

If it is true that the artist expresses in his work dreams that in less powerful, confused minds lie latent; and for that reason, only for that reason, for the lines of the bronze, the colors of the painting, the music of the poem, the notes of the score, to emboss, to paint, to express, to sing, what we would have said had we been able to, the love that some of us today profess for Mademoiselle Bashkirtseff has as its true and heartfelt cause the fact that the Diary, in which she wrote her life, is an accurate mirror of our consciences and our exacerbated sensibility. Why should you sympathize with the admirable dead woman whom Barrès venerates and whom several of us love, O grotesque doctor Max Nordau, if your faith in myopic science has suppressed in you the sense of mystery; if your spirit, devoid of curiosity, is not impassioned by the most conflicting forms of life, if your rudimentary senses do not require the supreme refinements of strange and penetrating sensations? . . . What is strange, by contrast, about a man for whom the twenty-four hours in the day and night are not enough for him to experience life, since he would like to experience and know it all, and who, situated in the center of the European civilization, dreams of a larger, more beautiful Paris, one richer, more perverse, wiser, more sensual, and more mystic, waxes enthusiastic over one who carried within her a violent impetus and a sensibility bordering on an imbalance?

There are sentences in the Russian's Diary that translate so sincerely my emotions, my ambitions and my dreams, my whole life, that I could never have found clearer formulas for putting my impressions to paper.

She then writes of a reading of Kant.

"I don't know where to begin, nor whom nor how to ask, and I remain thus, stupid, astonished, without knowing which way to turn and seeing interesting treasures on all sides; histories of nations, languages, sciences, the whole earth, all that I do not know; I who would like to see, know, and learn it all."

She writes six months before dying:

"It seems no one loves everything as I do; I love everything: the arts, music, books, society, dresses, luxury, noise, silence, sadness, melancholy, laughter, love, cold, heat; all the seasons, all types of weather; the frozen savannas of Russia and the mountains outside Naples; the winter snows, the fall rains, the joy and madness of spring, the mellow days of summer and its starry nights, all that do I admire and love. Everything in my eyes takes on interesting and sublime appearances, I would love to see it, possess it, hug and kiss it all, and made one with everything, die, it doesn't matter when, in two years or thirty years, dying is an ecstasy for experiencing the final mystery, the end of everything or the beginning of a new life. To be happy I need EVERYTHING, the rest is not enough! . . ."

Blessed are you, departed ideal woman who took from the Universe an intellectual and artistic vision and for whom a love of beauty and feminine modesty prevented your zest for life and insatiable curiosity from complicating that soul of modern life with sensual fevers of pleasure, with the morbid curiosity for evil and sin, with the villainy of calculations and schemes that will bring gold to one's hands and pile up in the depths of the coffers! Blessed are you who bound within the borders of a painting the work of art of your dreams and poured the essence of your soul into a book, if you are compared with your fervent admirer who, at twenty-six, feels thousands of contradictory impulses bubbling and boiling inside him as he writes these lines, impulses aiming at a single target, the same as yours: to possess EVERYTHING; blessed are you, admirable Our Lady of Everlasting Desire!

After believing for a time that the universe's purpose was to every so often produce a poet to sing of it in impeccable stanzas, and a few months after publishing a volume of poems, *First Verses,* which brought me ridiculous triumphs of literary vanity and two affairs that puffed up my twenty years with pride, the deep, close friendship I developed with Serrano with his high-flying intellectual superiority and passion for philosophy, changed the course of my life. It was an unforgettable year, in which, rid of all material concerns, of all worldly commitments, the days and nights flew by, divided between long morning walks down the University's avenue lined with pines, the reading of philosophers from all eras, till noon, in the silent library where only the turning of pages under the hands of the students could be heard, and the evenings spent in the silent bedroom of the noblest of my friends, speaking with him about the most fascinating issues that can attract the human spirit. The tranquility of nerves soothed by a calming diet and by isolation, conversations in which the names of Plato, Epicurus, Empedocles, Saint Thomas, Spinoza, Kant, and Fichte, mentioned in the same breath with the thinkers of today—Wundt, Spencer, Maudsley, Renan, Taine[54]—shone like stars unmoved in the black majesty of the night sky; vertigo of the mind, which, detached from the body, searches out the laws of being; the noble life of the thinker, in which the only figure of a woman that passed through my mind's eye as stripped of sensuality by lofty intellectual speculation was that of my grandmother, with her long silver locks falling down around her bosom and her profile like that of Leonardo's Saint Ann, how far you all are from the vertigo and hedonistic frenzy of my life today!

The sudden death of Serrano, the arrival of my old age, the need to administer a sizeable fortune invested in easily increasable stocks, rung the curtain down on that quasi-monastic period of my life. Back in the whirlwind of the world, sitting on a vast fortune to use for enriching my native soil, my instincts teeming in my veins, moved by the Andrades' rage for action; footloose, free, fatherless, motherless, brotherless, welcomed and courted everywhere, full of conflicting and intense aspirations, possessed of a mad passion for luxury in all its forms, I was the ridiculous Alcibiades[55] of that society that made way for me as one would for a conqueror. Years of madness and action in which the plans that consume me today began taking shape, in which my compressed sensuality burst like a vigorous shoot in the spring sun, in which my intellectual passions began to grow, and with them the infinite curiosity towards evil; a stroke of luck that made me hold on to my inherited wealth without fabulous squandering managing to diminish it, ambitions that by making me find the open country confining, romantic affairs lowly, and business narrow-minded, you forced me to leave the earth, where it was perhaps the moment to look down from above, and to become the ridiculous *rastaquouère*,[56] the grotesque snob that I feel like at times! How vain that you amuse yourself reading the item in *Gil Blas* announcing that the *richissime Américain don Joseph Fernández y Andrade* bought such-and-such little painting by Raffaeli, and you puff up like a peacock opening his electric green tail spangled with eyes, when as he rolls along in Lady Orloff's carriage to the rhythmic trot of the pair of Arabians down the Rue des Acacias, among the vague mist enveloping the Park at six in the evening, a *zute* rubber tree whispers, taken with the elegance of the horses or the eccentricity of the unchaste woman's dress, and says to his companion: "Tiens, regarde, ma vielle! Epatante la maîtresse du poete!"[57] . . . you should have your fill, Vanity! . . .

Yes, that is life, hunting with the nobles, more stupid and more dim-witted than my country's peasants, galloping along dressed in their red riding jackets, after the doddering, obtuse Duke's sorrel; dressing in a different white riding jacket, sporting a silk vest with colored trim and in women's shoes and stockings for cutting the capers of an acrobat and grotesque affectations when the Tres Estrellas holds the cotillion in

Madame la Princesse's house; escorting the uninitiated new bride who wishes to apprise herself of the latest fashions to the shops of the dress-makers and modistes, to assist her in tailoring dresses that she could not choose on her own; killing an hour in conversation with the shirt-maker to suggest to him the idea for a crinkly, pleated cambric shirt front, and five minutes choosing the rare flower that should adorn the tux's lapel; yes, Vanity, have your fill, that is life and those are the occupations of the man who spent his twentieth year reading Plato and Spinoza!

It is ludicrous. I write and give in involuntarily to my exaggerations. That is not my whole life. Together with that fatuous socialite is my alter ego, the lover of art and science who has collected eighty oils and four hundred artist's sketches and engravings, from the greatest painters ancient and modern, miraculous medallions, priceless bronzes, marbles, porcelains, and tapestries; implausible editions of his favorite authors, printed on special paper and bound in marvelous leathers from the Orient; the science-worshipper who has spent two whole months paying daily visits to the psychophysics laboratories; the philosophy maniac who follows the conferences at the Sorbonne and the School of Advanced Studies, and next to that intellectual self is another, the sensual self who speculates successfully in the stock market, the gastronomer of the lavish dinners, possessed of an athlete's physique, the unbridled, furious horses, of Lelia Orloff, of the precious stones worthy of a rajah or an empress, of the furniture in which the upholsterers have exhausted their art, of the thirty-year-old wines that infuse new life and fire into the blood; and on top of all that is an analyst who sees clearly into himself and who bears his many contradictory impulses, armed with an iron will, as the four horses of the quadriga drew the Doric chariots in the races at the Olympic Games!

So have you had your fill, Pangloss?[58] asks my inner voice, which speaks in times of self-reflection . . . No, never, this life that to so many would seem incredible for its intensity serves only to excite all the more my desire to live . . . More! Everything! shouts the Monster I bear within . . . You are no one, you are not a saint, you are not a bandit, you are not a creator, an artist who captures his dreams in colors, in bronze, in words, or in sound; you are not a wise man, you are not even a man, you are a puppet drunk in your blood and in your will who sits down to write stupidities . . . That worker going down the street with his blue shirt laundered by his dear, loving wife and who has coarse hands from hard work, is worth more than you, since he loves someone, and the anarchist they guillotined the day before yesterday for throwing a bomb that blew up a building is worth more than you because he acted on an idea that had been incarnated in him. You spend ten minutes polishing your nails like a courtesan, you useless wretch, your head swollen with monstrous pride! . . . Oh, a plan to devote my life to, regardless of good or ill, no matter, sublime or wicked, but a plan that is not the one I have now, neither the business firm in New York for large-scale speculating and doubling my fortune, nor the trip around the world to store up sensations and ideas, nor my life on the archipelago for pearl fishing, to add to my riches; no, a plan that has nothing to do with myself, one that takes me out of myself, one that carries me off like a hurricane, without feeling I am alive! . . .

Bâle, 23 June

From yesterday afternoon I have only two remaining impressions: the cuff of the blood-soaked shirt and the black border of the letter; and the night, the sound of the train as it passed through shadow . . . She must have died by now and the police are probably looking for me. I registered at the hotel under the fake name of Juan Simónides, a Greek travel agent, to throw them off the scent . . . From the state I'm in to madness there's but a single step! Mirinoni should wire me this very day and they'll send the telegram to Wyhl from the hotel . . . where I am going to hide in a small hotel a few miles out of town!

Wyhl, 29 June

In front of the sheet of paper on which I write lies Marinoni's folded telegram. I have read it twenty times and have needed two hours of reflection to awaken from the bloody nightmare. "You can come back," it reads, "the police don't know anything. She was there yesterday, fine as you please, in the Park, with a new dress. She ate in good company in la Cascada. Heartfelt congratulations." Where was the wound, then, if it left no trace? . . . I still feel the warmth of blood on my hand, and there in my traveling case is the shirt with the blood-soaked cuff.

The next day

The brutal scene, the idea of the murder, the getaway, the anguish, prevented me from understanding Emilia's letter as I read it. I understood only that the old lady had died, the only true family I had left in all the world; I felt as if a weight were crushing my chest, a knot were in my throat, and a blackness in my soul, but the particulars of the death I did not know, as if I had not read them. I want to copy the letter here in order to find it later, after a few years when I read this accursed diary, and relive the singular hours of these days in which that noble impression mingled with the anguish of a crime. The lines written by Emilia's feeble hand on the paper with the thick black border ran thus:

"My letter of the first of the month told you your dear grandmother was extremely frail and had suffered several spells of vertigo in recent days. The situation has worsened since the night of the second. Doctor Álvarez, whom I had sent for despite her objections, ordered her to bed from that day forward and informed me that all efforts to save her were in vain, since we were witnessing the tail end of the illness, just as she had been predicting for years. He merely prescribed total rest and a narcotic potion. On her own account she summoned the Archbishop, who was her confessor, as you recall, and after confessing received the communion with her usual fervor. In the days leading up to her death she accepted no visitors except for the Prelate, and she spoke continuously of you, and of death, which she awaited with absolute tranquillity. At eight at night began a strange, feverless delirium, a prelude to death, in which she rambled non-stop, alternating her favorite prayers with strange references to you. 'Lord, save him, save him from the crime that spurs him, save him from the madness that sweeps him away, save him from the hell that clamors for him. By your agony in the garden, and by your crown of thorns, by your sweat of blood and the bile of the sponge, save him from crime, save him from madness, save him from hell! . . . ' she would say, trembling on the pillows . . . 'You're going to save him: see he is good, see he's a saint. Blessed be the sign of the cross made by the hand of the Virgin, and the bouquet of roses that falls in his night as a sign of salvation! You are saved! See he is good, see he's a saint! Blessed be.' An expression of calm beatitude replaced what had been anguish on her thin face. Drifting off to sleep, her breath a death rattle, she returned her soul to God. Forgive me for giving you these painful details of her final throes. I know you and I know that they will make you suffer but that you want to know them.

"She died a saint, as she had lived. At the funeral home only don Francisco Cordovez, Doctor Álvarez, the Archbishop, and I went in. The Prelate kneeled for a long time at her coffin. The wake was a mystical experience greater than any I have felt in my life. I was sure that that corpse was that of a saint from the race of Monicas,[59] and that her soul had already received the reward of a stainless existence. The corpse's expression, with its thin head and features as if purified by death, framed by the white hair that seemed like snow in the candlelight, betrayed an infinite serenity. From within the Vázquez oil painting decorating the bedroom, the saints, her intimates, seemed to look upon her, leaning their heads out from the canvas and coming out through the faded gold of their old Spanish frames. That night spent beside the departed saint will give me strength to suffer[60] all the ills of life with the hope of dying thus.[61]

"The body occupies the main crypt in the family monument, near your father. The house is closed up and in her bedroom, all around you, if you return some day, you will still find the smell of the mortuary candles, for the key shall not leave my hands as long as I live. I share your pain. I am with you with all my heart and of God and of the Saint who watches over you today from heaven I ask for your happiness with all the fervor of my affection for you. Emilia . . ."

My happiness . . . good God! How easily I could be reading the previous lines in a prison, held for having murdered one of the most renowned hetaeras in modern Babylon . . . Ah, the feeling that reading that letter gave me the same day on which I had to go and commit a crime, on which I almost committed it! The saint having died, there in the bedroom draped in dark damask, and there I am, the very day I learned of her death, fleeing like a murderer, after trying to kill a defenseless woman!

I saw her for the first time while listening to the superhuman music of the Walkyries[62] in an Opera House box. She had arrived from Vienna the previous night. The crimson background of the box-seat wall brought into relief her pure Diana the Hunter silhouette[63] as a red velvet vanity case does the orient of a flawless pearl; among her pale blonde hair, in the lobes of her diminutive ears, around her slender round wrists, and on her short pale-green gauze bodice that left her bosom half exposed, shone, burned, the translucent emeralds of my country, the luminous emeralds of Muzo.

The dreamy expression on the face of that blonde head, the golden pallor of her complexion, the color of that aereal dress, the sparkle of those queenly jewels, gave her more the seeming of an unreal apparition than a flesh-and-blood woman, an undine[64] inhabiting the depths of a lake or a wood sprite from the black and mysterious heart of the forests. The ride of the Walkyries inhabited the air, the superhuman music filled the room with its superhuman vibrations, and she, as if held in thrall to the urgency of my eyes that devoured her from the box seat, looked at me again. The first gaze, slow and penetrating as a French kiss, sent a shiver of voluptuosity down my spine . . . Three days later she was mine.

That delicate creature, attired and idealized by designers, was the idol of these last six months. Oh, the first nights of sensual delicacy in the deep, wide bed, golden and ornamented like an altar; the amber pallor, the perfect lines, the aroma of magnolia, the silken gold down of that twenty-year-old body, stretched out in voluptuous postures on the black satin sheets! Oh, the leisurely caresses, knowing and insinuating from those thin, nervous hands; the lasciviousness of those lips that modulate kisses like a brilliant songstress modulates the notes of a musical phrase; oh, the sensual refinement, the furious pleasure, the well-nigh religious gravity of all those moments consecrated to love, as if instead of having the miserable modern notion of it, which relegates it to the taming of the filthy, she experienced it as grave and noble, an august performance! Thus Aphrodite's priestesses must have loved, they who believed in their Goddess and held the Act sacred.

A fortnight after the first night I knew what strange mystification that creature was, and yet understood her less than before. Her name was María Legendre, the other was her nom de guerre. Her father and mother lived in an alley in Batignolles, he, a longtime shoemaker, brutal and drunken; she, a poor woman, skin and bones, wan and with a sickly air, whom her husband beat every time he drank more than his share. They raised two other daughters of no account. By what mystery had she wound up four years before my finding her in the hands of a former president of a South American republic, who, cast out of his country by one of those revolutions that constitute our favorite sport, arrived in Paris bursting with gold and local color, on a quest for security and pleasures, and lavished her with gifts in one year? . . . Was the Russian duke, who on his way through Paris spent more time in her bedroom than anywhere else, and later took her to St. Petersburg, whence she emerged, reborn with a princess's surname and owner of the fabulous emeralds and the diamond necklace, the one who educated her senses and awoke in her that sybaritic sensuality,[65] which seduced me from the very first like a bewitching spell? Or was her educator rather the perverse Italian with whom she fell madly in love and on whom she lavished gifts, without the starving, complacent bard protesting at that role of lapdog? . . . I don't know, I don't want to know, nor shall I ever know. I found her settled into a small apartment whose balconies overlook Monceau Park and is furnished with an exquisiteness of taste unlikely even in a woman born on the steps of a throne.

The little room with the walls hung with a Japanese silk, yellow as a ripe orange[66] and with hand-embroidered gold and silver, was soberly appointed with furnishings that would have been up to the standards of refinement of the most demanding aesthete; the bedroom was hung with ancient church brocatelles, faded by time; with its authentic sixteenth-century furnishings and bathroom, where a bathtub made of opalescent glass like the windows of Venice stood sparkling alongside the dressing tables, all of crystal and silver plate, over the Pompeiian décor[67] of the walls and floor, suggested the idea that some poet who had devoted himself to the decorative arts, a Walter Crane[68] or a William Morris,[69] for example, had overseen its installation down to the minutest detail.

When visiting it for the first time I understood clearly that no aesthetic notion had determined the selection of all that; that she had it because she had liked it, as others like pink plush, six-franc terra-cottas, oleographs,[70] and artificial flowers, and when, at her insistence, I ate in her apartment, the succulence of the food, the unfamiliarity of the sauces, and the maturity of the wines made me see that she was possessed of the first fruits of artistic industry, only because she needed deep and refined sensations as a matter of course, and she spared no expense. But where in blazes had she gotten that aristocracy of the nerves, rarer perhaps than that of the blood or the mind, she being the daughter of a grimy shoemaker? . . . An insoluble riddle . . . The tea she drank in fragile Chinese cups, worthy of a museum display case, was caravan tea, had at an absurd price. She maintained ingenuously that it was the least bad she had found in Paris; she drank the only coffee free of all sophistication that I have drunk in Europe; she was forever complaining about the table, and on my proposing we go eat in one of the famed restaurants, she grimaced in disgust, as if in all of them combined one could not find an edible steak; she cultivated passionately the mania for old lace, and piled them up unused in the giant wardrobe made of fragrant woods, perfumed by Guerlain with aromatic herbs, in which, heaped up in enormous symmetrical stacks, the white batistes of her underclothes dazzled the eye, which was caressed by the pale shades of her nightgowns, fragile as spiderwebs, of the petticoats embroidered like ballroom handkerchiefs and the silk knickers olorous of Florence iris and frangipani.

In her strawberry mouth, that princess's phrase upon hearing the moans of the people begging bread: *If you don't have bread, why don't you eat cake?* . . . would seem natural; luxury is her element like water is that of fish, but an inborn, unconscious luxury . . .

"You study, don't you? . . ." she asked me one afternoon, both of us lying on a Turkish divan in the little room on the left. "What for?" she added innocently.

"To learn . . ." I answered, surprised.

"What do you get out of learning?" she added, kissing me. "Life isn't for learning, it's for enjoying. Enjoying, enjoying is better than thinking," she added with a tone of heartfelt conviction.

And it seems I had accepted her philosophy, judging by my last months, in which I have not opened a book and have forsaken Greek and Russian and my studies of comparative grammar and the outlines for my poems, my business dealings too, to spend my time concerned only with pleasures, sport, soirées, fencing, in an incessant hunt for sensations. . . . I was asphyxiating for lack of intellectual air, accustomed to the silence that also formed part of Lelia's nature, since for days on end not a word would pass between us, submerging me slowly into an incredible intellectual lethargy . . . Oh, the Circe who changes men into swine . . . ![71] In lucid intervals I agonized amidst matter like the Emperor thrown into the latrines by the Roman people.

The first time I found the de Roberto girl in Lelia's house, the monstrous suspicion plunged into my mind's eye. Tall, thin, bony, her eyes burning, her not prominent bust, dressed and shod after the masculine fashion, and with something mannish about her, in the peach fuzz shadowing her thin lip, in her brusque movements, in her voice full of serious modulations, just to look at the Italian girl was detestable to me . . .

"Who is she? Why do you have anything to do with her?" I asked Mademoiselle Orloff.

"Because I like her," she answered, and closed herself off into her customary silence.

One afternoon, when I went in, the lamps were unlit and the room was lulled in the darkness of the dawn. I heard whispering in one of the dark corners, and before lighting a match a form brushed by me and went out to the anteroom. Lelia, upon seeing light, sat up on the divan where she had been reclining . . .

"Who just left here?" I asked, nervous. "Angela de Roberto, am I right?"

"Yes," she answered with her unflappable tranquillity. "So why do you have her over if you know she's detestable to me?" I said, unable to contain myself.

"Because I like her," she answered, enclosing herself again in her enigmatic silence, and the night following that afternoon was one of the most delicious nights of my life . . .

On the afternoon of the 22nd I went to see her, to ask her for a cup of tea and to take her an enchanting miniature, mounted by Bassot, in a circle of diminutive pink pearls. The parlormaid answered the door, and when she saw me she made a strange face, of scorn, joy, fear, an outlandish expression that suggested everything to me. Upon knocking the bedroom door off its hinges, which smashed at the first brutal slamming, and wound up breaking, two cries of terror sounded in my ears and before either of the two of them could undo herself, I had reached the vile twosome, with the impulse of a madman redoubled by rage, thrown them to the floor on the black bearskin at the foot of the bed, and beat them furiously with all my might, eliciting shouts and blasphemy, with violent hands, with boot-heels, like one who is squashing a snake. I do not know how I retrieved the little Toledan blade, damascene and engraved like a jewel that I carry with me always, and buried it twice in the yielding flesh; I felt my hand soaked in warm blood, sheathed the weapon, bounded down the staircase in two jumps, hearing shouts, and got into a hackney coach, giving the coachman directions to Miranda's office.

From there, after requesting a sum from the teller and collecting my correspondence delivered an hour previous, I went to my hotel for Francisco to pack a travel kit, then left in another carriage hired by the concierge and reached the station to take the train, the first one bound anywhere . . . I caught the one that brought me to Bâle, where I slept, and since the next day I have been here, where, with supreme anguish, I have awaited Marinoni's telegram, which I have opened in front of the page I am writing . . . After all, I have not killed anyone, it was a scratch, yesterday she was eating in the La Cascada Restaurant, and I take a breath . . .

Now I mull it over with a cool head. Why did I commit that brutal act, the act of a highwayman, and attempt a murder from which I was saved by the size of the knife, which is more of a jewel than a weapon,[72] I the libertine curious for rare sins who has sought to see in real life, with voluptuous dilettantism, the strangest practices invented by human depravation, I the poet of decadences who has sung of the lesbian Sappho and the loves of Hadrian[73] and Antinous[74] in verses polished like precious gems? Jealousy? That would be grotesque . . . Hatred for the abnormal? . . . No, since the abnormal fascinates me like a trial of man's rebellion against instinct . . . Then? It was an unreasoned move, a blind impulse, unconscious, like the one that one afternoon last fall led me, having no call to do so, to insult the German ambassador who had been introduced to me ten days earlier, occasioning a stupid duel on the Belgian border and Marinoni's conviction that I was a madman.

Wyhl, 5 July

I found a hiding place to hole up and think, a hovel built out of rough wood and inhabited by an old peasant couple. It is an inaccessible place where no tourists go, a wild woodland gorge, full of the sound of a torrent that turns to spray as it runs amidst enormous black boulders, and shaded by pines and the tallest chestnut trees. I have written to Paris asking them to send to me in Interlaken a host of things I need, and I will go tomorrow to climb up to the peak, bringing no other books than some studies of South American prehistory, written by a German,[75] and some treatises on botany. I feel a strange emotion as I think of my hideout.

10 July

The old man and the old lady landlords have never been in a city, nor do they know how to read or write; they look at me like a strange animal, and only speak to me to say good morning or good night. Unable to eat their food, I feed myself with the milk of a few cows they have in a neighboring esplanade. My room, don José Fernández's room, the *richissime américain*'s room, has for furniture a bed the lowliest of my Paris servants would not lie in for any amount of money, a crude table on which I write, and an enormous wooden bowl, which in the morning they fill with ice water for me, collected from the torrent, in which to bathe. All that, luckily, cleaner than the best hotels in the world, probably. The thick sheets on the bed smell of the country, and the furniture shines as if just varnished. In these five days not one voluptuous image has passed through my mind, I have not felt any desires, and I have gotten drunk on air and ideas.

In the early hours I rise, and after a cold bath and milk still warm from the udder, I climb through the grey mist pierced by light, where the rugged mountain looks barely like bluish shadows, as far as a hill that towers over the landscape. It is a sea of white steam that slowly, slowly floods with light, until the sunbeams dissolve it and show the scene enshrouded in gentle mists, which float like shreds of a bridal veil over the blue of the faraway mountains, over the greens of the valleys, to come to rest on the silvery whiteness of a snowcapped mountain, on yonder horizon . . . Then everything comes slowly into sharper focus, the sky grows bluer, the mist disperses, the colors sharpen, the greens intensify, the black or red of every bare rock is in evidence. All that is heard are the birdsongs and the muffled, dampened torrent that bellows in its riverbed of rock. The air has a vegetable smell and is thin, rarefied . . . As I lie on the summit, on the blanket that is with me on all my journeys, I am overwhelmed by the penetrating and profound feeling of freshness that emanates from it all. I look around me and right in front of me I see by the yellowed, aereate verdure of a cluster of willows the old mill, whose great wheel, as it spins against the thick black wall moldy from the humidity, turns the current that moves it into thin streams and drops of transparent crystal and impalpable vapor, while the swallows that nest in the gable-ends and hollows of the ancient building criss-cross over it with the wide-wheeling semicircles and hostile zigzags of their incessant nervous fluttering. The goat trail that leads up to the top passes by the foot of the mill, and with a sharp turn disappears behind one of the mountain's first spurs, which at that hour, seen from where I am, is a mass of silvered blackish mist, ridged by the green thickets that stand out above the second spur, whose tangled mass of contours the mist blurs in a hazy blanket. Further on in the distance lay the bluish darkness of the far-off peaks, with their silhouettes of pointy ridges and jagged rocks that cut dark rough bends against the pale diaphanous blue of the sky and the dazzling white of the morning clouds.

expressions of the human fused in the black vastness, and lost to myself, to life, to death, the sublime spectacle entered my being, as it were, and I scattered into the starry firmament, into the peaceful sea, as if fused in them in a pantheistic ecstasy of sublime worship. Unforgettable instants whose description resists the word's every effort to capture them! The light of dawn that fades the starshine and returned to the ocean its sea-sickening blue-green coloring brought me back to the realities of life.

Though not feeling these ecstasies at the grandiosity of the scene, I did feel at times a supreme peace descending over my spirit in the hours spent at the summit to which I climb. The plan that called for the only purpose to which to devote my life has appeared to me as clear and precise as a mathematical formula. To reach it I need to make an effort every minute for entire years, and to have an iron will that does not relent for an instant. More or less it will be this. I have to increase my fortune two- or threefold in order to begin. If the engineers' commission sent from London by Morrell and Blundell gives a favorable judgment of the gold mines I have almost negotiated with them and that in my father's will were evaluated at a paltry sum, the mines will provide me with several million francs when they are sold. The English should be cabling Paris any time now and the Mirandas will let me know by telegraph to Geneva, where I will go to spend the month of August. Once that transaction is complete I will transfer all my capital to New York and I will establish the firm with Carrillo for conducting the business he has planned out. After Carrillo are the Astors, the millionaires who have not made one wrong move since they began trading, and in his hands my gold will work for me, while I devote myself body and soul to traveling the United States, to studying the inner workings of American civilization, to looking into the wherefores of the fabulous development of that land of energy, and to seeing what may be made use of as a lesson, to test it later in my experience. From New York I will go for a spell to Panama to manage the pearl fisheries in person, the exploration of whose shoals will yield hitherto-unknown marvels like those produced when Pedrarias Dávila sent the King and Queen of Spain the one pearl that adds the finishing touch to the royal crown. All the gold these explorations yield and what I possess today will be ready for the moment in which I return to my land, not to the capital but to the States, to the Provinces I will travel one by one, researching their needs, studying the best crops for the soil, the potential means of communication, the natural resources, the nature of the inhabitants, all this with a corps of engineers and experts that for all my compatriots know are probably Englishmen traveling in search of orchids. I will spend a few months among the savage tribes, unknown to everyone there and which appear to me to be exploitable members for civilization, given the awkward strength of some of them and the slovenly indolence of others. Afterwards I will settle in the capital and expend all my energy on intrigue, then push and shove my way into politics to gain any trifling office, of the sort that one receives in our South American nations by being friends with the president. In two years of devotion and incessant study I will have hatched a rational finance plan, which is the basis of all government, and I will learn administration down to its smallest detail. The country is rich, formidably rich, and has untapped resources; it is a matter of skill, of simple calculations, of pure science, to resolve the problems of the day. In a ministry, gained with my money and influence brought into the equation, I will be able to show something of what can be done when there is the will. Then I will be but a short step away from organizing a center where the civilized among all parties are recruited to form a new party, removed from all political or religious fanaticism, a party of civilized men who believe in science and place their efforts in the service of the great idea. Then to the presidency of the republic following the necessary campaigning, accomplished by ten newspapers that denounce previous abuses, after promises of contracts, brilliant jobs, big material improvements, another . . . All that willingly. If the situation does not allow for those Platonic ideals, as hereafter I presume, I will have to resort to supreme measures to spur the country to war, to the means that the government with its false liberalism gives us in order to provoke a conservative reaction, to make use of the unlimited freedom of the press that the current Constitution grants, to report theft and general abuses committed by the government and by the States, I will have to draw on the influence of the clergy to rouse the fanatic masses, on the pride of the old conservative aristocracy hurt by the mob rule of recent years, on the selfishness of the rich,

In that far-off place the decisive years lie, in which all will be energy and action.

Budgets balanced through sound economic measures will bring down customs duties, which in the long term, facilitating enormous introductions of capital, will double the income; the removal of useless jobs, reorganization of taxes on scientific grounds, economies of all types; in a few years the country will be rich, and to solve its current economic problems, an effort to instill order suffices; the day will come in which the current deficit of the businesses will be a surplus that is transformed into highways, indispensable railroads for the development of industry, bridges that cross torrential rivers, and into all the means of communication we are lacking today, and whose lack binds the country like a steel chain, condemning it to pitiable inaction.

Those will be the years of trading on the studies I have done, put to the test by the experts and engineers that traveled the country for years and were paid with my gold. In those climates that run from the heat of Madagascar in the deep equinoctial valleys, to the cold of Siberia, in the luminous upland moors whitened by eternal snows, all the enriching crops, from the plantain extolled by Bello in his divine ode[78] to the lichens that cover the polar ice caps, the husbandry of all work animals, from the ostriches that populate the burning plains of Africa to the polar reindeer, will emerge, incited by my employees and stimulated by the bounty of farming. Countless sheep will graze in the fertile meadows, the branches of the coffee bushes will bend under the weight of the purple clusters; in regular perspectives where the eye is lost in the green twilight made by the shade of the protecting guama tree, the vanilla vine will climb nimbly through the misshapen trunks of the rubber trees, hanging from its delicate lianas its aromatic urn-shaped sporangia, and in the steep mountainous terrain, the gold, silver, and iridium will shine in the eyes of the miner after a tiring excavation and the elaborate exploitation of the native mineral.

Doubtful of my own aptitudes, for however great my studies may have been until that point, I will call economists renowned in Europe and consult the greatest statesmen in the world in order to proceed according to their counsel as I arbitrate the measures that will crown the work.

These tasks having been devised and articulated, the new land will be unveiled, bursting with wealth in the European markets, owing to treasury agents who will cover them, and through the efforts of a wise diplomatic corps, handsomely remunerated and selected from among the crème de la crème of the national talents. The theretofore depreciated bonds will be an investment as solid as the consolidated English ones; colossal loans advanced by the Hutks and the Rothschilds, underwritten in favorable conditions, will allow for the obtaining of the sought-for results with dutiful labor. The immigration attracted by the minimal price at which the adjudication of wastelands in territories now deserted will occur will flow like a river of men, like an Amazon whose waves are human heads mixed with the indigenous races, with the old landowners that today are vegetating, sunk in a wretched obscurity, with savage tribes, whose native fierceness and courage will be a potent element of vitality, will populate down to the last barren desert, will work the fields, exploit the mines, bring new industries, all the human industries. To attract that civilized immigration, colossal steamers from government-sponsored companies with sums that allow the cost of passage to be reduced to a minimum, practically eliminated, will cross the Atlantic and go pick up the crews, eager for a new life, in the ports of old Europe, where hunger casts them, and in those of Japan and China, countries overflowing with a hungry population, and in the wide roadsteads of the Indian peninsula, wherefrom the poor native, the disinherited pariah, the Bengali of almost feminine gentleness, all will emigrate longing for a new fatherland, to avoid the sting of the English lash on their backs.

Monstrous factories where those unhappy souls find work and bread will then cloud with the thick plumes of their smokestacks the deep blue skies that shelter our tropical countries; on the plains will quiver the metallic cry of the locomotives that go down the rails, tying together the cities and little villages that sprung up where fifteen years earlier were rough-hewn wood stations and where, as I write, amidst the tangled virgin jungle the colossal silk-cotton ceiba trees stretch their secular branches, interwoven with vines that snake among them and offer shade to the boggy jungle floor, the nest of reptiles and of fevers; like an aerial network of telegraph and telephone wires shaken by an idea they will run through the air; they will cleave the dormant current of the great arteries of the slow, mighty navigable rivers, on whose banks will grow the leafy cacao plantations, fast white steamships that overcome distances and carry the shipments of fruit to the sea; once these are turned to gold in the world's markets, their gigantic forces will return to the earth that produced them to multiply in geometric progression.

Light! More light! . . . The last words of the sublime poet of Faust[79] will be the motto of the nation that thus embarks on the path of progress. Public education, overseen with special diligence and propaganda spread through all possible outlets—from kindergarten where the little children learn to spell among the roses, to the great universities in which the eighty-year-old men of learning, their hair greyed over their instruments of observation, give themselves over to the most audacious speculations they seek from human thought—will raise up the nation to an intellectual and moral level higher than the most advanced nations of Europe. Once the country is free of the dreadful problems that undermine the old European societies and erupt in them in nihilistic screams and exploding bombs, it will look calmly toward the future.

The capital transformed with pickax blows and with millions—as Baron Haussman transformed Paris—will welcome the foreigner bedecked in all the flowers of its gardens and all the greenness of its parks, it will offer in spacious hotels the creature comforts that let one forge the illusion he has not left his happy home, and will unfold a scene before him of wide avenues and small green squares, the statues of its great men, the pride of its marble palaces, the melancholy grandeur of the old buildings from the colonial age, the splendor of theaters, circuses, and the dazzling display windows of the shops; libraries and bookstores that bring European and American books together on their shelves will offer noble pleasures to his intellect, and as a flower of that material progress he could consider developing an art, a science, a novel with a clearly national flavor, and a poetry that sings of the old native legends, the glorious epic of the wars of emancipation, the natural beauties and the glorious future of the regenerated land.

It seems absurd at first blush to establish a conservative dictatorship like that of García Moreno[80] in Ecuador or that of Cabrera[81] in Guatemala, and to think that under that dark regime, with its dungeon gloom and inquisitorial evils, the miracle of the transformation I dream of will come to pass. It is not, if one thinks about it. The country is tired of windy demagogic speeches and false freedoms written in the constitution and violated every day in practice, and yearns for a clearer political model. It prefers the shout of a dictator whom one knows will follow through on his threats to platonic promises of respect for the law that are broken the next day. The success of the enormous enterprise depends on the skill with which, as the situation returns to normal after the victory, the modifications are launched that slowly will change the situation of the defeated party, and allow it to return to the political arena schooled in the harsh lesson of defeat, educated after the first years of running a tight ship in which its leaders learn the futility of armed combat. They will dream then of deals that will let them scale down subordinate positions, or they will raise their voices over abuses committed, but their speeches will have no impact, since the people will already sense the advantages of the new regime. Industrial development will absorb part of the forces that hitherto produced deep disruptions as they caused unrest in politics. Concessions, gradually granted, will steadily earn the administration the favor of the youth, who are disillusioned with the old ideals and the support of capitalists from all camps, who want security and well-being. To every advancement made in the material order, to every right respected, the opposing ranks will reply with a movement that draws them closer and allows new concessions. In the long term, their spirits soothed and the old caudillos with their overblown ideas gone from the scene, political bosses whose presence stood in the way of returning the necessary elasticity to the movement of the social body, a moderate, hardly viable opinion, since they will have no abuses to denounce or protests to raise like flags of war, an almost perfect balance will be struck between the demands of the most advanced and the foresightful prudence of the most backward.

O, slow apprenticeship in civilization by a fledgling nation, upon rendering you in my brain into a plastic, almost grotesquely reduced image, you remind me of the crawling tiny tot who babbles formless syllables; of the baby-walkers that keep him from falling as he ventures his first steps, of the upright toddling he does between chair and table, of the room he crosses, supporting himself on the furniture, of the thirty-foot walks that surprise the smiling mother, until the muscle hardened by exercise and the stamina of his nerves lets him walk clinging to the wet-nurse's hand . . . The little legs that barely hold him will later have tendons and muscles and formidable bones with which he will dig spurs into the frisky horse on which he will cross the plain, and with his little rosy-dimpled hands, whose little fingers strain to hold a favorite toy, he will raise the hoe to work the soil of the country and the sword to defend it! . . .

I have a mental picture of the transformation of the country in the protagonists who will accompany me in every age and in every scene of the undertaking, from entering the capital in blood and fire, bursting bombs all around and the discharges of rifle fire of the vanquishing army, dispatched by the most select of the conservative aristocracy, my cousins the Monteverdes. Athletic, brutal, and fascinating, they will serve as makeshift generals on the battlefields, owing to their audacity of savages. I can see the old commanders gone grey in their duty, General Castro and the two Valderramas, for instance, until the day when these venerable old men who stand in the way of my plan are resting peacefully in their tombs with the civil leaders of the defeated party, men who, shaking in their sexagenarian boots, witnessed the bloody victory on the day the dictatorship was installed. Those who then were insipid little kids, some becoming potbellied ministers of state and others skinny opposition-party journalists, will realize, in that far-off age my imagination reaches, that the problems that seemed insoluble to their fathers practically solved themselves once the stable government was founded and the idlers were given something to do, once the land was cultivated and tracks were laid that would facilitate the growth of the country.

Then, shorn of the power that will wind up in good hands, retreating to a country estate surrounded by gardens and palm forests, wherefrom the blue of the sea can be spied in the distance, the cupola of some chapel shaded by dark foliage rising not far off, having had my fill of humanity and contemplating my work from afar, I will reread favorite philosophers and poets, write singular stanzas shrouded in hazes of mysticism and populated with apocalyptic visions that, contrasting strangely with the verses full of lust and fire I wrought at age twenty, will set the poets of the future to prolific dreaming. In them I will pour, as if into a sacred vase, the supreme elixir[82] that the manifold experiences of men and life have deposited in the depths of my dark burning soul.

There I will live out the happiest disenchanted existence of a dethroned Dom Pedro II[83] who read Renan in evening meditation. My being stripped down of all human feeling and inaccessible to all emotion that does not derive from some truth, unknown to men and glimpsed by me in the calming of old age and with the serenity that dreams-come-true can bring, just as I lie dying, on my still-warm corpse the legend will begin to form that makes me seem a monstrous problem of psychological complexity to future generations.

As long as even the first part of this plan is not brought to fruition I will not rest easy. For it is large . . . Larger was that of Bolivar upon swearing the freedom of a continent on the Montepincio hillside, that of Napoleon, a poor unknown military man of no consequence when, enclosed at age twenty in a room at Dôle, he dreamt of changing the face of Europe and of passing out thrones to his brothers as if they were a fistful of coins.

"I was mad when I wrote this, wasn't I, Sáenz?" Fernández exclaimed, interrupting the reading, speaking to the doctor and smiling at him amiably.

"It's the only time you've been in your right mind," Sáenz replied coolly.

"I thought I had imagined all things possible and impossible with respect to you, except this, that you would get such poppycock into your head! You, president of the republic, how degrading to you," Rovira blurted with an indignant air. "*You*, president of the republic . . ."

"Tell me, the sale of the mines, the business in New York, and the pearl fisheries, did they produce for you the results you expected, José?" asked Luis Cordovez, deep in thought.

"Better than I expected," replied the poet.

"So then what stopped you, pray tell, what stopped you from doing what you could have been able to do, which was great, enormous?" asked Cordovez with his usual enthusiasm.

"Truffled goose liver pâté, dry champagne, tepid coffee, green-eyed women, japonaiserie, and wild literary schemes," answered Oscar Sáenz peevishly from his armchair somewhere in the shadows.

"You're a better psychologist than physiologist," responded Fernández.

"And you're a loon, for though you conceived that eight years ago, you are reading it to us now, instead of having carried it out by degrees. . . ."

The tea served by Francisco, the old manservant who was at the poet's side since he saw him being born, interrupted the reading for a few moments.

"You've had three cups of tea, three cups!" Sáenz shouted at Fernández, unable to contain himself upon seeing him fill for the third time his fragile little porcelain cup and stir the aromatic liquid with his teaspoon.

"Fernández, go on," said Cordovez, Sáenz, and Pérez as one, while Juan Rovira was rising to take his leave, saying:

"I'm an ignoramus . . . No one loves you as I do. I am enchanted when I hear the adepts recite your verses and call you a great poet: suddenly I fancy hearing you read something like tonight; I'm paying all the attention God granted me, and I give my word of honor I'm in the dark about the better part of what I'm hearing . . . What does all that you've read us have to do with the name of the estate, with the gallery painting or with the watermark on the white-leather-bound books? . . . I'm an ignoramus . . . Tomorrow I'll send you the parasites that arrived today from the coffee plantation."

"The odontoglossum?" asked Fernández, using the technical name of the orchid out of habit, acquired from speaking of botany with the Englishman who tended the hothouse.

"I don't understand that, the ones you wanted, they sent a ton . . . You'll have them tomorrow." And after shaking his friends' hands with his own large, strong, tan hand, he left grumbling under his breath: "Decidedly I don't understand any of this, I'm an ignoramus!"

"José, go on!" said Cordovez impatiently upon seeing the red portiere close behind the giant.

So Fernández read the following by lamplight:

Interlaken, 25 July

Drunk on ideas and tired of thinking, I left my hideout eight days ago to expend the energy that quietude, icy baths, and exercise had welled up in me, and from that morning to tonight it has been a riot of incessant movement, landscapes traveled, dizzying mountain-climbing and tireless hikes through cool valleys full of new verdure. Snowstorms, snowdrifts, high peaks where the lungs fill with the purest air, the eyes with unexpected lights, the brain with grandiose ideas; where the blood is infused with life and enriched better than with the most careful hygiene that could be followed in a city. A never-before-felt sensation of burning vigor and boundless muscular energy to exert in new exercises have made me aware of all the vitality my body holds despite all I have squandered in recent months, and at all times I have been ruminating on the details of my plan. Not one desire, not one sensual image has pursued me; unhealthy temptations are breathed in with the smell of fine food and perfumeries, of rice powders and of Woman, smells that waft through the air, laden with the effluvia of lust and with the germs of mental illness from the modern Babylon.

Nature, bless you! . . . [84] Your spectacles seen in complete solitude, without hearing a single human voice that would disturb our meditations, are like a calming, efficient bromide for sleepless souls!

The day before yesterday I was in a snowdrift, all white, bright, the ground diaphanous. The distances, where the morning sun played, were full of mist, the sky awash in light. I uncorked the smooth flat flask full of green Chartreuse that I carried on my belt and took back a long draught that scorched my palette with the tang of aromatic plants

Switzerland, the ardent sites of old Castille, full of noble fevers and the rosy vistas of the Mediterranean coastline; you old ladies who cross the countries that attract you as you drink the same lukewarm tea, devour the same bloody roasts, and write with your fine cursive the same ten-page letters, your backs to divine scenery; German canoness with your fourteen quarters in your coat of arms, you who turn upon the drawing room the insipid uncomprehending gaze of your big, grey melancholy eyes; you pair of French renters whom some travel agency shuttles from place to place for you to admire without understanding the sites and buildings pointed out by your guide, Johanne, for your harmless touristic titillation; you, honorable Mr. Woodding, who, missionizing for the trinitary sect, with a copy of the Gospels under your arm, lash with the tails of your long frock coat the honeysuckle blooming in spring, and walk your offspring—the four little blonde girls who look like something out of a Kate Greenaway[86] album—around all the flat walkways near all the hotels where it costs ten francs a day to register; the enormous Wallachian or Romanian count with the long curly locks dressed a la Caracalla[87] and lifeless, bovine eyes; you Italian prince, whose secular palace, where your glorious ancestors dwelled, was sold by creditors tired of trying to collect from you; O, specimens of the common run of the human species, made in haste by the Great Creator, without swelling of muscles or tuning of nerves, readers of Ohnet,[88] worshippers of Gaboriau[89] and of Montépin,[90] you who consider the supreme pinnacle of art the paintings in which smile the pink-pomade Venuses by Bouguereau;[91] you who are thunderstruck hearing the Italian ditties from thirty years ago and the idiotic pornography of the café-concerts, and you who are indifferent to the tender ingenuousness of the Pre-Raphaelite painters, the subtleties of Japanese art, the grandiose symphonies of Wagner, the pitiable characters that cross the grey shadow of Dostoyevsky's novels, the otherworldly creations of Poe; admirers of the mediocre and of the facile, whom Max Nordau would present as prototypes of perfect equilibrium, you all slurp down the same cosmopolitan noodle soup, the same suspect roasts, glazed with the same chemical-tasting Médoc, you soak up the same black plum raisin compote with which the friendly proprietors of the Swiss hotels nourish your beautiful selves in the summertime! May those indigestible delicacies go down lightly and become the blood of your blood and the bone of your bone, and may the thanksgiving uttered by the gaunt lips and the blessing the abbot Pazavillini's fingers scatter in the air help peptize you and ease your labored digestion, as he sits at the head of the table where the cadaver-colored Camembert cheese, the deliquescent Roquefort, and the decoction of bitter chicory now shine, and with which, believing you are taking in aromatic coffee, the liquor of Voltaire and Balzac, you finish your Pantagruelian luncheons!

Interlaken, 5 August, nighttime

Nini Rousset, the divette of a comic theater on the Boulevard, Nini Rousset, who, dressed like a wreath of grapevine leaves, drove wild a roomful of prostitutes and pleasure seekers by displaying nude her statuesque curves and the turgid coolness of her Venus body in a magazine last year, Nini Rousset, to whom I sent bouquets of gardenias and a pair of diamonds, eliciting no more than a sneer and a rude remark the day I sought to make her mine. Nini Rousset, for whom I would have given a month of my life before coming across Lady Orloff, has just left my room, leaving in it her scent of Cyprus and in my nerves the vibration of a violent jolt of pleasure. She arrived an hour ago, with six trunks full of hats and dresses and three lapdogs; upon finding my name in the hotel registry, after she was settled in her room, she came to mine, and coming in on tiptoe, she drew near me from behind and with her soft, smooth little hands covered my eyes, which at that moment were reading a page from Spinoza's *Ethics* . . . *Guess who, guess who, rastaquouère poet, you animal you, guess who,* she shouted, kissing me and biting the nape of my neck with her mouth redolent of mint. Like a satyr drunk on sex, I lifted her from the floor with my arms as I wrested loose from her lascivious embrace; the provocation having begun with her childish fun, it ended some minutes later in a double savage yowl of voluptuousness on the bedchamber divan.

I dislike her with all my heart and soul. She is a true incarnation of all Parisian rottenness and vice. A column in *Gil Blas* once related the craving she had upon seeing a half-naked strong man who lifted

250-pound weights, and her seducing the Hercules when the show was over, taking him in her coach, and holing up with him for two days and nights in her bedroom, where all those who have had a few thousand-franc bills at their disposal to pay for that night's whim have passed through. She's a Messalina with a price; coarse as a fishwife and beautiful as a Greek Venus . . . She has gone now to work out spending the night in my apartments without the manservants seeing her, and to have some bottles of champagne put on ice. The orgy will be worthy of my fifty days of abstinence and stupid study . . .

Geneva, 9 August

I have just risen after spending forty-eight hours under the lethargic influence of opium, of the divine, all-powerful, just and subtle opium, as De Quincey[92] calls it, who paid with his life for his love of the baneful drug, under whose influence millions of men in the Far East become depraved daily. It was absurd but I could do nothing else after the horrible scene. I wanted to flee from life for a few hours, to not feel it.

While we both were exhausted with lust and fatigue, drunk on chilled champagne, Lady Rousset beginning to slumber with her beautiful head on the soft bolsters, an unlikely fury, the ire of a Samson mutilated by Delilah, jarred me from head to toe as I thought, with all the stimulation of the alcohol in my body, of the coarse insults we had lavished on one another in the previous hour, mixing them with depraved caresses, and of my plans for a rational, abstinent life, undone by the night of orgy. A mad urge welled up in the depths of my being, unconsidered and swift as an electric shock, and like a tiger pouncing on its prey, I surrounded her with my hands contorted, clutching as if with two metal claws the round white throat of the divette. To choke her then and there, like a blood-thirsty animal, against the feather pillows! She gave a horrible cry upon wakening. Suffocating, she stared fixedly into my eyes, her pupils wide in an expression of superhuman terror. Upon surmising my murderous intent as I went on tightening my grip around her with my hands, she shouted in a hoarse voice, "Mad! Mad! He's mad!" and

German accent. They came in, she in front and he behind, they returned the greeting I performed for them by rising; she having rid herself of the traveler's overcoat and the hat that with its strange shape made her look somewhat like the portrait of a young princess painted by Van Dyck that is housed in the Museum[94] in The Hague, they sat down to eat.

Slowly, as I examined the strange figure of the man, she removed her Swiss gloves and rubbed her hands, two long, pale little hands with tapered fingers like those of Anne of Austria in Rubens's portrait, with which she tossed back the ringlets of her flowing, curly, silky chestnut hair, which, where the light fell on her from the front, had golden gleams. Her cool, silvery voice was heard then discussing the dishes of food . . . *For you, Rhine wine and cheese; no, daddy,* she was saying, *strawberries and milk for me* . . . The man, who was probably fifty, but whose head and beard were grey as an old man's, gazed at her with a father's tenderness, which made a strange contrast with the pained expression in the lines of his fine, admirably carved physiognomy of a nobleman or artist, and whose curly hair, sharp cleft chin, and impassioned faded green eyes added to his distinction. *You're going to eat alone,* he said to her, *I'm anxious to read the details,* and placed on the table, folded lengthwise, a newspaper printed in German typeface . . . *Read,* she answered him, drawing the candelabrum near so that the light fell on the page.

An irresistible sympathy had tied me to them in those seconds in which, they having forgotten my presence, I examined them with an insatiable curiosity. Doubtless they had wanted to escape the banality of their fellow diners at the table d'hôte by taking refuge in the reserved dining room. For those grey hairs to whiten his temples, for the deep wrinkles of suffering to thus furrow his yellowed thinker's brow, for that indelible painful expression to thus mark his features, he must have suffered horribly, for the vigor of his nature could be read in the lines of his body, molded by a grey suit of refined elegance, and his energetic profile put one in mind of a military man wonted to command and retired from service. The other profile, hers, naïf and pure as that of a Fra Angelico virgin, of a nonesuch grace of lines and expression, stood in relief against the dark background of the dining room wallpaper, fully lit by the candelabrum light. Completing her beauty was her hair, which came undone in front and fell across her narrow forehead in abundant curls, the feeble curves of her little fifteen-year-old body, her long, thin bust, her dress of red silk, her thin, snow-white hands. As she lowered her somewhat heavy eyelids, the shadow of her curly lashes fell on her pale cheeks, a pallor as healthy and fresh as that of the petals of a white rose, but a bloodless pallor, a profound, almost supernatural wanness, and around the harmonious curve of her rosy lips floated a supremely understanding smile. I had not seen her eyes, and spellbound as I was by the grace of her ideal figure, by the impression of equanimity and aristocracy that emanated from her everywhere, like the aroma emanates from an opening flower, I dreamt of seeing them. Suddenly she tossed her head back, and bouncing the silky ringlets of her chestnut-brown hair, turned toward my seat and directed her gaze toward me, staring at me fixedly with a stern expression. Hers were big, blue, penetrating orbs, *too* penetrating, whose gazes fell on me like those of a doctor on the body of a leper eaten away by ulcers, and sought mine as if to penetrate, with demeaning and icy insistence, to the depths of my being, to read the innermost recesses of my soul. For the first time in my life I lowered my gaze from that of a woman. It seemed to me that, in the seconds I held it, hers had read in me, as in an open book, the previous night's orgy, the opium binge, and penetrating deeper, the knifing of Lady Orloff, the debauchery in Paris, all the weaknesses, all the wretchedness, all the disgrace of my life. I hung my head in shame like a schoolboy caught in some misdeed, looking for some stanza in the book. I felt that her gazes had lit on it, that she knew it was a book of poems, the poems of Sully Prudhomme, gentle and penetrating as womanly moans . . . With the look I gave her I had wished to ask her forgiveness for having studied her with my eyes, which have seen human evil and have taken their pleasure in its spectacle, for the light of purity, of sainthood that irradiated in her eyes the first time our eyes met, suggested some strange impression of irresistible mystic respect. . . . When I looked at her again I chanced upon her pupils trained on me, and would have lowered mine had I not seen in the blue of hers, in the curve of her delicate lips, in her whole kindly countenance, an expression of infinite pity, of supreme compassionate tenderness, gentler than any sister's caress.[95] That gaze human love, but the luminous calm of divine love. In a choked-up voice I would tell her I had sought her for long years, that my lips, scorched by warm burgundies and burning champagnes from the orgies of the earth, were thirsty for her pure, childlike love, like that of water from a hidden source that reproduces the ferns and where the sky is reflected. Fray Luis de León's sweet, sweet stanzas poured her way from my mouth like a song:

> O soul divine, now lying
> Enchained in new limbs' feminine array,
> As earthward thou wert flying
> Through heaven, on thy way
> The riches of that realm became thy prey.[98]

I sought once more her blue pupils, and her gazes of mysterious tenderness told me she consented to my dreams. And an expression of supreme love shone over her pale face, turned my way. In my overheated imagination, my having lost all sense of reality, her flowing golden hair, on which the lamplight beat down, took on the brilliance of a halo that shone against the dark background of the dining room.

As he lifted his greenish eyes from the newspaper he was reading, the father spoke to her in Italian, breaking the spell. In the phrases in which she answered him in the same language, I caught the names of Malloggia, Silvaplana, and St. Moritz among the sweet singsong syllables of the language of Leopardi, which in her mouth had the sonorities of music.

"Serve us the coffee in the suite," the man with the white beard said to the manservant, rising and passing her coat to her and helping her place on the chestnut curls of untamed hair, with infinite delicacy, as a mother would do, the singular black toque that had attracted my gazes when they came in.

They left the dining room, he in the lead, she behind, and as she turned her head, casting me another long, deep, pensive gaze from her large blue eyes, their shine, the bloodless, almost luminous pallor of her face, and the slenderness of her long, thin body, gave her in my eyes, as

I saw her thus against the black background that framed the door, the seeming of an apparition.

Some minutes later, as I rose from the table, the shine of an object fallen at the foot of the seat where she had been sitting impelled me to draw in and retrieve it. It was a cameo. On its grey background in white relief was molded a branch with three leaves, and flitting around them, a butterfly with its wings spread. The stone was set in matte gold, in the form of a brooch, and the gem, which had been peerlessly worked, had surely fallen when she took off her coat.

I saved it to give back to her the next day, and to find a kindling of acquaintance on that coincidental occasion. I went to look in the visitors' book at the porter's lodge for the names of those singular travelers. They had arrived three hours ago and he had said they would be spending two days in the hotel, having taken the room marked number 9, a large drawing room with two adjoining bedrooms off to the side, situated on the second floor and with a view of the garden. They were coming from Nice, they had not written the place they were headed, and they were registered under the names of Count Robert de Scilly and Helen de Scilly Dancourt.

A strange idea crossed my mind. That name, Helen, did not evoke in me any figure of a woman that united with it, none of those who have passed through my life, leaving me the melancholy of a dying love gone cold after the fleeting thrills; that was her name, I dreamt of the princess Helen from Tennyson's idyll[99] and mentally I called her Helen, like a childhood friend.

A hand gloved in dark goatskin rested on my shoulder, wrenching me from my reverie. It was that of Enrique Lorenzana, one of my friends from adolescence, who lives in London and who, on his way through Geneva in the previous days, had come to see me, but had not succeeded in doing so, since my manservant, excusing me, on my orders, with the pretext of a serious illness, did not let anyone into the apartment while I was under the influence of opium.

"Man," he said to me, taking my hand between his hands, "I've come to see you three times, to no avail . . . Was your illness dire? . . . You look terribly disfigured and pale, and you have an air of dissipation, which if I didn't know you would give me a horrible impression of you," he added familiarly, and after conversing with me for half an hour in the smoking room, where two athletic, blood-red Yankees were infecting the air with the smoke from their Virginia cigarettes and poisoning themselves with whisky that smelled of motor oil, obliged me to dress and accompany him to a history lecture a local luminary was giving that night. He placed in his endeavor to take me out the earnest gentleness of a brother who wishes to break someone away from grievous ideas through practically forced amusement. Unquestionably, with his perspicacity of a born physiognomist, he read the ravages of opium on my face.

As I returned on foot to the hotel, midst a splendid midnight clustered in stars, the moon shining in the sky in its final quarter like a silver jewel in a black silk jewel box, the leaves on the trees, which rustled in the wind, the waters of the lake, with its deep transparencies where the reflections of stars trembled, were a scene worthy of the new emotion that filled my whole being and returned me to the pure and far-off days of my adolescence. The gaze of blue pupils, radiant in the deathly pale face framed by her chestnut brown curls, left my spirit aglow. Dreaming of her I jumped over the iron door of the hotel gate, and fearing certain insomnia in my bed, I took to strolling through the garden. The dark vegetation, speckled white here and there by the opened flowers, smelled like a bottle of rare essence. The stars shone above, and one could hear the silence in the midnight still. Of a sudden, as I raised my head to see the sky through the trees that stretched out the black masses of their giant branches against it, I saw one of the second floor balconies lit up in the building front, its windows open and white curtains drawn. A long shadow of a woman, as if enwrapped in a shawl that fell from her head down over her shoulders, stood in hazy relief over the misty white of the curtains. It was She; that was the bedroom on the left-hand side of apartment number 9. Surely the father was asleep by now in the right-hand side, where the light was out.

Spurred by an irresistible impulse, I pulled up some flowers from the thicket, calculated the weight necessary for the bouquet to reach its destination, attached my card to it, and went back down to the garden.

The light still lit the full-length white curtains, which lightly stirred in the evening breeze. The shadow had vanished. With my heart leaping in my breast, like a thief who fears being spotted, I hid in the shadow of a thicket, and standing on the stone bench, threw the bouquet, which soared through the air, through the opening in the curtains, and landed inside the room.

The curtains were raised a moment to reveal to me in the back of the dark bedroom the lamplight that burned copper-colored through the wide gauze shade. Turning its back to it, the long black silhouette walked forward, like that of a Fra Angelico[100] virgin, reached the balcony, and, with her head high, held heavenward, lifted her right hand to eye level, slowly tracing with it a cross in the shadows, while the left hurled something that crossed through the air and fell at my feet—white as a dove—on the dusky earth. It was a great bouquet of flowers, which shed pale petals into dark space as it passed through it, and bounced when it hit the ground . . . In the sound of its fall I think I heard my dying grandmother's mysterious words, "Lord, deliver him from the madness that sweeps him away, deliver him from the hell that clamors for him" . . . A profound shiver of religious fear shook my flesh, a slight chill ran up and down my spine, and as if death had touched me, I fell faint on the stone bench. When I came to and recalled the scene, I searched for the flowers, whose whiteness could be seen in the darkness, to convince myself that I had not dreamt it. It was a bouquet of pale tea roses that I raised to kiss. I looked up at the hotel's façade, which was now dark and still, and through whose shuttered balcony windows not a single ray of light filtered in.

When I woke this morning, after an unhealthy night's sleep, achieved with two grams of chloral and full of the images of the day, of blue eyes, that pale countenance, that chestnut hair, the ceaseless fluttering of a white butterfly over three green leaves and the bouquet of roses, the sun striped with gold my balcony blinds. It was ten-thirty. I searched with my eyes for the flowers, thinking the nocturnal scene was part of a chloral-induced nightmare. There they were, in the Bohemian jug where I had placed them upon retiring. Already somewhat withered, some were hanging above the table, and two of them covered the cameo set in greenish gold.

After the bath and the thorough toilette with which I sought to remove the traces of the opium and the chloral, I went down to the dining room to have my morning tea. I felt sad, my heart made heavy by a strange weight. The servant who had served me the previous night brought breakfast and with it a telegram from Miranda and Company that had arrived in the early morning hours. Overcoming a certain repugnance, I sent him to inquire of the hotel concierge if Mr. Scilly and the young lady had left. When he returned, I had already drunk the tea and read the telegram, and was waiting anxiously.

"The gentleman and the young lady left first thing this morning, carrying their bags to a private coach that came around to fetch them. The concierge heard him say *to the station,* but did not hear the name of the station . . . Would the gentleman like more tea?" he asked, looking at the empty cup.

Where to search for her while finishing up my business with Morrell and Blundell in London; where to search for her, for I need to see her as I need to breathe, to see her again, to bathe my soul in the light of her blue eyes, to kiss her long white hands, kneeling at her feet? Why the blessing and the bouquet of roses that match so extraordinarily with the delirious words of the dying old lady? . . . So then mystery can take on material form after all, mixing with our life, nudging us in the light of day? . . . The bouquet of roses is now enclosed in a glass box that will allow me to take it on my journey, and the box has been perfumed with the faint smell of dying flowers.

Miranda and Company inform me they have received word from Morrell, telling them they accept the price I set for the mines, in light of the report from the engineers' committee that has returned already and whose findings we were awaiting to cinch the deal.

I shall be in London on the 15th, as they require, in order to sign the deeds, and I shall leave here this very day so I might dream about her during my journey.

Where could she be? . . . In the Engadine, certainly . . . I heard her mention Malloja, Silvaplana, and St. Moritz . . . When my business with the English bankers is concluded I will go and find her there, and if I do not find her I will search over all of Europe, over the whole world, for I need to see her to live.

London, 11 October

Two months of life in the fantastic city, which I did not visit during my last stay in Europe and of which I still had a hazy impression from my visit eleven months ago; two months that have slipped by quickly between the countless errands that the sale of the mines required and the anxiousness with which I waited in vain for a reply to my telegrams, sent to all the grand hotels of Europe, and the letters in which I requested knowledge of the whereabouts of Scilly and his daughter from information agencies—to no avail.

His daughter . . . I smile to myself to think I have written that word . . . I do not call her that when, as I name her in my mind, I evoke her with all the sweet grace of her newly nubile curves made of long lines wrapped in the red silk of her bodice, with her bloodless mortal pallor, framed by the dark gold of her unbraided hair and lit by the luminous smile of blue pupils; I call her Helen, as if the intimacy with which I have lived with her image had drawn her close to me, and I name her with the tenderness that would quiver in my trembling voice were I to press her hands in mine, these hands unpolluted by a woman's touch from the night I picked up the bouquet of white roses until the instant in which I write these lines, her long alabastrine hands that as they make the mystic sign of the cross in the air cast the pale flowers into the darkness of night.

Helen! Helen! . . . Sometimes in the quiet of this midnight tucked away in millionaire London, seated before my desk on which a volume of the poems of Shelley or Rossetti lies open, which are paralyzing my senses with their supernal subtleties and the almost Italian music of their strophes, I raise my eyes from the book and consider in the lamplight the cameo set in gold that I could not return to her.

Then I say her name aloud like an incantation that would make her rise up and appear before me, there in the somber recesses of the estate where the green suede drapes hang in heavy, opulent pleats, and slowly move in closer, closer, not touching the carpet until coming to a stop in the circle of lamplight and looking at me with her overmastering eyes.

Why *not touching the carpet?* asks the analyst I carry within me and who perceives and distinguishes down to the shadows of my ideas. . . . Why *not touching the carpet?* Let the Mephistopheles we all carry within our soul laugh at this phrase, let the long plumes of his red cap commence to shake, let a diabolical grimace twitch in his ironic features, lit by a hellish glint, and let him burst into derisive laughter; *not touching the carpet* because when I think of her I see her uncontaminated by the earth's atmosphere, sexless and radiant as Milton's cherubs. The phrases that come to my lips to praise her then are not the inharmonious passages from my flat prose, but these verses from *La Vita Nuova,* in which Dante speaks of Beatrice:

> My lady is desired in the high Heaven:
> *Wherefore,* it now behoveth me to tell,
> Saying: Let any maid that would be well
> Esteem'd keep with her: for as she goes by,
> Into foul hearts a deathly chill is driven
> By Love, that makes ill thought to perish there;
> While any who endures to gaze on her
> Must either be made noble, or else die.
> When one deserving to be raised so high
> Is found, 'tis then her power attains its proof,
> making his heart strong for his soul's behoof
> With the full strength of meek humility.
> Also this virtue owns she, by God's will:
> Who speaks with her can never come to ill.[101]

Tonight it has been two months since that night at Interlaken; at this hour I was already asleep, under the influence of the chloral. The sixty days that have gone by since the time we met make for a peculiar story:

The first ten were spent putting the sale of the Mal Paso mines in order, and at the end of the next day the Bank of England already had credited my account with the hundred thousand pounds received in payment from Morrell and Blundell, and neither my imagination nor my senses, burning with the notion of that money earned almost effortlessly, suggested a single idea of pleasure-seeking or passionate emotions to procure with that gold that could be rendered into sensual lunacy. Withdrawn in my own house, whose terraces look out on Hyde Park, and where the upholsterers quickly installed the furniture and artworks that surrounded me in Paris, I have split my time between a task I am performing in the Foreign Office, visits to the most renowned hothouses, and a series of new studies undertaken here, in the peace and quiet of my office, with two famous scholars.

My extravagances during this period have not amounted to a thousand pounds: seven hundred spent on a painting by Sir Edward Burne-Jones[102] and the bookseller's bill for a little over two hundred, which I settled yesterday. I have not set foot in a salon, despite the fact the Lorenzanas, Roberto Blundell, and Camilo Mendoza, our great statesman, who lives in Richmond, have visited me persistently. I have not set foot in a restaurant or a theater, and my strolls have leaned toward the quiet neighborhoods of the well-to-do bourgeoisie, where the wide streets, shrouded in the autumn mists, at twilight stretch out the monotony of their mellow mansions, separated from the public thoroughfare by the greens of the little gardens in front of their façades.

How many times have I gone down them at that hour—I, an ingenuous passerby, standing somewhat outside myself to catch the British soul in its simple outward manifestations—and have I stopped when through the sash window of some half-open balcony I descry through the panes the lamplight that illuminates the evening gathering of family, from a lamp whose light falls on the wide table cover near which the bespectacled old lady in her bonnet and wig, of whom Pombo[103] sings, the old heavy John Bull, ruddy and phlegmatic, reading *Tit-Bits*[104] and guffawing as he looks at the *Punch* cartoons, and the two blonde, green-eyed, fresh-faced misses, the visitor dressed in the inevitable tuxedo to drink the endless warm tea, spoiled by generous amounts of milk; the insipid infusion into which the old well-to-do Albion has turned the nervous liquid that in their native land the mandarins drain, dressed in pink silk and with their smiling, slant-eyed *musumes,* in diminutive, fragile porcelain cups, eggshell thin and on which are depicted bunches of chrysanthemums, golden half-moons, hieratic cranes, and implausible pagodas.

Other times, to offset the contrast, wrapped in the black ulster that hides my suit, I pass through the horror of the poor neighborhoods, full of dark and degraded souls, peopled with beggars and where the autumn mist enshrouds the dim reddish light of the gaslamps to make out, through the greasy windowpanes of some third-rate store full of the ruins of things that are no more, the long, thin, hungry face of a Jew that looks like something out of a ghetto from the Dark Ages; and at the back of the taverns, reeking of rotgut brandy and nauseating beer, sinister shadows of ruffians, wrinkled faces of old procuresses, and withered faces of impudent little urchins, eaten away by vice, and which still have an air of innocence unbroken by the steady sale of their poor artless caresses.

Hovering over my spirit is the melancholic reclusion of autumn, of its leaves burnt and red from the cold, of the giant copper and violet storm clouds of its twilight, of the smell of abandoned nests and chloroform of the leaves that come loose from the branches and whirl in the humid air under the sickly rays of the October sun, which hardly warm them, then to fall to earth and await there, black and rotten, the solitude of the frozen winter and the fresh symphonies of spring.

At night my body is consumed with a sloth that makes me smile if, when entering my room to dress, I see the black tuxedo, the patent leather half boots, the resplendent shirt, the silk socks, the cambric handkerchiefs, the white gloves, and gardenias for the buttonhole, placed in little shining silver vases, which Francisco, my old manservant, carefully prepares without consulting me, and lays out on a low divan, in front of the enormous bright mirror with the bronze frame, in anticipation of a foray into the world. I smile at myself and put on a wide flannel suit; sensitive to the cold, I light a fire in the fireplace, whose gentle heat neutralizes the temperature that gives signs of the severest of winters, and with my legs wrapped in the Sevillan blanket, my inseparable travel companion, and breathing the opiated, aromatic smoke of an Oriental cigarette, I sit close to the fire in order to gaze at the tumbling black castles that the carbonized trunks form, the red caves of fire where the smoldering logs burn, and the blue blazes of the tongues of fire. Hours of infinite seclusion in which I mull over the plan that will immortalize my memory, readings of Shakespeare and of Milton in the silence of the sleepless dawns, how far you are from the hedonistic brutishness of my Parisian nights in which, after a dinner of lobster American style and extra-dry champagne, the bedroom of Miss Orloff would hear my cries of wild voluptuosity and her delicate frame would be hurting under the crush of my pleasuring hands! . . .

Enrique Lorenzana, the Botwell partner with whom I was in Geneva, came here last night and told me when he came in and saw me: "You're a different person from the one I saw in Switzerland; you've got some color in your face and you look as lively as a schoolgirl. Your eyes are laughing! . . ." I should *say* I was a different person . . . If I did not carry deep down in my soul the incurable longing for her blue eyes, if I knew how to find her, how happy I would be to feel regenerated by her!

London, 10 November

I spent a dreadful night and I cannot say why. An average day, half spent at the Ministry of Foreign Relations making photographic reproductions of the minister's documents that my country accredited in England to ask for the recognition of its independence, the afternoon in a rocket factory—I have thrown myself furiously into my military studies that the follow-through of my plan requires—and the night here, looking at a series of etchings and watercolors they are offering me for sale; after all was said and done not one strong emotion. Simple food, with a little aged, pale Bordeaux. So then, why the horrible nightmare that has had me screaming and shaken, the angst-ridden nightmare with no images crossing it but my falling through the blackness of an abyss, and away on high, the three leaves of the cameo and the flitting of the white butterfly against a blue sky criss-crossed with white clouds? . . .

Why today's depression, in which I feel uninspired to work or live, and I think of Helen as a little boy lost in the night of a forest would think of the caresses of his mother? . . . It is practically a morbid obsession; as I fall asleep I see her, dressed in the red silk bodice she wore in Geneva, motioning to me with her pale hand; the first thing I think of when I open my eyes is her, and as I strain to recall the impressions of the dream, to me it is as through the darkness of the dream that she has passed, clad in white, in a dress whose skirt falls over her bare feet, in the margin of a Byzantine drawing of embroidered gold on opaque canvas, with a handful of white lilies in the snow-white folds of the cloak wrapped around her . . . Certain syllables resound inside me when inwardly I perceive her image. "Manibus date lilia plenis"[105] . . . says a voice in the depths of my soul, and her figure, like something out of a Fra Angelico painting, commingles with the sober and musical words of a Latin hexameter.

All that is delightful, but it is a sickly obsession and I know the cure. I say "cure" because purchased pleasure repels me like a nauseating drug, and neither of the two English lady friends who could afford me a night of caresses is in London, neither that aristocratic Lady Vivian I met in Berlin a year ago, so fresh and sweet and mad and passionate; nor the other, Fanny Green, the professional woman whom I had for three weeks in Rome four years ago. She was as stupid as an ignorant peasant girl and sentimental as a Richardson[106] heroine, but unsurpassably beautiful.

They are not here in London. I understand what the cause of my strange nervous state is, in which inner images become almost hallucinations, and I wish to suppress it. I am tempted at turns to head out to Regent Street at eleven at night looking for one of those Jennys like she of Rossetti's poem:

Lazy laughing languid Jenny,
Fond of a kiss and fond of a guinea,[107]

to make of her my captive, to take her to my house, where, upon seeing the furnishings and the dinner service and the paintings, all the luxury of the installation, she would open her eyes wide and, not understanding the fancy I had taken to her weak little body, I would possess her for some weeks during which the feeble voluptuosities she might bring me would in my mind be mixed with a sense of pity for her and of charity to spare her the endless strolls down Piccadilly and the brutal treatment at the hands of her night-time customers, and once the fever that runs through my veins is stilled by excess, send her on her way, first giving her a sum equal to what I spend on a jewel I fancy and with which she could live worry-free until her declining years in some pleasant little house in the suburbs, married to the boyfriend who adored her before her fall, and remembering me like a demigod she stumbled upon one night . . .

I cannot. A female presence in the house where Helen's cameo brooch is and where I have thought so often of her, would be impossible. By the next day I would have thrown the poor lass out, adding insult to injury, and feeling a horrible hatred and deep disgust towards her.

London, 13 November

It was Roberto Blundell who arranged everything. He is Jewish on his mother's side, and with the planned business on the horizon, would have done more to keep me happy had I asked it of him. We were together on the day I found her for the first time, and I was astounded at his beauty, which up until two years ago had earned him the protection of a member of the royal family. It seems that Blundell and she are old friends, and I suppose something of the fat sum I paid him earlier on the condition everything be done according to my wishes will wind up in his gold-cornered, alligator-skin wallet.

As I entered the bedroom, my blood was burning my cheeks and buzzing in my ears and I saw, in the shadow of the sea-green curtains with a bluish sheen, the gold of the wide bed and the whiteness of foam and snow whence emerged her bust with her nearly naked breast, barely covered by her open cambric shirt, lit by the light of an electric lamp that simulated a miraculous rosy flower of light between the bronze leaves that supported it on the headboard. "Come," she cried to me, smiling, showing between her roseate lips the enamel of her marvelous set of teeth; "come," and she held out her arms, diffusing through the surrounding air the fragrance of a rosebush shaking in the warm spring air.

Yes! Come, my very blood cried out to me, ablaze with desire; my nerves stretched out from three months' continence, my muscles invigorated by chasteness, come, slake your thirst at this pure mother-of-pearl cup that longs to feel your lips, kiss it, satiate yourself, have your fill, die of voluptuosity in her arms, in a spasm of vibrations everlasting! . . .

Turning my eyes away from hers, I looked toward the dark depths of the bedroom, where shadow converged into the gloomy color of the tapestries, opposing the electric light, and I cried out . . . I had just seen together, up high on the wall, as on an old medallion, the elegant silhouette and grey hair of my dear grandmother, and above it, the preternaturally pale outline of Helen in a one-second hallucination.

"Why are you shouting?" . . . she asked, without the charming, voluptuous smile that arched on her tender lips vanishing. "Why are you shouting? What has fallen there on the carpet is a bouquet of flowers I received today from Nice; fetch it, bring it to me, and kiss me," she added, laying the blonde curls of her beautiful head on the frill of the cushions.

I picked up the bouquet, which I had not seen before, and with it in my hand approached the bed, where the shapely arm, soft, white, and fragrant, wrapped around my neck.

"You are beautiful!" she said, riveting her black eyes on me with their caressing gaze and alluring me toward her. "You are beautiful, but why are you looking at those flowers with the eyes of a madman? They are flowers I had brought from Nice and had forgotten there . . . Look at the white butterfly that flew into the box!" she shouted, looking at the insect, which took flight through the warm perfumed bedroom.

I feigned a dizzy spell and took my leave, kissing her hands, tarrying on them, and taking away on my own hands the smell of tea roses that filled the branch, and in my eyes the fluttering of the white butterfly, which flew there at that moment and in my dreams four nights ago, when in a nightmare of unspeakable horror I was tumbling to the depths of the vertiginous abyss.

Helen was on her way from Nice the afternoon I found her in Geneva

. . . The fresh tea roses from the bouquet I held in my hands tonight are tied with the same oddly worked, cross-shaped ribbon that binds those of the other bouquet, which is now but a cemetery of black and withered flowers in the glass box that holds them. As I leaned over to breathe in the smell of the fresh flowers, in the bedroom where I dreamt I left my sickness exhausting the vitality I accumulated over three months, the white butterfly from my dream took off flying from them, the butterfly from the cameo, for the two are a single creature . . . It goes without saying that it was a fevered hallucination to have seen together the two heads of the beings whose words and glances envelop me today in a skein of shadows, but . . . why these coincidences that in my mind form a question that opens into mystery? . . . Why the ribbon with the same strange handiwork of interwoven knots? Why do these flowers, probably grown in the same place as the others, arrive at the exact place and time that I was going to debase myself with a pleasure purchased so as not to think of Her? . . .

I feared madness as I came out of the brutish orgies of the flesh, and now the noble love of the enigmatic creature that seemed to bring in her hands a strand of guiding light that could lead me through the darkness of life, that fresh, charming love that has rejuvenated my soul, is the source of supreme anguish, for when I inquire into the reasons behind the mystery that shrouds it, I run out of explanations.

If I could manage to see her, to trade these dreams that drive me mad for the serenity that the first words exchanged with Her would sow in my soul! . . .

London, 17 November

My Greek professor, who comes daily, had spoken to me several times of his friend Sir John Rivington, the great doctor who had devoted his final years to experimental psychology and psychophysics and whose works, *Correlation of Larval Epilepsies with the Pessimistic Conception of Life*, *Natural Causes of Supernatural Appearances*, and, especially, *Moral Hygiene* and *The Evolution of the Idea of the Divine*, place him at the pinnacle of the great contemporary thinkers—Spencer and Darwin, for example. I was familiar with Rivington's books from days gone by and I read and reread them with great enthusiasm, since the direct and precise observation of the facts, the perfect logic of his reasoning, solid as a steel chain, and the few but very accurate general deductions that stem from them, make that reading a heady, fortifying food for my wavering spirit, curious about the problems of the inner life. These works will still be standing when many of the vast theories of other philosophers, who today enjoy more fame than he, are chipped away by subsequent research.

I obtained two letters of introduction for Rivington, reread his books before going to the consultation, thinking this useful for my plan, and as a very special favor I managed to arrange a meeting at night in which we conversed at length for hours on end, alone in his spacious consulting room full of odd instruments for observation and technical works on his specialty, and in his office, where I experienced an unforgettable emotion.

The first impression my doctor makes with the almost childlike freshness of his full, rosy cheeks, which contrast with his curly grey beard, and the singular vitality that his gazes and the agile movements of his robust, brawny physique reveal, a body unbowed by sixty-five years gracefully lived, is that of perfect health, body and mind. A benevolent smile of intelligence lights up those solemn features, and from the first I felt in his presence the sense of confidence a man grown old in the study of human miseries inspires.

"Doctor," I said to him as I sat down in an armchair he offered me, "you have before you an odd patient who, in perfect bodily health, comes to seek in you the aid that science can offer one to improve the spirit. Catholicism gives its devotees spiritual directors to whom they can give themselves over. I, lacking all religious belief, have come to request a priest of science, whose merits are known to me, to be my spiritual and physical leader. Do you accept the position?"

"I accept," he answered with smiling gravity, "by requiring, like the ministers of the noble cult you name, contrition for whatever sins against hygiene you have committed and your firm resolve to change . . . Tell me your sins. . . ."

With the ingenuousness of an adolescent who pours his soul out to the priest who is to absolve him, I related my life to him, holding nothing back, neither my idealistic impetus, nor my outsized ambitions for learning, glory, wealth, and pleasure, nor the debauched orgies, the womanly faintings and miserable inactivity that for spells overcome me. I told him of the last six months with more sincerity perhaps than I have used in these notes I have written for myself.

He listened, never taking his eyes off me. I lowered my own to the floor at times, not moving a muscle, his impassive Greek features not betraying the least emotion.

"Now tell me your family background, describe for me your country, the city where you were educated, tell me everything you think might make things clear for me."

I did so simply and spoke for some time, and all the while his attention to me never flagged for a second, nor did he take his eyes from me.

"Now be so kind as to lay out for me how your life today is organized, your plans for the future, everything having to do with the present."

I spoke, telling him of my almost monastic existence since my encounter with Helen, the plans I am nursing with respect to my country; I related to him the incident that took place in Constanza Landseer's bedroom, my studies of Greek and Arabic, the fruitless efforts I exerted to find the one who is now the whole life of my soul . . . until this question, put with the childlike innocence that wise men have in matters of feeling, ruffled me, for I did not know how to answer him:

"Do you intend to marry this beautiful young lady if you find her, and to start a family?" . . .

Upon my failing to reply, for I was confused and somewhat ashamed by the question, he rose to bring and place on the table several little devices, with which each in turn he subjected me to examination, making me stand, sit, lie down, count, covering my eyes in order to prick me with pins or lift weights strapped to my legs; squeeze a rubber balloon, clutch to my wrist a clock mechanism with one end attached to a pen that traced a wavy, rhythmic line on a long ribbon; lift several hunks of iron, search for the variable in an equation, and translate a text by Aristophanes from the original Greek, while he, bent over the chronometer as if taking the pulse of my intellect, counted the minutes.

"There's a mistake here," he said, examining the sheet of paper I held out to him. "These adjectives refer to the action the verb describes and not to the subject of the sentence . . ."

And then began another head-to-toe examination, my body nearly naked on a black morocco leather divan, during which I analyzed the strange effect his words had caused on me: "Do you intend to marry this beautiful young lady if you find her, and to start a family?"

Good God, I, Helen's husband! Helen, my wife! The intimacy of daily dealings with her, the details of married life, that vision deformed by maternity . . . All the dreams in the universe had passed through my imagination except the one suggested in the specialist's words.

"You would be a model physical specimen," he said when, after the checkup, we sat down again near the heavy mahogany desk, "were your thoracic cavity a little wider and if you did not have a certain disproportion between your muscular development and your nervous strength; it is strange that your system has endured the excesses to which you have subjected it.

"You have to begin," he continued with a low, measured, silky-smooth voice, "by normalizing all, absolutely all, your functions, without stopping to think that there are noble and base functions in the human being. Despite your obvious enthusiasm for science, which today does not allow any separation between the phenomena of life, and considers them all, from breathing and nutrition to the loftiest conceptions and the noblest sentiments, as manifestations of a single cause, the one understandable as falling under the domain of our current methods of observation and analysis, and the other incomprehensible still on account of the rudimentariness of the instruments we are only beginning to use to observe them, although you declare you have no religious beliefs, you are a confirmed spiritualist, a mystic practically, perhaps despite yourself. Your words have shown that. You can wish *to not believe,* but the atavistic influences that endure in you force you *to believe,* and you proceed in accordance with those influences as far as the classification of your actions goes; make an effort, triumph over yourself, get your life into a routine, give the same reign in it to the physical needs as to the moral ones, as you call them, the same to the pleasures of the senses as to study, care for the stomach and care for the brain, and I guarantee you will be cured.

"Schedule your life and give it a simple, precise direction," he went on, after another long silence in which I seemed to read a certain sympathy in the cold gaze of his eyes. "The first thing you must do is enjoy yourself, force yourself to alternate your studies with amusements, noble ones if you prefer; frequent the theaters and concerts; I would be delighted to take you to the house of one of my best friends, where they play excellent music by the old German masters and where you would find fine company. Return to sexual needs their role as needs, disgust you though they may, and do not mix your sensations of that order with sentimentalism or aesthetic emotions that get you overwrought; this until you find the young woman you love and marry her so you can bring the impulses of your instinct under control in married life.

"Don't be unnerved that I speak to you of your love in those terms," he said upon seeing my involuntary scowl when I heard the remark. "You have to turn that ideal into your wife; you need, above all, like a child frightened by the appearance of an object he has not had a good look at and whose fear dissipates as he touches it, to find that young lady, get to know her, see if her character and her ideas fit with yours, and if so, marry her so the apparition you have fashioned disappears. She is an apparition. What you saw under the influence of opium and the profound weakness caused by the previous night's orgy, the hold her gazes had on you in the dining room, and the whim she had in throwing you a bouquet of roses have worked an autosuggestion on you that has become drawn out because of the drastic change of regimen to which you have subjected your body, and to the isolation in which you have locked yourself away. There have been no external impressions to combat it and it continues to grow. Since it coincides with a phrase that had struck you, since a person in your family spoke it as she died, it has taken on supernatural appearances. . . ."

He fell quiet, bowing his head in thought, and raised it after a few minutes of silence, smiling.

"Kindly repeat to me the description of the young lady when you see her dressed in white and with the lilies in her hand, where she seems to recall to you a Latin phrase."

I did so with the patience with which a patient tells a common Æsculapius for the second time a symptom of the physical pains he is suffering.

"Feeling nervous tonight?" he asked me, still smiling with a frank smile that arched his lips and revealed to me the potent animality of his body.

"No, Doctor, I am perfectly calm, this conversation with you has relaxed me like a dose of bromide," I responded, smiling in turn.

"Do you want to see your vision painted in oil by a painter who died years ago?" he said, smiling all the while, thrilled by the perplexity my expression revealed as I heard his strange proposal.

"As you like," I replied, not knowing exactly what to say, and filled with a childish curiosity that was mixed with a certain strange anxiety.

"Excuse me, I am going to send word for the lights in my hall, where the painting is, to be turned on. What a strange coincidence," he added, talking to himself and rising to ring an electric bell, which a few moments later the tuxedoed servant heeded, appearing in the room.

"Are the ladies in the sitting room?" he asked him.

"No, sir; they have just retired to their bedrooms."

"Are the lamps in the sitting room lit?"

"No, sir," the servant answered.

"Put one where it will well light the painting on the right wall, and serve us tea there," he ordered, and turning back to me, familiarly, as if the prospect of a triumph had broken the ice between us, he slapped my back like an old friend and said:

"Ten years ago one of my wife's whims had me buy the canvas I am going to show you. It was a strain on me, to be sure, for my budget was so tight then it did not allow me fantasies like that. Were you in London when you were a child?" he asked me, suddenly animated.

"Yes, Doctor," I replied. "I came with my father and spent a month here, of which I have rather hazy memories."

"Where did you live?"

"In a hotel near Regent Street that I have not found on this trip."

"So the exhibition of the painting took place here near the gallery where I bought it," he said, talking to himself. "Come see it," he added, rising to show me the way, and raising the portiere that separated the study from a dark room that we crossed to enter the hall, where four lamps burned.

"Is there a likeness?" he asked from the armchair where he had settled in order to see the effect that studying the painting was having on me, after a long while in which, as if hypnotized by the reality of my vision, I could not take my eyes off the figure of Helen. She was wearing the fantastic dress and white mantle of my dreams, and carrying in her hands the pale lilies, she trod a black fringe that was at the bottom of the picture, and on which could be read in gilded characters like the crowns of a Byzantine painting, the phrase *Manibus date lilia plenis*.

"Is there a likeness?" Rivington repeated. " . . . Come sit down here, where you will see her well, and have your tea with me, and talk of her."

"It is she, Doctor, it is she," I said, already sitting in the place he indicated, and turning my gaze to the divine apparition that smiled on me, framed in gold against the dark wall. "It is she, Doctor, but how to explain this mystery that surrounds everything about her, that has me find this oil painting here, which is her portrait, the night I have come to talk to you about her, as it had me find the bouquet of roses and the white butterfly the night I went to seek out another woman to forget her for a few hours? How do you explain all that?" I added, unable to contain myself.

"You are again seeing the ghost and dreaming about the supernatural," he answered with an almost harsh gravity. "Apply yourself to finding causes and not to dreaming. You have described the young lady as a figure like those of the virgins of Fra Angelico, and this painting is by one of the members of the Pre-Raphaelite Brotherhood, the group of English painters that proposed to imitate the primitive Italians down to their slightest artistic mannerisms. Clearly the girl did not serve as a model since, as you tell me, at the most she is fifteen, and it was twenty years ago that the picture was painted; but tell me: would there be anything strange about it if the model were an aunt or the mother of the girl you met in Geneva, and if the two had a great resemblance? Now, why did a certain Latin verse and the figure you were seeing join in your imagination? . . . Because a memory of this painting and of the legend it bears below it, seen by you many years ago, revived in your mind, owing to the analogy that exists between the features of your beloved and those represented in this drawing . . . Memory is like a camera obscura that receives countless photographs. Many remain in the shadows; some circumstance draws them out of there, the plate is struck by a ray of sun that imprints it on the sheet of white paper, and here you are asking who did the portrait, forgetting the moment the negative was met by the ray of light that traced it in silver acetate. Come now, are you still seeing the ghost? Do away with those mystic ideas, which are a carryover from the Catholicism of your ancestors, prefer action to useless dreaming, look for the young lady as of this morning, marry her, and you will be very happy. Is it not so that you'll be happy?" he asked interestedly.

"Very happy, Doctor," I answered, pouring myself some tea that the servant had brought.

"Don't drink more than one cup, you should use moderation in the use of stimulants. One cup of tea per night, no more, and a small cup of coffee with dinner. Cut back on the wine, not all at once but gradually, replace it with beer, cut out liquors and condiments little by little, make abundant meals but without the least refinement; give up strenuous exercises like horseback riding and fencing, which are muscular stimulants, so to speak, and take long hikes on foot through the countryside. I would like for you, once you are persuaded you must shun all stimulation of any kind, to gradually abstain from your overindulgence in luxury and your artistic fixations. Channel your intellect and your energy toward some vast industrial venture instead, an ironworks, a factory, that would let you make continual adjustments to expand it and that kept your mind on the small concerns involved in running it. Think about it: rather than planning to go civilize a country resistant to progress on account of the weakness of the race that inhabits it and the influence of climate, where the lack of seasons makes it hard for the human plant to thrive, sign on with some large English firm whose business is related to art—makers of furniture or porcelain, glassware or luxurious cloth for making tapestries—and devote your talents to the aesthetic education of the consumers through that objective route. A single idea from art carried over to industry ennobles the latter like hectoliters of alcohol into which a drop of rose essence is placed. That would be a wonderful plan. I have another one for you. Go to your country and put your fortune to work in a giant agricultural investment that will make you immensely rich and will keep you entertained with all the experiments in acclimatizing strains, animals, and exotic plants you could carry out in those climates. It would also be a boon if it let you live in the country. Whether here in London, overseeing manufacturing, or there in America developing your businesses, you could live a life of ease, raising a family and making the girl you found in Geneva happy. But better give up your dream of returning to your country and put down roots here. Frankly, don't you feel more comfortable and more practical running a factory in England than going to take your dream role, that of Shakespeare's Prospero in a land of Calibans?

"And besides, that's the life that suits you," he went on after pondering a bit. " . . . Scrap those political dreams, they can't come true. You're not in the practice of following through on your plans, and that is an education, an *entraînement*," he said, using the French word; "you have to start by brainstorming and performing small, practical, easy things, to then, after many years, fulfill those enormous dreams of yours. You strike me as a child who feels strong, and when he sees a professional gymnast lift two-hundred-kilo weights, thinks he can do the same without any inkling that his muscles are barely strong enough to pick up the rubber ball he is playing with.

"Give up those dreams," he went on, "give up those dreams of glory, of art, of sublime love affairs, of lofty pleasures, universal science, all your dreams. Dream is the enemy of action. Think, make a modest plan, carry it out at once, and move on to the next one. The delight in living, which you are experiencing now, diluted with violent bouts of depression that put you out of commission, is at once the cause of your unbridled ambitions and a potential danger to you; the cause, because it is what makes you continually seek new sensations in the hopes they are pleasant, a danger, because this delight reveals a sensibility out of all proportion, a kind of hyperaesthesia that renders you unfit to endure pain when it comes knocking. Have you known pain?"

"I have suffered, Doctor, perhaps less than most, and since we've agreed that you be told every detail of my inner life, I must tell you that in moments of suffering a pleasure greater than pain itself arises within me, that of *feeling the pain,* that of experiencing the new sensations that it brings me."

"That is the symptom that completes the scene," the doctor continued. "Right now there is such life-intoxication in you that I'm reminded of Goethe's line: 'Youth is an intoxication of the blood.' Everything seems beautiful, smiling, grandiose to you, everything attracts you, everything cries out for your attention. The day when your system, worn out by abuses, weakens, your nerves preferably will transmit disagreeable or painful sensations, deadly apathy will rule you, inhibiting you from action, your wasted, powerless stomach will digest poorly, your brain will scarcely function, and then you will be the flip side of the coin: your misanthropy, your blanket hatred, your disenchantment will be limitless. Every young pleasure-seeker is an old melancholic in training, rosebuds become withered roses; only the strong keep the form that defies time. If you think about it you will find that asceticism, which is the last word in religions, is the secret to inner peace: hardening man through the voluntary privations to which he is subjected, desensitizes him to suffering.

"That fantastic notion you have concocted of mastering everything, of enjoying with your senses and being at the same time a man of the world, an artist, a scholar, warrior, and leader of men, is the ultimate absurdity. For as long as you do not lock yourself into a specialization and forget about the rest, you will feel bad. Perhaps you will protest that there have been men that have almost managed to do it, that Leonardo had a command of all the sciences and arts of his time, and perhaps there was no realm of human thought in which Goethe did not exhibit his powerful intelligence. I will permit myself the observation that science in Leonardo's day was but an embryo, and the man from Weimar[108] lived seventy-odd years studying methodically. The simple act of thinking is exhausting; look at my dear friend Herbert Spencer, who has stuck to the prescriptions of the most absolute hygiene, and is now compensating for his lack of strength with colossal studies; recall the many contemporary French men of letters, neuropaths or those prevented from producing in the fullness of their youth, and you will understand that an excess of mental labor is the worst of excesses.

"I am honor-bound to tell you that heredity and the life you have lived make me fear for your future if you do not change your way of life. There is an odd, twofold atavism in you: one of almost unconscious impulses and brains united. If you succeed in balancing out those tendencies that fight amongst themselves, and manage to get your mental faculties to control your instincts, you are saved; if you persist in living alternately in asceticism and dissipation, with your unsystematic studies, with your impossible plans, when you least expect it, you'll run up against an unforeseen circumstance, and wind up an imbecile or a madman. Needless to say, the stimulants and narcotics that you have used have brought you halfway to your current state. You are predisposed to it, and it's you at-risk types that give to morphine, opium, and ether a bumper crop of victims. Search for her starting tomorrow," he said, looking at the painting, to which I had turned my gaze, "and when you find her, marry her and set up house, where in twenty years' time you will find your children succeeding you in the business and you will have the satisfaction of looking back on youthful missteps, like one who recalls danger after he is free of it. That love could be your salvation . . ."

"So you've held up under eight years of the same lifestyle, and now when I talk to you like Rivington talked to you, now when there's still time, you laugh at me and pay no attention," Oscar Sáenz said gravely from his chair, which was lost in the crimson semidarkness of the luxurious chamber.

"Now is different," Fernández replied with a certain superiority. "I have distributed my efforts among pleasure, study, and action, I have turned political plans from the time into an amusing bit of sport, and I have no strong sentimental impressions since I have thorough contempt for women, and I never have less than two amorous trysts at the same time so that the feelings toward each offset the other, and . . ."

"And so to create a contrast in the heroines," Luis Cordovez piped in. "One blonde and languid, a reader of Heine, and the other brunette and fiery, a reader of Pardo Bazán;[109] one sentimental like a schoolgirl and the other sensual from the tips of her nails to the marrow of her bones . . ."

A smile of vanity lit up the tired countenance of the poet . . .

"Go on, José, your reading has made me a better man," said Máximo Pérez from the neighboring divan where he lay.

London, 20 November

"That love could be your salvation!" was the materialist physiologist's last sentence . . . "Save him, Lord, from the hell that is clamoring for him! Blessed be the sign of the cross made by the hand of the Virgin and the bouquet of roses that falls in her night like a sign of salvation! He is saved, take a good look at him, he is a saint!" were grandmother's words in the mysterious delirium that took the shape of an almost divine reality. The reason of science, the intuition of sainthood, the cry of feeling, all the voices of life blend in a sublime chorus to call you, O mystery child of the curly chestnut locks, which are golden where the light plays on them; of the captivating blue eyes and the soft, pale cheeks like the petals of white camellias and the long alabastrine hands that, as they traced the sign of redemption in the darkness, tossed the bouquet of roses that fell through the darkness of the garden, as your gazes fell in the shadows of my soul! O you, immaculate, you most pure, everything calls to you, come save the weak and sullied soul that feels beating above it the black wings of madness and that invokes you now from the edge of the abyss!

Totally self-focused like a pilot who in time of supreme peril gathers all his depleted strength to consult his compass and steer clear of the storm, I have found in Rivington's words food for thought for hours on end. While being analyzed I produced an impression in *moral anatomy*, as Bourget[110] says in the preface to his marvelous *André Cornélis,* and I was appalled by it. It runs thus:

I am the only son of the loving marriage of two beings of opposing origins; within my soul the clashing instincts of two races battle and quarrel, like the biblical twins in the maternal womb. From the Fernández family's side come the pensive coldness, the habit of order, the view of life as if from a height inaccessible to the storms of the passions; from the Andrades, the intense desires, the love of action, the violent physical vigor, the tendency to overpower men, the pleasure-seeking sensualism. To what extent does the memory of my father, his delicate physique, his feeble frame, his silent seclusion, his passion for the exact sciences, throw a strange light on the appearance of certain moments in my mental life? My dear old grandmother, the poor saint, who died without me there to close her eyes for her, learned from that family of ascetics her asexual scorn for the weakness of the flesh. "She's a vile creature, whom neither God nor man shall forgive," she once said when she heard the name of a poor adulteress, and a flash of indignation lit up her lifeless eyes and violent rage made her wizened lips tremble. Abstention from all luxury and the almost monastic modesty of the father's house, where the silver service slept tucked away in the old mahogany cupboard and the help would desert their tasks to go to church. When I engulf my gaze in the far reaches of time, before my eyes the figures of the family well up: on my father's side, doña Inés Fernández de Sotomayor, the twenty-two-year-old virgin who, back at the turn of the eighteenth century, the night before her wedding, broke her engagement to devote herself to God and enter the convent of the sisters of Santa Inés with the name Sister Mary of the Cross; the third grandfather to be educated at Salamanca was captain of the royal armies and in my country served detestable posts appointed by the Inquisition; and more distant, towering over all the others, the brother of the first forebear who came to the Americas in his company, Alvaro Fernández de Sotomayor y Vergara, the wise archbishop and commentator of Tertullian[111] who, once back in Spain, died a virgin at seventy in the odor of sanctity. Delicate framed miniatures of diminutive diamonds, old Spanish oil paintings where emaciated figures stand out, moved by an intense spiritual life; moth-eaten, yellowing short chronicles, royal letters, parchments hand-lettered by distinguished artists, on which the gothic characters of the legend mix with the colors of elaborate coats of arms, tell the glories of that race of intellectuals with flabby muscles, delicate nerves, and deficient blood whose faded corpuscles run through the bluish branches of my veins. The Catholic piety that motivated them endures in me, transformed into an atheistic mysticism, as the holy malady of the epileptic atavisms revives in certain degenerates in the form of morbid duplicities of conscience.

Ah, yes, but in the dimples on my mother's cheeks laughed fleshly flowers, her milk had the savor of that of a tough country woman; my maternal grandfather was a big, simple, strapping man who at the age of seventy had two sweethearts and with his ax uprooted the stumps of the tangled forests; and back on the plains of my country they still talk about the black legend of defilements, fires, and murders at the hands of the four Andrades, Páez's savage companions in the Los Llanos campaign, who cut a victorious swath, sowing fear in the Spanish masses, with the rough-riding gallop of their colts, their lances raised in their arms of iron, madness in their soul, their blood scorched by alcohol, and blasphemy on their thick kiss-hungry lips . . .

These compressed and conflicting instincts live on in me, and determine my impulses; my bogus acquisitions of education and reason are powerless to contain them. A religious feeling has me in its sway, making me get down on bended knees if I go into the semidarkness of a temple at dusk, and on the day I felt my hand soaked in the warm blood of Lady Orloff, I could not hold back a cry of pleasure.

In order for the antinomy of those conflicting impulses to be transformed into permanent balance, I would have needed to harness them with a truly scientific plan of study. Circumstance decided that I would spend my early years under the most contradictory influences. I lost my mother when I was a child; when my father died when I was seventeen, I left the Jesuit school where my adolescence slipped the bonds of severe discipline, the state of my health undermined by my poor hygiene at the boarding school, and my kinship with the Monteverdes, nephews of my mother and owners of the rural estates neighboring ours, took me to live in contact with nature, right in the brutal rural life of the country estates, where under the twin influence of youth and diet, my muscles strengthened and my blood grew healthy. At that singular time of life, deer hunting and physically demanding athletic exercises were varied with delirious orgies in which Humberto Monteverde, drunk and with his curly head resting on some bare breast, would shout to me at the top of his lungs while his father, don Teodoro, would eye the gathering with his amazed eyes clouded by alcohol: "Hey, José, you and I weren't made for society, we're savages, we're Andrades, we're the nephews of plainsmen." That was a strange time in which the reading of the greatest poets and the sentimental and sensual boil of youth and the abandon of the body after nights of dissipation made me write my *First Verses;* stranger still if one compares it to the following year in which my close friendship with Serrano, the noble friend who had devoted his life to transcendental speculations, revived in me the pensive philosopher who from his grandparents was heir to an intense love of the moral life. Strange influences that engendered four souls in me, as I entered the salon where at twenty-one, cravated in white and with my bust molded by a Poole[112] tuxedo, I made my first aristocratic conquest: that of an artist enamored of things Greek, and who bitterly sensed the banality of modern life; that of a philosopher disbelieving in everything as a result of overstudy; that of a pleasure-seeker weary of common pleasure, who would seek more profound, more refined sensations; and that of an analyst that discriminated between them in order to experience them the more ardently. All these moved my heart, which beat under my resplendent shirt front, flirtatiously fastened with a black pearl.

Protean and multifarious, ubiquitous and changing, resistant to the sway of environments, tough from athletic exercises, the consumption of succulent morsels, and mellow liqueurs, enervated by sensual delicacies, my personality progressively developed and within me alternated times of pleasure-loving savagery and long passionate days of meditative detachment from tangible realities and of ascetic continence.

An intellectual cultivation undertaken without rhyme or reason and with mad pretensions to universal knowledge, an intellectual cultivation that wound up in the lack of any faith, in scorn for all human conventions, in a burning curiosity about evil, in the desire to take part in all possible experiences of life, rounded out the workings of other influences and wound up paving this dark road that has brought me to this dim region where I now make my way, seeing no more on the horizon than the black abyss of desperation, and way up on high, in the inaccessible reaches, her image, from which, as from a star on a stormy night, a ray of light, a single ray of light, is shed.

Terror? . . . Terror of what? . . . Of everything, in flashes . . . From the darkness of the room where I spend a sleepless night watching a procession of evil visions; terror of the herd, greedily running after pleasure and riches; terror of the bright, sunny scenery that smiles on noble souls; terror of the art that freezes the appearances of life in eternal poses, as if by means of some sinister spell; terror of the dark night in which the infinite stares down at us with its millions of eyes of light; terror of feeling myself to be alive, of thinking I could die, and that in those moments of terror, stupid, spine-chilling thoughts echo in my wearied mind: "What if there were a God? . . . Poor humanity is alone on the earth."

No, it is not terror of those things, but of *madness*. For years the chloral, the chloroform, the ether, the morphine, the hashish, mixed with stimulants that restored to the nervous system its tone, lost through the use of evil drugs, gave me an account of that idea of mental virginity being more precious than the other kind, of which Lasegue[113] speaks. Then the dissipation of the body, persisting in experiencing new sensations, the dissipation of the soul bent on discovering new horizons, after all the vices and all the virtues, practiced by indulging in them and feeling their influence, have brought me to the state I am in today, in which some days, when kissing a new pair of lips, when I breathe in a flower's perfume, when I see the iridescence of a precious stone, when my eyes range over a work of art, when I hear the music of a verse, I take such passionate, intense pleasure, I throb with such profoundly pleasurable vibrations, that with every sensation I seem to absorb all of life, all the best of life, and I think that never has a man taken such pleasure as that; and that other days, tired of it all, disdaining, hating everything, feeling for myself and for existence a nameless hatred that none has felt, I feel unable to make the slightest effort, I remain lethargic, stupid, inert, for hours on end, with my head in my hands and calling out for death, since I do not have the strength to bring to my temple the steel muzzle that could cure me of the horrible, dark *mal de vivre* . . .

Madness! Good God, madness! Why not say it sometimes, if I am only thinking out loud? . . . How many times have I seen her passing by, dressed in shimmering rags, her teeth chattering, shaking the rattles in her ridiculous scepter, and making mysterious faces at me, beckoning me into the unknown! In a hallucination that seized me for a few minutes the other night, the gems that shone on the black velvet of the enormous jewel case turned into the magical trappings of her queenly dress; another night into a nightmare in which she was clutching me in her black claws; I woke up bathed in a cold sweat. She had a horrible head, half twenty-year-old woman, smiling and healthy but crowned with thorns that bled her smooth brow; the other half, a desiccated death's-head with hollow black eye sockets, and a crown of roses that wreathed her skull-bone, all silhouetted against a halo of pale light, a horrible head that spoke to me with its mouth, half pink-flesh lips, half pallid bones, and was saying to me: "I am yours, you are mine, I am madness!"

Mad! . . . The madman in his dark seedy madhouse room, reeking of rat urine, swathed in his straitjacket! . . . the madman with his close-cropped hair, being showered with an icy jet down his skin-and-bones back, under the impassive eye of the man of science who jots down his violent actions and the blasphemies he chokes out, then to turn them into a detailed and precise monograph . . .

Mad? . . . Why not? That is how Baudelaire died, to true men of letters the greatest poet of the last fifty years; that is how Maupassant died, feeling the night creep in around his spirit and reclaim his ideas . . . Why shouldn't you die that way, sorry degenerate that you are, you who did everything to excess, who dreamt of mastering art, of possessing knowledge, all knowledge, and of draining all the cups in which life offers its supreme intoxications?

But no! You sweet angelical vision who in my dreams has her hands full of white lilies, who in my presence traced the sign of redemption and cast the pale flowers into my night, that is not how the soul you favored with your sanctifying gazes shall come undone.

When I think of you, Beatrice, you who make me ascend from the depths of my hell to the heights of your glory, Alighieri's verses sound in my soul like a song of hope and of comforting certainty:

> . . . as she goes by,
> Into foul hearts a deathly chill is driven
> By Love, that makes ill thought to perish there;
> While any who endures to gaze on her
> Must either be made noble, or else die.
> When one deserving to be raised so high
> Is found, 'tis then her power attains its proof,
> making his heart strong for his soul's behoof
> With the full strength of meek humility.
> Also this virtue owns she, by God's will:
> Who speaks with her can never come to ill.[114]

Oh, come, arise, appear, Helen! What is still good in my soul appeals to you for its life.

I am oversated with lust and I want love; I am weary of the flesh and I want the spirit. In my soul were foul dunghills that the spring tide, set flowing within it by the untenable gaze of your blue eyes, washed away. To receive you, what today is withered undergrowth will thrive with perfumed flowers and the noble dreams of my adolescence will all come back to life when your diminutive feet tread the dark doorway of my spirit, and will be by your side like a procession of angels; where there remain only pools of poisoned emanations, there will be slumbering lakes, barely ruffled by the wings of white swans. If searching, lascivious hands roved over my body tense with voluptuous contractions, if I sought forgetfulness in all the intoxications and all the orgies, if I fell tumbling like a drunkard down the dizzying staircase of vice, it was because I had not seen you yet. Have mercy on me. To achieve your sainthood—for I perceive you as a saint and you appear to me encircled with an aureole of mysticism, nearly holy—to achieve your sainthood, I have tried to be good. There has been no stigma in my life after your eyes' gazes met mine. But to be good I need you, I need to see you. Come, arise, appear, save me, come free me from the madness that moves forward in my skies like a dark cloud fraught with storms, come save what remains in me of the saints of my stock, of the wise archbishop and the gentle, gentle nun who in the earth unknown to you dream their final dream in the shade of the Gothic arcades in their old stone tombs!

London, 5 December

The thread of light that will lead me to her resides in the mysterious likeness of Rivington's painting, I thought two weeks ago. A phenomenon common in me makes me always take the long road and lose my way on it when I try to investigate something that interests me; instead of going straight to the old man, or asking him the name of the artist who painted the mystery work, and going on making inquiries until getting to the bottom of it, I threw myself with mad verve into the study of the origins and development of the Pre-Raphaelite school, the lives and works of its leaders, and the causes that brought about its appearance in the art world.

I have come away from my task with a few new perceptions on beauty, and my spirit retains something like the perfume and the soul of the ideal that moved the noble artists that made the Brotherhood famous; like a smooth and mellow aroma of incense emanating from the gentlest, ingenuous piety of the pre-Renaissance painters, and like a dazzlement caused by the coloring of certain timeless paintings. In short, I had never felt more ridiculous inside; I tried to find out about Helen and I have found out details of the life of Fra Angelico, read letters from Rossetti and Holman Hunt,[115] *canzones* by Guido Cavalcanti and by Guido Guinicelli,[116] verses by William Morris and by Swinburne, seen canvases by Rossetti and Sir Edward Burne-Jones. In sum, it all gets tangled up inside me and takes on literary appearances, one curiosity gets added to another, the attractions of the work of art make me forget the most serious interests of life, and without the brutal wake-up call Doctor Rivington gave me the other day, God knows how long I would have gone without looking for her, dreaming of Her, with my imagination spinning around her radiant image and my eyes searching poems and paintings for phrases and lineaments that evoke her.

I am not practical. Rivington has told me so in demeaning tones and I, who know it better than he does, smile to think of the scorn his voice betrayed as he told me. I should *say* I am not practical; practical men give me the strange impression of fear that the unintelligible produces. *To perceive reality well* and to act harmoniously is *to be practical.* To me what is called *perceiving reality* means *not perceiving all of reality*, to see only a part of it, the worthless part, the useless part, the part that does not matter to me. Reality? . . . *Reality* is what people call all things mediocre, all things trivial, insignificant, and worthless; a practical man is he who, placing scant intelligence in the service of mediocre passions, sets up for himself an annuity of impressions that are not worth the trouble of experiencing. That conception of the individual gives rise to the current organization of society, which the best-known of its detractors calls a "limited liability company for the production of a life of limited emotions," and that conception of life serves as the basis for the aesthetics of Max Nordau, who classifies true works of art as pathological products, and for the disgusting socialist utopia that in the phalansteries he dreams of for the future will dole out equal rations and clothing to geniuses and idiots.

Reality! Real life! Practical men! . . . Horrors . . . To be practical is to apply oneself to a lowly, ridiculous undertaking, one of those that you all scorned, O jealous ones! O, creators! O, fathers of what we call the human soul, you in your sublime madness prevented our eyes, lit up by some reflected light that your spirits shed, from being the atonic eyes of ruminants! You were not practical, sublime warrior, poet who dreamt and won the independence of five semi-savage nations, then to come to death under a strange roof, feeling within you the ultimate melancholy of disillusionment, on the seacoast where the waters bathe your native shores; nor you, poor daydreaming Genovese who gave a world to the Spanish crown, to die in chains; nor you, immortal maimed one, who suffered countless wants; nor you, sublime Florentine, who with your soul saturated with the ardent visions of your *Divine Comedy* begged for your exile's bread; nor you, Tasso, nor you, Petrarch, nor you, poor Rembrandt, nor you, enormous Balzac, hounded by heartless creditors, nor you, all of you, O poets! O geniuses! O beacons! O fathers of the human spirit who passed through life loving, hating, singing, dreaming, begging while the rest got rich, took their pleasures, and died sated and peaceful!

But I digress. Each one of those men, in forgetting the miserable material realities of life, did so to carry off some grand master plan to immortalize his memory. I am wasting my time in fruitless pursuits, entertained like a child in somewhat pretty trifles, without looking for the only one that will restore peace to my troubled spirit.

When I set foot in Rivington's consulting room, all the impressions from the last two weeks came flowing back to my memory, and oblivious to the details of real life, my mind moved in an atmosphere of ethereal refinements, of supernatural and delightful feelings produced by the incessant contemplation of Rossetti's paintings and the reading of his verses. That environment of ardent, melancholy mysticism filled with daydreams of Helen and her scent, like the sumptuous feminine dressing table with the aroma of flowers that impart their fragrance as they die, had enveloped me for hours like a spiritual mist, preventing any contact with the outside world. It lifted as if a spell were broken when I sat in one of the armchairs in the doctor's office and surveyed the crowd waiting their turn to seek the man of science's assistance. In front of me an obese, apoplectic old coot, bundled up in a heavy fur coat, with the scruff of his neck as red as a ham and wrinkly as an alligator hide, his eyes covered by double-thick black glasses and big chunky boots on his enormous feet deformed by gout, was soundly snoring. He had fallen asleep waiting his turn. In one corner of the room a greying, hungry-looking woman with an angular profile watched with her big grey hate-filled eyes a poor little girl of twelve or thirteen with sparse dirty-blonde hair, a colorless complexion splotched with freckles and discolored, half-open mouth, which showed her chipped teeth and faded gums. In another chair sat a little sickly olive-colored man, who kept perfectly, unnervingly, implausibly still, and among those four individuals of miserable and pitiable appearance, a fantastic figure, disproportionately tall and skinny with a caricatural appearance, paced around the office with great strides. He would furiously twist the hair on his long waxed mustache, and his unpleasant gestures were followed with indulgent concern by a thirty-year-old man dressed with refined elegance, but in whose delicate and beautiful features, of an extraordinary paleness, the signs of a definite and irremediable exhaustion could be read.

The little blonde-haired girl shook from head to toe and gave a sharp cry like a wounded bird, and a nervous trembling put her weak limbs in a flutter; the character with the fur coat awoke with a rasping snore and rubbed his apoplectic face with his enormous hand, ruddy and plump as a fencing glove; the olive-green individual who looked like a waxworks statue made not the slightest movement, and visibly humbled, the elegant patient who a moment earlier was roving his tired eyes over the whole room, as he felt himself in that assembly of incurables, returned his gaze to a ruby ring that graced the pinky of his left hand.

Stirred by the sight of those wretches, the pride of life, of youth, and of vigor welled up deep within me, and with an involuntary movement I squeezed with my practically twitching right hand the biceps of my left arm, which jutted out, springy and strong, forming something of a mass of iron under the thick cheviot wool of my winter coat; the blood rushed to my cheeks and with a brusque movement I got up to leave . . . No, I was not ill, I was not an incurable, a human tatter like those poor devils. I, ill? With what? With an excess of life, with an excess of ideas, with an excess of strength, and as if I had seen death as I looked on those human ruins on their way to seek relief for their miserable days, at that moment I desired all the pleasures of life, all the flavors, smells, colors, lines, music, delightful touches; I had a mind to hasten it all then and there, right then, before my body grew deformed and fell into wretchedness like those I was seeing . . .

So profound was the impression that when the person whose appointment had ended left, it did not register, nor did I see Rivington at first. Through the half-open office door, he looked at me from head to toe with an unsettled look in his eyes.

"Doctor," I said by way of hello, forgetting that there were patients that should have gone before me.

"Come on in," he said, somewhat sharply, ushering me in the room.

There proceeded a grotesque scene in which, unable to get a hold of myself, crying like a woman, hugging that big hulk of a man, who was virtually a stranger to me, I told him the dreadful impression that his horrible clientele had made on me, and begged that he assure me I was not ill, that I would not go insane, and in stupidly sentimental words I begged him to let me send a painter to his house for a copy of the painting. As gently as a mother handling a sick, spoiled, capricious child, the specialist overrode my wish, and with his customary gravity, pointed out everything that was abnormal and unhealthy in my spiritual state at the time.

"I had thought your case less serious than it is. You must harness the energy you have left to look for a cure immediately; head out tomorrow to find that young lady, enjoy yourself, amuse yourself, stop dreaming; dreaming is poison to you. Play, get drunk rather. That would be more hygienic in your current state. Do not waste a minute, go after her. You will find her and if you wish, you will make her your wife. You are young, you possess a tidy fortune, you have all the basic elements to be happy; do not waste your time in ravings that get you nowhere . . . Be happy . . ."

I rewarded the old man for that strange consultation, which ended with that fantastic prescription, with a king's ransom. I thought he would return my check, but no, he kept it, and no doubt he will use it well. All the better.

Ten days from now I will be in Paris, reinstalled in my hotel and devoted to looking for her. I am horrified to think of returning to the city where my life slipped away for so long amidst revolting delights. You smell of factories and smoke, my sooty London; the aerial network of telegraph wires crosses your opaque sky; your underground railroad has the appearance of a grotesque nightmare; the people that inhabit you know nothing of smiles; you, Paris, caress the traveler with your wide elegant avenues, with the Latin charm of your residents, with the harmonious beauty of your buildings, but in the air that one breathes in you are mingled smells of women and rice powder, of cooking and hairdressers' salons! You are a courtesan. I love you while scorning you, as we worship certain women who seduce us with the spell of their sensual beauty, and well I know that Helen's feet shall not trod your soil, O treacherous, voluptuous Babylon!

From my time in London I will take away with me a delightful impression of withdrawal and of inner life exacerbated to an indescribable degree; two languages that to me were dead letter, Greek and Russian; two branches of human activity that were strange to me: all the arts of war and of agronomy, with all the advancements made in the last half-century, are completely familiar to me. A bountiful harvest of impressions of art, readings of the original tragic Greeks that I knew previously in poor translations, of the poets before Shakespeare, of the whole modern pleiad, from the sensual and vibrant Swinburne to the mystical Cristina Rossetti; ineffable daydreams inspired by the paintings of Holman Hunt, Whistler, and Burne-Jones; all that have you given me, fantastic city that looks almost ideal to me since, while I have lived in your heart, I have lived with your memory!

As the upholsterers began to take apart the house, I was surprised at the number of luxurious objets d'art I bought without realizing it in these six months and have looked them over again one by one, lovingly, for in times to come they will remind me of days in my life more noble than recent years. You will decorate the foyer of the hotel in Paris, you giant Etruscan vase boasting in your bas-reliefs a beautiful procession of satyrs and nymphs, and above the ram's heads that form your handles, the tropical orchids will tangle their snowy vegetal butterfly shoots, splotched with violet and purple; you will cross in warring panoply over the halberd, chiseled like a gem, you Arabian swords with your polychrome hilts and your shiny blades of intricate quillons and twisted coquilles that the sixteenth-century Toledan masters tempered in the waters of the Tagus, the Arab spearheads and dangerous Frankish battle-axes with their fine gold damascene daggers; against your faded, moribund colors, you old heavy brocatelles, the two paintings by Gainsborough and by Reynolds I bought in last month's sale will smile; you, copies of Shelley, Burne, Keats, Tennyson, and Rossetti, that have on your exquisite white morocco bindings the three imprinted leaves and the butterfly cameo, you will wait on the Venetian malachite nightstand for someone to inspect your pages, their eyes startled to find the design of their lost jewel there, and you, unique Burman ruby, for which a fortune was paid at Bentzen, ruby that burns like a live coal and shines like a ray of light, you shall shine like crystallized blood, holding together the wedding ring, and making paler the supernatural pallor of her tapered fingers, on her queenly pallid hand!

Paris, 26 December

From the moment I set foot in this city I have been overcome by an indescribable malaise. It is not a moral impression, since I feel better, my mind having been put at ease by the idea of searching for Helen and comforted by the hope of finding her; it is not a disease, since no outward symptoms manifest it, nor is there any pain accompanying it, and my body is overflowing with life. I have a virtual plethora of strength at my disposal of which I cannot find a way to make use. The day before yesterday I spent doing strenuous physical exercises, horseback riding, cycling, boxing, fencing with the foil, which, instead of tiring me out, gave my muscles a sensation of essential strength that, as absurd as the image may seem, I think to compare with that of a well-made machine if one becomes aware of the solidity of its steel gears and the power of the motor that makes it run. "You're a regular Hercules," old man Miranda said to me the other day as he punched me in the shoulder, his eyes shining enviously while I was in his office.

A regular Hercules, and it seems that excess strength is the cause of the strange state I am in. Yesterday I could hold off no longer, and went to a doctor, to whom, without going into details on any other topic, I told my complaints. It was Professor Charvet, the scholar who has summed up in the six volumes of his admirable *Lessons on the Nervous System* what science today knows on the matter. It is he who has known me and looked on me with extreme benevolence since I heard his lessons at the university and witnessed his curious experiments in hypnotism at the Salpêtrière.

"You have followed Spencer's counsel: 'Let us be good animals,'"[117] he told me. "You are a beautiful animal," he added smiling. "I hope it won't turn out to be a serious illness. To what do I owe the pleasure of this visit? . . ."

"To a dreadful sense of anxiety and anguish I've been living with since I arrived in Paris; anguish for no reason and therefore the more detestable, anxiety that has no object, and to which I would prefer the most intense pain . . . Has it ever happened to you, Doctor, that you're running late to a pressing engagement, you're counting the minutes, the seconds, opening your pocket watch, not seeing the time, opening it again, seeing that the second hand is moving, checking to see if the timepiece is working by pressing your ear to it, thinking it has stopped, looking for the time on the clocks in the street, feeling that the train or the coach is not running, and having no respite from the horrible impression that sends an icy sweat down your temples and chokes your epigastrium until you have reached your agreed-upon place? . . . Prolong that for six days, exacerbate it, make it more intolerable by removing its cause, and you will have an idea of what I feel."

He questioned me skillfully and discreetly until forcing a confession of my five months of sexual abstinence, to which the impossibility of enduring the touch of a woman since the afternoon of that blessed tryst in Geneva has sentenced me.

"Come, now," he burst out with a joyful smile that lit up his whole smooth-shaven face, and when he shook his head made his smooth grey hair shine, which combed back, falls in a thick mane around the neck of his big long black frock coat. "Come, now, why the whim? A vow of chastity from you, at your age and with those looks?" . . . he asked with a kind expression.

"It's no whim; it's for reasons that would take too long to explain," I said, mincing words. "So you think that's the cause?"

"I should say, my friend," he replied with caressing gentleness. "I should say that's the cause. With that athlete's build of yours, and you're twenty-six years old! Imagine yourself as a powerful battery building up electricity; a boiler producing steam, electricity and steam that go unused! These first months must have been terribly uncomfortable, and I feel admiration for the willpower that has allowed you to spend them thus. Drugs are unnecessary, my friend, you know the cure, apply it . . . in small doses at first," he added, smiling all the while.

"If you don't give me another," I answered, using a tone analogous to the one he was using, "I won't be cured soon, you can be sure of that."

"Ah! So you persist with your regimen? . . ." he asked with an expression of marked curiosity. " . . . That's admirable . . . Come now, spend your energy in every sense, as you have done in recent days, and finish off the work of vigorous exercise with long hot baths and high doses of bromide. Bromide in ordinary water," he added, handing me the formula. "And . . . mind the beast you have managed to tame does not awaken suddenly and go off on a rampage, eh? . . ." he said to me as he shook my hand in the doorway of his office.

All in vain. I have stayed hours on end in the enormous white marble bathtub, made drowsy by the hot water; on my palate I have the saline flavor of the sedative and in my nostrils the smell of the lemon balm essence that the professor added to the salt. All in vain. Anguish oppresses me, exhausts me, brutifies me, makes me break out in a cold sweat, prevents me from thinking. In the last forty-eight hours I have not been able to get a wink of sleep and my brain, tired out from insomnia, is working feebly. I can hardly think, and I am dying of anxiety. Over what? . . . Over nothing . . . This morning I had the most fiery of my horses saddled up, an Arabian, refined and nervous as an artist, who gets riled and stamps when he sees me. Running away from the Park exposition and disobeying the regulation easy trot, I sped feverishly away at full gallop on the spirited animal, which drank in the winds of the winter landscape laid waste by the cold . . . It seemed that furious ride had some goal I would never attain, and the anguish was growing and growing, and in the sound of the horseshoes pounding the road, deserted and white with snow, I seemed to hear a voice that shouted: "Hurry, hurry, you're going to arrive too late; faster, hurry, hurry!" And under that impression I arrived four hours later at the hotel, bathed in sweat, worn out and trembling in fear as if some bad news were awaiting me there . . . "Any letters?" I asked the doorman, who handed me two. As if they were something unexpected and of the utmost seriousness I opened the envelopes with a fright; they were a note from Morrell and Blundell, informing me of one hundred pounds paid to my tailor in London, and a short note from Alberto Miranda letting me know they had finally acquired some watercolors I had been after for some months . . .

For six hours I have been shivering, soaked to the marrow, stretched out on the divan in my office, on which Francisco has accumulated blankets and pelts that fail to warm me, as does the bright fire burning in the fireplace. I am freezing to death and dying of anguish. To keep my mind off it I write these lines, and as I reread them and find them intelligible, I experience a strange amazement. The mental weakness I feel is so great that I could not add one hundred more. My brain refuses to think. A thick fog envelops my intellectual horizon; deathly dejection overcomes me, and if it were up to me I would not make a single move, in order not to drain what little strength I have left. It is as if through an invisible wound my blood and my soul were leaving me at the same time. Thus must Seneca have died with his open veins, in the warm water of his marble bath. In my mind, where images lose their relief and commingle, are floating two verses from a Rossetti sonnet in which a vision speaks to the poet through the brume of night:

> Look in my face; my name is might-have-been;
> I am also called, No-more, Too-late, Farewell;[118]

And I cannot rise and I am dying of anguish and weakness . . . Death! . . . I am unmoved by thoughts of it; I am sure it is no more horrible or mysterious than Life!

17 January

I am better now, still lying down, and until Professor Charvet arrives at three in the afternoon, I will pass the time by describing, possessed by my eternal mania of turning my impressions into literary works, the symptoms of my strange affliction.

The last lines penned here are dated the 26th. I spent that day and the two following ones in the same state of indescribable ill-ease I felt as

I wrote then. The sense of anguish became so intolerable that, despite my efforts to get hold of myself, it became an involuntary moan like the one a neuralgia might have elicited, and my prostration had become so acute that efforts to rouse and dress me were for naught. Francisco, frightened by my illness and without my telling him to, ran to the Mirandas' office and to Marinoni's shop. A few hours later, upon hearing voices, I opened my eyes, which I had kept closed, and through the mist that filled the room I saw six faces that were leaning over mine; I could make out don Mariano Miranda's big white mustache, Vicente's little Arab face, his son Marinoni's big blond head and the lilac-colored tie of one of the doctors, an important person, pink and smelling of Cyprus, who auscultated me frenetically, tapping me with his ring-filled fingers.

I struggled to sit up, and my head, as if disconnected from weakness, rolled back on the pillows on which they had settled me. Those people's presence there had restored a bit of my energy, as they irritated me with the pitying faces they were wearing. I managed to sit upright, say my helloes to them, and I nonchalantly answered the doctor with the lilac tie, blond sideburns, and curly hair, who was asking how I felt.

"Weak and tired, sir . . . Weak and tired," I complained because my head hurt somewhat.

"I think we are in the presence, dear colleague," said the effeminate figure, turning to his associate, a chubby, round-faced individual with a little brown beard and bald head, who looked at me with an expression between ironic and disdainful, "of neurasthenic phenomena attributable to the patient's state of profound weakness. There are certain points relative to the diagnosis and treatment in which your learned opinion would help clarify my impressions, dear colleague."

"If you gentlemen wish to speak in private, come into the salon," don Mariano Miranda suggested, showing the way. They say it is nothing serious. That is all I caught; the rest I cannot make sense of: asthenia, neurasthenia, anemia, epidemia, syringomyelia, camelia, neurosis, coriloporo[119] . . . "How should I know," he grumbled under his breath, chewing on the ever-present cigarette, whose blackish ash was falling on the Aubusson tapestry covering the floors and whose nauseating smoke turned my stomach.

"Your problem is you lead a vagrant life," he continued, settling into a chair and making me sick with the smell of tobacco. "You're doing fine, boy; you have money, you're young and strong; but don't overdo it, don't overdo it."

"Listen to the news of the earth," began Vicente, with his simian vivacity and the insufferable enthusiasm he expresses in telling other people's business. "Have you not received today's mail? . . . Of course not. In the office we opened it half an hour ago. The Reyes girls, who, as you know, tell Victor everything that happens there, gave him a batch of news each more unforeseen than the last; the first, the marriage of your madcap cousin Heriberto Monteverde, that harum-scarum Heriberto, and guess to whom . . . Inés Serrano. Doesn't that surprise you? . . . Monteverde, a man of pure fire, marrying Miss Serrano, so cold and dumb and of a lower social station than his, because, in short, be that as it may, the Monteverdes are the Monteverdes! I guess they will spend their honeymoon in Buen Retiro, on don Teodoro's country estate. How dull, eh? Tell me, just between you and me, don't you think that that marriage was sheer calculation on Monteverde's part? . . . The Reyeses tell Victor that he is badly off and that he owes a great deal to Spínola. Maybe that's true. Who knows, eh? . . . My father thinks it's quite likely; Alberto too," he added with a malicious look . . . "We received orders for the bridal trousseau; the mother is commissioning a diamond brooch that will be the finest that has been sent out in recent years . . . and one of the brothers, a prayer book . . . A ridiculous wedding gift, don't you think?—a prayer book! . . . Ah, but why am I telling you news from abroad when here in the colony there is news that will interest you greatly . . . Eduardo Montt arrived finally, right?, and I have it on good faith that he did not bring more than four thousand francs; but you should see him! . . . He has had shirts made at Doucet's shop; clothes at Eppler's; he ate last Sunday at the Paris Cafe with a famous coquette and yesterday was going around the Park in a hired coach . . . All that on four thousand francs! It's incredible, eh? He probably gambles, don't you think? . . . What do you say to that? . . . Could it be he gambles? . . . My father thinks it's likely."

"We'll have to buy him his ticket back down to earth, like that Muñoz with his disputed bills of exchange," don Teodoro said philosophically, chewing on his ever-present cigarette. "The one who supposedly isn't doing too well in business either is that countryman of ours who's married to a Chilean, the one who bought titles of nobility and boasts of his being on intimate terms with the Orléans and the dukes of la Tremaouille . . ."

"The thing is, not everyone has don José Fernández's income," Vicente interrupted him, believing he was telling me a kindness; "the tidy little private income that lets him lead the good life without having to go begging for spare change . . . And while we're on the subject of income, how outrageous those prices for those watercolors they sent you today at the office were! . . . And you should know Alberto thought them dreadful, and he knows about painting! You have really odd taste!"

The doctors came in; the potbellied one with the ironic face and the knitted brow, he of the lilac tie and the gold sideburns, was more happy-faced and swollen with pride than ever.

"My kindly and good-natured colleague has been so good as to give me the honor of authorizing me to tell you the opinion we have formed with respect to the change you have undergone. The disorders in your nervous system are serious . . . ," he began, putting on a solemn voice, and embarking on an endless dissertation in which he listed every labeled and classified neurosis of the last twenty years and all the classified ones since the beginning of time. He spoke to me of mental vertigo and epilepsy, of catalepsy and lethargy, of chorea[120] and paralysis agitans, of ataxias and tetanus, of neuralgias, of neuritis and of painful tics, of traumatic neuroses and neurasthenias, and with particular indulgence, of the newly minted diseases, of *railway brain* and *railway spine*,[121] of all the morbid fears, the fear of open spaces and enclosed spaces, of filth and animals, of the fear of the dead, of disease, and of stars. To all those miseries he gave technical names: kenophobia, claustrophobia, misophobia, zoophobia, necrophobia, pasophobia, astrophobia, which seemed to fill up his mouth and leave it tasting of honey as he pronounced them . . . The other individual, the potbellied man with the brown beard, remained silent, smiling, and had the face of one who was enjoying himself endlessly at his *dear colleague*'s exhibitionist talk.

"And which of those diseases do you gentlemen think I have?" I asked, now enjoying this character.

"A diagnosis at this time, in which the irresolution of the symptoms and the scant notions we possess of the etiology of disease prevent the necessary precision, would not be safe to say," he said with sacerdotal gravity. "The symptoms would point to somnosis or to narcolepsy, but we can say nothing with certainty until the digestive tract is working normally. *Ingeniis largiter ventris . . .*" [122]

"We have to purge him," blurted the bald-headed doc, firing off that sentence like a shot, and as if he were talking about a horse.

The lines from the Spanish comic operetta sang to me in my memory, and brought an involuntary smile to my lips:

> Judging by the symptoms
> the animal shows,
> it could well be hydrophobic,
> or just as well not.
> And the great Hippocrates asserts
> that the dog in a case like that
> either is wont to bark a great deal
> or is wont not to bark at all. [123]

There was a disagreement between the two notable men about who would write the prescription, and finally the man with the brown beard traced signs on the paper that amounted to one dose of English salt, calculated to purge a Durham bull.

"You will take this early tomorrow, and one equal dose the day after tomorrow, and another every morning for six days," he told me rudely. "On the seventh, you will be fine, I give you my word of honor."

"I'm glad it's nothing . . . Use but don't abuse," said don Mariano, rising. "Good advice, eh?" he hinted, pointing out to me the man in the lilac tie. "He's Vicentico's doctor."

"And hers," he whispered in my ear as he took his leave. "She recommended him."

She is an actress in the comic opera who is eating up the Mirandas' fortune, served in the form of diamonds and coaches by my well-informed friend, who was born a newsmonger as others are born blind.

"Remind me to tell you another piece of news the mail brought," he said with a naughty air as he shook my hand upon leaving.

They left. Why had those good friends come around? . . . One to smoke a nauseating cigarette, lounging in a more comfortable armchair than the ones he has in his office; the other, to bring me his crop of trivialities; the two doctors, one to charge for his talk, the other for his stupid prescription.

"Your countrymen are delightful!" said Marinoni, emerging from the corner where he had stuck himself since he came in. "Delightful! But what's the matter? You're disfigured," he added upon seeing my pallor, the deep circles under my eyes, and my weak, trembling hands. "What's wrong with you? . . . You're in a bad way. Charvet needs to come here; I'm going to bring him; I don't like the look of you," he added after I had told him of the last few days' martyrdom.

At midnight, after a sleep that had sapped more than restored my strength, the sleep of a child dying of weakness, I woke, victim of a deathly fright, in a cold sweat and crying out in anguish.

"What's this, my friend?" asked Charvet, who, seated alongside the divan, was watching over my sleep, adjusting the pillows that held up my head. "What's this? Try and tell me what's happened to you."

"I'm dying, Doctor," I said to him, stretching out my hand to him; "I am dying for no reason, dying of anguish and of a lack of strength."

"You committed some act of lunacy after going to my office, didn't you? While I watched you sleeping, I ended up imagining that you'd had an abundant hemorrhage . . . Let me examine you," he said, drawing the light closer. "Prop yourself up a bit so I can hear your heart; there you go . . . Fine. Now lie back . . . , put the thermometer there, don't get uneasy; know that I will do all that is in my power to make you better.

I am truly interested in you . . . Your family isn't living in Paris, now, are they?"

"I don't have any family, Doctor; I live alone with my servants."

"But you have many, many friends who care for you," he said as if to console me. "This evening when I came in I found people in the vestibule and in the drawing room . . . So you live alone, completely alone?" he asked again. "One degree less than normal temperature," he said, looking at the thermometer; "the pulse of a dying child; that pallor, that prostration, and the day on which you were in my office, I was awestruck at your vigor . . . Your heart is as weak as that of a seventy-year-old man . . . Come on, you can confide in me; confess what it is that happened to you . . . Was the hemorrhage that abundant? . . ."

When I replied that I had been following his prescriptions to the letter and told him what my life had been like since we had last seen each other, he rose from his chair and began to pace across the room with slow, measured steps, with his hands in his pants pockets and his head tilted forward to his chest.

"I can't endure what I feel any longer," I said, sitting up. "Give me something that makes me sleep or drives me mad. Inject me with morphine, make me drink chloral, put me to sleep at all costs, though it take my life."

"I cannot do that, sir; my duty forbids it," he answered, stopping himself, with an air at once ceremonious and unpleasant. "Besides, artificial sleep will not prevent you from feeling what you feel. I only know two things about you: first, that if I gave you the smallest dose of narcotics, it would poison you, because you are in an incredible state of extreme weakness; second, that I have to get your strength up, since your heart is pumping very slowly and your entire system is showing serious and inexplicable signs of depression and exhaustion that I do not understand."

"Is this terminal, Doctor? Tell me sincerely, straight out," I said to him, my voice shaking.

"My poor friend," he began, sitting down again near the divan, "you are talking to an ignorant man. You have followed my directions, you have seen my experiences; as I understand it, you have read my books, you know that I enjoy a certain fame in the scientific world . . . Do not be surprised at what I am going to tell you. Listen . . . I don't know what you have. If I were a charlatan, I would give you a name categorically; I would make up some pathological entity to which to refer the phenomena I am observing, and I would pump you full of drugs . . . The most I can do on your behalf is call one of my colleagues for him to come with me to study your case . . . Perhaps he sees more clearly than I do. Shall we do that? . . ."

I openly refused, and he seemed to appreciate my doing so. The next morning he returned and had me drink two glasses of cognac, which burned my throat and made me somewhat dizzy. The old man surveyed with interest the effects of the liquor. He administered an injection of ether and made me take some caffeine granules. He promised me he would immediately prepare a medicine for me to begin taking every hour, and agreed to return before evening.

"Promise me this: however great the malaise you feel may be, that you will not budge from this bed nor will you take anything but your draught."

I assented and drained the contents of the dark bottle hourly. It was a honeyed, reddish liquor, aromatic and bitter, in which ten strange flavors were blended. At the fifth spoonful, as if burned by an internal fire, I felt my blood coursing through my veins, and quivers of life vibrating up and down my spinal cord. It prompted me to rise. I was taking the sixth when Charvet came in with Marinoni.

"You revived already?" the old man asked me, offering his hand.

I began to speak to him in a loud, vibrant, full voice, and thanked him for his care. "I felt I was dying and now I'm full of life, Doctor," I said to him. "You have restored my lost strength in a matter of hours; now you are going to rid me of this cursed sense of anxiety that has me at wit's end, isn't that right? . . ."

"That will be gone in three or four days, if all goes well. Will you be brave enough to spend them without turning to narcotics? . . . If so, I will venture the prognosis of a speedy recovery. Still, I should not hide from you a fear I have had since yesterday; from one moment to the next a violent neuralgia could take hold of you that would drag out your illness several weeks. You can get up tomorrow if you don't feel any pain, and spend a few hours in the office. Mind the cold . . ."

On the afternoon of the thirty-first he assured me he found me fine and that in a few more days I could go out. Feeling as if I had strength to spare and despairing at being shut in, during which time my excited nerves had not withstood more company than that of the gentle Marinoni, whom a surfeit of activities prevented from being at my side, I prevailed upon Francisco, worn out by sleepless nights, to go to sleep, and prepared my nocturnal exit. By noon what I was feeling was unbearable. The malaise that took me the first time to Charvet's house, the mad anxiety of the gallop on the Sèvres path, the horrible anguish of the past days were child's play next to that afternoon's martyrdom . . . The prospect of a sleepless night on New Year's, that long tolling of the hours of the old hall clock, that nameless melancholy that had washed over my soul since the morning, all made the idea of reclusion unacceptable to me. I wanted to hear the noise of the crowd, lose myself for a few minutes in the human tumult, forget myself.

The hotel door slammed behind me. An icy breeze beat against my face and sent a chill running down my spine. Anxiety took the concrete form of an idea of movement, and I had to contain myself to not act on my wish, which loomed from the depths of my being, to run like a madman, frenetically, until falling out of breath against the icy sheet that winter stretched on the ground in the silent street.

It was twenty minutes to twelve when I went out to the boulevard and disappeared into the human river that was flowing by. The appearance of the New Year's stalls, black against the whiteness of the snow, of the windows of the restaurants, reddish in the light that filtered through the unpolished windows and the small transparent lace curtains, the clean skeletons of the trees, which raised their emaciated branches toward the low, leaden sky, the same bustle of the happy, noisy crowd, heightened the horrible impression that was coming over me. I walked for a quarter of an hour at a fairly steady clip and . . . I stopped a moment near a gas lamp, whose flame was burning in the darkness of night like a butterfly of fire . . . "Peekaboo cards?" a boy said to me, who put away the obscene pack as he looked at it again.

The light in a bronze shop's windows caught my eye. Walking slowly, since I felt my strength waning, I wound up standing at one of them.

A pale, thin woman, looking hungry, her cheeks and mouth tinged with crimson, made me shiver from head to toe when she touched the sleeve of the heavy fur coat I was wrapped in, and the *psst psst* that she directed at a sanguineous, obese Englishman sounded ominous in my ears. He was covered with grey cheviot wool, and had stopped alongside me and now went after her. When I turned my head, the red-glass lamps of a horse-drawn carriage crossing the nearby intersection distracted my attention for a few seconds. Whereupon I looked in the window, and at the very moment when I saw the great black marble clock with its alabaster dial and externally mounted balance wheel hanging from the hand of a bronze figure, suspended by a thread of golden metal, I understood what the horrible anguish I had been feeling in the previous days and nights referred to: ah, doubtless it was the unexamined, ill-omened, and lugubrious terror of the year that was about to begin! It was five minutes to twelve. The gold second hand moved along the alabaster face. The balance wheel kept turning: tick tock, tick tock, tick tock, a luminous strand on a dark background: tick tock, tick tock. The two mirrors on opposite sides of the window, as they copied each other, reflected with the greenish coloring of a decomposed corpse my horribly pale, disfigured features, my profile made thin by the previous days' suffering and the tangled mass of my unkempt beard. I felt I was trapped between two glass walls and could never get out. The balance wheel kept turning: tick tock, tick tock, and every oscillation marked one more degree of anguish, of terror, and of desperation in my soul. My body rigid, my nerves on edge, my senses working overtime. The murmur of the human river that ran at my back changed to my deluded ears into an infinite sobbing that would die off in the large leaden storm clouds that overcast the sky. Tick tock, tick tock, tick tock: the balance wheel spun and spun against the dark background of the window. With every passing second, the supernatural drew closer and closer to appearing to me in the depths of the abyss of shadow that would open up behind the alabaster dial as the hour of the new year chimed. The hour drew nigh. Tick tock, tick tock . . . I tried to flee to avoid seeing it, but my legs did not obey the urging of my will. A mortal chill ran up me from my feet to the nape of my neck. In the nameless nightmare that was the undoing of my being, I saw the marble clock moving towards me like a living thing. Terrified, I took four steps backwards. The twelve strokes sounded slowly, gravely in my ears, muffling all the street noise with the sharp, deafening metallic din of gold bells. The clock-hands having blurred into one to mark the tragic hour of supreme horror, the balance wheel stopped, motionless, as if obeying a command from the unseen. A thick mist floated before my gaze, a violent neuralgia crossed my head from temple to temple, and I collapsed onto the ice.

When I came to I was in my room, dressed, with my shirt open, and stretched out in bed. Marinoni was close at hand, and Francisco was down on his knees saying the prayers for the dying. On the bedside table burned a candle at the feet of a Christ figure. The sullen light of dawn was filtering in through the bars of the terrace grillwork. A horrible neuralgia was gripping my head as if in a circle of iron; but the sense of anguish had lifted.

"Marinoni!" I shouted, "I've been saved; come here close."

"It's a miracle you're alive. You're a madman. If you knew what you've put us through all night. How is it you're all right?"

"I'm all right. I have a horrible pain that might kill me, but I don't feel the anxiety I have had in recent days." After saying this, I fell into a kind of profound lethargy.

I have blurred impressions from those first ten days of fever. My eyes, being unused to the grey half-light of the bedroom, dimly perceived the black and white dress of a sister of charity seated at the head of the bed, and the outline of her snow-white cornet, which, standing out against the dark wall, looked to my poor brain like a heron with its wings open, and by association evoked the memory of the bogs of Santa Barbara.

When my fever was allayed I felt extremely weak. Now I am in full convalescence, I feel life returning to me with every cup of the mature

Spanish wines that I imbibe, with every mouthful of them, which I wash down with a Pantagruelian appetite, and Charvet is delighted to see the speed with which I am regaining my strength.

It seems the old man took a liking to me. He is sensual down to his fingertips; he has passion for works of art, exquisite taste, and they say he has the most beautiful collection of Persian tapestries in all Paris. When he comes to see me he settles into an armchair near the fire, sips a forty-year-old discolored sherry, savoring it, looking at its color as he raises to eye level the fragile Salviati glass in which they serve it to him, and smells it delightedly. Sometimes, as if by way of apology for draining his third, he says "excellent," pressing to his mouth his fingers curled in a fist, then opening them and extending his arm to raise the wine with a gentle motion that seems to scatter in the air the aroma of the aged liqueur.

"How sorely you're lacking a wife among the art treasures you've piled up in your house! Not a sweetheart, who would be unable to understand any of this, but a very young, well-bred woman who could enjoy every sumptuous detail and liven up with her freshness the gloomy magnificence of these bedrooms, where you must miss, sometimes, the delicate female presence! . . . Marry, my friend . . . Marriage is one of man's beautiful inventions, the only one able to channel the sexual instinct.

"You smile at what I say? . . . You should know that medicine has been but a necessity for me, a means of earning a living. I have the nerves of an artist, not of a man of science; therefore you and I don't see eye to eye. Just between the two of us, I confess that one of the bitter pills of my life is that my name is going to be linked for all eternity to a nasty irregularity of the nerve cords of the medulla oblongata. That thought turns my stomach. A botanist unearths a beautiful plant with sweet-smelling flowers in some tropical undergrowth; an astronomer observes a comet, and humanity in the future cannot separate its memory of the image from the fresh petals, or from the luminous rays that fall from on high . . . One of us, bent over the bleeding corpse, poking around in it with a scalpel, sees an ugly little spot that looks anomalous, puts the tissue under a microscope, wears out his poor eyes observing it, writes a monograph in which he makes up what data he is missing, and as a reward for his efforts he is given this: some quack, upon giving up hope on some poor sap whose malady he does not know, has just buried him by telling him: you have the beginnings of Bright's disease.[124] I can do nothing for his health; these symptoms indicate Krishaber's[125] cerebral-cardial neuropathy, science is powerless; convince yourself that Charvet's disease is consuming you . . . Does that seem very amusing to you that they give one's name to an ignoble thing?" he concluded, his hands deep in his pockets and shaking his head disgustedly. "Enjoy life at your ease, marry, my friend, be happy. . . ."

10 March

Rivington's gift, a sumptuously framed copy, custom-made by a master's hand, of the painting that decorates his sitting room, arrived at my hotel four days ago. It was in the drawing room that I opened the crate, removing the screws myself, lifting the wooden lid, tearing the wrapping papers, until gazing upon the ideal image of Her Worship. I could never let a menial hand perform that task. The painting is a perfect specimen of the Pre-Raphaelite Brotherhood's method; the noble figure, placed at three-quarters view and facing forward, was almost devoid of movement; marvelous for their design and color were the little bare feet that peeked out from under the gold of the intricate Byzantine hem of the white gown and the long tapered hands that, detached from the wrist in the style of the Parmesan's[126] figures, come together to hold the bunch of irises, and her arms covered to the elbow in the white folds of the long cloak, and then bare. The shape of the head, the slightly excessive brilliance of the colors, grouped by hue—the overall composition labors under the mannerism for which the imitators of the quattrocentists established a fashion. The work is detailed with supreme minuteness, with all the *finish* that would satisfy the most demanding Ruskin;[127] the viewer can make out one by one the rays that form the aureole that encircles her brown curls, the strands of gold of the embroidered edging, the giant branches of the flowering peach trees, the pink petals of its flowers, the leaves of the yellow roses against the green of the thickets, and in the shoots and grasses of the soil a botanist could recognize one by one the plants copied there by the artist. Below the painting, on the black edging, in golden Latin characters shines the phrase:

MANIBUS DATE LILIA PLENIS

Who was the painter, that J. F. Siddal, whose name is at the bottom of the painting, and who with such utter love put the mystic expression of supreme, almost ecstatic, unction in the oil painting that now inhabits my house and my life of sweet, sweet reverie? . . . The critics that have written on the Pre-Raphaelite Brotherhood fail to even mention him, nor is his name included in any gallery or museum catalogue.

Why should I care what ideal of art his meticulous technique proclaims to him if before my eyes you smile with the gentle grace of your delicate body's long lineaments, with the mysterious irradiation of your blue eyes that illuminate the unearthly pallor of your visage, framed by the silken, chestnut-brown curls of your unbraided tresses, image that fills my life, my soul? . . .

This is what I have found so that, in the room next to the office, where a wide curtain of ancient weave and faded tints drapes its folds on both sides of the balcony, framing it, the best of myself is all together. On the walls hung with dark cordovan leather only two canvases catch the eye: the copy sent by Doctor Rivington and the portrait of grandmother, with her St. Anne profile and her grey hair, standing out against a dark background, which James McNeill Whistler painted for me, the strange artist who, in the words of one critic, uses extraordinarily lucid intuition to give off in his works, steeped in mystery, the suprasensory part of reality.

Below Helen's portrait, a heavy sculptured bronze table holds up the jardinières full of flowers I ordered from Cannes by telegraph. The aroma of red roses, yellowish roses, and white roses, of the bouquets of Parma violets that languish in tall opalescent crystal goblets, of the heaps of white, golden, rosy, and purple carnations commingled with the sweet emanations of the mimosas and the lilies, wafts up to her feet. That opposition of vivid, singing tones would tempt the palette of a colorist.

The green of the malachite candlesticks stands out against the white of the bindings, ornamented with the three leaves and the butterfly, of the volumes of verse that I bought in London and had bound to suit my taste. A single armchair, where under the pacifying gaze of her blue eyes, I am going to read Shelley and Longfellow, and the heavy iron chest where I keep the gems, her cameo, and the bouquet of roses from Geneva, make up the room's furnishings.

This spiritual environment is the kind you need, my darling, to live with intense life, and the only kind I find breathable today, when my tenderness aspires to you with all its might, like a feeble plant that turns its leaves toward the sun!

10 April

Charvet, annoyed with waiting for me in the office while I dressed, was settled into the armchair, his big head against the backrest, his gold pince-nez perched on his noise, and the poems of Keats in his hand, when I entered the little room.

"Atheist poets, when young, do not believe in God, but in the angels and the Holy Virgin," he said, rising when he saw me. "To date this is the place where I have breathed the atmosphere thickest in mysticism . . . for as long as I have paraded my carcass through this vile world. If poor Scilly Dancourt were to come in this room, he would kneel at the sight of the portrait placed in this chapel-like environment. You are becoming uneasy . . . What's wrong?" he added, looking surprised. "Have I committed an indiscretion by coming in here? . . . Forgive me; I saw the door ajar and couldn't resist the temptation; let's go to your study."

Seated near me, Charvet, encouraged by who knows what mad words of mine, explained to me what he meant by what had made me tremble in shock, telling me roughly this:

"It was twelve years ago at the end of January; I was in Provence escaping the winter cold, when I received a telegram from a Nice hotelier offering me a tidy sum to go spend a few days there and lend my services to a seriously ill patient. The offer was so attractive that I did not think twice about setting out, to witness upon my arrival one of the most anguishing scenes that I have looked on in my professional practice, all the more so since my science could do nothing to prevent it. Now as I see that painting, of which I have a photograph given me then by Scilly Dancourt, I feel I am looking at the poor thing with the admirable beauty of her twenty-three years, and as if they happened yesterday I remember the horrible sufferings of the poor soul when, kneeling at the foot of the bed, drinking in her poisoned breath and kissing her, he turned his eyes toward me, as if asking me to protect her against death. 'Doctor: Save her and I will serve you on my knees all my life; I am rich; use my fortune, but save her!' he begged me; and I would understand the paroxysm of pain that contorted him when he saw the ideal figure and the superhumanly tender gaze with which the blue eyes of the consumptive woman enveloped him.

"The disease had been a cold, caught the night they left Paris; but the patient's fragile constitution and some unknown family history of tuberculosis caused a galloping consumption, against which my efforts were in vain. It would be an impossible task to tell you what kind of pain, of madness, the husband went through upon being convinced she was dead.

"'Apart from this child,' he told me days later, showing me a little four-year-old girl who seemed to understand the horror of what had happened and looked at him with her mother's same blue eyes, and had a delicate appearance like that of a sick flower, 'I don't have anyone in the world. I journey to Africa, to the Far East, through all of the Americas, I travel for entire years to keep from dying of melancholy here.' Poor man! It moved me so to see him in that state, that I even remember his last words:

"'Doctor, don't be surprised to see me suffer this way, to see my despair; you don't know that she was a saint, you don't know that all the women of her family line have been worshipped this frenetically. Haven't you heard the story of Rossetti, the poet-painter who married Elizabeth Eleanor Siddal, who was from the same family as my wife, twenty-odd years ago . . . and who never painted in his pictures anyone but *her,* and that once *she* was dead he deposited in her casket the manuscript of his poems so they could rest alongside her who had inspired them?[128]

. . . Rossetti, when Elizabeth died, was nearly mad; and if years later chloroform and sadness polished off his life, it was because he did not do what I am going to do, to ask of the travels and the study of religions the necessary strength to not leave this little girl alone in the world,' he said, showing me the girl.

"And the photograph, Doctor? . . ."

"Ah, yes! That painting you have is a portrait of Scilly Dancourt's wife, done by a brother who gave up the painting later to go to India, as Dancourt told me at the time . . . And listen . . . The mannered imitator of the Pre-Raphaelites did nothing more than damage the model by subjecting it to the inventions of his school, for the dead woman was even more beautiful; she had chestnut-brown hair with golden glimmers, the color the English call *auburn,* and blue eyes unlike any I have seen since. Poor man; I never saw him again."

"Have you not even heard from him, Doctor? . . ." I asked him with barely concealed impatience.

"Not one word. I think the only person whom he writes to in Paris is General des Zardes. He served under his orders as a captain in the war with Prussia in 1870, and the latter holds him in high regard for his bravery . . . And how's our health?" he inquired, turning to his ossuaries.

Charvet authorized me from that day forward to go back to the life I led before the illness:

"You are stronger today than on the afternoon you came to my office for the first time. Enjoy life at your ease. Be happy," he told me, punching my shoulder as he left.

Enjoy life without her! I will enjoy life when I am kneeling at her feet. Bless you, ray of light that has fallen in the night of my soul and that will allow me to find her!

20 March

"All I can tell you is what I have already told you; contact Professor Mortha, whom Scilly Dancourt writes frequently about his crackpot orientalist ideas and religious history," old General des Zardes said with his rough voice, rising from the chair in the Circle Salon. "Go find Mortha . . . Now you're preoccupied with esoterism and religions too. I thought the barracks life you lead had kept you from those vagrant ideas. And you're too young to be a general," he added with an ironic expression, twirling his greying mustache.

"I am no general," I answered him, laughing, when I heard that witticism.

"Well, it's strange . . . All your countrymen I have met in the Circle are generals," he grumbled by way of good-bye.

I had made little headway with the conversation I had with him, which ended with that reference to how easily gained epaulettes are in our Latin American republics. During it he told me of the campaign both he as colonel and Scilly Dancourt as captain carried on in the fifth division of the army led by General de Tailly, the marches and countermarches, the irresolution and mistakes of the ill-fated campaign; he depicted the poor emperor as atonic and crestfallen, plunged in uncertainty and silence; he praised Trochu to the skies, he who, to hear him tell it, would have saved France had he carried out his plans; he called Rouher, Montauban, and Chevreau idiots; he insulted Bazaine, glorified MacMahon, described to me in shouts and technical terms the battles of Saint-Privat, Wisenbourg, and Froeschwiller, and the air of mortal sadness and brutishness about Napoleon as he saw Ducrot, then Douay, and finally Lebrun enter in turn the prefecture of Sedan;[129] the brutal dialogue between Ducrot and Wimpfen and the latter's exit to parley with the enemy.

"Scilly Dancourt," he said to me, getting excited, "did not see the end of the battle, nor does his name appear in the register of the shameful capitulations, nor did he take away from Sedan the horror in his eyes of seeing our ninety thousand soldiers who, unused through the days that they spent in the miserable field, with their feet stuck in the mud, soaked through from the rain, trembling with hunger and thirst, cold and shame, and sensing the tragic upheaval of the crumbling empire, awaited the battalions of German recruits that were to take them prisoner to Prussia. No, Scilly Dancourt did not see any of this. After lifting our spirits with his lionheartedness, rousing us with his cry, with his gesture and his example, and weathering three wounds, upon seeing the battle was lost he dropped out of sight, no one knows how. His heart rent by France's ill fortune, he made for England, where he contracted marriage some years later with the daughter of an actor and a renowned musician. When she died, he took his leave of Europe . . . And I'm telling you, the only one who hears from him is Mortha, whom he writes this religion and crazy orientalist business."

My heart was leaping out of my breast the last time I entered the low-roofed, vile-looking mezzanine on a back alley in the Latin Quarter, where the author of *The Religions of the East* receives the few visitors that go to divert him from his habitual concerns, the interpretation of sacred secular texts, old liturgical hymns, and the primitive cults of humanity. "I am going to speak to him of Scilly Dancourt and he will tell me where I will find Helen!" I thought to myself, seated now on a settee in the poor, tidy little room preceding the study, and looking deeply at an Assyrian sculpture, a body of a winged lion with a human head and a long, curly beard, crowned with a priestly tiara, which, facing the pot-bellied Buddha smiling against the dingy blackened chimney, makes up the only décor in the room.

Mortha is an adorable little old man, with a long, long face on whose yellowing, wizened skin cross deep vertical wrinkles, and a head of white silky unkempt hair, from which long loose hair falls down his enormous brow and over his lively black eyes. When he laughs, there is something childlike in the joy that livens up his face; grey hair, wrinkles, and eyes, everything laughs. His books and the need to get observations on a lapidary inscription were the excuse I used to introduce myself to him several days ago. He spoke to me in the first interview of some Egyptian parchments that were up for sale in London. I had them bought there through Morrell and Blundell, and sent them to him. I am to be his guest; he believes me to be a consummate Egyptologist.

When I entered the room full of papers, stones, remains of statues, and inscriptions, he was writing something in his little spidery handwriting, and a ray of sunlight that was filtering through the window made his white, white hair shine like silver.

"Were you writing, dear master?" . . . I asked him.

"Yes, I was annotating the translation by my brother Maspero of the hymn discovered by Grebaut[130] near the necropolis of Zawiyet el-Aryan. Listen how sublime:

You arise, beneficent Ammon Ra Harmakuti.[131]
You awake, true Lord of the two horizons,
You burn, shine, rise, and culminate.
Men and gods kneel before that which is your form, O Lord of
    forms!

A full hour passed, during which I made him speak and I said nothing, so that he would not grow wise to my deception, and after which I took him down twisting, turning paths to the matter in which I have invested my entire soul.

"Ah, yes! Scilly Dancourt," he said; "but Scilly Dancourt is not a specialist, he is a man who wishes to know everything to do with all religions. He knows fairly well the Egyptian rites of the Ancient Empire. Six years ago I received his last letter, addressed from Abydos,[132] where he was studying the temple's bas-reliefs. He had good data to offer for an amateur, but his strength lies in the religions of India. He is one of the few Europeans to have managed to enter into the depths of the sanctuaries at Benares and cultivate close relations with the Buddhist priests in the southern pagodas; but do not believe him a man of science, and above all, a man impartial in his studies. What he is pursuing is the very essence of religion, the supernatural, with which those of us that act in good faith will have nothing to do. There is no religion he has not studied, taking huge trips and making outrageous outlays to that end, visiting sanctuaries and traveling around the places where he was born. He knows the latest humbuggery with its psychic powers and telepathy, long-distance hypnosis and luminous apparitions, like Crookes[133] does, and I believe he laughs at them. He attended the Parliament of the World's Religions in Chicago in 1893, not taking part in it, and I am sure he could have taught each of the attendees something. We wrote each other up until six years ago, and suddenly he stopped answering me. I found out later through my colleague Chennevières, who bumped into him in Rome, that he was there with one of his sons. It seems that young man has done the same studies as his father, and it was he who induced him to abandon them, to devote himself to the Catholic rites with a rare fervor. Chennevières informs me that they were living near the Vatican, that the Pope received them frequently, and that they received the Holy Communion every day in the mass given by His Holiness. I went on writing Scilly, in keeping with the promise I made him to tell him the findings from my studies of the ancient religions of Egypt, but he has not written me back."

"So you write him at Rome, knowing he travels continually? . . ." I asked him.

"No, it's his bankers that see to forwarding his letters; I send them to the office of Lazard, Casseres and Company. My patient investigations must not interest my friend, since what he searched for in his journeys was not the science of the origins and development of religions, but a faith to practice, and finally he wound up with Catholicism, for which all the going round on journeys was unnecessary. When I tell you that Scilly Dancourt has never been a scholar and his investigations were never selfless, I mean it!"

Finally I come upon the strand of light I seek, with the clue I follow to find you, oh, path that will take me to her! I thought, startled at the happy coincidence that had me place in the hands of Lazard, Casseres and Company the sums I had held in the Miranda firm until the year before last. Bless you, light comedy actress, idol of my friend don Vicente, the instinctive reporter, with your appetite for diamonds and the authority you wield over him and the fear I felt that my gold would wind up in your little pink hands, together with don Mariano's money, you prompted in my mind the idea to transfer my funds to the Jews' firm! I thought, climbing the monumental staircase to the latter's office. A Jewish banker is useful for everything . . . even to tell one where lies the image about which one dreams. O Israel! I murmured to myself as I pushed the office door.

Nathaniel Casseres, doubled over, his aquiline nose, his greenish eyes, his ring of blond beard, entirely *delighted* to see me, stretched out his hand with an affectionate gesture and swore that his family had been dismayed by my illness. The man lived for four years in Buenos Aires and speaks Spanish, a Spanish learned in Frankfort, that exhausts the ears.

"To *vat to ve owe ze honah of zeeing* Mr. Fernández here at his home? . . . Do you have purchases to make or *odahs to gif*? . . .

And when I explained to him that I wished to know where his client was and that he please give me information on him:

"Ah, yes! *Goot* client, *goot* man, *goot* person Mr. *Chilly* . . . *Goot* client, *goot* man, *goot* person, but I cannot inform you of *vat you vich* . . ." and roughly this was his explanation: The only business that the firm of Lazard, Casseres and Company has with the count consists of receiving from a life insurance company a fat sum that the latter pays out, to which he gave his capital in order to receive traveling money. When I heard this, an icy chill ran down my spine. And should he die, what would become of Helen, forsaken, alone, fortuneless and friendless? . . .

"Another service we perform for him," continued the obliging Nathaniel, "is to pay premiums on a life insurance policy for a daughter of his, so she receives it when she turns twenty; a hefty policy, which will return to Miss Scilly Dancourt the capital that her father invested in the company, a clever move, but that above all is in keeping with the tastes of our client, who does not wish to deal with business or money, and wires to our account for any sum he wishes, from any point in Europe, Asia, America, Africa, or Oceania, where our bankers accept his checks, since the firm has agents the world over," he added, pleased. "No other correspondence arrives here than that of his friend the scholar. Three years ago we received a telegram from Rome from Mr. Scilly, instructing us not to send him those letters, and the firm, following orders, keeps them here. He never writes."

"So where is Mr. Scilly's latest check dated?" I asked.

"I have given you all this information in the strictest confidence, and likewise shall I give you that fact. Allow me to speak with the bookkeeper to inquire.

"It's from Alexandria and for a tidy sum. He will likely continue on to the Orient . . . Last year around this time, we received a check from Benares . . . *Goot* client, *goot* friend, *goot* person, Mr. *Chilly Tancourt!*"

Then bowing and promising the firm forever at my service, he accompanied me as far as the door, where I left, despairing.

My God, one month wasted like that, cultivating imbeciles, hearing the story of the battle of Sedan and reading the hymns to Ammon Ra Harmakuti, and knowing through the Jews how the father's fortune is situated, all this without finding the path that takes me to Her! Now I know the history of the Scillys perhaps better than does the count, who does not look like those vanities matter to him. All the books I have found that could shed light on Helen's ancestors I have read with the patience of a Benedictine. My head is full of names and facts running from the year 48, in which one Scilly, a close friend of Lamartine, took part in politics, until 1327, when another left on the first Crusade. I know his weapons and blazons, his battle shield and his war cry. My God! And what is all of that to me if I lose the hope of finding her and if I despair at losing that hope? Helen, my love, Helen, love of my soul, come, arise, appear before my eyes weary of searching for you and immerse your penetrating blue-eyed gazes in mine, see into my soul so that in it only you are reflected, like the starry heavens in the waters of a slumbering lake!

12 April

Only one advantage did I reap from the interviews with General des Zardes, with Mortha, and with the obsequious Jew: that my love for Helen, whose family I already know, the history of the father and the investment of his fortune, has grown sweeter, undiminished, but is becoming more human, so to speak. Only love understands, your Worship, of whom through intuitive divination I know even the most hidden secrets of kindness and nobility, only love understands! For General des Zardes you do not exist, only the image of your father lives in his imagination, just as he saw him in the days of the ill-fated campaign; to Professor Mortha you are a young man involved in studies of religious history;

the Jew only knows of you the gold you will receive upon turning twenty! Only love understands! Charvet, for whom the practice of his profession has not hardened his soul like so many of his beloved colleagues, knows the agony of the existence that life gave you, recalls the horrible pain your father felt during the tragic incident, and glimpsed in your eyes of a child the sparkle they have today, the terrible sparkle of saintliness and gentleness that lit up my soul that night in Geneva. Only I, who wish to search in you for the light that shines on me and the anchor that saves me, I know about you as much as all of them together, and I divine you as you are . . . Only love understands!

Today there are two places on earth where human feet do not tread. The atmosphere that is breathed in them enshrouds a holy silence; they are the abode where the silver-haired saint died, she whose profile smiles six paces from this site in Whistler's painting, and the room, rented out for ten years to the Swiss hotelier and whose key is in the iron box near the cameo; the room from whose balcony she flung the bouquet of roses that unforgettable night.

13 April

I was saying yesterday how my love was growing sweeter, becoming more human . . . Ah, yes! . . . Only my spirit clamored for her a few days ago, and now my whole being clamors for her! . . . Before finding her I did not know what love was and had kissed my poetic ideals only in my mind's eye, with my flesh-and-blood lips the lascivious, half-open mouths of my loose, idolized women. Now my soul and my lips dream of her, and if I think of her my whole being quivers, like the strings of a sonorous instrument under the inspired bow of the artist that conveys his soul in them.[134]

Now that you have come into my life, most gentle, immaculate virgin vested in mystery and the beyond, our life will be ecstasy. Ennobled by you, the particulars of daily existence will be transfigured and every step taken down the roads on Earth will be a step heavenward. For you I will forsake the plans to have my name go down in posterity. What greater glory than spending my life kneeling at your feet, feeling the caress of your hands and drinking in from your lips the very essence of life!

Hear me this: in the land that saw my birth there is a mighty river that rushes headlong from the heights of the high frozen plateau to the depths of the warm valley where the sun warms the greenery and gilds the fruit of flora unknown to you. Niagara Falls, profaned by railroads and by the human riffraff that goes in search of a good time in the surrounding hotels, is a grotesque place near the rustic setting with its templed majesty where the powerful torrent falls in a sheet of foam, and shoots deafening echoes off the age-old hills. Sheer above the abyss, where the mist iridesces and the waters glitter at sunrise, rears an enormous rigid basalt rock. That rock is the property line of one of my estates.

On it I will build for you a palace that on the outside takes on the appearance of a blackened feudal castle with its moats, its drawbridges, and its high fortified towers covered with dark-green ivy and greyish mosses, and that inside holds the treasures of art I possess and which you will enliven with your presence. We will live, when life in Europe tires you and you require new impressions of the grandiose horizons of my country's plains and mountain ranges, in that eagle's lair that within shall be a nest of white doves, full of cooing and caresses. There will be sunny mornings on which we will be seen riding by on a pair of Arabian horses, down the paths that stretch out into the savanna, and the coarse peasants will kneel as they see you, believing you an angel, when you fix on their bodies, deformed by rustic chores, the resplendent gaze of your azure orbs; there will be nights in which in the perfumed air of the room, where the golden-yellow tea in the China cups is steaming and the lamplight shines on the sumptuous furnishings, attenuated by lace shades, the sublime phrases of a Beethoven sonata are vibrating, wrested by your pale hands from the resounding keyboard; nights on which, faint with pent-up emotion, you rise from the piano to gaze at the moonlit falls from the stone terrace. Whereupon you will rest your head on my shoulder, your chestnut curls from your unbraided hair falling over me, you will turn your radiant blue eyes toward mine, and the supernatural pallor of your semblance, the mortal bloodless pallor of your cheeks and your brow will flush with kisses from my lips!

Helen! Helen! Fire flows through my veins and my soul forgets the earth when I think of the times that are to come if I can find you and unite your life with mine! . . .

14 April

Yesterday another building exploded, wrecked by a bomb, and the society gathering in a boulevard theater clapped until their hands hurt for Ibsen's *A Doll's House,* a new-style play in which the heroine, Nora, a run-of-the-mill woman of no account with an everyday soul, leaves her husband, children, and relations to go fulfill the obligations she has to herself, to a self she does not know and that she feels emerging one night like a mushroom sprouting and growing in a brief period of time. So, with melanite explosions in the footing of palaces and shovel-blows at the depths of moral foundations, which were the old beliefs, humanity marches on toward the ideal realm of justice that Renan thought he glimpsed in the end of days. Ibsen and Ravachol[135] help him, each after his own fashion; the president of France falls wounded by Santo Caserio's[136] blade, and Sudermann[137] writes *The Woman in Grey,* where self-denial and love of family take on grotesque overtones, without the fairy-tale ending, tacked on by the novelist to his work as a skillful pharmacist would toss syrup into a concoction that contained strychnine in order to sweeten it, managing to cover up the bitter taste of the lethal drug.

Art is becoming a medium for antisocial propaganda, a curious symptom that coincides with the negating trend of pseudoscience, the only one to which the rabble has access. The purer the form of the amphora, the more poisonous can the contents be judged; the sweeter the verse and the music, the more terrifying the idea they entail.

Hugo, father of the modern lyric, you died at the right time;[138] had you lived fifteen more years, you would have heard the roaring laughter that greets the reading of your poems inspired by an enormous gust of optimistic fellow-feeling; you died on time; poetry today is an amusement for enervated mandarins, a riddle whose solution is the word *nirvana*. The cold north wind, which brought to your country the compassion for human suffering that is brimming over in the novels of Dostoevsky and Tolstoy, today bears the terrible voice of Nietzsche.

You there, worker who spends your life doubled over, you whose muscles grow impoverished with hard work and a deficient diet, but whose calloused hands still make the sign of the cross, worker who gets down on bended knee to pray to heaven for the owners of the factory where you are poisoned with the vapors from explosive mixes, listen, worker, do the hard syllables of that German name, Nietzsche, suggest nothing to your rudimentary brain when they vibrate in your ears? . . . The echoes of the North reverberate them, they ring throughout Europe, and his disciples preach the gospel of tomorrow. Do not think it like the gospel that tells the story of the pale Nazarene imparting his consolatory blessings by the blue waves of the tranquil lake of Tiberias and breathing his last up on the cross, with his body bruised from the blows and his pale brow torn up by the crown of thorns; it is a gospel that tells the story of Zarathustra in a cave, meditating, between the eagle and the serpent, on the transvaluation of all values. Does this phrase not suggest anything to your obtuse mind either? . . . It's like this: Humanity had been taking false notions about its origin and destiny as true, and the profound philosopher found a touchstone on which to prove his ideas, as one tests coins to determine their gold content. That is what is called the transvaluation of all values. What you call *conscience*, the thing that tortures you when you believe you have committed some misdeed, is nothing more than the instinct for cruelty that you can inflict on others, and that by not wielding it, because society prevents you from it, containing you in the notion of duty like a lion in an iron cage, it torments you as its useless claws would torment the tawny animal were it to sink them in its own flesh upon being unable to tear out the unyielding iron bars nor rip its delicious prey to shreds. Those very duties you believe in are but the invention with which a powerful and noble race of joyful men that laughed at fires, ravishings, murders, and robberies subordinated the races of the vanquished weak, which they made their slaves. The *good* among the victorious were the most cruel, the most brutal, the hardest, and the slaves imagined as virtues the qualities contrary to those they saw in their masters: continence, self-sacrifice, compassion for another's suffering. In the slave revolt, which took place centuries ago, a victim was needed so they could have a flag to hoist, a man that could unite and embody all those false virtues and die for proclaiming them, so Israel crucified the Christ, he whom you believed to be God, and the morality of the weak prevailed, the one your father taught you, the one upon which today's society is founded.

Did you know none of that, worker, who, with your hands calloused by work, still make the sign of the cross and kneel to pray for the owners of the factory where you are poisoned with the vapors from explosive mixes? Well, know it, and, regenerated by the teachings of Zarathustra, profess the master morality; live beyond good and evil. If conscience is the claws with which you hurt yourself and with which you can rip apart what comes your way and take your share of the spoils of victory, do not sink them in your flesh, turn them outward; I know the superman; the *Übermensch* free of all prejudice, and with your calloused hands with which you still stupidly make the sign of the cross, gather some of the explosive mixes that poison you when you breathe their fumes and set off the fulminate of picrate, and blow to smithereens the house of the rich man who is exploiting you. Once the masters are dead, the slaves will be the masters and shall profess the true morality in which lust, murder, and violence are virtues. You follow that, worker? . . .

So, with melanite explosions in the footings of palaces and shovelblows in the depths of moral foundations, which were the old beliefs, humanity marches on toward the ideal realm of justice that Renan thought he glimpsed in the end of days. Ibsen and Ravachol help him, each after his own fashion.

Away in the most lofty heights of intellectuality, a noble group of selfless philosophers inquires, investigates, sounds the ineffable mystery of life and the laws that govern it, and transforms its patient studies into books that lack for categorical assertions, that scarcely record what is common knowledge, what falls under the domain of observation; in books that show at the limits of human science "two black waves in the ocean of mystery to embark upon with neither a boat nor a compass," in Littré's[139] grandiose phrase. The religious impression those great spirits experience in considering the eternal problem, and express in their works, coincides with the idealist renaissance in art, spurred by the inevitable backlash against the narrow, brutal naturalism that was in favor a few years ago. Instead of prostitutes and kitchen-maids, odd-jobmen and petty clerks that earn a hundred pesetas a month, the novelists delight in depicting grande dames who move in the most pleasant of atmospheres, sages who work the miracles of the ancient theurgists, and wise men who possess the supreme secrets. Music, of a sensual modulation that caressed the ears and suggested voluptuous temptations, becomes a mysterious voice that speaks to the brain; mystical shadows pass through the dawn that houses the strophes of the poet, and visions of the beyond take shape in oil paintings. The explorers who return from the ideal Canaan of art, bringing in their hands fruits with unknown flavors and dazzled by the horizons they could glimpse, are named Wagner, Verlaine, Puvis de Chavannes,[140] Gustave Moreau.[141]

In the hands of the masters, the novel and criticism are means of presenting to the public the terrifying problems humanity must confront, and of distinguishing psychological complications; the reader no longer asks of the book that it amuse him, but rather that it make him think and see the mystery ensconced in every particle of the Great All.

Do you persist in doubting the idealist and neo-mystic renaissance, you spirit who inquires into the future and sees the old religions toppling? . . . Look: from the dark depths of the Orient, land of the gods, Buddhism and magic are returning to reconquer the Western world. Paris, the metropolis, opens its doors to them as Rome opened its own to the cults, to Mithra, and to Isis; there are fifty theosophical centers, hundreds of societies that research mysterious psychic phenomena; Tolstoy forsakes art to perform practical propaganda for charity and altruism. Humanity is saved, the new faith sets its torches burning to light the gloomy way!

Ah, yes! But do you not know, optimistic critic who harps on the mystic Renaissance, and upon seeing these symptoms cries hosanna on high and peace on earth to men of good will, what is it that reaches the people, the masses, the human flock, of all those sparkles that dazzle you, of the inharmonic choir made up of those voices praying the "Our Father who wert in heaven," which is the prayer in fashion among the intellectuals of today? . . . Well, I will tell you: what the people are coming to understand is what the popularizers of pseudoscience teach them, the only one popularizable, the Jules Vernes of psychology and of evolutionary doctrine: you see, man had the monkey for an ancestor, and duty is merely the limit of the strength at our disposal. There are voices that shout into the mobs: "Behold: that pale little old man dressed in white, who walks around as a prisoner of the Vatican, is a charlatan; that puppet there up at the top of the social pyramid, an imbecile." And while the neo-mystics make up their religions for poets, for millionaire innkeepers or scholars purified by study, the rabble lifts its gaze and sees. Thus did they lift their gaze one hundred twenty years ago to see, in the atmosphere of the court, perfumed like a marshal's wife, the red heels of the favorites, the powdered wigs, the lace frills, the bright-colored dress coats of the courtesans that surrounded the syphylitic monarch. Voltaire had not yet laughed; Rousseau had not yet cried. The beast of a sudden heard the blasphemy and the sob, shook itself from the lethargy in which it was sleeping, sank its clutches in the golden prey, and Terror's pool of blood revealed the power of its claws and the destruction wreaked by its bloody ire.

In recent years, what the lion has seen upon turning its gazes aloft is the imbecilic face of Father Grévy,[142] and behind it the Jewish profile of Daniel Wilson,[143] who, like a thief, kept the gold for himself, the fruits of the sale of glorious insignia; what it has seen is the *brave général* prancing on his black horse; what it has seen is the Panama affair, that mudstorm that splattered Lesseps's[144] grey hair and the brows of so many of his distinguished senators.

Do you believe, optimistic critic who harps on the mystic Renaissance and sings hosanna on high, that the classifying science of the Taines and the Wundts, the religious impression that emanates from the music of Wagner, from the paintings of Puvis de Chavannes, from the poems of Verlaine, and the morality that Paul Bourget and Edouard Rod[145] teach you in their prefaces, are sufficient chains to bind the beast when it hears the Gospel according to Nietzsche? . . . Santo Caserio's blade and the bursting of nitroglycerine bombs may suggest the answer to you.

15 April

A powerful wave of sensualism runs through my body, inflames my blood, puts my muscles right, brings the most faded images in my mind into sharp, colorful focus, and sets my nerves vibrating endlessly on contact with the slightest pleasurable sensation. Not outside my body, but in the depths of my soul, is where the sap is rising, where the birds are singing, where the green shoots are bursting forth, where the waters are running, where the flowers are perfuming as they receive the warm kisses of spring. Love has made its nest in my soul. You, music that floats on it, lines, colors, aromas, touches, sensations of unbounded power, you blood that ignite my cheeks, you dreams that flutter in the shadows, you *delectatio morosa*[146] that brings before me the voluptuous sight of pleasures past and plagues me with the memory of your biting delights, you all dance a bacchic chorus, a Saturnalia in which the kisses are bursting and the bodies commingle and fall intertwined on the soft, aromatic grass! Helen, Helen! I thirst for your whole being and I do not want to sully my lips, which have not alighted on the mouth of a woman since your smiling lips brought light into my life, nor my hands, unpolluted by all female touch since they picked up the bouquet of roses thrown by your hands! Helen! Come, arise, appear, kiss me, and allay with your presence the sensual fever that is devouring me!

19 April

There in the little shop, Bassot's, on Rue de la Paix, my eyes were feasting on the glitter of the stones heaped in front of me on the glass counter by the aristocratic jeweler's hands.[147] It is told of the great Balzac, who, enamored of the rose-colored glimmers of two twin pearls, worked for a year to acquire them; of a dying Richelieu, who sunk his feeble hands in a box brimming with precious gems, and as he made them shimmer, his lifeless eyes lit up. May such famous examples serve in my own mind to excuse my passion, which is greater than theirs, for you, mysterious minerals, more solid than marble, harder than metal, more durable than human constructions, more radiant than the light you reflect, increasing it a hundredfold and coloring it with the nuances of your essence. Oh, shining stones, splendid and invulnerable, vivid gems that slept for whole centuries in the bowels of the planet, delight to the eye, symbol and sum of human riches! The diamonds iridesce and shine like droplets of light; the dark sapphires are like unto bits of tropical sky in the starry night; you, ruby, burn like a crystallization of blood; the emeralds boast in their luminous crystals the diaphanous greens of my country's forests; you amethysts and topazes, who decorate the thick episcopal rings, have subtle colorings of the sky in the springtime dawn; bluish, blush, and pale green are the flames that burn inside your luminous milk, ever-changing opal; greenyellow: you shine with a golden glow, like the phosphorescent eyes of a cat; who could describe the delight you bring to those who see you, O pearls, more discreet in your shine than the radiant gems, pearls that form in the murky deeps of the oceans, white pearls of the smoothest orient, pink pearls from Visapur and Golconda, fantastic black pearls from Veraguas and Chiriquí, you pearls that adorn the crowns of kings, that quiver in the rosy little earlobes of women, and rest like a kiss on fresh, palpitating bare breasts! More artistic, more credulous, humanity from other times attributed the sacred character of amulets to you and mixed the sensual delight your sparkles spread with veneration for your magical power, diamonds conjured with curses and poisons, you sapphire that protects against shipwrecks, you emerald that helps in difficult childbirths, you ruby that gives chastity, you amethyst that guards against drunkenness, you opal that will pale if Her Worship forgets us! O shining stones, splendid and invulnerable, vivid gems that slept for whole centuries in the bowels of the planet, delight to the eye, symbol and sum of human riches!

There I was, in Bassot's shop, when at the door out front the simple, elegant coach stopped. With agile movements and anxious looks, like those of a startled deer, she stepped out, took ten steps, while through her dark black silk dress, adorned with jet trinkets, I read the delicious curves of her bosom, of her shapely arms and her long thin legs, like those of Jean Goujon's[148] Diana the huntress, and she stopped next to the jewel counter. My sharp sense of smell picked up, all commingled, the smell of fresh bread emanating from all of her, a charming aroma of health and life, and that of the bouquet of carnations she wore in her bodice. I scented her like a hunting dog sent after a trail, and after she spoke a single word, my gazes had already undressed her and I had kissed her with my eyes on the nape of her neck full of golden down, the thick, dark, kinky hair with reddish sheens gathered up under her large felt hat adorned with black feathers, her large grey eyes, her thin little nose, and her mouth, red as a pepper, where her blood ran to her lips pink and fresh like that; with her aroma of leaven and carnations, she looked like a haughty, fleshly flower that had just opened.

"Do you have white diamond necklaces?" she asked the jeweler with the purest American accent and with a childish smile that made the pearly whiteness of her teeth shine between the pinkness of her lips.

"This is all too expensive for me," she murmured when she heard the prices, while on her countenance a sudden expression of ill humor and sadness replaced the excitement that had opened her eyes and had flushed her lips upon seeing the costly stones.

"There is nothing too expensive for you. This jewel will be in your hands this evening, if you allow me to offer it to you," I said softly in English, practically in her ear, in a hoarse voice vibrating with temptation.

"It's beautiful," she said in the same language, which sounded like music in her mouth, as she looked me up and down and saw my hand tense on the black silk case. "Really?" she added, fixing her bright eyes on mine and with her whole face lit up by an expression of indescribable happiness such as I have never seen on any face.

"Come at nine in the evening and we'll talk. Do not ask the doorman my name; I myself will wait at the door, as if I were returning home; we'll go in together," she said, handing me a piece of paper that she tore out of the tiny wallet bound in Russian leather and on which she feverishly wrote the directions to a quiet street off the Champs-Elysées. "At nine sharp I'll go in with you, as if I were returning home," she added in a low voice, looking me in the eyes.

The clerks at Bassot's were looking at us, whispering, surprised at the conversation held in low tones and in a foreign language that had been struck up between us, two strangers, since I had not greeted her upon entering.

"These jewels are magnificent, but too costly for me; sorry, sir," she said to the clerk, who was devouring her with his eyes.

"I'll be expecting you at nine," she said turning back to me, with the serious expression of a person who knows what she is doing and is used to important business.

So with her agile movements and deer-stares she crossed the space that separated her from the coach, which left when she got in. She did not look back at the jeweler's.

"Haughty young thing! Those American girls . . . eh?" the clerk, a greying man in his fifties, insinuated to me. His eyes were full of malice and he had a goatee and a pointed mustache, twisted like Napoleon III's. "Haughty young thing! Her husband's a big clean-shaven American brute with a Quaker physique. She's driving him crazy wanting a diamond necklace, and he doesn't want to buy it for her. Last week they were out at all the jewelry shops, he against his will, scolding her, she employing every kind of cajolery to win him over. Now she is out on her own, but certainly she does not have the full amount. These American girls . . . You can bet she won't rest until she has the necklace. Ah! So you'll take it, eh? . . ." he said, opening his eyes wide . . . "It's the best we've had in recent years . . ." he added nonchalantly, "one of those jewels that doesn't sell."

You all are going to be converted into one of those stones, faded blue thousand-franc notes! You came to me unbidden in the three nights in which, staving off my hunger for kisses with the dizzying swindle in which you flew over the green table cover, I collected you with icy indifference while the other players rose from the table with their pockets empty, their eyes exasperated, and their hands trembling!

And now I am writing of my escapade. What did she mean by telling me to go pick her up, after my blunt remark? . . . I do not know. I only know that the diamonds, fit for a princess, shine from the bottom of the flowers' calyxes, where I had them placed in order to take her the bouquet, and that she will be mine. I see her bare flesh, her slender curves offered to my kisses, and I burn. It is eight in the evening; within two hours she will be in my arms, I am feeling it, and the repressed desires built up in me from eight months of mad continence and stupid sentimentalism, suggested from seeing an anemic girl while I was under the influence of opium, will be fulfilled. Hurrah for the flesh! Hurrah for kisses that alight like butterflies on the suede of rosy skin, hurrah for kisses that enter like asps through the aromatic satin of the lips, for kisses that penetrate like honey-drunk insects deep into the flowers; for the aroma and taste of the female body that gives itself over! Hurrah for the flesh! Outside, the voice of my three Andrades, bloodthirsty and drunk on alcohol and sex, you who, galloping on wild colts, spear in hand, crossed the burned-down villages, deafening them with our cry: "God is for laughing at; whisky for drinking; women for getting pregnant, and the Spanish for quartering!" Cry, voice of my wild plainsmen: Hurrah for the flesh!

28 April

Oh, strange and charming creature! We went in together, she unlocked the door to the foyer, which she crossed quickly, and when I reached the pleasant little room, after taking off my coat, in one of the pockets of which was the diamond necklace hidden among the flowers, she had already lit the lamps. The bareness of the cramped room, furnished with only two chairs, a divan, a nightstand, and a lamp, and the expression on her serious little face, dispelled my last doubts. No, this was not a comparable woman; who knows what mad fancy for the valuable jewel had made her receive me, and what she had understood by my blunt remark.

"Take a seat," she said to me, already sitting in a greyish brocatelle armchair, beneath a tall lamp from which a square of light, softened by a faded green gauze shade, fell on the carpet.

It was she who first broke the silence. I was content, until then, to send my eyes into raptures looking at her, from the thick mass of dark hair that crowned her head, to her delicate, spirited features, to her long, narrow little feet that, in low, shiny patent leather shoes, allowed a glimpse of her whiteness through the openwork of her black silk stockings as thin as lace.

"Have you ever lived in the United States? . . ." was the first comment that, after another silence, her fresh, incarnadine mouth directed at me in harsh, guttural French that made me smile involuntarily when I heard it. "No? . . . That means, roughly, that you don't understand me and that perhaps you misjudge me, and there's probably nothing we can do . . ." she went on, the same sadness of a spoiled child who has been denied a toy showing in her eyes, an expression I had seen in the jeweler's when she heard the prices of the diamonds. "Oh, but you speak English better than I do! Maybe we can understand each other; forgive me for leaving you alone a second," she added, rising.

These American girls! I thought to myself, echoing the remark by the Bassot's clerk I had heard that morning.

"Here they are," she said, placing some satin and suede boxes on a little table that she drew closer, and then lit two candles to make the evaluation easier for me. "Look at them, appraise them, and then I'll make you my offer."

"They are worth half of what the best of the necklaces you saw on Rue de la Paix is worth," I answered her unsmilingly and with unflappable calm after examining the contents of the cases, some marked with the name of Tiffany, others with those of several second-order Parisian jewelers, and wherein there was not a single flawless stone. "This was chosen more for size than for quality; you probably agree that the diamonds either are straw-colored or have flaws, lines, or cracks that make them compare unfavorably; and that the rubies are not of the same hue, and that one of the emeralds in the brooch is paler than the others and has a flaw," I said to her, fully taking on the role of gem dealer.

"That's John for you, he can't tell the difference! I prefer a diamond this big," she said, showing me the end of a pink, white, and shiny fingernail, "but one without spots, to a cork with a straw-colored sheen." Then, smiling for the first time: "You are a master, and how refined!" She added "how refined" in English, never taking her eyes off the black pearl that fastened my shirtfront. "But anyway, you agree with me that these jewels are worth half of what the necklace is worth; well, listen to my proposal: I'll give you my name, which will serve as a pledge, and this," she said, showing me the cases, "and a promissory note for the difference of the price of the necklace. In three months I'll send the total amount for the necklace, and you will return my things, together with the cancelled promissory note, delivering it all to the United States consulate, where we will make the transaction official, first thing tomorrow. Do you accept?" she asked, smiling happily.

"I don't accept, Ma'am," I replied with studied coolness, enjoying the sight of her lowering her eyes, which were brimming with tears, and of how the shadow of her long curly eyelashes fell over her cheeks. "What do I stand to gain with that deal?"

"Seeing how you told me this morning you could get me the necklace . . ." she answered with an indignant grimace.

"But you've misconstrued me," I began, in a voice that I tried to make sound firm, unsuccessfully. "There is a deal by which you will have the jewel tonight, without paying one cent for it," I hinted, looking deep in her eyes, which had risen from the floor, and, now calm, looked at me fixedly.

"You've got the wrong idea, mister," she answered, her cheeks aflame. Standing up suddenly with a brusque movement of her entire body, she glared at me with a profound expression of disdain and anger. "You've got the wrong idea, mister! So you dare think my passion for stones would go so far as to make me forget who I am, and that those diamonds can buy me? . . . But don't you see, you wretch, that those boxes of jewels I offer you are mine, all mine? . . . Oh, you just don't know my name and you think I'm going to steal the difference," she shouted; "I'm Nelly————!" and then a German name with a bogus English ending, that of a Chicago millionaire, known worldwide as one of the most powerful American railroad magnates. "It's only too clear you haven't lived in my country when you misunderstand my behavior and judge me like that!" she continued, not sitting down and wearing the anguished expression of one who feels tarnished by vile, undeserved suspicion.

I picked up the fine batiste and lace handkerchief perfumed with carnation that she had dropped when she rose, and in a gentle voice said to her, breathing in the aroma:

"Madam: do me the honor of allowing me to remain here a few more moments, and believe you are speaking with a gentleman." I put the kerchief on the bedside table and nervously looked for my billfold. Opening it, I handed her one of my calling cards. "If you feel offended when our conversation is over, let your husband send two witnesses to arrange with mine the conditions for a meeting . . . You shall tell him that this evening I came in after you, who was returning home, and I tried to kiss you and possess you. Do that, but allow me to speak to you," I practically shouted at her, possessed by the fury to crown the plan that I had hatched in those minutes.

"What! You're Mr. Fernández, don José Fernández, the author of the *Pagan Poems* that Murray translated?" she said, seated now and lifting her eyes from the tiny piece of bristol board . . . "And here I didn't recognize you . . . It's also that your portrait is really old, right? You didn't have a beard then . . . I was completely unaware you lived in Paris. Sit down, Mr. Fernández; you're going to have tea with me and we're going to talk about your verses. So let's forget this business with the stupid necklace . . . "

"Ah! So you read that little article published in a Boston magazine and written by the Yank who visited my country and who paid me the five hundred dollars I lent him, calling me a great poet in it, translating a part of my verses and having it run with the portrait that appears in the second edition of *First Verses*? So you've read it, my adorable and frenetically arrogant Yankee, and you want for us to talk about my *Pagan Poems*?"

"Let's talk about your verses, about *Pagan Poems*. I know them in Murray's translation published in *North American Review*.[149] How beautiful, they're fascinating!" she said, then again in English, smiling at me, "Let's talk about your poems, Mr. Fernández."

"No, Madam; let's talk about you and the necklace you want and that your husband does not want to buy you, that is making you do foolish things and that has made me appear at your house and have the honor of speaking with you."

"Back to the necklace again . . . So be it . . . What is it you're trying to tell me?" she said to me with poorly concealed impatience and an expression of pride. "It is my hope that you think me a lady and that you are not going to prove my believing you a gentleman to be a vain hope."

"What I'm trying to tell you," I began, my voice trembling with emotion, "is that I beg you, in the most respectful way, to accept this jewel, which I place at your feet without asking more from you than, whenever you wear it on your goddess body, you remember the man whom you made happy by allowing him to satisfy a whim of his. If you accept my proposal, the necklace will be in your hands in one minute and I will leave without having kissed them, never to see you again, should you require that."

"Are you serious?" she asked me, with deep and inexplicable agitation, when she heard my answer.

"Madam: I only hope that you allow me this, and for me to leave, for I fear I am imposing."

"My God, my God! This one looks for the way to make me happy and he just met me this morning; and the other one insults me when I beg him and he leaves me alone so he can go find loose women in New York! What a life!" . . . she articulated between the sobs that choked her, resting her head against the armchair's backrest and covering her tear-filled eyes with the little batiste handkerchief smelling of carnations.

The sobs shook her all over; nerves were getting the better of her lovely, energetic nature.

I went out into the anteroom, fetched the bouquet, and, entering on tiptoe, went and knelt next to the armchair where she was crying, as the serpent crept to innocent Eve's foot when he offered her the apple. The sobs and tears continued, and I kept silent.

"Nelly!" I said to her when she began to calm down, wrapping an arm around her slender waist, caressing her forehead with the flowers in the bouquet, and singing her a monotonous little song that the wet nurses in Florida use to sing little children to sleep. "Don't cry, Nelly; the flowers are kissing you to make you happy; the diamonds want to see you, Nelly, pretty and fresh like the flowers, Nelly, radiant and cold as the diamonds, who are worth less than those tears."

Defeated by that coddling and surprised to hear it, she pulled away the handkerchief and sunk her eyes in the purple calyxes of the gloxinias and in the white leaves of the gardenias, where the diamonds shone like droplets of light.

"No, no," she said, with a smile that lit up her wet eyes like a ray of light on a spring landscape recently wet by the rain. "No, no; if you don't accept my proposal, don't say another word to me, that's worth a crazy amount. My father, who's a millionaire and who adores me, never would have given them to me. No, take them and give me the flowers. They're pretty," she said, breathing in the bouquet. "Keep this," picking up the platinum strand, given luminous life by the white, red, and blue palpitation of the radiant gems that iridesced in the light of the candles and the lamp. "Fernández, why do you want to give me this? . . ."

We spoke, she with her adorable head, whose dark curls caressed my brow, bent over mine, which practically rested on her knees, since I was positioned firmly at her feet, breathing in her aroma of flowers and encircling her with my arms.

"Because poets go through the world only to fulfill the whims of goddesses like you," I replied, covering with kisses her smooth, cold hands, with which she strove to push me away. "Nelly, those diamonds are going to make you remember me when you see them later; don't deny me the delight of thinking I am going to live in your memory in your nights of triumph . . ."

And my lips, moving along the bluish branches of her veins, which shone through the thin skin of that slender doll, went up her nicely rounded, white arm, bare to the elbow of her opaque black silk sleeve decorated with jet trinkets.

"And why do you want me to remember you for the diamonds? I'll remember you because I know your charming verses and because I have seen you kneeling at my feet, wishing to indulge a whim of mine at the cost of an enormous sum and telling me things that no one had ever told me . . . The things you say to me! You can tell you're a poet, a great poet," she added in a tone of conviction. "Do you want to hear your verses recited by me in my language? It's not as beautiful as yours. I know them by heart. Listen . . . And she recited with her golden voice the lines to "Song to Venus," which tell of the glories of Aphrodite as she is born amidst the ocean waves.

"Now say them to me in your language; I don't understand it, but it sounds like music." Then placing her rosy little ear near my mouth, which gently, very gently, recited my best hendecasyllables, she said in English: "How noble, how musical."

We spoke thus, lost in the delight of savoring the essence of the verses and of feeling each other close, without her, the prideful girl of a few minutes before, or me, the respectful admirer who had sworn to her he would leave without kissing her fingertips, realizing the giddiness that was overcoming us both. Before I knew it, I was sitting in the armchair and had her sitting on my knees. One of her little feet was dangling onto the carpet. The whiteness of her long, slender foot and the swollen curve of her thigh, revealed by the black skirt where the dull jet trinkets twinkled, shone through the black silk lace of her stocking. I was kissing the back of her neck full of golden down, and I felt all her nerves quiver under my lips. Her firm little hand that was clutching mine sunk, contorting, its pointed rosy nails into my flesh. In the silence we heard only the sound of our blood pounding.

"More poetry, slower . . ." she said with a caressing expression, drawing her cold, velvety cheek in close to my burning one, and intoxicating me with her smell of fresh bread and moist carnations.

I told her the verses that depict the groups of white doves on the altar of Cyprus, enveloped in the aromatic smoke of the sacrifice and winging among the roses, and told them to her in her language, as I encircled her wrist in the necklace, which entwined her pale arm like a serpent of light and began to radiate with the sparkle of its hundreds of facets.

"How old are you? . . ." she asked me suddenly, running her white hand gently over my hair and beard. " . . . Twenty-six? I'm eighteen; he's forty-two . . . Who do you live with? . . . By yourself? No father, mother, wife, or children? Nothing? Alone in that hotel? . . . The other day I stopped to look at the façade. It's old, isn't it? . . . And majestic. So you live alone there? . . . You live like a prince. So doesn't it make you sad to live alone? . . . So what do you do? . . . How you must enjoy life, eh?"

"No. I worship beauty[150] and strength and I write those verses that you know," I said to her in a sad tone of voice, lying to complete my spell over her.

"And do you receive women? . . ." she asked me, laughing with delightful roguishness.

"No, because I don't find them as beautiful as Nelly," I replied, enfolding her in a gaze of mad desire. It had been eight months since I had given a kiss or received a caress.

"It's impossible! It's unreal[151] . . . Swear to me that that's true," she said, her voice muffled and speaking in my ear.

"I swear it. I want what is perfect and cannot find it. Everything else sickens me. And when I find a woman whom I fall in love with in an hour with all my heart and whom I beg to keep some paltry stones so that she remembers me, one at whose feet I would spend my life kneeling and for whose kisses I would give my soul, she refuses my love and throws back in my face the gift with which I dream of making her happy for a moment."

"No," she said, "let me go. Wait . . ." Whereupon she rose to leave the room.

"You're leaving, Nelly?"

"But I'll be right back," she responded, lifting the portier, which fell behind her.

"She will be yours, she will be yours!" the plainsmen's voice shouted inside me. "She will be yours!"

"Do you like me in this?" she asked me, sitting back down on my knees in the corner of the room where there was more shadow and a Turkish divan spread out its soft cushion, as wide as a marriage bed. "I haven't worn it yet. Look."

The black suede bodice of a ball gown, fastened at the shoulders by two ties, one of which sported the bouquet of gloxinias and gardenias, revealed the turgescent whiteness of her bosom, which undulated with a rhythmic movement under the platinum strand given luminous life by the white, red, and blue palpitation of the gems that shone like a rainbow in the dusky half-light. "Do you like me in this?" she asked, leaning over to see the diamonds and allowing me to sink my gaze in the treasures that the velvet bodice barely concealed.

"If we had only met earlier! I'm leaving tomorrow for New York,

Fernández, my poet," she remarked, resting her head on my shoulder and wrapping her bare, fragrant arms around my neck.

"If only we had met a month ago! Perhaps you would have loved me . . . How happy we'd be, wouldn't we?"

"We'd be no happier than now, Nelly, since I love you with all my soul. But you won't leave tomorrow; you'll stay here and I will live on my knees, divining your thoughts."

"I'm leaving tomorrow morning; everything's all ready, the trunks are shut, the passage bought . . . This afternoon I sent a cablegram notifying him. My father will be expecting me very soon. I'll ask for the divorce and I'll live in peace."

"He's a swine, isn't he, my love? . . ." I said into her ear. "He doesn't love you and he doesn't give you the jewels you want."

"He's a swine, a brutish man, and he doesn't love me. What do the jewels matter? *You* give them to me . . . You know, and if you don't give them to me, you say sweet, charming things to me, don't you?" she answered, clinging to me. "I'll take the necklace. What do you ask of me in return?" she asked, letting go and holding my hands in hers. "What do you ask of me in return? . . ."

"I don't ask anything; what I want is for you to have a moment of happiness and that you remember me. Tell me you'll keep it forever and I'll leave happy, without giving you a single kiss."

"So you want to make me happy and leave? . . . The necklace is mine . . . Will you accept a gift that I'm going to give you? . . ." she said into my ear with a triumphant expression. "I'm going to give you a gift too, but an unlikely one, worthy of you who are a poet; a gift that you yourself are going to think is a dream. I too want to make you happy by being happy. I want to be happy one night. I never have been. I hate time. Time is a stupid thing—a stupid thing!—that only exists for the body," she added, looking at me with an inspired face, like that of a pythoness. "In my country we want to suppress it with electricity, with steam, with the intellect. There we created, in one decade, cities larger than those of Europe, which are six centuries old, and we have made a two-hundred-year-old civilization. Time is a stupid thing that drags. I

191

want to suppress it in my life . . . You know? . . . I love you, Fernández . . . I'm leaving tomorrow. Any other woman would leave and take her love away with her; I want to give it to you; I love you," she sighed in my ear, kissing me.

"And I adore you, Nelly," I replied, madly searching for her lips first, and then plunging my forehead into her soft bosom, perfumed and fresh . . .

"No; stop it, stop it; not here; take me away; don't you live alone? . . ." she articulated, holding me tight and with desire; "we'll walk, wherever you want to go . . ."

"My coach is waiting at the door . . . Come on," I said as if in a dream, an instant later in the foyer, wrapping up her bare shoulders and switching off the lights.

All I have left from that night is the memory of her smiling beauty under the wide velvet canopy of my bed, in the bedroom lit only by the Byzantine lamp with dark red glass; the impression of tenacious freshness, the perfume of her adolescent body, and the cooing of her voice urging me to go to the United States. "Come in the summer," she was saying; "John won't be there. You'll meet us in Newport[152] and I'll introduce you to my father and all our friends . . . We'll look for a place to see each other, a cottage surrounded by trees and flowers, and I'll be happy . . . If you offer to come, I won't ask for the divorce; I'll tolerate today's events in exchange for your peace of mind and your love. Swear to me you'll go . . . Kiss me!"

Her delirium for pleasure was getting close to the same level as mine, and the night was a single kiss, interrupted by sobs of voluptuosity.

"Everything has been unreal and adorable . . . Unreal and adorable . . . You are unreal and adorable . . . I'll wait for you in June in Newport," were her final words, shouted from the railing of the giant steamship that cast off and released a black column of smoke, blackening the Le Havre sky to where I saw her off.

My eyes still see her slender silhouette wrapped in the long grey traveling overcoat, and the palpitation of the little white handkerchief that she shook as the boat pulled away on the blue-green waves of the Atlantic, under a cloudy sky, leaden and gloomy as a soul full of regrets.

1 September

Five months without having written a line here. The night of delights spent with Nelly was but a stimulus, a drop of liqueur for one dying of thirst, *sed non satiata!*[153] She excited me, we drank, I got drunk, and now in my soul I have the slackness that remains in the body after a drinking bender. The ball was supposed to dazzle them, and it dazzled them so much that come morning, when the final notes of the orchestra vibrated through the rooms saturated with human emanations and the melancholic perfume of moribund flowers, I had already kissed the three coveted mouths and elicited from them the promise of three trysts.

A sumptuous party, in the words of the newspapers on the boulevard, which annoyed me with the details of the luxury displayed there by *le richissime américain don Joseph Fernández et Andrade.* A sumptuous party? I do not know about that, but in any event, a bit more elegant and more artistic than those I have managed to see up until now. I say more artistic since in the sitting rooms, which are furnished and decorated with museum-caliber objects, and in the hall, decorated with exotic plants and rare flowers, the penetrating sounds of Sarasate's[154] magic violin and the moans of Jiménez Manjón's[155] incomparable guitar were heard, and the warm notes of the fashionable tenor cost, in Monteverde's phrase, a pound sterling each. I say more elegant since one part of the frivolous, mundane Paris, which is exhibited on the Rue des Acacias in the evenings and where one meets on opening nights at the grand theaters, hobnobbed at the party for a few hours with the artistic, pensive Paris, which is forever cooped up in the workshops, in the laboratories, or hunched over the pages that the day after tomorrow will be the fashionable book. They say the gathering was left in shock at the exquisiteness of the table and the quality of the aged liqueurs. A murmur of approval ran through the rooms when, as the cotillion hovered around, flapping its wings of ribbons and crêpe in rhythmic rounds, the little gifts were given out to the dancers.

The most truly pleasant sensation I had was when I saw the most distinguished and charming elements of the Spanish-American district mingling with the most highborn and upper-class members of the aris-

tocratic neighborhood. I managed to have the compatriots who honor
the country with their learning, Serrano the philologist and Mendoza
the statesman, leave their claustral seclusion to put in an appearance
here for a few moments' time. Doddering old duchesses of the greatest
importance and with highfalutin names, whose origins hark back to the
Rome of the Antoninos, promenaded on the arms of generals, former
presidents of our republics, who boasted uniforms that were more gold
than fabric; there was a member of the Jockey Club who courted a newly
arrived young waif, who still had the memory of tropical skies in her
eyes, and the sound of the breeze through the coffee plantations in her
ears. Also in attendance were the group where shone the bald Manouvr-
ier, the spiritualist philosopher, Mortha—my old professor of Egyptian
archeology—and his wrinkles, and the monocle of the psychologist-
novelist, author of *The Feminine Profiles,* who, shunning women that
night, who were asking for him in order to woo him, went and hid
amidst those old relics and talked to Doctor Charvet, who told me as I
passed by him, punching my shoulder:

"This is how it's done. Enjoy life at your ease, my friend; enjoy life
at your ease."

What did I care about the success of the party . . . if my lucidity
of an analyst made me see that, to my elegant European friends, I'll
never cease to be the *rastaquouère* who tries to rub elbows with them, by
towering up his bags of gold; and to my compatriots I will not cease to
be a swanky show-off who wants to show them to what extent he has
managed to insinuate himself into the grand Parisian world and the
cosmopolitan highlife?

That did not stop the three women from attending nor prevent my
plan from being carried out.

And what is that to me, if not one of the three has been able to
give me what I ask of love, and today all I have left is the pride of having seduced in a few hours the three beauties whom no one would dare
suspect and that the entire gathering designated as the three belles of
the ball?

And what is that to me, if I do not live for others, but for myself, and if that victory does not satiate me, since I know that perhaps they themselves do not know the reasons each had to give herself to me and to lavish me with wild caresses? . . .

And what are those ideas about love to me, and what do I care about anything, if what I feel within me is weariness and disdain for everything, dreadful surrender, horrible spleen, the taedium vitae that, like an inner monster whose hunger cannot be appeased with the universe, begins to eat away at my soul? . . .

You all experienced that nameless, cureless malady, you Roman nobles who, oversated with the pleasures of the flesh, having had your fill of the philosophers' declamations and the poets' verses and the creations of Hellenic and Latin art, forsook the purple-covered marble tricliniums on which the aromatic essences and Paestrum roses rained down, you cast to the floor the golden chiseled cup full of Cyprian wine, and the crown of roses that girds your brow, and, scorning the sensual delight the naked courtesan at your side afforded you, you ran to seek in the spurned teachings of the coarse disciples of the Nazarene, in the practice of poverty and humility, a new faith and a sublime hope that made you change your life, embrace the cross, defy the ire of the emperor, and, transfigured by ecstasy, to go and await the hour of death under the claws of lions in the bloody sand of the amphitheater!

Ah, yes, that was then. In our base and mediocre era, there is no avenue left open for souls of your mettle, O nobles, who feel what you felt. The sublime has fled the earth. The blind faith that in its lap of shadow those weary of life might find a pillow whereupon to rest their heads, has vanished from the universe. The human eye, when applied to the lens of the microscope that looks into the infinitesimal and into the lens of the enormous telescope that, turned heavenward, reveals to it the sky, has found, above and below, in the atom and in the incommensurable nebula, a single matter, subject to the same laws, which have nothing to do with the lot of humanity. Keen exegetes and conscientious commentators studied the old sacred texts and analyzed them, discovering in them not words, which are the way, the truth, and the life, but the wise prescriptions of the civilizers of the primitive nations and the legend forged by a nation of poets. The corpse of the Redeemer of men lies in the tomb of incredulity, on whose stone the human soul weeps as Mary Magdalene wept on the other tomb.

"Our Father who art in heaven, hallowed be thy name . . ." The prayer that the silver-haired saint taught me on my knees, when I could hardly babble it, comes to my lips as a man and I cannot say it. You are empty, O heaven where prayers and sacrifices rise!

Neo-mysticism of Tolstoy, Western theosophy of the crackpot duchesses, white magic of the magnificent hairy poet at whom Paris laughs, Buddhism of the dandies who use monocles and wield the foil; cult of the divine, of the philosophers who destroyed science; cult of the self, invented by the *literatos* bored with literature; spiritism, that believes in dancing tables and knocking spirits; grotesque fin de siècle religions, revolting parodies, pastiches of the ancient cults, let a child of this century as it dies enfold you all in a single scornful guffaw and spit in all your faces!

It is that hunger for certainties, that thirst for the absolute and for the supreme, that tendency in my spirit toward the heights, which I have been cheating with my amorous affairs, as I was staving off my thirst for the latter with the dirty tricks played during my last nights of chastity. But there is nothing to sate the hunger to believe, except belief itself . . . And in what will you believe, my melancholic, fervent soul, if men are that miserable fidgeting mob, committing wicked acts, searching for gold, cheating on women, flouting greatness, and if the gods have all died?

Perhaps Love had bitter and ecstatic flavors that could replace faith. That matter of the mystical came in the coarse medieval times, and in the grandiose expansion of passions that was the Renaissance. To love while trembling, since through the door of the bedroom, warm and perfumed by kisses, one could hear the sound of footsteps and the guns of the toughs sent by the husband, who were coming up to avenge the affront; to love while praying, for the Lady took on the appearance of the Madonna; to love without satiating love, and immortalizing Her name in songs or in statues, to be Benvenuto Cellini or Godofredo,[156] Dante Alighieri, Petrarch, or Michaelangelo, when She was called Beatrice Portinari, Laura, or Vittoria Colonna, was a man's undertaking, but today, in these decrepit societies, in which adultery is simple, indulged in out of harm's way, like a sport; in which the life of the woman is in its entirety a slow and gradual preparation for the fall, and in which the husbands come to visit the fortunate one to ask favors of him, is a misfortune unworthy of a man.

Perhaps my misanthropy leads me to judge those deluded wretches harsher than they deserve to be. They likely thought that what they saw the night of the ball was an inconsequential flirt, to their minds easily taken advantage of on account of my youth and my money; but the truth is the circumstances have intertwined so strangely that one would need the benevolence of a saint not to judge them as I do, at best as imbeciles.

"Hey, Pepillo," my friend Rivas said to me, using the disagreeable name he calls me; "I've come to ask you a favor that only you can do for me."

"I'm at your service," I replied, believing it was about a duel in which I had to go along with him as a witness, and surprised to hear him talk that way. . . . "You having coffee?" I added, offering him some, because I was having mine, finishing eating in the smoking room, when he came in like a hurricane, with an upset look about him, and gasping for breath.

"No, I don't drink it; it makes me nervous. Listen, Pepe: you are going to do me this *huge favor,* the kind that you can only ask of a close friend. You won't say no, will you?" he added, faltering. "Swear you won't say no."

"I'm telling you I'm at your service . . ."

"So you'll miss *Faust* to help me? You don't have plans for tonight? . . . All right, you don't know how I appreciate this! Well, look: four of us, Amorteguí, Rodríguez, Saavedra, and I, have a dinner planned with four women, *choice* ones, you know? . . . four *horizontals* that would make your mouth drop open if I told you their names . . . four select ones! And just guess who I'm stuck with! Consuelo is indisposed and I don't have anyone to keep her company, and I feel bad leaving her by herself. You know . . . And the idea of talking to one's wife because she feels weak, and to retire at eleven after drinking tea, when one has a dinner going on with four fellows like Rodríguez and four women as dandy as that . . . No, I was desperate. From thinking it over while we ate, it came to me, know what I mean? . . . I'll go back home, because I told her I was going out for a minute; you come in and pay a visit and make like you're hectic; you tell me that Amorteguí was looking for me urgently in the boulevard because he has to talk to me tonight about some business. I swear it's her that's driving me to go out! I'll leave and you go with her until as late as possible, right? so that she doesn't notice the time I get back if she stays awake, as happens almost every night. How about that plan, eh? What do you think of my scheme? Admirable, isn't it? . . . Help me out . . ."

"Admirable . . ." I said. "With the greatest pleasure; you'll have me there within half an hour at the most," and he left happy as a lark, twisting his mustache and feeling like Machiavelli.

"What lovely thing have you brought me? . . ." the listless and languid creature asked me when, after the other man had gone out, we were left alone in the little room where she greets her close friends. "Any of those things that only you find? . . ." she said to hide the alarm she felt upon feeling herself alone with me after the delicious kiss tasted in the back of the deserted hothouse where I took her away for a few moments the night of the party, and after the pledges of love I made with it.

"What lovely thing have you brought me, José? . . . Flowers? Good gracious, pink flowers from the Guaymís![157] . . . The same," she said, shaking all over, as if caressing with her eyes the bouquet of orchids that had been placed on her knees and that I had just cultivated in the hothouse when I left home. " . . . My gracious! . . . where did you get flowers from our country in Paris, José? . . ."

"At home, Consuelo," I said to her, sitting alongside her, on the same Turkish divan from which she had risen when she saw me come in a few moments before. "At home, Consuelo . . . Ever since one afternoon nine years ago, I have had, no matter where I might be, some plants that I care for a great deal so they give me flowers like those . . . for nine years, ever since one afternoon," I said, looking at her to see the effect of the suggestive phrase that I had rehearsed since the moment in which the cunning Rivas told me his plan in the smoking room.

She turned paler, paler than she is normally; her hands and lips trembled, and she lowered her eyes to the floor.

Nine years earlier, she and I being practically children, one delightful afternoon, one of those tropical afternoons conducive to dreaming and loving with the aroma of the warm breezes and calm falling from the sky, roseate from the dawn, we were returning down a narrow path, shaded by corpulent trees and choked by weeds, to the little village where her family would go to spend the summer. We had gotten ahead of the group of walkers. Telling her I adored her, I recited stanzas from Núñez de Arce's *Idyll,* and felt like Paul to her Virginia[158] dressed in white muslin, her little arm resting on mine.

"I want some of those flowers," she said to me, showing me a bunch of pink parasites that hung from the branch of a bush, and as I gave them to her, in the semidarkness of the path, where the air was warm and the fireflies flew and the orange trees exhaled their aroma, I took her in my arms and kissed her with all the ardor of my eighteen years, and she returned the idyllic kisses with her fresh, virgin mouth.

"They're Guaymis flowers, Consuelo," I told her. " . . . Ever since that afternoon I always have had those plants in my house so I can breathe that kiss in their fragrance, which was the happiest minute of my life. From then until the night when, now living here, I found out you had married Rivas, not a single day went by that I did not think of you with the same tenderness. Had your father not laughed at my love then, since I was a child, and forbade me to return to your house, as he did, how happy I would have been and how different my fate! You loved me then, do not deny it; let me believe that it was so; then you forgot me. If only *I* had done the same. Before last night, when I saw you at the house, among the hothouse verdure, with that white muslin dress that made you look like the child who made me happy with her girlish affection, and as I felt close to you, I forgot everything, I felt like that boy from long ago, I felt the same love for you as I felt in that instant, grown through nine years of thinking of you, and I had the audacity to steal a kiss, and it was ecstasy . . . Now I have come to ask your forgiveness, Consuelo, for that unspeakable audacity, and I ask for it in the name of our childhood love, and on my knees . . . Consuelo: do you forgive me?" I went on, kneeling now at her feet and kissing her hands, which she surrendered limply to me. "With all your sweetness, will you be able to forgive a man who has adored you his whole life and who does naught but dream of you, who speaks to you thus because he can no longer hold his tongue? Tell me," I added, reverting to the charming informal form of address we used when we were children; "tell me, Consuelo: don't you see that I adore you with all my soul? Didn't you see that the party the other night had only one purpose, to see you at the house, to feel you near me a few minutes, to feel your hands in mine? Don't you think that these flowers have the same fragrance as our Guaymis flowers? . . . Breathe them in; don't you feel the aroma of that kiss in them? . . ."

Now I had her wrapped up in my arms, mesmerized, captivated by my sentimentality act, which transformed inside me into sensual delirium upon sensing that she was returning the kisses I was giving her, and hearing her tell me: "The other night I was dying in the hothouse when you kissed me. I've done nothing else but think about you since then. If I married it was to come to Paris to see you. I've never given Rivas a kiss. Swear to me you adore me, for it seems like a dream to hear you say it . . . José, José! For goodness' sake! But this is a crime to adore each other this way; an appalling crime, since I'm his wife."

"No, it's not a crime, my love; it would be a crime if he were to love you, if he were not who he is, if he had not married you for your fortune, if he did not abandon you as he does, if I did not adore you as I do. Consuelo, is it not madness for me to stay here one moment longer," I said, controlling myself to gain the promise I was seeking, "when he can return at any moment to catch us unawares, with something showing in our faces of the delight these moments have been? Isn't it true that it's madness, when tomorrow we can spend hours on end together, where we do not have to be afraid, at home, where we can pretend we're not in Paris and we'll breathe in the aroma of our forests in the hothouse? . . . What?" I persisted when I heard the reply. "What? You're afraid to go? And you don't remember we're in Paris, where no one looks at anyone else, and we live a stone's throw away from each other? . . . Has Rivas ever come home at noon, while you were out shopping, or has he asked you where you've been? We can be together six hours, which to me will be worth six years of happiness . . . Are you afraid of me? . . . Don't you know that my love is as pure as it was back then, that it is enough to see you, to hear you, to be happy, and that I won't give you a kiss if you don't want it? . . ."

And she came over and was mine. And thereafter she came over twice, practically without my asking her to, because she wanted to, because she needs caresses as she needs to breathe, and because the other man, the cunning one with the Machiavellian schemes, is out having dinner with his *horizontals* who are having him as the main course, and he has abandoned that flower of sensuality and innocence, who whiles away many days and nights alone, since she has almost no relationships in Paris.

With different weapons the other women fell, the blonde German baroness, who has the golden robustness of Titian's Venuses and is free of all bias, by her own account, and a reader of Hauptmann[159] and of Hermann Bahr.[160] With that one I affected absolute coldness the night of the ball and merely spoke to her in German and told her simply of the duel with her relative, the Embassy Secretary, and assured her of my scorn for men. Believing me of marble, while we were walking together through the halls, she struck up a conversation probably intended to make sure of my meager powers of love and to shock me with the profound disdain she displayed toward all social order and all prevailing ideas on morality. I let her talk at length. I listened to her as if I did not understand her, not answering more than necessary so that she would go on talking, and fixing my gaze on Juno's breast, half naked in a dark green velvet bodice on which shone magnificent diamonds, and on her red lips like a ripe strawberry. She fixed her gaze on me, as if searching for the effect of her bold words and her majestic beauty, and would smile a defiant smile upon seeing me blanch more and more as the temptation that was fraying my nerves grew stronger in me.

"Those are all theories, Madam; simply theories. In practice you are a strict Puritan and respect even the most stupid ties with which society binds us. If you lived truly beyond good and evil, as Nietzsche says, it would be another matter; but that is not the case. If I gave you a kiss now," I said, having her sit in a little room with no one around, "you would have your husband send me a couple of witnesses; and if I invited you out to eat alone with me tomorrow, at seven in the evening, you would not so much as acknowledge my existence thereafter."

"Try it and see," she replied, taking her boldness and my excitement to climax and using a phrase that said it all.

I kissed her frenetically, and she turned up at the tryst the next evening.

"What I have loved about you," she said as we left the house, "is your scorn for prevailing morals. We two were born to understand one another. You are the superman, the *Übermensch* I was dreaming about."

With Lady Musellaro it was a whole different story. On the pretext of a love of pagan art and my keenness for modern poets from Italy, in the previous while we had had unspeakably libertine conversations. I had started seeing her three months previously, on Tuesday evenings, on which she receives in her home the crème de la crème of the ruined counts and marquises and of the painters and musicians from the district. She had recited to me the most passionate poems in which D'Annunzio sings the glories of the flesh, with a slightly harsh, veiled voice and half-closing her dark eyes, which, with the lusterless whiteness of her skin, the purity of her profile, and the thickness of her black hair, make one dream of a Roman woman from the days of the Empire; she had heard me unblushingly tell her unmentionable things. Her sculptural lines and queenly gestures attracted men's gazes the night of the ball. As she had come over to the house several times with her husband to see my collection of medallions, cameos, and engraved stones, she felt at home and did the honors. That night she gave off a tepid smell of Cyprus, which, mingled with that of her body, enveloped her when she danced as if in an atmosphere thick with voluptuosity. On her round arms of ideal whiteness, on her square-cut neckline, and burning on her black, shiny, wavy hair, were blood-red rubies, which were of the same hue as the opaque silk of the dress she had on, which was embroidered with silvery *passementerie*.

"Julia," I said, taking her toward the corner where a copy of the Venus de Milo brought out its marmoreal whiteness against the heavy background drapes, "tonight your beauty is intoxicating, like a Falerno wine drunk in a golden cup. If you could see yourself with a man's eyes, you would fall in love with yourself. Upon seeing you one dreams of not living in this sad and listless century, in which even pleasure is measured and appraised, but in the age of the Borgias; seeing you causes one to imagine you presiding over an orgy of princes, in which the savor of kisses mixes with that of poison."

"You dream of that because you have the muscles of a he-man and the nerves of a Renaissance artist; I seem common to all these Parisian men, for sure; to them distinction consists of being skinny and pale. We two should be closer, for we are quite alike; we are both pagans," she told me, burning me up with her fiery gazes and making me feel sick with her perverse and suggestive scent.

"That closeness is up to you. If you were to come see me on Thursday morning, we would feel pagan down to the marrow; I would read you some verses and show you some etchings by Félicien Rops,[161] which you have not seen, but they are worthy of the Secret Museum in Naples . . ."

"I'm awfully keen on seeing them," she said, her face lit up with happiness and stretching out my arm across her bosom, the bosom of a goddess. "I'll come at eight. Musellaro never gets up earlier than eleven."

And a kiss sealed the tacit pact that contained those words; a kiss given behind the drapes, to which the partygoers had turned their backs, involved as they were in seeing Sarasate, who was rising to begin to play the violin, from which he drew mysterious groans.

Philandering? Seduction? . . . With respect to Consuelo, perhaps, in whom I touched the most hidden fibers of feeling by reminding her of our sweet, sweet childhood idyll; not with the other two, debauched sensation-collectors, schooled by heaven knows whom before me, corrupted by art and literature and each of them determined to see in me the figure that the poisonous, moldy old books they have read without understanding them have shown them as ideal. Seduction? No; no one seduces anyone. It is the idea of pleasure that seduces us . . . Desire was as ardent in them as it was in me; after a few years they will not remember the affair, and if they do, it will seem to both as innocent as it seems to me now.

And *this* the strict moralists call a crime, they who preach their morality in three-act dramas? Crime? To flatter a woman, to idealize her vices, to place her before a mirror where she looks more beautiful than she is, to make her enjoy life for a few hours and end up feeling disdain for her, disgust with oneself, hatred for the grotesque parody of love, and longing for something white, like a peak of a glacier, to rid one's soul of the smell and taste of the flesh!

Musellaro called me the other night in the Circle, where they had cleaned out his pockets the night before, and with a great display of groveling and cajolery and praising my knowledge of art to the skies, he told me of a little silver box chiseled by Pollaiuolo,[162] which a friend of his was selling in Florence.

"The price is seven thousand francs," he told me. "As soon as I found out they were selling it, I thought about letting you know, certain you'd take it. My friend doesn't want his name to be known. It is an object that has been in his family for three hundred years and which circumstances are forcing him to part with. You know how it is in Italy."

"Only too well. Telegraph him first thing in the morning and tell him he's found a buyer for it and for him to send it to me," I replied. "I'll send you the check as early as tomorrow."

A box chiseled by Pollaiuolo—what a laugh! I will get some junk right out of the mold. How the fortunate husband of Petronius's admirer will laugh at me!

Olga's husband, the sad, skinny German baron, who has the postage stamp craze and collects them with the enthusiasm of a schoolboy, has just left here to ask me a special favor. He wants the Bust of the Liberator, a decoration that the government of Venezuela confers; so to that end, he wishes for me to speak with the likeable boy author of *Smoke Spirals,* who represents that nation in Paris and with whom he knows I have ties of friendship. Within a few weeks he will have his medal and he will pin it to his uniform so it stands out next to the seven he decks it out with when he wears it, and he will receive a stamp from my collection.

"You have always been this way, haven't you?" he asked, looking at her again, as if annoyed by my request.

"Always," she answered him, stretched out on the ottoman and wrapped in the folds of the loose pink silk negligee that smells of white heliotrope . . . "Always," she replied, smiling that sweet, dying-girl smile she has.

"It's also that she doesn't want to go out; look Pepillo: you're not busy, take her around; business doesn't give me a moment to myself; if I had it I'd do it. You know so much about paintings and statues, take her to the museums for me; I don't have time. Why don't you go to the Louvre tomorrow with Fernández?" he asked her. "Weren't you saying you felt like going?"

"We'll go, won't we, José? It's just that when one isn't used to life in Europe, one doesn't think to go out with a friend, you know? . . ." And her Arabian eyes looked at me delightedly, and her head, resting on the soft cushions of the ottoman, held the promise of millions of kisses for the next day.

"Fact is, women have no inkling of how business consumes a person," the other man continued. "You know about the complications in mine, just imagine if I have the time to take her out and show her a good time as I'd like to . . ."

"And you *do* have time to play billiards and baccarat at the club and to spend weeks on end with your famous *horizontals* and to go have dinner with them, you senseless bedlamite?" I thought to myself when I heard that.

"So, Paco, you're giving me formal authorization to take her out and show her a good time?" I asked him with the coldness of a seventy-year-old man.

"I've been begging her since she got in to go out and see Paris, and she doesn't listen to me one damn bit!"

"Listen, Consuelo: your husband is giving you to me to take out and show you a good time; afterward don't claim he hasn't given you permission to go to such-and-such place."

"No, take her wherever you want to; go with Fernández wherever he takes you, you hear? . . . Oh, ten o'clock," he said, taking out his watch;

"I have to go; you'll excuse me, won't you? I have a meeting with Amorteguí about an important matter."

Apparently the next day she asked him if those who know us would not start to talk when they saw us together in my carriage, and he said to her, letting loose a guffaw:

"No: everybody knows Fernández . . . You know what they call him? *José the chaste.*[163] Don't trouble yourself over what they may say, they won't say anything."

And she was the one telling me this, laughing with her delicious, fleshy mouth, and stretched out on one of the divans in my library! "I'm going to spend whole days with you, if you want," she told me; "so you can spoil and love me; if not, I'll die . . . I'm quite sick, you know? I've had a bit of a fever every night since a year ago when I came. Don't study so much," she added, looking at atlases, maps, the thick volumes open on the desks and the enormous shelves of the library; "you'll die if you go on studying like that. Look: you're going to rest by taking me around, starting tomorrow I'm locking up this old room and we'll start our outings . . ."

Said and done. As I did not want her to be seen with me, the favorite places were the outskirts of Paris, the merry little villages full of greenery, the halls of the museums, the churches furthest from downtown.

"I don't like Cluny; there's so many old gaffers, and it smells like a sacristy. What I love is Luxembourg, which has new paintings, and those pretty gardens nearby. So is this what they speak so highly of?" she asked me, looking at the very dark stone arches and the mysterious sculptures in the towers of Our Lady. "How much prettier the San Francisco is, which is new and has so much more gilding! I started to read a novel once that had the same name as this church, and I didn't read on because I didn't understand a thing. Have you heard of it? . . . I think it's by Dumas."

She came back to life with my love. She took to not wanting us to go out and spent her days enfolded in the loose pink silk negligee, looking at sanguine drawings, etchings, the steel engravings and watercolors housed in my crates; examining the cameos one by one. "Look at this painting," she said, pointing it out to me, lolling her curious gazes and swaying through the empty rooms with the listless, rhythmic languor of her delicious body, which undulated like the palms from my country in the ocean breeze. Should I have her eat something nourishing? . . . No; sweets and fruits, jam-filled little pastries, sweets, caramels, and almonds from Boisier's, and clingstone peaches and muscat grapes, which played havoc with her bluish-white teeth.

"You're going to die of anemia, Consuelo," I told her one morning in which, while both of us were seated at the dining room table, she did not want to try a chicken wing I offered her, begging her.

"Now you *know* I never eat meat. Give me black coffee; yes, and a little glass of maraschino," she continued, holding out the Sèvres glass to me and the fragile lily-shaped cup. "Tell me: I'll wager you've never thought about this. What do they have here that's as good as what we have back home? Look at the coffee, the chocolate, the pineapples, the vanilla, the emeralds, the gold, all that, which is the best, comes from our country. Do you remember the Guaymis pineapples? . . . One sends the blacks to go pick them, and they bring back heaps of them . . . Here only the millionaires and princes eat them! . . . What are you laughing at?" she asked me, seriously, upon seeing the smile I could not hold back in listening to her.

"The thought that not even princes get the women born back there," I said, alluding to her roaring with laughter at Prince Pontavento the night of the ball in which he tried to kiss her hand.

"No, those are for men who have known them since birth and spoil them like you do me. Women from here may be prettier and more elegant," she said, "but they don't know how to love. Here nobody loves anybody else. You know what the Parisian girls seem like to me? Living dolls . . . ," she added, bursting out laughing. "Do you think that any of them is able to love as we do? . . ."

Thus have nearly three months passed, in conversations like that, in *siestas* taken in the two hammocks I had hung between the two hothouse palms, in strolls from which we would return with our eyes full of color and the smell of the countryside, where we would spend the mornings strumming a mandolin that I had in my office as decoration, and fill the Paris air with the lazy songs from the land where we were born . . .

I have offered to go to San Sebastián and Biarritz, where Paco took her to see bullfights.

"Hey: we'll even hear Spanish spoken there and they won't call me Madame. We'll be happy; you'll come, won't you?"

"You've cured her for me, Pepillo! Look how rosy and fat she is . . . It was the strolls with you. I don't know how to thank you for it. If you could see the high spirits she's in now. Before, she was forever sighing. Come to San Sebastián and you'll finish the job there. Can we really expect you? Talk him into it, Consuelo," her husband told her this morning as he left us in the station, where we exchanged the last gaze and I stretched out my hand to her, for I will not feel her in my arms again for quite some time since, weary of kisses, pampering, enervations, and lasciviousness, I will leave in three weeks' time for New York to see if business American style and hard work can cure me of my *mal de vivre* and the repulsion I am feeling toward life.

18 September

So I have not left! If she returns, I will close the door on her brutally and have someone tell her husband not to let her go out alone, since he runs the risk of getting laughed at if she continues to be seen with me. Since her departure I have devoted myself to reviewing my plan conceived in Switzerland last summer in the days in which I lived on the steep peak where not even the noise from the human pack of rotters could reach me. My senses calmed by the excesses of the past months, I have gone back to living the true life and to feeling that my wings are growing back, which had been cut off by the three Delilahs: the reader of Nietzsche, the sensual Roman, and my lazy, sentimental friend, who has not read, thank God, any books that would take away from her soul the perfume of simplicity that makes her adorable.

She is a dim little soul, thoughtless and fresh, who preserves all her scent of undergrowth and nests and roses like Guaymis parasites, like the pink orchids that I gave her the evening on which I kissed her for the first time!

1 October

Camilo Monteverde, my first cousin, who is in Paris now, and I have never spoken of art. In literature he is stuck back in the naturalism of Zola, which is for him the supreme school. He knows I consider him fourth rate as a sculptor, in spite of the fame he enjoys in my country, and he does not understand my poetry, by his own confession. "That is music of the future, pure Wagner," he tells me when he reads anything of mine. "In my opinion Spain's top contemporary poet is Campoamor[164] . . . he is clear and I understand him . . ."

We never speak of art. We speak of ourselves, or rather, he speaks of himself and of me, given the type of modesty that prevents me from letting him see certain ways of feeling that I have, at which he would laugh. On the other hand, he overdoes his cynicism a bit; when he confides in me, he takes *la pose canaille*,[165] as a painter would say, and he shows me a very different character than the one the public knows and very like the one Luis Montes describes, who despises him and hates him vehemently and does not even acknowledge his good points.

"Are you always hunting the bluebird?" he said to me the other day in the smoking room. "I've got a thousand dollars that says you're in love platonically and that everything I've seen in your house you've bought and paid for."

"I don't know another way to acquire what one wants," I said to him. "Have you found another?"

"I should say I have; one has it given to him and he takes it away with him. Here in Paris my procedure must be difficult; but in my country it has worked famously. All the tapestries, the old furniture, the weapons and paintings that I have came out of convents and churches. How, you ask? Well, doing such vile deeds to get them; saying such things about them, that their owner, an old-timer who knew one as a boy, or a boy who admires one and wishes to please him, after little thought sends the painting, the bronze, the historical object, telling himself: 'This doesn't look that good here, and besides Monteverde will consider it a gift from me . . .' Is it that you're not practical? . . ." he continued after a silence and as if thinking out loud. "You are excited by things, you fall in love with women, you do foolish things for them, you have manias for work and knowledge. What has your life been up till now? . . . A hunt for the bluebird . . . Look: the secret is, with the least possible effort achieve the greatest possible results, virtually without lifting a finger and by means of the imbecility of other men and women, of the adulation of those who do not expect it and of insolence toward those who do. Thus does everything begin to rain down on a person from heaven: friends, fame, money, and women. Women!" he continued in his monologue, draining in long draughts a large glass of whisky he had poured himself; "women! all of them incoherent: George Sand and Cora Pearl,[166] Sarah Bernhardt and Joan of Arc; all charming, all disgusting, and all women! Do you know Rousselot's tavern in Montmartre? . . . Why would you go there! . . . You, the dreamer of aristocratic utopias! . . ."

"So why do you ask if I know it?" I asked, laughing . . .

"Because before last night I found a wonder there, one of the girls who sells the beer. She's charmingly stupid and stupidly charming. You don't know anything about that. You go around dreaming always of some Dulcinea, like the Knight of the Woeful Countenance; I am more practical . . . We two are from the same tree, the Andrades of old, you know? . . . with two different grafts, yours Don Quixote . . . and mine Sancho; you go off tilting at windmills, freeing the prisoners, putting on the Mambrino helmet and looking for the wizard Merlin . . . Tell me you don't spend your life reading books of chivalry . . ."

Thus does he call all those who are a bit abstruse in science, psychological in novels, long-winded in poetry, subtle and personal in criticism.

"I'm leaving now for Normandy to buy some cows; then I'll go to England to pick up some Durham bulls. Do you believe in my passion for art? . . . I don't give a damn about sculpture. Come with me to England."

"I can't," I said to him. "I have a lot to do."

"You've got a lot to do, living in Paris, and at twenty-six, with your millions? . . . Well, then, you're beyond all hope . . ."

Monteverde is a practical man, no question about it.

In the isolation in which I have lived during these weeks, all recent memories have become hazy around me, and the image of Helen has been reviving until it has been more vivid than ever. Yesterday, as I opened the door to the room where the portraits are, the door, whose key only I have and which I had not used again since my encounter with Nelly, a strange, nauseating odor prevented me from entering. The evening was dark, and the somber hue of the cordovan leather that covers the walls increased the darkness of the room. I could make out in it only the whiteness of the tunic and the cloak, standing out against the somber background.

I returned with slow steps, preceded by Francisco, who entered with the candles of a candelabrum lit to light my way. The nauseating odor was that of the last flowers ordered from Cannes, which, when they decomposed, had putrefied the water in the vases. It smelled of the tomb, and the many dry leaves and petals, little black bouquets, some with hard calyxes and wizened like mummies, others rotted by humidity, lay in the Murano flower vases and in the jardinières on the dust-covered marble tabletop; the roses, detached from their stems and practically black, suggested a flower cemetery.

The servant opened the terrace to freshen up the stale air. Through it came in the diffuse light of the violaceous and copper-colored dusk, and the cold drizzle, which shook the curtains melancholically. A ray of sun shone on the frame of the portrait of the saint with the long white hair, and I shivered when I felt an icy gust of the autumn wind.

On the malachite candlesticks the dust obscured the greenness of the stone, and some dead flies spread their inert little wings and their stiff feet. The dust and the flies had spotted the white morocco and the gilt of the books I bought in London last winter; and in the double light of the candles in the candelabrum and that of the dusk, which filtered its cold dreariness in through the terrace, the colors of the Oriental carpets that cover the floor looked faded and shabby.

My soul at that moment was gloomier than the abandoned room and more withered than the flowers. The pitiful specked books have wound up in my library, and the heavy iron jewel box, in my study. The copy of Rivington's painting and the portrait painted by Whistler are in my bedroom. I sleep under the gazes of the saint with the long silver hair and the figure who holds in her hands the bunch of white lilies, and I sometimes think that, if the two oils had always been on the dark tapestry covering the walls, neither Nelly, nor Rivas's wife, nor Lady Musellaro, nor Olga would have come into my life, or my bedroom.

25 October

These have been ten days of mad activity, with nothing to show for it. For five days there has been an employee of mine in each of the European capitals, with nothing else to do but scour the hotels and telegraph me. Through Marinoni and under the pretext of very important business I have gotten the Charnoz agency to transmit to its correspondents worldwide the name of Scilly for them to inquire after him, and I pass the time in my office, awaiting, minute by minute, the arrival of the telegraphic communications or of the telegrams. A vain undertaking; a vain undertaking, and nevertheless I have the certainty of finding her and that some day, when I tell her of my impatience during this time, her blue eyes will have a sweeter glow when they look at me and her slightly pink lips will smile, giving life with that smile to the unearthly bloodless pallor of her cheeks, framed in her curly, untamed auburn hair, which has golden glimmers where the light hits it!

Helen! Helen! Today it is not the grotesque fear of mental imbalance, as it was when I wrote of the ridiculous analyses in London, that makes me call on you to ask you to save me. It is an unearthly love that rises toward you like a flame where all the impurities of my life have fused. All the strength of my spirit, all the powers of my soul turn to you like the magnetic needle to the unseen magnet prevailing on it . . . Where are you? . . . Arise, appear. You are my last belief and my last hope. If I find you, my life will be something like a glorious ascension toward the infinite light; if my desire is for naught and my toil fruitless, when the supreme hour tolls in which my eyes are closed forever, my being, mysterious composite of fire and mud, ecstasy and moans, will be undone in the fathomless darkness of the tomb.

16 January

I spent ten days out of my head. The first thing I saw when I opened my eyes, in the shadow of the velvet curtains of the bed and in the artificial half-light of the bedroom, was Charvet's giant head leaning over mine. He sank in my half-opened eyes his sharp, penetrating gaze, and had his eyes so close to mine that I could distinguish each of his grey lashes.

"You recognize me, Fernández?"

"Yes, Doctor," I managed to articulate in a weak voice.

"He's recovered!" I heard him say, and when I closed my eyes again to sink into a heavy lethargy, I glimpsed the heads of two women who were whispering in the shadows.

Then, nothing, not the least thought, not the least image crossing the unconsciousness in which I was plunged. From time to time some hands that would lift my head up, the light from a candle, the gleam of a silver spoon, and the taste of a drug that burned my throat; sometimes a pain that crossed my head from temple to temple, and incessantly, the sensation of falling, like a rock through the blackness of a starless night.

When my whole body started hurting as if bruised and wounded, and the external sensations were increasing, I complained like a child and flailed like a man possessed to avoid taking the spoonfuls.

"There's the recovery now; he's coming back," Charvet's caressing voice said. "His will has returned. He has an iron constitution!"

"My friend," he said to me the first day on which, after a long, long dream and feeling alive upon waking, I attempted to move. "You have diseases that could disconcert the man most secure in his knowledge. You have been between life and death; there was a moment in which your heart was so weak that, with my ear pressed to it, I awaited the final beats, and in which your temperature dropped a degree and a half below normal. Now your heart is working well and your temperature indicates a mild fever. It was the same faint as a year ago, but much more serious. You are in the same state as you were then, as if you had had a copious hemorrhage. We have to draw blood, my friend! . . ."

And I had blood drawn, as he says, in my convalescence, which has seemed speedy to him and endless to me, for I did not see the day when I would regain movement; my youth and the drive of my organization, assisted by his learned suggestions, triumphed over the horrible faint-ness in which vertigo left me.

I have just now passed by the hotel, which is vacant, completely vacant, with the walls and floors bare. My steps echo in the deserted rooms, which seem larger for want of furniture. All of it, lit by the cold winter sun, has the desolation of the places where we lived, leaving be-hind something of ourselves, and that we will never see again. Tomorrow another will come and live between its four walls, perhaps one who is less unfortunate than the one who is leaving it.

Furniture and objets d'art, horses and carriages, the whole lavish train that was like the decoration in which I moved in these years of life on the old continent, all await me now in the steamship, which at daybreak will begin to cruise the green waves of the vast Atlantic to drop anchor in the bay, where, electric torch in hand, the Statue of Liberty, modeled by Bartholdi, stands tall.

I am going to ask of common commercial operations and of the incessant employment of my material activities what neither love nor art could give me: the secret of enduring life, which would be impossible in the place where, under the earth, a part of my soul has remained. The carriage that will take me to the station to take the train that will separate me from Paris forever, will first go to the place where I spent the mornings on my last days.

When I got there on 28 October, on a damp, intemperate after-noon, Marinoni went off, begging me to wait for him a few moments. Surely he wanted to be alone to commemorate the anniversary. I walked a few steps, and as I felt the wet ground, I stopped under the branches of a tree, near a column whose inscription was partly worn away by the years and the rain. I ran my gaze along the coppery horizon, on which, like the perforations of a piece of lace, the treetops at the entrance, shaken by the wind, cut out their delicate black shapes. Away in the distance, amidst the shadows that began to engulf the countryside, gilded by a ray of sun, shone the cupola of Les Invalides. Above the city, the nebulous black masses of the towers of Our Lady stood out, and the copper-colored sky was reflected in the river's current.

As I lowered my eyes toward the ground carpeted in wilted leaves, whose melancholic odor I was inhaling in the desolation of the landscape, my gazes chanced on a branch that hung, broken, from the neighboring rosebush and whose three leaves were grouped in the same arrangement as that in which Helen's cameo has them.

A white butterfly paused above them an instant, and taking flight, came and touched my brow.

Upon seeing it, I was overwhelmed by the superstitious terror that seized me when I saw the other one rise up out of the bouquet of white roses, in Constanza Landseer's bedroom; my nerves were set on end by the memory of the nightmare in London, in which, falling toward the pit of a black abyss, I saw three leaves of a branch and the fluttering of a white butterfly against the blue clarity of the sky, high, high above; and as I recalled the horrible dream, a nameless anxiety, a sensation of irrational and unbearable fear, made my legs go slack and robbed me of my strength. I realized I was going to fall in that instant, there in the mud, and die of the same malady that felled me on the boulevard the last night of the previous year, as the flywheel stopped and the golden clock-hands met on the alabaster dial. The twelve deafening tolls that I heard that night began to echo in my ears. Turning around to find a place to hold myself up on the monument behind me, and closing my eyes, I managed to clutch the low iron railing and the pilaster that formed the corner. I fell to my knees, holding myself up with my right hand on the ground and grabbing with my left the cold metal railing. The fainting fit was passing and the sense of terror abating. Finally, I opened my eyes. I saw white; I made a dreadful attempt to pick myself up and, now standing, grabbing hold of the balustrade, closed my eyes again instantly, for I felt that the dizziness was coming back. Suddenly I gave a cry of terror. I had felt some hands that were resting on my shoulders. I turned my head around. It was Marinoni, who had returned and grabbed me from behind.

"What's the matter?" he asked me, frightened.

"Vertigo . . ." I succeeded in answering.

"Stay still; let it pass; I've got you so you don't fall," he said, and he held me up with his whole body . . . "Let go of the railing; that's it; put your weight on me. Stay still . . ."

"It's gone," I said as I felt the anguish subside gradually, and I raised my head. As I did, I read the black inscription on the white marble inside the railing; I gave another cry, which resounded throughout the cemetery, and collapsed.

From then until my waking up in the bedroom with my head propped up on the big pillows and Charvet's eyes fixed on mine, I have no memory.

Twelve days ago I went out for the first time to go to the cemetery, where I have later returned every morning to cover with flowers the tombstone that bears her name and states the time and date of her death. It is the final hour of the year, in which I was in the death-throes of anguish in front of the black marble clock, watching the golden clock-hands meet to mark the supreme minute on the alabaster dial, after which I thought I felt the Unknown was going to reveal itself to me. The time for the train is nearing. I hear the sound of the carriage stopping in front of the hotel door.

It is coming to fetch me to take the last flowers I shall place on her tomb.

Her tomb? Dead, you? . . . You, turned to flesh that rots and that the worms will eat? . . . You, turned into a black little skeleton that decomposes? No, you have not died; you are alive and will live always, Helen, to enhance the mystical delirium of dying grandmothers, tossing into the soul of the atheist poets, darkened by the orgies of the flesh, the pale bouquet of roses, and to make the sign of salvation with your tapered fingers and your alabastrine hands.

You, dead? Never! You are making your way through the world with the gentle grace of your virginal contours, your pallid face, whose deathly bloodless pallor lights your blue eyes and frames the unruly hair that falls in dark curls over your shoulders.

You, dead, Helen? . . . No, you cannot die. Perhaps you never have existed and you are but a luminous dream of my spirit; but you are a dream more real than what men call Reality. What they call thus is but a dark mask behind which the eyes of mystery loom up and look out, and you are Mystery itself.

José Fernández, as he broke off the reading, closed the book bound in black morocco, and adjusting its golden keyhole with a nervous hand, placed it on the table.

The four friends stayed silent, an absolute silence in which could be heard the oscillations of the pendulum in the old hall clock, the whisper of the rain, which shook the thick branches of the trees in the garden, the mournful moan of the wind, and the fluttering of the dry leaves against the terrace windows.

The crimson semidarkness of the room grew drowsy. The tenuous smoke from the Oriental cigarette curled in subtle spirals in the circle of lamplight, dimmed by the old lace lampshade. The fragile china cups were whitened against the blood-red velvet of the rug, and in the bottom of the cut-crystal bottle, amidst the transparency of the Goldwasser, the gold-leaf particles stirred, dancing all in a luminous ring, as fantastic as a fairy tale.

NOTES

1. The first critical article was probably Jorge Zalamea's relating of José Fernández to Dorian Gray, Des Esseintes, and (Lorraine's) Phocas (Orjuela, *De sobremesa*, 13). But it was Juan Loveluck who "salvaged" the work in the 1960s with his article on the "lost novel" of modernismo. Another major early study was Hector H. Orjuela's *De sobremesa y otros estudios sobre José Asunción Silva* in 1976. It was not until the 1990s, particularly the latter half, that the work saw a thoroughgoing renaissance in the criticism, which continues unabated.

The first edition of *Precursores del Modernismo* (Calpe: Madrid, 1925) by Torres-Ríoseco already begins the tradition of unproblematically equating Silva with the implied author, calling the work the Colombian's "spiritual biography." Countless authors would follow suit, incurring the fallacy of attributing to Silva (the "alter ego" or mouthpiece for) Fernández's asystematic theories and even contradictions. As an almost arbitrary example, the Editorial Sopena Argentina edition of 1941 features an introduction called "Poeta yo!" ("I, a Poet?!"), the very scene in which Fernández rejects his eligibility to be called by the same name as the immortals; the prologue, however, is not sourced, and is attributed to Silva.

2. Allegedly the fragments of the original text were salvaged (See Cobo-Borda, *El bogotano universal*).

3. For Silva's principal life events, see Camacho Guizado, 282–313, and appendix to Fernando Charry Lara. I am also relying on Miramón's early *José Asunción Silva*, which addresses the earliest biographies. See also the three major modern studies of his life: Cano Gaviria's, Orjuela's, and Santos Molano's. The best compilation of bibliographical secondary sources is Jaramillo Zuluaga's "Bibliografía cronológica de José Asunción

Silva (1871–1996)," available at *www.banrep.gov.co/blaavirtual/letra-c/ csilva/silva/bibliogr.htm*. See also Cobo Borda, *El coloquio americano*, 34– 41. I refer the interested reader also to *José Asunción Silva: Cartas* and *Páginas nuevas*. All translations in the introduction are the translator's, unless otherwise noted.

4. Roll call according to D. Arias Argáez (Camacho Guizado, 304).

5. For any student of *After-Dinner Conversation,* this loss is particularly acute: this theme of will and energy permeates the novel (see *homo economicus* section). We could offer passages of the novel as attempts on Silva's part to recover or rework these ideas, but it would not go beyond mere speculation.

6. Miramón cites five lost novels apart from *De sobremesa* (hereafter referred to as *After-Dinner Conversation*) (256).

7. This literary transformation of insanity supports the argument later in the introduction that insanity is a prestige ailment for the artist, and reacting to it a ritualized pose.

8. *Obra completa* 100. It may be worth observing that Leonardo is the anti-type of the Decadent.

9. For more on Silva's finances, and the influence they had on his work, see Camilo de Brigard Silva.

10. The best introduction to the early "machine aesthetic," the changes of the first decades of the twentieth century, is surely Marshall Berman's *All That Is Solid Melts into Air,* which includes Marx's critiques of the startling coexistence of industry and decay at the root of capitalist culture. For *modernismo,* see Jrade.

11. Cytherea. Island associated with Aphrodite.

12. The settings in the novel, then, depend on ideas about them; the *sobremesa* occurs in a place ostensibly of deprivation (recollection), the search in a place ostensibly of fulfillment (Paris's plenitude and stimulation); neither is "real": the "perpetual desire" is exacerbated in part by this environment. See Guerrieri, who shows how London is figured in the novel as a dark counterpoint to modernity, depicting the suffering underclass.

13. Aníbal González makes much of the novel's recollection of the *Symposium.*

14. See Phillipps-López for more on the novel as diary.

15. While the artist-hero Fernández wilfully does not write poetry, he cannot help but testimonialize his impressions in the diary form.

16. Henri Frédéric Amiel (1821–1881). Swiss writer famous for his self-analytical *Journal intime.*

17. A study of the "superfluous man" (*lishni chelovek*), a stock figure

in the Russian literature of the day, might reveal commonalities in the psychological dilemmas then characterized in the verbal arts. Much like Fernández, the superfluous man cannot act concertedly; he is trapped in his idealism. Cuddon (933) notes Turgenev's employment of the figure as "a compound of Hamlet and Don Quixote, unable to reconcile the impulses of heart and head, given to over-much introspection, intellectualizing and indecision." Both Hamlet and Don Quixote are referenced quite pointedly in Silva's novel.

18. Implied are the Platonic orders of archetype and copy; searching for "not its semblance but itself," in Browning's phrase, Fernández achieves only the artificial Helen. Yet one may advance the argument that *it is precisely—and only—art that is salvational* in the novel; the cameo, for example, serves as an amulet or charm—virtually a relic in religious terms.

19. A few words on dandyism. Dandyism is akin to Decadence; in Baudelaire's words, it is "like a setting sun; like the declining star, it is magnificent, without heat and full of melancholy" (Baudelaire, *Selected Writings*, 421–422, cited in St. John, 215). It is a "heroic" stance *in opposition*, man in open revolt. (By *man* I have to mean "man" instead of "humankind" here; Baudelaire explicitly defined woman as natural, and therefore abhorrent, an "anti-dandy." The misogyny of this stance is apparent in representations of women in art of the period, a well-studied aspect of the era. In Silva's case, there is a double dehumanization of Woman working in the novel: the idealized, etherealized woman on the one hand, and the "prey," or "carnalized" woman on the other. Moreover, in the dandy's values and in his aloofness he reflects an attitude "close to spirituality and to stoicism" [Baudelaire 420, cited in St. John 220].) For more on the dandy, particularly his relationship to modernity, see Habermas (10), Boym (66–69), Adams, and Glick.

20. Bourget was the author of the landmark *Essais de Psychologie Contemporaine* (1883). I have seen this description of Decadence erroneously attributed to Havelock Ellis, who translated Bourget some decades later.

21. We can take this idea even further and suggest that every reference in *After-Dinner Conversation* is a kind of digression, pointing to another text and derailing any horizon of expectation. Too, many of the names are ornamental, and many too are shibboleths, passwords that test, while asserting, affiliation. In this sense Decadent works are self-consciously historical, and polemically so.

22. This schema bears a striking resemblance to the stages which Nietzsche outlines in explaining "How the 'Real World' at last became

a Myth," in *Twilight of the Gods* (Watson, 208n15). See also chapter xix in Gordon. Lacan could also be useful in reading the bibelot. Aching's chapter on the "Reino interior" ("kingdom within") is apropos here, though the book avoids all mention of Silva.

23. In context, *recogida* is also "focused" or "collected," a key topos of concentration (versus dispersal) in the novel. Consistent with the photographic reading, *recoger* is also used to describe an instantaneous capturing, as with a photographic impression. The first image of the novel is of light, appearance, and the visible/invisible; the final (virtual) image—"fantastic as a fairy tale"—is an appeal to an inner visual, the mind's eye: fantastic (*phantastikós,* able to show to the mind; *phantázein,* to make visible; *phanós,* light, bright). By contrast, almost immediately the narrator begins fragmenting—we see parts of actions, even parts of bodies ("A man's hand ran along . . .").

24. See Moreno-Durán, 57–58, in the parallels he draws to *Axel.*

25. See Serrano Orejuela ("Silva destornillado . . .") who takes the novelist to task for his disillusioned ("spoilsport") rereading of Silva.

26. See Poe, "The Philosophy of Furniture," wherein he discusses the ideal composition of a room.

27. Rachilde was the pen name of Marguerite Eymery (1860–1953), a prolific French transvestite writer. Jullian does not note the source of the excerpt, though *Monsieur Vénus, La Jongleuse,* or *La Marquise de Sade* are possibilities.

28. It is a misconception that *After-Dinner Conversation* is a novel of aristocratic scenes; Silva even uses contrasts to create painterly grotesques as well.

29. Serrano Orejuela ("Narración, discurso . . .") addresses time, but more as it intersects with diagetics and planes of experience.

30. Jullian (113), while allowing that the "mauve nineties" wandered into both Lesbos and Sodom, points out that they did so only with circumspection; those who did not—Wilde, Mendès—paid the price: ostracism.

31. See also Giorgi on this score.

32. The point of interest is perhaps, as Jaramillo Zuluaga notes, that Fernández inhabits a mutually acceptable space of the law-giver power position (money and politics) and the bohemian (travel and art) (48).

33. Notes on Edgar Allan Poe: José Asunción Silva had internalized many of Poe's structures in his poems, his musicality, and his poetic theory; this has been shown more-or-less amply in Englekirk (1934). This author mentions speculation, not his own, that Silva even translated Poe, though there is no evidence. He mentions the inevitable "death of

a beautiful woman" motif (214) that has its echo in Poe, although arguably Silva detains himself very briefly on Helen's demise; the action of
the work revolves around the *search* for her. Silva's affinity for Baudelaire
would be enough to suggest a connection to Poe, this author argues. As
for *After-Dinner Conversation,* he sees little in the way of direct influence,
although the settings of "Usher" and "Ligeia" seem to him to have had
an impact on the opening of Silva's novel, as well as the creation of
Helen, in particular her *ojos dominadores* ("overmastering eyes") (220).
He suggests a relationship—not causal, necessarily—between Silva's
poem "Estrellas fijas" ("Fixed Stars") and Poe's "To Helen" (presented
below) and Becquer's Rimas XIII and XIV.

Many, however, completely overlook Poe's influence on *After-
Dinner Conversation.* Only Smith discusses Silva's affinity with Poe's
claustrophobic scenes and spectral horror (100–104). Speculatively, let
us consider Poe's possible effect on Fernández's creation of Helen.

Villanueva-Collado ("La funesta Helena . . ." 69) has identified Mallarmé's note on Poe (in the latter's *Oeuvres Completes* [Paris: Bibliothèque
de la Pleiade, 1945]) explaining the origin of the poem "Estrofas a Helena," which likely is the second of two poems titled "To Helen." The first
of these dates from 1831. The longer "To Helen" (1848) finds still more
convergences with *After-Dinner Conversation*: the protagonist anguishes
over having seen his beloved once, only to be left in her absence with
her luminous eyes for guides; the apparition takes place in summer (July
in Poe, August in Silva); the notion of salvation ("saving") via Woman;
the enchanted-garden setting; the division of spheres of action into ter-
restrial and supernal, their degree of mutual (in)accessibility forming
the crisis. Here, then, are excerpts:

TO HELEN

I saw thee once—once only—years ago:
. . .
What wild heart-histories seemed to lie enwritten
Upon those crystalline, celestial spheres!
. . .
And thou, a ghost, amid the entombing trees
Didst glide away. *Only thine eyes remained.*
They *would not* go—they never yet have gone.
Lighting my lonely pathway home that night,
They have not left me (as my hopes have) since.
They follow me—they lead me through the years.

They are my ministers—yet I their slave.
Their office is to illumine and enkindle—
My duty, *to be saved* by their bright light,
. . .

They fill my soul with Beauty (which is Hope),
. . .

[The Poems, 16–18]

In the final lines she has acquired a reality "unextinguished by the sun"—in other words, she holds up to reason (the light of day); similarly, in the final lines of Silva's novel, Fernández denies Helen's death, declaring her undying, superreal, inhabiting a higher existence. Both are kinds of apotheosis.

34. See Ortega (90) for more on the gaze as organizing principle. The author recommends a Lacanian reading.

35. These three novels, or novellas, engage the issues of modern alienation and abnormal psychology. *El pozo* ("The Pit") is a cameo portrait of angst equal to that of any of the Existentialist novels. *El túnel* ("The Tunnel") explores dementia, nothingness and meaninglessness, incommunication, and the psychology of crime and punishment. Like *After-Dinner Conversation,* it significantly involves a painting and the real-life effects of its interpretation, or rather, the interpenetration of art and life. *La tregua* ("The Truce") is a meditation on God, women, and the existential experience of time and solitude.

36. This same critic (*Quimera,* 44) sees Eduardo Mallea's *La bahía del silencio* (*The Bay of Silence*) as the descendent of the novel of the "spiritual aristocrat" and artist.

37. "For spiritual consolations overcome all delights of the world and the voluptuosity of the flesh. For all earthly things are vain or vile" (translation mine). In the conclusion to his "Carta abierta" ("Open Letter"), Silva describes these versicles from the *Imitatio* as consolatory. In that final passage of the short prose piece, which seems to be of the exact tenor of *After-Dinner Conversation,* the narrator admits to "worldly temptations" and enumerates the train of regal distractions that assail him. Finally he is brought to inner peace, cured of "spiritual aridity by my lay confessor, an old psychologist who has in his cell, as its only adornment, a copy of Dürer's *Melancholy.* . . ." See "Carta abierta," *http://rehue.csociales.uchile.cl/rehuehome/facultad/publicaciones/autores/silva/jasilv12.htm,* p. 2.

38. Ingwersen has unproblematically attempted to show Alan Kardec's profound influence on Silva. The Colombian, however, is ambivalent on the pseudosciences; here he mocks them, claiming authen-

ticity in the ancient cults, but elsewhere he deploys them as if finding some worth in them.

39. Villanueva-Collado pioneered readings of the book's spiritual-symbolic repertoire in several articles. See also Marún.

40. Note treatments of this topic in the poem "A un ateo" ("To an Atheist"), which relates the redemption of a sinner, and the recently discovered poem originally from *Gotas amargas*, "Puntos de vista" ("Points of View"). In the latter, an atheist patient dies in the arms of a doctor and a priest. He converts in his final minutes. The priest notes the conversion triumphantly in his notebook. The doctor in his own book writes: "The patient has been out of his head since yesterday at two."

41. One could argue that desire in itself, while not an earthly sin, is a purely secular value, in contradistinction to renunciation and humility. Note that Fernández reacts largely to Barrès's treatment of Bashkirtseff, rather than the diary; the Frenchman called her "Notre-Dame qui n'êtes jamais satisfaite" ("Our Lady of Eternal Insatiety") (Meyer-Minnemann, 60).

42. Canto XXX of the Purgatorio contains many of the outlines of Fernández's relationship to Helen. For example, the mother/child motif, the lowered gaze in shame, penitence, and the deviation of reverence to pleasures of the world: "And into ways untrue he turned his steps. / Pursuing the false images of good, / That never any promises fulfil." http://www.kalliope.org/digt.pl?longdid=longfellow2001081464 (Translation by Henry Wadsworth Longfellow.) Zuleta (125), stressing the death-of-God theme in Silva's novel, argues that Helen is the ultimate belief, there being no God behind her as there is behind Beatrice.

43. Another apparent contradiction, since his hero, Sir John Rivington, is the author of such works as *Natural Causes of Supernatural Appearances*.

44. See Jrade's careful and nuanced discussion of the ambiguity of the Nietzschean passages, and of Fernández's problematic relationship with the masses' access to a freedom born of Zarathustrian self-creation (59–63).

45. Fernández is a reader of Loyola and of the mystic Fray Luis de León.

46. Chapter XXXIII of Pater's *Marius the Epicurian*, "Anima Naturaliter Christiana," depicts the antiheroic: "In his case, at least, the Martyrdom, as it was called—the overpowering act of testimony that Heaven had come down among men—would be but a common execution: from the drops of his blood there would spring no miraculous poetic flowers . . ." (261).

47. For the phenomena of "hyperaesthesia" and neurasthenia, see Greenslade.

48. Among them, in Navarro. See the excellent background on Modernism in Karl, chapter 3. See also G. B. Shaw's refutation of Nordau's school.

49. "Charcot, Jean Martin (1825–1893). French physician who studied hypnotism in relation to hysteria. . . . He was responsible for notable researches in the fields of muscular disease and mental disturbance. His work . . . marks the serious medical and scientific study of the phenomenon of hypnotism in place of the earlier occult connotations of Mesmerism" (Shepard, 36). Silva attended his lectures while living in Paris.

50. See also chapter 5, "Madness as a Goal," in Feder.

51. The grotesque is typified by disharmony; for instance, the irresolution of Fernández's death wish with the erotic or pleasure impulse. Freud's *Beyond the Pleasure Principle* could most certainly offer a framework for these impulses.

52. Even in the novel, Fernández inspires the admiration and disgust of secondary characters in equal measure.

53. Principally Villanueva-Collado, Navarro Marín, and Giorgi.

54. One could speak of "French" nerves, "bad nerves," etc.; hypochondria and hysteria began to be demarcated as gender differences marked by the nerves (although later, by the nineteenth century, hysteria, which was tied to repression of emotions, was attributed to men as well as women); further, "the 'otherness' . . . of women was now newly attributed to a defect—discursively represented as an inherent weakness, a lingering form of exhaustion, a fundamental lack of tonic vigour—in female nerves and fibres" (Rousseau, 222). Indeed the whole patriarchy of discourse lay in this differentiation of the strength of nerves. The Decadent, then, is a feminized male, made "other" by inherited nerves aggravated by study.

55. See Rousseau, 224.

56. Consider not only the previous illnesses—spleen and the like—but modern ones such as "stress," which likely will be studied a century hence as an indicator of late-twentieth-century lifestyle, anxieties, desires, and urban realities.

57. Cf. Baudelaire: "Le savant qui lui fait de l'or n'a jamais pu / De son être extirper l'elément corrompu" ("The alchemist who brews him gold has failed / to purge the impure substance from his soul" ["Spleen (III)," trans. Richard Howard]). Note the overlapping semantic fields (alchemy/medicine).

58. See discussion of hands in Aching, chapter 5.

59. Villanueva-Collado ("Gender Ideology . . . ," 113–125) stresses the emasculating effect of art on the protagonist's status—thought is conceived as inaction, and therefore is associated with unmanliness. Similarly, Amiel, in *Philine*, during a bout of chastity, feeling the "lure of voluptuousness," writes of his retreat from the useful in terms of a "sterilization":

> . . . the horror of decisive action, the agonies of the imagination which destroy the real through the image of the possible, everything [sic] combines to deprive me of the strength demanded in the present instance. I am never at grips with reality, never serious, aroused, willing, possessing. Hence my moral impotence. . . . Desire and will characterise males; I seem to have lost my sex.

60. It is just this will to power that Machado de Assis satirizes in "O Alienista" ("The Psychiatrist"). In this classic Foucaultian work, the naming function, diagnosis, is linked to political power and its abuses; the Brazilian's contemporary novella sends up the ideology of stigmatization, and questions, as Sontag would, and as the Decadents exploited, the identification of illness with criminality or immorality.

61. See also Burton's *Anatomy of Melancholy;* Julia Kristeva's *Black Sun*.

62. The topos of nature-as-curative is to be found especially in his early poems, such as "A una enferma" ("To a Sick Girl") (*Poesía completa,* 215).

63. The mystery of diagnosis takes Silva (and Fernández) not only into the "over-naming" by specialists but also into the topos of the *nameless malady*. The poem "Psicopatía" ("Psychopathy"), for example, features an innocent child asking her doctor father what ill a certain man—the narrator—suffers. The reply: the disease of thought, "curable" only by death.

64. For a discussion of "elitist consumption" see Rosalind Williams.

65. Angel Rama describes the growing, but still limited, possibilities for the writer to gain exchange value for his work, though the latter may suffer an improvisational hurriedness, while the writer himself is torn over a lack of time, transformation into a consumer, or lack of specialization (284, cited in Loveluck, *La novela,* 229–234). Fernández's production is not affected by the exigencies of the market; Silva's, however, decidedly was. García Márquez draws the important contrast that Silva could never have afforded Fernández's vices or indulgences—in money or time (28).

66. I am using this term as an alternative to *equivalents*, which has become fraught with misunderstandings.

67. The modern terms are used here, traceable most directly perhaps to Friedrich Schleiermacher. Cf. Goethe's *Oration in Memory of Wieland* (1813).

68. By *strangeness* I mean *ostranenie*, the Russian Formalist term. The strange word heightens effect by calling attention to language (which, as Jakobson reminds us, is the very hallmark of poetic language).

69. I find the image of translator as actor to be useful. Better still would be translator as dramaturge, insofar as research into a role authenticates a performance.

70. In Leppihalme's discussion (113), defenders (footnotes as marks of a "democracy of knowledge"; Oksala 1990: 94) and detractors (heavy notes can turn literature into "an ethnographic source-book"; Dagut 1987: 80) must, she argues, consider the function of the target text, usually a weighing of what role entertainment plays versus instruction for the readers of the fictional work. (Recall from the epigraph to this study: "The reader no longer asks of a work that it amuse him . . .") Pater's *Marius the Epicurian* (Oxford ed.), incidentally, has 266 explanatory notes.

71. Silva himself performed some excellent transpositions and translations, which apparently have not been studied systematically.

72. It is the rare translator, of any stripe, who does not use the word *preserve* at some point in discussing his or her aims. This is, however, a mere figure, since *preserving*, literally speaking, would mean *not translating*. To say "I have striven to preserve x, y, or z" would mean keeping the source verbatim. What one means is "reproduce," "reconstitute," "re-figure"—in essence, re-write.

73. I am not of the school that believes translation alienates interest in the source language; on the contrary, a translation advertises its intertext (archetext); if that plays on the superstition that the source text is truer and better, so much the better for the source. In such cases the translation is a favorable book review for it. Furthermore, fetishizing the uniqueness of a language by disparaging translation as deforming (Schopenhauer et al.) misses a number of points.

74. A writer can and does become "strange" or "estranged" in translation; translation can activate features of a writer that his or her own language left latent. Also, if critics are key to making reputations, why should not translators also be part of creating literary identity? If "the death of the author" implies a new life in the text, translations are that life, and the author will die many deaths. To coin a ghoulish image,

the translated text is the lost soul, or the text in search of its author; as J. Hillis Miller has it, "Translation is the wandering existence of a text in a perpetual exile" (Devy, 182).

75. With the exaltation of the Author has come the necessary repudiation of the Translator.

76. The English translation was based on the Hiperión edition, Madrid, 1996.

77. I believe as of this writing that the importance of making allowances for this feature escaped me; I rendered this phrase as "blood" in the text to avoid awkwardness, but this may be an undertranslation. On other occasions, I have maintained even absurdly marked medical discourse (e.g., Paris, 26 December, ". . . the horrible impression that sends an icy sweat down your temples and *chokes your epigastrium . . .*") (emphasis mine).

78. The word *carnal* in English has the feeling of sin, which is perfectly appropriate as well.

79. Doubly anachronistic—in our era and in the 1890s.

NOTES TO THE TEXT

1. García Márquez judges this name to be a poor choice (26). In fact, we might contend, it is perfectly *nondescript,* suggesting—wittingly or not on Silva's part—that the Decadent hero is nameless to the world. His dissolution, his inability to act concentratedly, all divest him of individuality, of a name.

2. Note that nothing "happens" until the promise of a *sobremesa* is attended to. Artistic impotence for the writer is manifested, or prefigured, as *textual inertia.* Inaction is one of the major leitmotifs of the work.

3. Italian: "fully lit," as daylight.

4. An aromatic Hungarian wine made from Furmint grapes.

5. Disciplinarian doctor in Miguel de Cervantes's *Don Quixote* who ministers to Sancho Panza (Chap. 47) while the squire governs his own island. *Recio* means hard, robust, or stupid; "Tirteafuera" likely is an instance of antonomasia (proper name for a quality) or antanaclasis (homonymic pun) from *tirarte afuera,* "to throw you out." The name is meant jocularly here to convey censure.

6. Worth, Charles Frederick (1825–1895), Parisian dress designer. Born in England, he was a powerful arbiter of women's fashion well into the second half of the nineteenth century.

7. According to Richard Milner's *Encyclopedia of Evolution* (New York: Facts on File, 1990, 341), orchids were the rage in England in the

mid-1800s, and collectors—before anyone knew how to grow the flower from seeds—ventured into uncharted regions for the sake of lords' and ladies' greenhouses. The subject of Charles Darwin's first book after the *Origin of the Species* (1859) was the orchid. Darwin was instrumental in the shift in thinking of flowers as merely "divine artistry" to a conception of them as the product of adaptation, that is, sex and history, in particular how these forces interact parallel to the evolution of insects. Darwin used the plant to explain how nature must cross-pollinate if it is to perpetuate itself. Revelations of the sexuality of the orchid—the flower, nature's femme fatale, often imitates the female insect to attract the male and deliver its pollen—were shocking in the day.

8. Tibullus (Albius Tibullus), ca. 54?–18 BCE, Roman poet. Master of the Latin elegy. (T. James Luce, ed., *Ancient Writers No. 1: Greece and Rome* [New York: Scribner's, 1982], 765–782.) Frequently erotic, his poems are often tinged with the sufferings and melancholy of romantic love, particularly for two objects of affection he calls Delia and Nemesis.

9. Leopardi, Giacomo (1798–1837). Italian poet, scholar, and philosopher. He is among the great writers of the nineteenth century. Suffering long neglect, frustrated love (for his married cousin), and physical disability, he reflects in his work his bitterness, sadness, and especially despair.

10. Quental, Antero de (1842–1891), Azorian poet.

11. Title recalls the "Fleshly School of Poetry," an epithet disdainfully "applied to a group of late 19th-century English poets associated with Dante Gabriel Rossetti. The term was coined by Robert Williams Buchanan [in 1871 to castigate] the poetry of Rossetti and his colleagues, notably Algernon Swinburne, for its 'morbid deviation from the healthy forms of life.' In Buchanan's view, these poets exhibited 'weary wasting, yet exquisite sensuality; nothing virile, nothing tender, nothing completely sane; a superfluity of extreme sensibility.' He reviled their decadence, their 'amatory forms' and 'carnal images'" (*Merriam Webster Encyclopedia of Literature* [Springfield, Mass.: Merriam Webster, 1995], 421). It is of interest to recall that "Poems of the Flesh" ("Poemas de la carne") was the very title of a collection of Silva's poems lost in the 1895 shipwreck. Spaniard Salvador Rueda's *Himno a la carne* ("Hymn to the Flesh") dates from 1890.

12. Silva used the English words *hard work* in the original Spanish text, betraying, as Orjuela suggests (234n7), the Modernist penchant for using—not always appropriately if suggestively—barbarisms and anglicisms to give a cosmopolitan air to their verbal repertoire. Silva also introduces one of the key oppositions—work and leisure—that will

predominate in the novel, as well as positing the Yankee as embodiment of the former ethic.

13. Ca. 1477–1549, Italian painter.

14. Sensorial intoxication is a motif common among the Symbolists and their disciples, often extended to the trope "drunk on life." We find drunkenness in Baudelaire's "Le Voyage" ("The Voyage") and Rimbaud's "Le Bateau ivre" ("The Drunken Boat"). For both poets, drunkenness functions as an emblem of sensorial derangement and its consequent transcendence—the ecstasy and headiness of freedom. Nietzsche considered drunkenness the analogy of the Dionysian force in art.

15. Ancestor of the guitar.

16. Andre Gide's *The Immoralist,* appearing in 1902, and exploring psychopathological states, echoes this idea that comfort is a debilitating force.

17. Book of hymns based on the Book of Common Prayer, published anonymously by poet and vicar John Keble (1792–1866).

18. *Hamlet,* II, ii, 195: POLONIUS: What do you read, my lord? / HAMLET: Words, words, words.

19. Cf. *Hamlet,* V. i, 201: "Alas, poor Yorick." Fernández has much in common with Hamlet, a figure taken up too by the Pre-Raphaelites and Symbolists (e.g., Rossetti's Hamlet and Ophelia, or Jules Laforgue's 1887 re-imagining of him as a Decadent: "Hamlet, or, The Consequences of Filial Piety," in *Six Moral Tales* [New York: H. Liveright, ca. 1928]).

20. Two important precepts occur in this sentence: the first, clearly an echo of the Symbolists' penchant for suggesting ("le chanson grise") rather than naming; the second, the aesthetic responsibility of the receptor, a forerunner to late-twentieth-century notions of "reader-response." Baudelaire had already codified this obligation when he wrote on more than one occasion of the critic's imperative to respond to poetry with poetic criticism.

21. Motif: contempt for the philistine. Insensitivity was the target of a Silva poem, "Un poema" ("A Poem"), in which a critic reads a poem six times and still doesn't understand ("I showed my poem to a tremendous critic / and he read it six times, and told me . . . I don't get it!").

22. Waltz by Hungarian Romantic composer Franz Liszt (1811–1886). The Mephisto Waltz for piano dates from 1860, no. 2 from 1881. It forms in part the composer's "symphonic poems," which sought to transpose great works by such writers as Byron, Goethe, and Hugo into music. I disagree with Orjuela's (237n15) reading of this reference as Arrigo Boito's Italian opera *Mefistófeles.*

23. Núñez de Arce, Gaspar (1832–1903), Spanish poet and play-

wright, a contemporary of Campoamor. In *La selva oscura* (1879), he interprets Dante's search for Beatrice as the search for eternal verities in an ever-changing world (Philip Ward, ed., *The Oxford Companion to Spanish Literature* [Oxford: Clarendon Press, 1978, 420]), and as a call for faith in an ever-more-materialistic age (*El haz de leña*, ed. Rudolph Schwill [Boston: Heath's Modern Language Series, 1903]), a sentiment echoed in his fretful "Discurso sobre la poesía" (in *Gritos del combate* [Madrid: Librería Deferando Fé, 1891]), wherein he takes a conservative line against the new "decadents," ridiculing their sensorial penchant for words with color, shape, and free rhyme, dismissing these writers as "quintessentialized bards" and pathological melancholics. Incommensurately, Rubén Darío was an admirer, perhaps largely because the Spaniard had "passed the torch," literarily speaking, to the Spanish American.

24. Scheffer, Ary (1795–1858), Dutch. Early leader of the Romantic movement. After 1830 he moved from idealized sentimental scenes to illustrations of literary topoi, including the work of Byron and Schiller but especially that of Goethe. (Geraldine Norman, *Nineteenth Century Painters and Paintings: A Dictionary* [Berkeley: University of California Press, 1977], 188–189.)

25. Pereda, José María (1833–1906), Spanish novelist from Santander. Known for his regional-traditional works such as *Sotileza* ("Fine Spun," 1885) and *Peñas arriba* ("The Upper Peaks," 1845), set in his native north, which was an innovation at the time. He extolled simplicity and attacked encroaching materialism and urbanization. The Generation of '98 would fiercely attack Pereda as anachronistic (Lawrence H. Klibbe, *José María de Pereda* [Boston: Twayne, 1975]).

26. Principle of phrenology, 1795–1805, the belief that mental faculties and even character traits—particularly antisocial ones—can be determined by the features of the skull.

27. Graphonomy: a practice especially in vogue in Victorian times involving the analysis of character through the handwriting. Roughly the same as graphology but for its "scientific" connotations.

28. Valdés Leal, Juan de (1622–1690), Spanish Baroque painter known for moral works.

29. Ribera, José de (1591–1652), El Españoleto, or "Lo Spagnoletto." Among his more famous works are "Jacob's Dream" ("El sueño de Jacob," 1639) and "The Martyrdom of St. Bartholomew" ("El martirio de S. Felipe," 1639). He essentially worked in Naples, Italy, and received the influence of Caravaggio and his tenebristic tendencies.

30. Barrès was the author of a study of Joan of Arc as well (*Autour de Jeanne d'Arc* [Paris: E. Champion, 1916]), the subject of one of Bash-

kirtseff's favorite paintings (by Jules Bastien-Lepage, who is mentioned later in this entry).

31. French site of a porcelain manufactory, 1800–1847.

32. The verb here is typically *modernista* in its imposition of artistic technique on the experiential phenomena of nature; e.g.: "glaze: *v., Fine Arts.* to cover (a painted surface or parts of it) with a thin layer of transparent color in order to modify the tone" (*Webster's Encyclopedic Unabridged Dictionary*).

33. Greuze, Jean-Baptiste, 1725–1805, French painter.

34. Récamier, Jeanne-Françoise-Julie-Adélaïde (1771–1849), French socialite and wit.

35. Renan, Joseph-Ernest (1823–1892), French philosopher and historian of religion, author of *Origins of Christianity.* He is best known for his controversial *Life of Jesus* (1863).

36. Taine, Hippolyte Adolphe (1828–1893), French historian. A father of the naturalistic school in that he provided determinism and positivism their theoretical underpinnings, Taine was a key intellectual figure of his day.

37. Daudet, Alphonse (1840–1897). "French short-story writer and novelist, remembered for his *Lettres de Mon Moulin* (1866) . . . and his egocentric Frenchman Tartarin from *Tartarin de Tarascon* (1872), the boastful, loud, vulgar 'Don Quixote' from the Midi. Daudet wrote also under the influence of Zola. . . ." Books and Writers, *http://www.kirjasto .sci.fi/daudet.htm.*

38. French painter (1838–1917), a.k.a. Charles-Auguste-Emile Durand, specialist in portraiture.

39. Rohault de Fleury, Charles (1801–1875), distinguished French architect and archaeologist. Known for his design of artistic buildings in Paris, including the Ópera in 1846, and the Conservatory.

40. Theuriet, Claude Adhemar André (1833–1907), French poet and novelist. See Theuriet, André, George Clausen, et al. *Jules Bastien-Lepage and His Art / Bastien-Lepage as Artist / A Study of Marie Bashkirtseff.* Three monographs. New York: MacMillan, 1892. The study of Bashkirtseff in this volume is by Mathilde Blind.

41. Colonna, Vittoria (1492–1547), Italian poet of noble birth. She is better known today for the intellectual company she kept—including that of Michaelangelo—than for her poetry.

42. Antonomasia for "physician," from the Greek *Asklepios,* god of medicine and healing. His attribute became the snake twined around a staff.

43. "The Holy Women by the Grave" (1884) is an unfinished paint-

ing by Bashkirtseff placed at her mausoleum in Passy Cemetery, Paris, France. See Alfredo Villanueva-Collado's virtual gallery of the Russian's work at *www.geocities.com/mbashkirtseff/02_virtual_museum_english.htm*. A striking portrait of her can be found at http://perso.wanadoo.fr/marie. bashkirtseff/Sans%20titre-3.JPG.

44. Saint Marceaux, Carlos Renato (1845–1915), French sculptor.

45. Grandson of Poseidon in Greek mythology. He is the king of the Phoenicians on the island of Scheria (Corfu) and receives the Argonauts in a subsequent legend. He appears in Book 6 of the *Odyssey* and elsewhere.

46. Daughter of Alcinous in the *Odyssey*.

47. Character in the *Odyssey*, the blind minstrel to King Alcinous. In Book 8 he sings at a banquet of Odysseus's exploits in the Trojan War, prompting the hero's tears.

48. Attican hero famous for slaying the Minotaur and waging war on the Amazons.

49. Daughter of Minos, the Cretan king, in Greek myth. She helped Theseus escape the labyrinth; later married Dionysus.

50. Tiepolo or Tiépolo (Giovanni Battista or Giambattista), Venice 1696–Madrid 1770, Italian Baroque painter and engraver.

51. From the Sermon on the Mount, Matthew 5:6, Authorized Version.

52. David Friedrich Strauss's *The Life of Jesus* (1835) was one of the earliest contributions to scholarship about the Nazarene, and was extraordinarily controversial for what he called his "mythical" approach to biblical exegesis. The work was perceived—erroneously—as denying Jesus's divinity.

53. Sylvia Molloy devotes considerable attention to Bashkirtseff's myth. The critic notes that the Russian's house became a reliquary for adepts, particularly Barrès:

> In Barrès' piece the place of devotion and the object of devotion were articulated jointly: the site spoke of Marie Bashkirtseff but Marie Bashkirtseff, or rather her journal, itself was a site. To reflect on Marie Bashkirtseff was a spiritual exercise, claimed Barrès; it was necessary to *envision* her through her journal, in what Ignatius Loyola called a *composición de lugar*, a composition of place. Marie Bashkirtseff *in situ*, Marie Bashkirtseff as site, became, in Barrès' incredibly suggestive words, a *"station idéologique,"* an ideological retreat. . . . (14)

See also Barrès.

54. Wundt, Wilhelm (1832–1920), German. The "father of modern psychology," he was a pioneer in studies of human sensory experience. Spencer, Herbert (1820–1903), British philosopher of evolution, sociologist, and advocate of a radical degree of laissez faire government. Maudsley, Dr. Henry (1835–1918), was a psychiatrist and criminologist who wrote on the theory of degeneration. One of his influential books was *The Physiology and Pathology of Mind* (1867).

55. Athenian general and student of Socrates, Alcibiades was raised by Pericles. His ambitious imperialism resulted in his recall for impiety after the mutilation of the Hermae, or Herms (square pillars supporting busts of the god Hermes standing as protective guardians in ancient Greece). Silva uses the image as one of sacrilege, overweeningness, and ill omen.

56. The term is French; in Spanish, *arrastrar cueros* (lit. "hauling hides," a reference to novices in the leather trade). Orjuela (*José Asunción Silva: Obra Completa*, 249n30) lists this as the name for Spanish Americans of lavish but unknown means. Jaramillo-Zuluaga (*El deseo*, 48–50) notes that its original application—*rastaquouère* or *rastacouère*—was to censure the indiscretion of Spanish Americans in Paris who displayed aristocratic pretensions.

57. ". . . Hold on, old man, the poet's mistress is a sight to behold!" (translation mine).

58. Protagonist of Voltaire's *Candide,* the unflinchingly optimistic tutor who declared this "the best of all possible worlds."

59. Reference is to St. Monica (North Africa, 322–387 CE), St. Augustine's mother. She prayed devotedly for her then-profligate son to convert; Monica is the patroness of mothers and those with wayward children. Augustine addressed her virtues and death in Book 9 of his *Confessions.*

60. Suffering is aestheticized, as we will see in ensuing chapters.

61. Silva depicts the topos of the *bel mourir,* here in a Christian context, though by no means exempt from secular treatments; a notable example in Spanish American letters of the time is Manuel Gutiérrez Nájera's "Para entonces" ("When My Time Comes"): "I want to die when day is on the wane / my face turned toward the sky, far out to sea; / where the throes of death seem but a dream, / and my soul, a bird that's taking to the sky" (translation mine). In this narrative fantasy sequence of the diary, *art* is responding to *life* and taking an interest in the affairs of humans.

62. Maidens of Norse mythology, literally "choosers of the slain." Both guardian angel and harpy, a Walkyrie, or Valkyrie, is a harbinger

of war. Here the reference is to Wagner's operas of *The Ring of the Nibe-lung, Das Rheingold,* and *Die Walküre* (1854 and 1856). The evocation of Wagner (see also 3 June 189– . . . diary entry) may serve as a model for the man of transvaluated values, or a Superman, in keeping with his "superhuman music" heavily steeped in larger-than-life literary themes; Wagner, more Romantic than the Romantics, sought to unite all the arts, and was a hero to the Symbolists. See also Baudelaire's important essay on him (in Richard Wagner's *Tannhäuser* [Frankfurt am Main: Insel, 1979]). Critic Teodor de Wyzewa sums up Wagner's conception of the artistic process:

> The soul first receives Sensations, which it organizes into Notions, which mixed with other and more powerful Sensations give way to Emotions. Art has attempted to reflect each of these modes of the soul—plastic art the Sensations, literature the Notions, music the Emotions. Wagner has sought, by creating a total work of art, a unity of these elements to reflect the total life of the soul.

(Wyzewa, "Notes sur le peinture wagnérienne," *Revue wagnérienne* 2 1886: 102, quoted in Carlson, *Theories of the Theatre* [Ithaca: Cornell University Press, 1984], 286–287.)

There are obvious veins of this "unification angst" in our hero, and a sense of Wagnerian leitmotif, if we were to read the novel as if it were a libretto for an opera.

63. Arguably the silhouette, while not a Victorian invention, reflects a fixation in evidence throughout the period, and naturally figures in novelists' use of light and darkness, as it also evinces art's growing interface with science and scientific phenomena; in art, the silhouette is a mere outline, or shadow, a feature with obvious appeal for an era that valued the fragile, the dreamlike, the aethereal, and especially the merely suggested (in contradistinction to the overtly and vulgarly material). Like the landscape, the silhouette is a privileging or selecting of visual signifiers; the silhouette derives its name from a real-life minister of France, Etienne de Silhouette (1709–1767). Not coincidentally, Roentgen captured the secret silhouette of the body in 1895: the X-ray. Meanwhile, Freud and his nascent school sought an even more elusive profile—that of the psyche.

64. A water-nymph, Undine married a mortal to gain a soul and all that a soul implies. From Parcelsus's treatise on *Elemental Sprites (Brewer's*

Dictionary of Phrase and Fable, ed. Ivor H. Evans [New York: Harper and Row, 1989]).

65. Again the Pygmalion motif emerges, here in an erotic and so-cial-class context.

66. Silva's image likely is of the *Citrus sinensis* or sweet orange, a tor-rid-zone variety. Comparing a color of something inedible to the color of something edible is a subtle way of transferring the latter's properties to the former; it arguably is an instance of synaesthesia, allying the vi-sual with the gustatory in a stroke.

67. Evocation of the ruin, a Romantic commonplace and emblem of decadence. Cf. Bulwer-Lytton's *The Last Days of Pompeii,* a highly stylized proto-Decadent romance in three volumes (1834). Marie Bash-kirtseff reads it in Volume 1 of her diary.

68. Crane, Walter (1845–1915), English painter, designer, and writer. He was key in the development of the Aesthetic movement, particularly in matters of decoration. His patterns for Jeffrey and Co. wallpapers are notable. Crane believed in the utility of art, a notion fol-lowing Ruskin (*The Dictionary of Art,* vol. 8, ed. Jane Turner [New York: Grove's Dictionaries, 1996], 121–122).

69. Morris, William (1834–1896), poet and artist of the Pre-Raphaelite movement. His wife, Jane Burden, was an important model for the artists of the day. Morris was the force behind the "Firm," which was devoted to improving craftsmanship and design, and produced fur-niture, wallpaper, and textiles. He famously said: "Have nothing in your houses that you do not know to be useful, or believe to be beautiful," the tenet of the Arts and Crafts Movement. (Eleanor Van Zandt, *The Life and Works of William Morris* [New York: Shooting Star Press, 1995], un-numbered pp.)

70. Oleographs (1873): chromolithographs printed on cloth in imitation of oil paintings.

71. Reference is to the epic enchantress on the palindromic is-land, Aeaea (Ææa), where Ulysses (Odysseus) was held entranced along with his crew, turned into swine. The mythical herb *moly,* presented by Hermes (Mercury), saved him after a year. The New Testament employs the same image, wherein Jesus performs an exorcism and runs the de-mons to the sea, to drown, in the form of swine. The dehumanizing force of the choice of animal is apparent in both, as in Silva.

72. It is significant here that an object of beauty is confused with an instrument of death. Note that in the end of this scene our protago-nist describes how he was forced, for a similar unprovoked attack, into a

highly *codified* form of violence, the duel, a convention involving honor and rules, not impulses and unreason.

73. For a modern-day treatment of Epicurean ancient Rome, see Marguerite Yourcenar's *Memoirs of Hadrian* (1951), a historical novel on the life of the second-century hyperaesthetic emperor.

74. Companion of Hadrian, much-remarked for his beauty.

75. It may be reasonable to guess the identity of that German as Alexander von Humboldt, or perhaps Adolf Engler or Karl Prantl.

76. The monster, a dominant motif of the novella, takes various manifestations. In all his guises the monster is the Other, even self-as-other, a constant in Spanish American literary consciousness.

77. Moloch, or Molech, to whom children were sacrificed, is the god of the Ammonites; symbolically he is a figure of any great sacrifice. In the American poet Allen Ginsberg's work, for example, Moloch figures prominently as a governmental leviathan-like force that is appeased by feeding on its children.

78. "Silva a la agricultura en la zona tórrida" ("To Tropical Agriculture," or "Ode to the Agriculture of the Torrid Zone," in Donald Walsh's rendering), verse poem by Venezuelan poet Andrés Bello, and one of the landmark works of the Spanish American nineteenth century. Ironically the poem was inspired abroad—Bello was strolling along the docks in London, where the tropical imports brought thoughts of the Americas (E. Rodríguez Monegal, *The Borzoi Anthology of Latin American Literature* [New York: Alfred Knopf, 1977], 200). In it, Bello praises the paradisiacal qualities of the torrid zone, catalogues its tropical riches (topos of the *cornucopia americana*), and praises country life over the "false glitter, / the pestilent idleness" of the city while urging youth to partake in the national good of agriculture and to forsake war. The city-country dialectic would be a defining one through *modernismo* to the present day.

79. The reference is to Goethe, whose dying words (attributed) were "Mehr Licht!"

80. García Moreno, Gabriel (1821–1875), Ecuadorian president noted for his autocratic stances.

81. Estrada Cabrera, Manuel, dictator of Guatemala from 1898 to 1920. He helped pave the way for the United Fruit Company's dominance in the region and the country's integration—to the detriment of many—into the global economy. Miguel Angel Asturias's masterpiece *El Señor Presidente* is based on his rule. Since Silva's suicide occurred in 1896, it is inexplicable that Cabrera is mentioned in Silva's work two years before the fact, though he held a powerful government position as

Silva wrote. I can offer no possible explanation, apart from the reference being added by a later hand.

82. Line corresponding transparently, as critics have pointed out, with the image of poetry as sacred nectar, seen in Silva's "Ars." See note 96.

83. Second emperor of Brazil (1831–1889) and great lover of knowledge. He had ample time to pursue culture after his overthrow and banishment to Europe in 1889.

84. The ancient polarity of city/country here is in evidence; it was José Martí in poems like "Amor de ciudad grande" ("Love in the City"), who perhaps most famously depicted the "impure love of the city" (in Julián de Casal's phrase) and its markers of corrupted, fallen pursuits. See note 78 on Andrés Bello.

85. Baedeker guidebooks are tourist guides, published since 1827.

86. Greenaway, Kate (1846–1901). British watercolor illustrator for children's books in the second half of the nineteenth century, chiefly with children as her subject.

87. Named for Marcus Aurelius Antoninus, emperor from third-century classical Rome whose curls inspired a unisex hairstyle of the day.

88. Ohnet, Georges (1848–1918), French novelist.

89. Gaboriau, Émile (1832?-1873, Paris), the "Edgar Allan Poe of France," a pioneer of the *roman policier* and of the detective character type. www.kirjasto.sci.fi/gaboria.htm

90. Xavier, Comte de Montépin (1823–1902). Pulp fictionist of the *roman populaire* or *feuilleton* school. (J. P. de Beaumarchais, *Dictionnaire des Littératures de Langue Française* [Paris: Bordas, 1987].)

91. Bouguereau, Adolphe-William (1825–1905), French. Artist noted for his coloring and draughtsmanship. He produced such important works as *The Youth of Bacchus* (1885) and his depiction of children, usually in pastoral settings.

92. De Quincey, Thomas (1785–1859). Author of *Confessions of An English Opium-Eater*, 1822, enlarged ed. 1856. For its intimacy the book was important in the psychological trajectory of the novel genre.

93. Sully Prudhomme, René-François-Armand (1839–1907). The *Solitudes* dates from 1869. He was awarded the first Nobel Prize in 1901 for his "scientific" verse.

94. Likely the Museum Gevangenpoort, The Hague, Netherlands.

95. This figure is one that critics—save García Márquez—have missed as "proof" of Silva's erotic obsession with his sister, a subtext read in (or into) "Nocturno" as well; in fairness to Silva, the line in itself bespeaks no more than an expression of closeness.

96. The *modernistas,* obsessed with issues of form and content, were naturally fond of the receptacle-liquid (container-contained) metonymy; perhaps for the alchemical, classical, or Dionysian connotations, but clearly it proceeds from the Platonic line: the soul as occupying—and distinct from—the host vessel of the body. These are also associations of the eroticist-gourmet savoring some libation; in this vein see Gutiérrez Nájera's "Para un menú": "Las novias pasadas son copas vacías . . ." ("Yesterday's loves are cups now drained . . ."). Gustavo Adolfo Bécquer's Rima LVIII (Rhyme LVIII) employs the same image, as does José Martí's "Copa con alas" ("Winged Cup") and Amado Nervo's "La sed" ("Thirst").

97. Greek prophetess who theorized an ideal love, teacher of Socrates.

98. Ponce de León, Fray Luis (1528?–1591), was an Augustinian mystic poet, writing in the Counter-Reformation, between the Renaissance and the Baroque periods. His translations brought him imprisonment at the hands of the Inquisition.

Reminiscent of Helen's otherworldly, nourishing radiance in *After-Dinner Conversation,* the Friar's 1569 poem extends the image to include the eyes as guiding lights to heaven, a conceit implicit in Silva's Helen. The poem ends with the organic image of the girl as a budding plant, a suggestion not of romantic love but of genetic promise of a greater destiny. Gutiérrez Díaz-Bernardo (*Fray Luis de León: poesía original,* ed. Gutiérrez Díaz-Bernardo [Madrid: Editorial Castalia, 1995], 91n) places the work in the genre of *genethliacus* or *genethliacon,* a neo-Latin form that is written as a horoscope upon a birth or birthday and hypothesizes the zodiacally ordained virtues of the subject. As with Silva's Helen and her mother, there is a theme of biological continuity, as there is in a perverse atavistic sense with Silva and the Andrades.

The translation of these lines, poetic if periphrastic, is the work of Aubrey F. G. Bell (*Lyrics of Luis de León* [London: Burns, Oates and Washbourne, Ltd., 1928], 53). The stanza is excerpted from the poem "Canción al nacimiento de la hija del marqués de Alcañices." The original lines (1569) read thus:

Alma divina, en velo
De femeniles miembros encerrada,
Cuando veniste al suelo
Robaste de pasada
La celestial riquísima morada.

Gutiérrez Díaz-Bernardo (92n) glosses these lines as following the Platonic-Pythagorean doctrine of the soul hidden away in the body. The poem implies a descent to material form after a planetary journey in which the soul takes on (in the original, "Robaste," or "Stole Away") the faculties of the gods—Jupiter, Venus, Saturn, Mars—that rule each sphere or heaven. The topos of woman as sun is at work in the poem (91n), which parallels Luis de León's "Noche serena," in which the narrator urges the human gaze heavenward. This would serve as a fitting remonstrance to Fernández: "What deadly madness / so alienates the senses from the truth that / forgetful and lost / to your divine good, / they follow this empty shadow, this feigned good?" (*Lyrics*, 158, trans. J. M. Cohen).

99. Silva could be referring to the poem "Helen's Tower" (*The Poetical Works of Alfred, Lord Tennyson* [New York: Thomas Y. Crowell and Company, 1897]):

Helen's tower, here I stand,
Dominant over sea and land.
Son's love built me, and I hold
Mother's love engrav'n in gold.
. . .
Would my granite girth were strong
As either love, to last as long!
I should wear my crown entire
To and thro' the Doomsday fire,
And be found of angel eyes
In earth's recurring Paradise.   [637]

Villanueva-Collado ("Funesta . . . ," 68) cites "Lancelot and Elaine" from *Idyls of the King*—the name Elaine is a variant of Helen—as the idyll in question. One of Sperelli's great loves in D'Annunzio's *Il Piacere* ("The Child of Pleasure") is named Elena. Silva may have been inspired, too, by another of that book's characters—Constance Landbrooke—for his own Constanza Landseer.

100. Fiesole, Frà Giovanni da (Beato Angelico) (ca. 1400–1455). He created masterpieces such as his renowned *Annunciation*. Fra Angelico made the Pre-Raphaelite Brotherhood's list of the "Immortals," which served them as a manifesto and portrait of kindred spirits; it is worth reproducing here in its entirety for its relation to Silva and *After-Dinner Conversation* (for example, Silva was planning a study of Leonardo before his suicide):

Jesus Christ
The Author of Job
Isaiah
Homer
Pheidias
Early Gothic Architects
Cavalier Pugliesi
Dante
Boccaccio
Rienzi
Ghiberti
Chavier
Fra Angelico
Leonardo da Vinci
Spenser
Hogarth
Flaxman
Hilton
Goethe
Kosciusko
Byron
Wordsworth
Keats
Shelley
Haydon
Cervantes
Joan of Arc
Mrs. Browning
Patmore

Raphael
Michael Angelo
Early English Balladists
Giovanni Bellini
Georgioni
Titian
Tintoretto
Poussin
Alfred
Shakespeare
Milton
Cromwell
Hampden
Bacon
Newton
Landor
Thackeray
Poe
Hood
Longfellow
Emerson
Washington
Leigh Hunt
Author of *Stories after Nature*
Wilkie
Columbus
Browning
Tennyson

(Robert A. Rosenbaum, *Earnest Victorians: Six Great Victorians as Portrayed in Their Own Words and Those of Their Contemporaries* [New York: Hawthorn Books, 1961], 224.)

101. Translation is by L. Binyon from *The Portable Dante,* ed. Paolo Milano (New York: Penguin Books, 1977); reprinted 1978.

102. Burne-Jones, Edward (1833–1898). English painter and companion in the arts to William Morris. Burne-Jones was a major influence on the development of Symbolist painting and art nouveau, and was in turn an admirer of Rossetti. Romantic, lyrical, and medieval, he stands as one of the preeminent Pre-Raphaelite painters, designers, and leaders

(Erika Langmuir and Norbert Lynton, eds., *Yale Dictionary of Art and Artists* [New Haven: Yale University Press, 2000], 112–113).

103. Pombo, Rafael (1833–1912), mainly Romantic poet from Bogotá whose themes covered love and nature; known for 1864's *La hora de las tinieblas* ("The Hour of Darkness"). Orjuela (*Obras*, 228n76) mentions the referenced poem, "La pobre viejecita" ("The Poor Little Old Lady").

104. Magazine. American prudishness at the time forced a title change to *Tidbits*.

105. Line from Virgil's *Aeneid*, VI:

. . . Manibus date lilia plenis:
purpureos spargam flores, animamque nepotis
His saltem accumulem donis, et fungar inani
Munere.—

Translated "Give lilies with full hands" or "Give handfuls of lilies," the verse often is invoked as a funeral lament, such as in Brant's woodcut, which features mourning at the tomb of Marcellus. Hector Orjuela (280n84) attributes the phrase to Dante, by whom it is used to hail the arrival of Beatrice in Canto XXX of the *Purgatorio*. (Incidentally, the Beatrice-narrator relationship in it bears a strong resemblance to Helen and Fernández's in several respects: the maternal image, the chiding and penitent guest the ideal woman inspires. This parallel is worth studying more fully.) The Latin line bodes an early death in the *Aeneid*, and elsewhere in iconography is invariably freighted with ideas of faith and the spiritual. It figures in Hopkins's poem "Lines for a Picture of St. Dorothea," Thomas Wentworth Higginson's "Decoration," and of course, Rossetti's "Blessed Damozel." See also George Bataille's text of the same title ("Manibus . . .") in *Inner Experience* (trans. Leslie Anne Boldt [Albany: State University of New York Press, 1988]).

106. Richardson, Samuel (English, 1689–1761). Pioneered the epistolary form of the novel. Best known for *Clarissa* (1747–1748) and *Pamela* (1740).

107. See *The Complete Poetical Works by Dante Gabriel Rossetti* (Boston: Little, Brown and Company, 1917).

108. The German Romantic actually was from Frankfurt am Main. Goethe died in Weimar, Saxe-Weimar, not in his seventies but at eighty-two.

109. Pardo Bazán, Emilia, Countess (1852–1921), Spanish naturalist known for her psychological novels and short stories.

110. Bourget, Paul (1852–1935), French novelist, poet, and critic who wrote one of the key studies of Decadence. Silva's reference to a preface later (14 April) is probably Bourget's own to the novel *Le Disciple* (1889), in which the writer turns traditional; he converted to Catholicism in 1901. For a study of the influence of Bourget on Silva, see Rafael Maya, *Los orígenes del modernismo en Colombia* (Bogotá: Biblioteca de Autores Contemporáneos, 1961), 68–79.

111. Ca. 150–ca. 230, Roman theologian.

112. Henry Poole and Co., tailors to the Prince of Wales, ca. 1880s, among the originators of the tuxedo dinner jacket.

113. Lasegue, Ernest Charles (1816–1883). Former teacher of Baudelaire and student of Victor Cousin, Lasegue was an important doctor, clinician, and psychiatric theorist in medical pathology and, in particular, in mental alienation, which he saw as deriving from morbid states of the brain. He was the first to define (1882) the persecution complex, and published key early studies on alcoholism, legal-medical issues, and hysterical anorexia, the foundation of later work on mental anorexia. *http://www.herreros.com.ar/lasegue.htm*

114. See *The Portable Dante*, ed. Paolo Milano, trans. Lawrence Binyon (New York: Penguin Books, 1975), 574–575.

115. Hunt, William Holman (1827–1910), English painter. One of the founders of the Pre-Raphaelite Brotherhood. His work is characterized by religious themes and the use of bright light. Hunt's unquestionable masterwork is "The Light of the World," which features Jesus holding a lantern. He also produced a notable "Lady of Shalott."

116. Cavalcanti, Guido (ca. 1255–1300), major Italian *dolce stil nuovo* poet and best friend to Dante. His love sonnets and *canzoni* survive. Guinicelli (Guinizelli), Guido (ca. 1230–1276?), Italian poet, precursor of Dante.

117. "To be a nation of *good animals* is the first condition of national posterity" (Haley, 22). Note that national health, in this view, is the raison d'être of personal health. Spencer had noted, further, that "disease or degeneration in society is characterized by a *loss of wholeness and a dispersal of energy*" (Haley, 85–86, emphasis mine).

118. Fernández-Silva misremembers the sonnet's opening as "Look at my face, my name is might have been / I am also called, no more, farewell." The poem likely was written between 1847 and 1853, and reads in part as follows (from Dante Gabriel Rossetti, *Sonnets and Songs* [Boston: Roberts Brothers, 1870], 232):

SONNET XLVI.
A SUPERSCRIPTION.

Look in my face; my name is might-have-been;
    I am also called No-more, Too-late, Farewell;
    Unto thine ear I hold the dead-sea shell
Cast up thy Life's foam-fretted feet between;
Unto thine eyes the glass where that is seen
    Which had Life's form and Love's, but by my spell
    Is now a shaken shadow intolerable,
Of ultimate things unuttered the frail screen.

Mark me, how still I am! But should there dart
    One moment through thy soul the soft surprise
. . .
Then shalt thou see me smile, and turn apart
Thy visage to mine ambush at thy heart
    Sleepless with cold commemorative eyes.

119. I have not come across any names, ancient or modern, that serve in English for *corilóporo. Chlorosis,* the former name both for an iron deficiency and for leukemia, is a very remote possibility. Silva may be either transliterating or inventing freely.

120. St. Vitus's dance.

121. See note in Villanueva-Collado's "Arte, ciencia . . ." (366), in which he discusses these two new diseases, at bottom legal terms with which to fight the railroad companies (citing George Frederick Drinka, *The Birth of Neurosis: Myth, Malady and the Victorians* [New York: Simon and Schuster, 1984], 110).

122. Latin, "One's nature is largely in the belly." Aníbal González (*La novela,* 101) notes that the *sobremesa* itself, in the tradition of Plato's philosophic banquet, is a moment not only of exchange of ideas, but of *digestion.*

123. I have not come upon the source of these verses, though it should be of interest to know that *hydrophobia* was used in ancient Rome to denote a symptom of rabies. http://www.umdnj.edu/Umcweb/hstate/fall97/phistory.html.

124. A morbid state whose symptoms were defined by the English doctor Richard Bright (1789–1858) (Orjuela, 310n). A kidney disease causing albumin to appear in the urine. Nephritis (inflammation of the kidneys), when chronic, is termed thus.

125. Krishaber, Maurice (1836–1883), Hungarian doctor and early researcher into the nervous condition Freud later called "anxiety neurosis" and what we call "panic attacks" today. Krishaber's actual term was *cerebro-cardial neurosis*.

126. Silva must mean Parmigianino (1503–1540), who was from Parma. The Italian Mannerist produced a self-portrait (1524) in a convex sphere that has the almost monstrous right hand occupying the foreground. The hands are predominant in his most famous painting, *The Madonna with the Long Neck,* in which the hand is artificially elongated and otherwise distorted, contributing to a "remote" beauty (H. W. Janson, *History of Art* [New York: Abrams, 1986], 466).

127. Ruskin, John (1819–1900), British critic and artist, important arbiter of taste in Victorian England.

128. Rossetti, Elizabeth Eleanor Siddal ("Lizzie"), 1829–1862, overdosed—possibly accidentally or forced by circumstance—on laudanum, to which she was addicted, and died after suffering a mysterious illness for some time, which was complicated by grief and depression over her stillborn child. Rossetti, then still struggling to gain his reputation, tucked his early unpublished poems—for the most part, the only copies—in Lizzie's fabled hair before the coffin was closed. Ne'er-do-well Charles Howell persuaded him to dig them up seven years later, under cover of darkness, apparently to find Lizzie, in the eerie light of a bonfire, preserved almost lifelike. Rossetti was haunted by the conviction that he had somehow killed her and was especially guilt-ridden after having the poems exhumed. Indeed, he had a predilection for experimentation with prostitutes and models, and a rumor persists that there was a culpatory note—later destroyed—pinned to the dying, long-suffering Siddal's nightgown. Violet Hunt's early biography perpetuated this rumor (see speculation on this score in Dobbs). In 1872, Rossetti, himself no stranger to drugs (including the compound chloral, which figures in *After-Dinner Conversation*), attempted suicide. (There is something of Fernández's dilemma in Rossetti's conception of Elizabeth in that he preferred her as a remote beacon of the eternal feminine.)

Adding another dimension to the already fantastic story, Rossetti's sister's tale "Maude," which gave a fictional account of just such an occurrence, had come out twelve years before the Rossetti poem incident actually happened. Dumas's *La Dame aux Camélias* features a similar sacrifice (Doughty, 417).

Siddal posed for one of the Pre-Raphaelite Brotherhood's most enduring works, Millais's "Ophelia." In death she was immortalized again by Rossetti in "Beata Beatrix" (1863–1870), in which her apotheosis has all the appearance of a rapture.

"J. F. Siddal," the painter of the portrait in Dr. Rivington's collection, is fictitious.

129. Sedan was the scene of France's defeat in the Franco-Prussian War (1870–1871), and Napoleon III was captured there in 1870.

130. G. Maspero and El Grebaut were actual Directors of Antiquities at the Egyptian Museum in Cairo during the last decades of the nineteenth century.

131. Ammon Ra or Amen Ra, the "father of the gods" and sun king of Thebes: conflation of Egyptian god Amen with older sun-cult god Ra of Heliopolis.

132. Abydos (Abtu). Egyptian pilgrimage destination on the west bank of the Nile, a sacred site of the earliest known or recorded dynasties, hieroglyphics, and tombs.

133. Crookes, Sir William (1832–1919); British physicist, discovered thallium.

134. Curiously, the familiar conceit of the self as instrument apparently relinquishes the creator's role; here it is not She who is acted upon, but who inspires action upon him.

135. Koeningstein, François-Claudius (1859–1892), known as "Ravachol." An important hero to French anarchists, Ravachol was enraged by the French government's use of the new Lebels machine gun against a May Day rally in which women and children participated, and against an anarchist labor demonstration in Clichy. Ravachol bombed the homes of the judge and prosecutors of those among the latter who were punished. Octave Mirbeau, author of the notorious *Torture Garden,* defended him in an 1892 article, but the martyr-activist was beheaded at Montbrison. (Jean Maitrou, *Ravachol et les anarchistes* [Paris: Julliard, 1964]).

136. Santo Caserio, Jeronimo, Italian anarchist revolutionary who stabbed French President Sadi Carnot to death at Lyons in 1894 to avenge the execution of another revolutionary, August Vaillant. Caserio was guillotined.

137. Sudermann, Hermann (1857–1928), German dramatist and novelist.

138. The very notion of dying "at the right time," posited as an act of dignity and will, clearly derives from Nietzsche (XXI, "On Free Death," *Thus Spoke Zarathustra,* 183), who explicitly informs the rest of this entry.

139. Littré, Paul-Maximilien-Emile (1801–1881), French philosopher/lexicographer, translator of Hippocrates, and lifelong student of the sciences.

140. Puvis de Chavannes, Pierre-Cécile. French muralist, 1824–1898.

141. Moreau, Gustave (1826–1898), one of the great French painters. Fernando Vallejo (*Cartas de José Asunción Silva* [Bogotá, Colombia: Ediciones Casa Silva, 1996], 70n) notes that he was a "precursor of Impressionism, Symbolism, Expressionism and . . . all modern painting. . . . 'Painter of History' as his calling card said. His themes, taken from classical mythology, the Bible, the divinities of India, Byzantine jewelry, the Zodiac and fantastic animals, had a nocturnal atmosphere in accord with the sensibility of the Silva of 'Nocturnos' and the 'Serenata'" (translation mine). The Colombian met Moreau in Paris and later wrote him an admiring letter (1 February 1890) requesting information on reproductions of his work. See also Geneviève Lacambre's unsurpassable *Gustave Moreau: Between Epic and Dream* (Chicago: Art Institute of Chicago, 1999).

142. President of France (1879–1887).

143. Grévy's son-in-law; he caused the president's ouster by trafficking in decorations of honor.

144. Lesseps, Ferdinand Marie, Vicomte de (1805–1894). French engineer and diplomat whose most notable feat was the conception and construction of the Suez Canal.

145. Swiss psychological novelist (1857–1910).

146. One of the internal sins, essentially the pleasurable contemplation of a sinful thought. The others are *gaudium*, obsession over past sins, and *desiderium*, the actual desire for sin (Porter, 109n1). Technically, Fernández means *gaudium* here, although it is arguable that *gaudium* can produce present delectation of still-imaginary sins. *Delectatio morosa* is perhaps the most purely "imaginational" dimension of sin and so held great allure for the artists of the day.

147. For comment on the vocabulary of gems in Modernismo and on this scene in particular, see LoDato.

148. Ca. 1510–1565?; French Mannerist sculptor represented generously at the Louvre.

149. *North American Review* was founded in Boston in 1815 and is still in existence, publishing such literary lights over the years as Walt Whitman and Henry James.

150. According to Anthony Synnott, *The Body Social: Symbolism, Self and Society* (London and New York: Routledge, 1993), 94, Freud argues for the erotic connotation in the love of beauty: "There is to my

mind no doubt that the concept of 'beautiful' has its roots in sexual excitation and that its original meaning was 'sexually stimulating' (1977a: 69n2)." However, Freud seemed mildly perplexed by beauty: "Beauty has no obvious use; nor is there any clear cultural necessity for it. Yet civilization could not do without it," apparently because the enjoyment of beauty can compensate for the threat of suffering. He suggests that "the love of beauty seems a perfect example of an impulse inhibited in its aim (1985: 270–271)," offering us a context for Fernández's consumption of beauty: the unfulfillment of some desire in a setting that assures that privation. (Synnott's 1977a is *On Sexuality;* 1985 is *Civilization, Society and Religion.*)

151. Silva's original has Nelly say *irreal,* a false cognate, as part of an English phrase. Though the word exists in English, it is relatively of very low frequency and not a likely translation for the Spanish *irreal.* Moreover, the English word *irreal* was not coined until the 1940s.

152. Silva writes "New Port," presumably for "Newport," likely Rhode Island.

153. Latin, "but not satiated." "Sed non satiata" is the title of one of Baudelaire's sonnets (XXX) from *Les Fleurs du mal* (see Blackmore, 155). The poem treats of a devil-woman conjured as if by Faust.

154. Sarasate, Pablo (1844–1908), Spanish composer-violinist.

155. Jiménez Manjón, Antonio (1866–1916), blind Spanish Romantic guitar maestro.

156. Cellini, Benvenuto (1500–1571), Italian sculptor, writer of an important autobiography; Sommavilla, Godofredo, Italian artist (1850–1944).

157. Guaymi Indians, native to Costa Rica, Panama, and northern Colombia and known for their agriculture. www.aup.org/lista/pr8115.htm

158. Rousseauesque, tragic characters in the once-popular romance (1787), *Paul and Virginia,* by Jacques-Henri Bernadin de Saint-Pierre.

159. Hauptmann, Gerhart (1862–1946), German dramatist dealing with the conditions of the lower class. He was merely a novice at the time of this novel's first writing, but went on to win the Nobel Prize in 1912.

160. Bahr, Hermann (1863–1934). Austrian dramatist and critic. He is credited with establishing modernism as a literary term (1890).

161. Rops, Félicien (1833–1898), major Belgian Symbolist painter who lived mostly in Paris. He is notable for his marriage of Eros and Thanatos, and for unbridled fantasy. Well-known works include "Incantation" ("Maleficiorum") and "The Supreme Vice." For Rops's etch-

ings, see www.ciger.be/rops/tech/etching. He is also featured in Jullian (101–106).

162. Pollaiuolo, Antonio de (1429–1498): Florentine engraver.

163. The sobriquet given Silva himself. There is wide disagreement about the nature and extent of the Colombian's erotic experience with women. (See Miramón, chapter 7.) Parenthetically, Miguel de Unamuno's praise of Silva in the introduction to the early editions of his work extends to calling the Colombian's poems "chaste," unlike those of his "carnal" successors (see Unamuno, "Prólogo"). Unamuno was almost certainly unfamiliar with *De sobremesa*.

164. Campoamor, Ramón de (1817–1901). Once-popular traditionalist Spanish poet who fell into disfavor among the *modernista* generation.

165. French, "the scoundrel's pose."

166. Sand, George (1804–1876), nom de plume of Amandine-Aurore-Lucile Dupin. Prolific French Romantic writer notable for her frank literary treatments of women's sexuality and gender identity. She carried on love affairs with many well-known artists and celebrities, including Musset and Chopin. Pearl, Cora (1837–1886), nineteenth-century English society diva wooed by some of the most powerful men in the world at the time, including Prince Napoleon.

SELECTED BIBLIOGRAPHY

NOTE: I have listed here the major reference works, secondary sources, and criticism used in this scholarly translation. I also include primary texts cited in the introduction. For reasons of space, some works less central to the project's critical apparatus as such have not been listed again here.

Aching, Gerard. *The Politics of Spanish American Modernismo: By Exquisite Design*. New York: Cambridge University Press, 1997.

Adams, James Eli. *Dandies and Desert Saints: Styles of Victorian Masculinity*. Ithaca and London: Cornell University Press, 1995.

Alighieri, Dante. "Canto XXX." *Purgatorio*. http://www.ccel.org/d/dante/purgatorio/purg31.htm

Amiel, Henri-Frédéric. *Philine*. Trans. Van Wyck Brooks. Boston and New York: Houghton Mifflin Company, 1930.

Balakian, Anna. "Andre Breton and Psychiatry." *Medicine and Literature*. New York: Neale Watson Academic Publications, Inc., 1980. 160–170.

Barnstone, Willis. *The Poetics of Translation: History, Theory and Practice*. New Haven: Yale University Press, 1993.

Barrès, Maurice. "La légende d'une cosmopolite." *Huit jours chez Monsieur Renan. Trois stations de psychothérapie*. Paris: Emile-Paul, 1913. 125–163.

Bashkirtseff, Marie. *I Am the Most Interesting Book of All: the Diary of Marie Bashkirtseff*. Trans. Phyllis Howard Kernberger with Katherine Kernberger. San Francisco: Chronicle Books, 1997.

Bataille, Georges. *Visions of Excess: Selected Writings*. Ed. Allan Stoekl. Minneapolis: University of Minnesota Press, 1985.

Battilana, Carlos. "Itinerario y construcción en *De sobremesa* de José Asunción Silva." *La novela latinoamericana de entresiglos*. Ed. S. Zanetti.

Buenos Aires: Instituto de Literatura Hispánica, Facultad de Filosofía y Letras, Universidad de Buenos Aires, 1997. 33–42.

Baudelaire, Charles. *Selected Writings on Art and Literature*. Trans. P. E. Charvet. London: Penguin, 1992.

———. "Spleen." Trans. Richard Howard. *http://www.poets.org/poems/poems/poems.cfm?prmID=1957*

Beckson, Karl, ed. *Aesthetics and Decadents of the 1890s: An Anthology of British Poetry and Prose*. Chicago: Academy Chicago, 1981.

Benjamin, Walter. *Charles Baudelaire: A Lyric Poet in the Era of High Capitalism*. Trans. Harry Zohn. London: Verso, 1983.

Berman, Marshall, *All That Is Solid Melts into Air: The Experience of Modernity*. New York: Simon and Schuster, 1982.

Blackmore, E. H., and A. M. Blackmore, eds. *Six French Poets of the Nineteenth Century*. New York: Oxford University Press, 2000.

Boym, Svetlana. *Death in Quotation Marks: Cultural Myths of the Modern Poet*. Cambridge, Mass.: Harvard University Press, 1991.

Camacho Guizado, Eduardo. *La poesía de José Asunción Silva*. Bogotá: Universidad de los Andes, 1968.

———, ed. *José Asunción Silva: Obra completa*. Caracas: Biblioteca Ayacucho, 1977.

Cano Gavira, Ricardo. *José Asunción Silva, una vida en clave de sombra*. Caracas: Monte Avila, 1992.

Charry Lara, Fernando. *José Asunción Silva, vida y creación*. Bogotá: Procultura, S.A., 1985.

Cobo Borda, J. G. *El Carnero, María, Silva y Arciniegas*. Bogotá: Presidencia de la República, 1997.

———. *El coloquio americano*. Antioquia: Otraparte, 1994.

———. *José Asunción Silva, bogotano universal*. Prologue by Fernando Charry Lara. Bogotá: Villegas Editores, 1988.

Comfort, Kelly. "Art(ist) for Art's Sake or Art(ist) for Capital's Sake: Aesthetic Production and Consumption in Turn-of-the-Century Literature." Ph.D. diss., University of California at Davis, 2005.

Cooke, John D. *Minor Victorian Poets*. New York: Charles Scribner's Sons, 1928.

Cronin, Vincent. *Four Women in Pursuit of an Ideal*. London: Collins, 1965.

Cuddon, J. A. *The Penguin Dictionary of Literary Terms and Literary Theory*. London: Penguin Books, 1991.

D'Annunzio, Gabriele. *The Child of Pleasure*. Trans. Georgina Harding; verse trans. Arthur Symons. New York: Boni and Liveright, Inc., 1925.

———. *The Triumph of Death*. Trans. Arthur Hornblow. New York: Boni and Liveright, Inc., 1923.

Darío, Rubén. *Los raros*. Buenos Aires–México: Espasa-Calpe Argentina, 1952.

Davis, Lisa E. "Modernismo y decadentismo en la novela *De sobremesa* de José Asunción Silva." *The Analysis of Hispanic Texts: Current Trends in Methodology*. Jamaica: Bilingual Press, 1976. 206–220.

des Cars, Laurence. *The Pre-Raphaelites: Romance and Realism*. New York: Harry N. Abrams, Inc., 2000.

Devy, Ganesh. "Translation and Literary History: An Indian View." *Post-Colonial Translation: Theory and Practice*. Ed. Susan Bassnett and Harish Trivedi. London and New York: Routledge, 1999.

Dobbs, Brian, and Judy Dobbs. *Dante Gabriel Rossetti: An Alien Victorian*. London: Macdonald and Jane's, 1977.

Doughty, Oswald. *Dante Gabriel Rossetti, A Victorian Romantic*. New Haven: Yale University Press, 1949.

Ellis, Havelock. Introduction. *Against the Grain*. By J. K. Huysmans. New York: Three Sirens Press, 1931. 11–49.

Englekirk, John E. *Edgar Allan Poe in Hispanic Literature*. New York: Instituto de las Españas en los Estados Unidos, 1934.

Feder, Lillian. *Madness in Literature*. Princeton, N.J.: Princeton University Press, 1980.

Franco, Jean. *La cultura moderna en América Latina*. México: Joaquin Mortiz, 1971.

García Márquez, Gabriel. "En busca del Silva perdido." *José Asunción Silva: poesías completas / De sobremesa*. Santa Fé de Bogotá: Casa de Poesía Silva, 1996. 9–28.

Giorgi, Gabriel. "Nombrar la enfermedad: Médicos y artistas alrededor del cuerpo masculino en *De sobremesa* de José Asunción Silva." http://www.lehman.cuny.edu/ciberletras/v1n1/ens_04.htm

Glaser, Hermann, ed. *The German Mind of the Nineteenth Century: A Literary and Historical Anthology*. New York: Continuum, 1981.

Glick, Elisa. "The Dialectics of Dandyism." *Cultural Critique* 48 (Spring 2001): 129–163.

Gómez Gil, Orlando. "El modernismo." *Historia de la literatura hispanoamericana*. New York: Holt, Rinehart and Winston, 1968. 401–407.

González, Aníbal. "'Estómago y cerebro': *De sobremesa, El simposio* de Platón y la indigestión cultural." *Revista Iberoamericana*, vol. LXIII, no. 178–179 (enero–junio 1997): 233–248.

———. "Modernist Prose." *Cambridge History of Latin American Literature*.

Ed. Roberto González Echevarría and Enrique Pupo-Walker. New York: Cambridge University Press, 1996. 69–113.

———. *La novela modernista hispanoamericana.* Madrid: Editorial Gredos, 1987.

González Echeverría, Roberto. "Sarduy, the Boom and the Post-Boom." *Latin American Literary Review* 15, no. 26 (1987): 57–72.

Goodwin, Neva R., Frank Ackerman, and David Kiron, eds. *The Consumer Society.* Washington, D.C.: Island Press, 1997.

Gordon, Rae Beth. *Ornament, Fantasy and Desire in Nineteenth-Century French Literature.* Princeton: Princeton University Press, 1992.

Greenslade, William. *Degeneration, Culture and the Novel, 1880–1940.* Cambridge: Cambridge University Press, 1994.

Guerrieri, Kevin. "Paris in Four Colombian Novels at the Crossing of Centuries." *Literary Research/Recherche Littéraire* 19, nos. 37–38 (2002): 29–45.

Gutiérrez Girardot, Rafael. "José Fernández Andrade: Un artista colombiano finisecular frente a la sociedad burguesa." *José Asunción Silva: obra completa.* Nanterre, France: ALLCA XX, 1990. 623–635.

———. "La literatura hispanoamericana de fin de siglo." *Historia de la literatura hispanoamericana,* v. vii. Madrid: Cátedra, 1985. 495–506.

———. "Prólogo." *De sobremesa. http://www.banrep.gov.co/blaavirtual/ letras/sobrem/lsobrem1.htm*

Habermas, Jürgen. *The Philosophical Discourse of Modernity: Twelve Lectures.* Trans. Frederick Lawrence. Cambridge, Mass.: MIT Press, 1987.

Haley, Bruce. *The Healthy Body and Victorian Culture.* Cambridge, Mass., and London, England: Harvard University Press, 1978.

Hanson, Ellis. *Decadence and Catholicism.* Cambridge, Mass., and London, England: Harvard University Press, 1997.

Hardin, Terri. *The Pre-Raphaelites: Inspiration from the Past.* New York: Smithmark, 1996.

Hazera, Lydia D. "The Spanish American Modernist Novel and the Psychology of the Artistic Personality," *Hispanic Journal* 8, no. 1 (Fall 1986): 69–83.

Heilman, Robert. "Variations on Picaresque (Felix Krull)." *Sewanee Review* 66 (1958): 547–577.

Hustvedt, Asti, ed. *The Decadent Reader.* New York: Zone Books, 1998.

Huysmans, J.-K. *Against the Grain.* Trans. John Howard [pseud.]. New York: Lieber and Lewis, 1922.

Iffland, James. *Quevedo and the Grotesque.* London: Tamesis Books Limited, 1978.

Ingwersen, Sonya A. *Light and Longing: Silva and Darío: Modernism and Religious Heterodoxy*. New York: Peter Lang, 1986.

James, William. *The Varieties of Religious Experience: A Study in Human Nature*. New York: Penguin Books, 1985.

Jaramillo Zuluaga, J. Eduardo. "Bibliografía cronológica de José Asunción Silva (1871–1996)." *Leyendo a Silva*, v. III. Ed. Juan Gustavo Cobo Borda. Santafé de Bogotá: Instituto Caro y Cuervo, 1997. 536–663.

———. *El deseo y el decoro (puntos de herejía en la novela colombiana)*. Bogotá: Tercer Mundo Editores, 1994.

———. "Desire and Decorum in the Twentieth-Century Colombian Novel." In *Bodies and Biases: Sexualities in Hispanic Cultures and Literature*. Ed. David William Foster and Roberto Reis. Minneapolis and London: University of Minnesota Press, 1996. 37–73.

Jennings, Lee Byron. *The Ludicrous Demon: Aspects of the Grotesque in German Post-Romantic Prose*. Berkeley: University of California Press, 1963.

Jiménez, José Olivio. *Antología crítica de la poesía hispanoamericana*. Madrid: Hiperión, 1985.

Jrade, Cathy. *Modernismo, Modernity, and the Development of Spanish American Literature*. Austin: University of Texas Press, 1998.

Jullian, Philippe. *Dreamers of Decadence: Symbolist Painters of the 1890s*. New York: Praeger, 1971.

Karl, Frederick R. *Modern and Modernism: The Sovereignty of the Artist*. New York: Athenaeum, 1985.

Kayser, Wolfgang. *The Grotesque in Art and Literature*. Trans. Ulrich Weisstein. Glouster, Mass.: P. Smith, 1968.

Kristeva, Julia. *Black Sun: Depression and Melancholia*. Trans. Leon S. Roudiez. New York: Columbia University Press, 1989.

Landow, George. "Aesthetes and Decadents of the 1890s—Points of Departure." http://65.107.211.206/victorian/decadence/decadence/html

Lathers, Marie. *The Aesthetics of Artifice: Villiers's L'Eve Future*. Chapel Hill: University of North Carolina Department of Romance Languages, 1996.

Lasowski, Patrick Wald. "Le Faux Joris-Karl Huysmans." *Revue des Sciences Humaines* 170–171 (1978): 158–172.

Lears, T. J. Jackson. "From Salvation to Self-Realization: Advertising and the Therapeutic Roots of the Consumer Culture, 1880–1930." In *The Culture of Consumption*. Ed. Richard Wightman Fox and T. J. Jackson Lears. New York: Pantheon Books, 1983. 3–38.

Ledger, Sally, and Roger Luckhurst, eds. *The Fin de Siècle: A Reader in Cultural History, ca. 1880–1900.* New York and London: Oxford University Press, 2000.

Leppihalme, Ritva. *Culture Bumps: An Empirical Approach to the Translation of Allusions.* Clevdon (U.K.) and Philadelphia: Multilingual Matters, 1997.

Lievano, Roberto. *En torno a Silva.* Bogotá: Editorial El Gráfico, 1946.

Lodado, Rosemary C. *Beyond the Glitter: The Language of Gems in Modernista Writers Rubén Darío, Ramón del Valle-Inclán and José Asunción Silva.* Lewisburg, Pa.: Bucknell University Press, 1999.

Logan, Peter. *Nerves and Narratives: A Cultural History of Hysteria in Nineteenth-Century British Prose.* Berkeley and Los Angeles: University of California Press, 1997.

Lorrain, Jean. *Monsieur de Phocas.* Trans. Francis Amery. Sawtry, Cambridgeshire, England: Dedalus; New York: Hippocrene, 1994.

Loveluck, Juan. *La novela hispanoamericana.* Santiago: Editorial Universitaria, 1969.

———. "De sobremesa: novela desconocida del modernismo." *Revista Iberoamericana* 31, no. 59 (1965): 17–32.

Martin, Gerald. "Literature, Music and the Visual Arts, 1870–1930." In *A Cultural History of Latin America.* Ed. Leslie Bethell. Cambridge: Columbia University Press, 1998. 47–130.

Marroquín, Lorenzo. *Pax.* Bogotá: Prensas de la Biblioteca Nacional, 1946.

Marún, Gioconda. "'De sobremesa': El vértigo de lo invisible." *Thesaurus: Boletín del Instituto Caro y Cuervo* XL, no. 2 (May–August 1985): 361–374.

Maya, Rafael. *Leyendo a Silva,* v. III. Santafé de Bogotá: Instituto Caro y Cuervo, 1997.

———. *Los orígenes del modernismo en Colombia.* Bogotá: Biblioteca de Autores Contemporáneos, 1961.

Mejía, Gustavo. "José Asunción Silva: Sus textos, su crítica." *José Asunción Silva: Obra completa.* Madrid: CEP de la Biblioteca Nacional, 1990. 471–500.

Meyer-Minnemann, Klaus. *La novela hispanoamericana de fin de siglo.* México: Fondo de Cultura Económica, 1991.

Miramón, Alberto. *José Asunción Silva.* Bogotá: Litografía Villegas, 1957.

Molloy, Sylvia. "Voice Snatching: *De sobremesa,* Hysteria, and the Impersonation of Marie Bashkirtseff." *Latin American Literary Review* 25, no. 50 (July–December 1997): 11–29.

Montero, Oscar. "Escritura y perversión en *De sobremesa.*" *Revista Iberoamericana* LXIII, nos. 178–179 (enero–junio 1997): 249–261.

Moreno-Durán, R. H. "La poesía en *De sobremesa.*" *Casa de Poesía Silva* 1 (January 1988): 50–64.

———. "*De sobremesa,* una poética de la transgresión." *Quimera (Dossier José Asunción Silva)* (1996): 42–50.

Navarro, Javier. "*De sobremesa:* genio y enfermedad." *De sobremesa: lecturas críticas.* Santiago de Cali: Universidad del Valle, 1996. 61–97.

Nietzsche, Friedrich. *The Portable Nietzsche.* Trans. Walter Kaufmann. New York: Viking Press, 1972.

Nordau, Max. *Degeneration.* Nebraska: University of Nebraska Press, 1993.

O'Hara, Edgar. "*De sobremesa,* una divagación narrativa." *Revista Chilena de Literatura,* nos. 27–28. Santiago: Departamento de Español, Universidad de Chile, April–November 1986: 221–227.

Orjuela, Hector, ed. *José Asunción Silva: Obra completa.* Madrid: CEP de la Biblioteca Nacional, 1990.

———. *De sobremesa y otros estudios sobre José Asunción Silva.* Bogota: Instituto Caro y Cuervo, 1976.

Osiek, Betty Tyree. *José Asunción Silva.* México: Ediciones de Andrea, 1968.

———. *José Asunción Silva.* Boston: Twayne, 1978.

Pater, Walter. *Marius the Epicurean: His Sensations and Ideas.* Oxford/New York: Oxford University Press, 1986.

———. "Preface from *Studies in the History of the Renaissance.*" In *Aesthetes and Decadents of the 1890's: An Anthology of British Poetry and Prose.* Ed. Karl Beckson. Chicago: Academy Chicago, 1981. 280–291.

Peschel, Enid Rhodes. *Literature and Medicine.* New York: Neale Watson Academic Publications, 1980.

Phillipps-López, Dolores. *La novela hispanoamericana del modernismo.* Genève: Editions Slatkine, 1996.

Phillips, Allen W. "Dos protagonistas: un poeta y un escultor." *Temas del modernismo hispánico y otros estudios.* Madrid: Gredos, 1974. 264–271.

Picon Garfield, Evelyn. "De sobremesa: José Asunción Silva: El diario íntimo y la mujer prerrafaelita." *Nuevos asedios al modernismo.* Ed. Ivan A. Schulman. Madrid: Taurus, 1987. 262–281.

Pierrot, Jean. *The Decadent Imagination, 1880–1900.* Trans. Derek Coltman. Chicago: University of Chicago Press, 1981.

Poe, Edgar Allan. *The Complete Poems.* Ed. Louis Untermeyer. New York: Heritage Press, 1943.

———. "The Philosophy of Furniture." http://xroads.virginia.edu/
~HYPER/POE/philfurn.html

Poggioli, Renato. *The Poets of Russia, 1890–1930*. Cambridge, Mass.: Harvard University Press, 1980.

Porter, Laurence M. "Decadence and the *Fin-de-siècle* Novel." *The Cambridge Companion to the French Novel from 1800 to the Present*. Ed. Timothy Unwin. Cambridge: Cambridge University Press, 1997. 93–110.

Rama, Angel. "Diez problemas para el novelista hispanoamericano." *La novela hispanoamericana*. Ed. Juan Loveluck. Santiago: Editorial Universitaria, 1969. 277–336.

Reed, John R. *Decadent Style*. Athens, Ohio: Ohio University Press, 1985.

Rivas Groot, J. M. *La lira nueva*. Ed. Ignacio Chaves Cuevas. Santafé de Bogotá: Instituto Caro y Cuervo, 1993.

Rossetti, Dante Gabriel. "The Portrait." *Minor Victorian Poets*. Ed. John D. Cooke. New York: Charles Scribner's Sons, 1928. 262.

Rousseau, G. S. "Towards a Semiotics of the Nerve." *Language, Self and Society*. Ed. Peter Burke and Roy Porter. Cambridge, UK: Polity Press, 1991. 220–245.

Sanín Cano, Baldomero. *El oficio del lector*. Caracas: Biblioteca Ayacucho, 1978.

Santos Molano, Enrique. *Corazón del poeta*. Bogotá: Nuevo Rumbo Editores, 1992.

Schwartz, Marcy E. *Writing Paris: Urban Topographies of Desire in Contemporary Latin American Fiction*. Albany: State University of New York, 1999.

Serrano Camargo, Rafael. *Silva: Imagen y estudio analítico del poeta*. Bogotá: Ediciones Tercer Mundo, 1987.

Serrano Orejuela, Eduardo. "Narración, discurso y tiempo en *De sobremesa*." *De sobremesa: lecturas críticas*. Eds. Orejuela, Eduardo, et al. 11–59.

———. "Silva destornillado por García Márquez." http://www.geocities.com/semiotico/silvadestornillado.html

Shaw, George Bernard. "The Sanity of Art: An Exposure of the Current Nonsense about Artists Being Degenerate." *The Fin de Siècle: A Reader in Cultural History, ca. 1880–1900*. Ed. Sally Ledger and Roger Luckhurst. New York: Oxford University Press, 2000. 20–21.

Silva, Camilo de Brigard. "El infortunio comercial de Silva." *José Asunción Silva: obra completa*. Bogotá: Editorial Bedout, 1980. 103–124.

Silva, José Asunción. "L'après-dînée." *Œuvres*. Trans. of *De sobremesa* by

Jacques Gilard and Claire Pailler. Paris, Rome, Madrid: Stock/Unesco/ ALLCA XX, 1996.

———. "Carta abierta." *http://rehue.csociales.uchile.cl/rehuehome/facultad/ publicaciones/autores/silva/jasilv12.htm*

———. *Cartas (1881–1896)*. Bogotá: Ediciones Casa Silva, 1996.

———. *Cuentos negros*. Ed. Enrique Santos Molano. Bogotá: Seix Barral, 1996.

———. *Obra completa*. Prólogo de Miguel de Unamuno. Bogotá: Editorial Bedout, 1980.

———. *Páginas nuevas: textos atribuidos a José Asunción Silva* / prólogo y compilación de Enrique Santos Molano. Bogotá: ESPASA: Planeta Colombiana Editorial, 1998.

———. *Poesía completa / De sobremesa*. Bogotá: Casa de Poesía Silva, 1996.

———. *De sobremesa: novela*. Prologue by Gabriel García Márquez. Madrid: Hiperión, 1996.

Smith, Mark I. *José Asunción Silva: contexto y estructura de su obra*. Bogotá: Tercer Mundo, 1981.

Sontag, Susan. *Illness as Metaphor*. New York: Farrar, Straus and Giroux, 1978.

St. John, Michael, ed. *Romancing Decay: Ideas of Decadence in European Culture*. Aldershot: Ashgate Publishing Company, 1999.

Stanford, Derek, ed. *Pre-Raphaelite Writing*. London and Melbourne: Dent, 1973.

Steiner, George. *After Babel: Aspects of Language and Translation*. Oxford/ New York: Oxford University Press, 1998.

Torres Ríoseco, Arturo. *Precursores del Modernismo*. Madrid: Calpe, 1925.

Trigo, Benigno. "La función crítica del discurso alienista en *De sobremesa* de José Asunción Silva." *Hispanic Journal* 15–16 (1994–1995): 133–145.

———. *Subjects of Crisis: Race and Gender as Disease in Latin America*. Hanover and London: Wesleyan University Press, 2000.

Trilling, Lionel. *The Liberal Imagination*. New York and London: Harcourt Brace Jovanovich, 1979.

Trotter, Thomas. *A View of the Nervous Temperament*. London: Longman, 1807; reprint, New York: Arno, 1976.

Unamuno, Miguel de. "Prólogo." *Obra completa de José Asunción Silva*. Medellín: Editorial Bedout S.A., 1980. 5–15.

Venuti, Lawrence. *The Translator's Invisibility: A History of Translation*. London and New York: Routledge, 1995.

Villiers de L'Isle-Adam, Auguste, Comte de. *Axel.* Trans. June Guicharnaud. Englewood Cliffs, N.J.: Prentice Hall, 1970.

Villanueva Collado, Alfredo. "Arte, ciencia y la creación de estructuras narrativas por José Asunción Silva," *Encuentro de la literatura con la ciencia y el arte.* Ed. Juana Alcira Arancibia. Buenos Aires: Instituto Literario y Cultural Hispánico, 1990. 353–378.

———. "Gender Ideology and Spanish American Critical Practice: José Asunción Silva's Case." *Translation Perspectives* 6: 113–125.

———. "La funesta Helena: intertextualidad y caracterización en *De sobremesa,* de José Asunción Silva." *Explicación de textos literarios* 22–23, vol. xxii–i (1993–1995): 63–71.

Watson, Janell. *Literature and Material Culture from Balzac to Proust: The Collection and Consumption of Curiosities.* United Kingdom: Cambridge University Press, 1999.

Weber, Max. *Economy and Society: An Outline of Interpretive Sociology.* Ed. Guenther Roth and Claus Wittich. Trans. Ephraim Fischoff et al. New York: Bedminster Press, 1968.

Weir, David. *Decadence and the Making of Modernism.* Amherst: University of Massachusetts Press, 1995.

Wicks, Ulrich. *Picaresque Narrative, Picaresque Fictions.* New York: Greenwood Press, 1989.

Wilde, Oscar. *De Profundis.* New York: Modern Library, 1926.

Williams, Raymond Leslie. *The Colombian Novel, 1844–1987.* Austin: University of Texas Press, 1991.

———. *Novela y poder en Colombia: 1844–1987.* Trans. Alvaro Piñeda-Botero. Bogotá: Tercer Mundo Editores, 1991.

Williams, Rosalind. *Dream Worlds: Mass Consumption in Late Nineteenth-Century France.* Berkeley and Los Angeles: University of California Press, 1982.

Wilson, Edmund. *Axel's Castle: A Study in the Imaginative Literature of 1870–1930.* New York: Charles Scribner's Sons, 1969.

Yúdice, George, Jean Franco, and Juan Flores, eds. *On Edge: The Crisis of Contemporary Latin American Culture.* Minneapolis and London: University of Minnesota Press, 1992.

Zuleta, Rodrigo. *El sentido actual de José Asunción Silva.* Frankfurt am Main: Peter Lang, 2000.